Patrick Hamilton was one of .... gifted and admired writers of his generation. Born in Hassocks, Sussex, in 1904, he and his parents moved a short while later to Hove, where he spent his early years. He published his first novel, *Craven House*, in 1926 and within a few years had established a wide readership for himself. Despite personal setbacks and an increasing problem with drink, he was able to write some of his best work. His plays include the thrillers *Rope* (1929), on which Alfred Hitchcock's film of the same name was based, and *Gaslight* (1939), also successfully adapted for the screen (1939), and a historical drama, *The Duke in Darkness* (1943). Among his novels are *The Midnight Bell* (1929); *The Siege of Pleasure* (1932); *The Plains of Cement* (1934); a trilogy entitled *Twenty Thousand Streets Under the Sky* (1935); *Hangover Square* (1941) and *The Slaves of Solitude* (1947). The Gorse Trilogy is made up of *The West Pier* (1951), *Mr Stimpson and Mr Gorse* (1953) and *Unknown Assailant* (1955).

J. B. Priestley described Patrick Hamilton as 'uniquely individual ... he is the novelist of innocence, appallingly vulnerable, and of malevolence, coming out of some mysterious darkness of evil.' Patrick Hamilton died in 1962.

BY PATRICK HAMILTON

Fiction

Monday Morning
Craven House
Twopence Coloured
Twenty Thousand Streets Under the Sky
Impromptu in Moribundia
Hangover Square
The Slaves of Solitude
The West Pier
Mr Simpson and Mr Gorse
Unknown Assailant

Plays

Rope
John Brown's Body
Gaslight
Money with Menaces
To the Public Danger
The Duke in Darkness
The Man Upstairs

PATRICK
HAMILTON

TWOPENCE
COLOURED

ABACUS

First published in Great Britain in 1928 by Constable
This paperback edition published in 2018 by Abacus

3 5 7 9 10 8 6 4 2

A CIP catalogue record for this book
is available from the British Library.

ISBN 978-0-349-14160-2

Typeset in Sabon by M Rules
Printed and bound in Great Britain by
Clays Ltd, Elcograf S.p.A.

Papers used by Abacus are from well-managed forests
and other responsible sources.

Abacus
An imprint of
Little, Brown Book Group
Carmelite House
50 Victoria Embankment
London EC4Y ODZ

An Hachette UK Company
www.hachette.co.uk

www.littlebrown.co.uk

Introduction

It is a mystery that for many years the work of one of the century's most darkly hilarious and penetrating artists fell into near obscurity. Doris Lessing declared: 'I am continually amazed that there is a kind of roll call of OK names from the 1930s ... Auden, Isherwood, etc. But Hamilton is never on them and he is a much better writer than any of them'.

Recently, however, Hamilton's novel *The Slaves of Solitude* was adapted for the stage, and the films of his taut thrillers, *Gaslight* and Alfred Hitchcock's adaptation of *Rope*, are now considered classics. He is regularly championed by contemporary writers such as Sarah Waters, Dan Rhodes and Will Self.

Patrick Hamilton was one of the most gifted and

admired writers of his generation. With a father who made
an excellent prototype for the bombastic bullies of his later
novels and a snobbish mother who alternately neglected
and smothered him, Hamilton was born into Edwardian
gentility in Hassocks, Sussex, in 1904. He and his parents
moved a short while later to Hove, where he spent his early
years. He became a keen observer of the English boarding
house, the twilit world of pubs and London backstreets
and of the quiet desperation of everyday life. But after
gaining acclaim and prosperity through his early work,
Hamilton's morale was shattered when a road accident
left him disfigured and an already sensitive nature turned
towards morbidity.

Hamilton's personality was plagued by contradictions.
He played the West End clubman and the low-life bohe-
mian. He sought, with sometimes menacing zeal, his 'ideal
woman' and then would indulge with equal intensity his
sadomasochistic obsessions among prostitutes. He was an
ideological Marxist who in later years reverted to blimpish
Toryism. Two successive wives, who catered to contradic-
tory demands, shuttled him back and forth. Through his
work run the themes of revenge and punishment, torturer
and victim; yet there is also a compassion and humanity
which frequently produces high comedy.

In 1924 Hamilton gave up his job as a shorthand typist,
working for a sugar producer in the City of London,
and began work on the novel that would become his
first work of published fiction, *Monday Morning*. The

book went through a number of working titles, including 'Immaturity', 'Adolescence' and 'Ferment'. By the end of the year it was finished.

An introduction via his sister, Lalla, led to the book being taken on by the distinguished literary agents A.M. Heath. After rejections from Jonathan Cape and Heinemann, the rights were bought by the respected Michael Sadleir at Constable, and a very happy personal and professional relationship began. Hamilton received a £50 advance against future royalty earnings. Within a year *Monday Morning* was published to good reviews and in an American edition from Houghton Mifflin. Hamilton's career had begun.

After the success of his second novel, *Craven House*, came *Twopence Coloured*, his witty satire on the theatrical profession, published in 1928.

In the 1930s and 40s, despite personal setbacks and an increasing problem with drink, he was able to write some of his best work. His novels include the master-piece *Hangover Square*, *The Midnight Bell*, *The Plains of Cement*, *The Siege of Pleasure*, a trilogy entitled *Twenty Thousand Streets Under the Sky* and The Gorse Trilogy, made up of *The West Pier*, *Mr Stimpson and Mr Gorse* and *Unknown Assailant*.

J. B. Priestley described Hamilton as 'uniquely individual ... he is the novelist of innocence, appallingly vulnerable, and of malevolence, coming out of some mysterious darkness of evil.' Patrick Hamilton died in 1962.

PROLOGUE

Prologue

1

Shortly before midnight, several years ago, a pretty but unusually foolish girl, for her age (which was nineteen), was walking by herself along the Brighton front. It was raining slightly, and the movement of her even strides made little thunders with her mackintosh, and the rain spat with a kind of sullen suddenness upon her glistening white face and mouth, and she was very full of her quiet self and her quiet decisions.

She had just been to the Theatre Royal in this town. That is to say, she had been one of a large crowd of people who earlier in the evening had fled in a state of unnatural excitement and seriousness from their dinners, spent two hours and a half shut up in a stewed atmosphere of ardent illuminations and rippling facial darknesses, poured out into a distressed vestibule amid the uneasy superciliousness of the frustrated taxi-seeker, and the maddened importunities of the professional umbrella-holder, and at last dispersed to their respective homes again, in good order, but with their taste for such ebullitions temporarily damped, if in no way permanently satisfied.

But this girl was in no way damped. She was braced and wrought up by it, on the other hand (why, else, should she have gone home and changed her clothes to walk by the rainy sea at midnight?): and the thick sights and sounds of the echoing evening behind her – the restless resplendence of the audience in the plush of the stalls, the hot whisperings, the lemon glare from the stage, the ring of actor's voices and the hard roar of applause – were still in her eyes and ears, were still an intoxication to her, and were the very stuff from which she was making her decisions. And her decisions were very clearly defined, and most charmingly and alarmingly simplified, and yet a little defiant and tremulous withal (for she was by no means quite sure of herself as yet), and they amounted to this – that she intended – or rather that she *intended* – she was underlining tremendously to-night, which shows how insecure she was down below – that she *intended* – to Go upon the Stage.

2

For in the calculations of the youthful, light-hearted, and in every respect untheatrical circles in which she had hitherto moved, you had no difficulty in Going upon the Stage like that. The Stage (whatever that was) had no say in the matter. It was, presumably, just waiting somewhere, like a bus, or a tram, or the Giant Racer at Wembley, to be Gone Upon ... That the cold testimony of Science might one day succeed in cumbering the situation with whispers of an Agent (or some such coarse reality), she was, of course, vaguely aware; but such a thing never entered her head as a serious barrier. If there were any deterrent at all, it came from the character of the Stage itself, which was conceived by this girl as being unalterably, lamentably, and yet also a little enthrallingly inseparable from a nebulous kind of Wickedness. This Wickedness was obscurely collective, of course, rather than actively individual – otherwise you would naturally have little desire to Go amongst it – but that did not alter the fact of this Wickedness. Wickedness, indeed, confronted you at the very opening of your negotiations in this quarter, inasmuch as it was another unalterable and lamentable axiom (much impressed upon this girl by her various girlish and sympathetic discouragers) that you were not likely to Succeed upon the Stage unless you Carried On with the Manager.

With respect to this Manager, it seems that the poor man had no more say in the matter than the Stage had in the first place; and that just as there was some placidly receptive Stage, to be Gone Upon at will, so there was some kind of ideal and all-embracing Manager, pleasantly and professionally intemperate, simply waiting in an iniquitous flat somewhere to be Carried On with.

It is believed that those actually concerned in this connection would not defer to this outlook. That is all very well, they might say, but the thing's not so easy as all that. The enigma hitherto has been to find your Manager. We shouldn't mind Carrying On with him a bit if you could only tell us where to look him up. And they would surely be justified in thus casting disparagement upon questionable data. For experience has exhibited, with respect to Managers, that although there may yet be a certain quantity extant who (as this girl imagined the greater part of them to do) relieve their daily energies in a nefarious round of cigar-eating, champagne-drinking, being bloated, buying souls, and turning beautiful (and trusting) creatures into Things and so forth – that although there can never be any natural guarantee against the acquirement of any of the above-mentioned characteristics by Managers – they are a great deal more likely to appear in everyday affairs as middle-aged and heavily married bodies, in the habit of returning to their wives punctually for supper, with a severe talking-to if they forget the greens, and not without the threat of a strong mustard bath and a pot of gruel if there's any sneezing and the weather's on the chilly side ... For the domesticity of the average Manager, experience would affirm, is as pious as it is proverbial.

But once get on to experience, and what experience

would have had to say on the subject of the profession this girl was choosing at midnight with such tremulous audacity, and instances of her general bemusement might be multiplied indefinitely. Her misinterpretation of managerial intention was but a preliminary misinterpretation.

3

Jackie Mortimer, for that was this girl's name, was the product of a late Edwardian and early Georgian Brighton, which was not really Edwardian, and not really Georgian; and she belonged to an indeterminate society which was dominated from no particular quarter, but conspicuously active in Cutting itself. This was a golden era for the Cut, in fact, and that naïve bludgeon of social consciousness and rectitude was wielded judiciously but lavishly on all sides. But then, from the standpoint of the present time, it was a naïve and simple-hearted Brighton altogether. It is impossible to say why it should have been so; but it was so, in its very artless Edward-Georgian self. It was a naïve Brighton merely because Horse Cabs are naïve things, and the spectacle of people whistling like blazes in the night for them is a spectacle of naïveté, and because people who can still make conversation on Ankles, and get into a great state about Glad Eyes, and speak derisively of Knuts, and wear straw hats, and play Coon Can, and try to get thin on Antipon, and consider themselves on the road to becoming

7

fast, and talk with strong conceit about Motoring, are fundamentally and necessarily a naïve people.

In this Brighton, or rather in the Hove lying ponderously and residentially to the west of this Brighton, the whole of Jackie's life had been spent. In the last days on earth of King Edward the Peacemaker, when that lovable yet imposing monarch was allowed to come out, laboriously and without molestation from the populace, into the King's Gardens, and there take the sun with surly receptivity and asthmatic silence, Jackie Mortimer was a little girl of about five or six, herself playing with a ball in those gardens. And in the early part of the reign of King George the Fifth, just before the war, when all Brighton and Hove was going out on excited steamers to the fleet of battleships that lay peacefully off the coast, and the front was festive with pink and green and blue electric bulbs, hung all the way along, Jackie was a very composed and full-grown girl of about sixteen, who walked in twilights on the lawns of those same King's Gardens, and was loved – walked up and down on the twilit grass, harangued, beseeched, peacefully worshipped, kissed, and withal very calm and friendly under the importunities of her straining young adorers.

Where and when Jackie was first taken with the idea of adopting a theatrical line of business, it is difficult to say; though there can be no doubt that it was her nurse who, in the very first instance, Put Ideas into the child's head. For Jackie was an exceptionally alluring little girl, and had just that kind of thoughtful-eyed and champagne-haired head into which it is a great pleasure for nurses to Put Ideas. But inasmuch as, among other ideas, Put, at this time, into Jackie's head, there was always a positive and unequivocal understanding that she was one day (and if Good) to be the Queen, it is doubtful whether anything of so professional a nature could ever have entered into her mind as a serious project. But she must have acquired it somewhere, and that very young, for it had always been a tradition at Jackie's day-schools, from the earliest and satchel-carrying times, that that, somehow, was Jackie's line, and that one day Jackie was coming back, in her glory, to play at the Theatre Royal. 'You won't know us then,' the other girls used to say. (That was the way in which people spoke to Jackie. She had just that quality of inspiring enthusiasm without resentment, and popularity without jealousy. She was always rather fêted and made much, was Jackie – in these days anyway.) Also, whenever there were any private theatricals in progress, she was always the leading figure, and naturally given the principal part, and played, it has been said, superbly. Indeed in a certain play, given by the school in her last term there, and called, you will not be surprised to hear, 'The Dream Man,' Jackie came on in a sweet boy's dress and with a large bag (purported to contain dreams), and took by storm the dark little hall that was specially hired for the entertainment. There was hardly one who did not join in the general applause of Jackie, then: and when she came up to take her prizes afterwards – for Jackie was as clever as Macaulay, as well as being so talented and beautiful (The Headmistress said that Their Youthful Siddons seemed to possess historic as well as histrionic talent (Laughter)) – such a roar of clapping and cheering and footstamping arose, that signs of tears became apparent not only in Jackie's eyes, and not only in the eyes of her closest friends, but even in those of her few detractors, so carried away were they all, by the occasion. Indeed one impassionable person of twelve years of age, celebrated for having nourished a Crush on the figure in the limelight, was positively observed to be no longer in command of herself, and compelled to withdraw to the back of the hall, with an accommodating companion of the same years, until such time as she could again face the world with a dry and sober countenance.

And then, of course, quite apart from her demonstrable dramatic skill, Jackie's adorers and Jackie's beauty must in themselves have been incitements to some sort of theatrical aspiration. And as for the quantity of those adorers, and the high quality of that beauty – the latter was proved by the former, and proved beyond question. Very possibly no other young girl in the whole history of those King's Gardens could lay claim to quite so much admiration and quite so much of soft intrigue as Jackie had drawn towards her in those days. But whether or no she could actually and objectively have been styled a beauty in these days, and what kind of beauty she would have been if she fell under that category, are different questions. It need only be said that to the world at large she was certainly recognizable in her looks as one belonging to a type aiming distantly at some racial ideal, and she could not go abroad without making this fact subtly manifest in whatever quarter. Old ladies in buses were to be discovered either gazing with lost and dim-smiling benignancy, or frowning with fierce absorption at her, as she sat opposite: ticket-collectors, carpenters, porters, and their ingenuous kind were either reduced to almost emotional direction-giving and professional exposition, or braced to misanthropic curtness, in her presence: factory hoydens, when they passed her in the street, at once began to nudge, and giggle, and cry 'La-di-dah!' and tumble about with similar derisive and envious expressions until she was out of sight: and she was, in general, considered in the course of nature to be unequal to carrying anything, of any weight whatever, or to standing up on the two legs which God had given her for any decent length of time, or to transacting any daily business with ordinary care or efficiency. Whether it was defined or not, Jackie introduced a new and slightly strained and slightly elevated atmosphere wherever she went; and it was taken for granted that she was constructed on slightly different principles.

You must figure Jackie in these days as being very modest, but very bright-eyed and serene, and full of the most high-minded intentions of Knowing her old friends when she came back to the Theatre Royal in her glory, and with all the unhurried air of one who knows that the world is at her feet, and that the world's prizes are for her leisurely picking. She had, at the time, the most curious credibility towards life as an occurrence, and success as a thing that would happen to her from the outside. Success, and the admitted obstacles to success, were alike to fall upon her as the natural results and indications of her talents. She had no sense of having to seek or make anything, to thrust, and watch the results, and thrust again. She had certain gifts, and the world would show the fit and normal worldly reaction to such gifts.

Indeed at this time everything hung so deliciously and yet so very much in the air, that the whole thing seemed likely to remain in the air for ever, and finally dissolve into its own element: but two events occurred which brought her projects down to earth, where they still remained phantasmal, and delicious, and vague, but were down to earth for all that. The first of these was the outbreak of the war, and the second of these was the death of her father. Her mother had died when she was very young.

Possibly there was no decline in Jackie's popularity at the outbreak of the war, but there was, of course, a war to think about, and she could not expect, had no notion of expecting, to be the talk and pet of her circle to the same extent. Her circle, in fact, towards the end, showed every sign of getting itself involved in war-work and war-marriage and dispersing altogether. At war-work proper Jackie herself was utterly incompetent. She fainted instantly on being confronted by a day's work at a canteen; she was the wretched and scared origin of a deplorable scene (involving a Tram) in the Dyke Road while trying to learn how to drive a car; and apart from a little rather strained singing and cigarette-bestowing amongst well-disposed wounded soldiers, and apart from a little estimably patriotic vilification of the Germans, whom she declared, with conviction, to be Brutes (or even, after great outrages, Swine), she was hardly any true support to her country in its hour of need. Indeed Jackie was always rather out of it as far as the war was concerned.

It was three months before the Armistice that Jackie's father died. Jackie's father is only of interest to this story in so far as he claimed to be immortal, but was not. At least that is the only interpretation that can be made of his incessant reiteration to Jackie that If Anything *Should* Happen to him, she would be well provided for. It was never supposed for a moment that anything could happen to him, but it did. Furthermore, she was not well provided for. Apart from that, Jackie's father was a much-loved father, who was a *Punch* artist, and who wore a close grey beard, and who was large, and tolerant, and a little guttural, and a figure in the neighbourhood: and when he died there was a great deal of him in the local papers, and much private commiseration for Jackie, to whom, it was affirmed by those in the know, he had left nothing but the Clothes she Stood Up in.

This was practically true; but however that may have been, she did appear to be standing up with very tolerable success in those clothes. Also, even if there had been any decline in

the cult of Jackie in the early days of the war, there was a
kind of Jackie Renaissance on her father's death, and from
all quarters there came the most astounding and unforeseen
remembrances and kindnesses and sweeping invitations to
stay indefinitely and be second daughters and so forth. The
world, in fact, seemed to open its protective arms to Jackie
on her father's death, and hardly a trace of misgiving as to
worldly circumstance ever entered her head. From the very
first evening of the disaster that had fallen upon her, when
she went over to sleep under the roof of old Lady Perrin,
the widow of an Indian judge, who lived two doors away
in First Avenue, and with whom she had remained until the
commencement of this story, she had never been able to feel
any true perturbation in that direction.

What Jackie found to be a trifle curious in all this,
though, was that now she had fallen upon more evil days
and was so placed that some sort of profession seemed a
bare necessity for her, the idea and her own suggestion of
adopting a profession, and most particularly a theatrical
profession, was slurred over by all her friends in a very
strange and misty manner – by all her friends who had
until that time incited her most whole-heartedly on those
lines. But to Jackie, the more they slurred it over, the more
her resistance, and even her slight resentment, arose. It was
hence that she had come to be walking along the Brighton
front *intending* to Go upon the Stage like that.

Indeed the thing which her best friends had in view for
Jackie at this period was, without any doubt whatever,

a Match. 'Oh, I wouldn't worry about it all, Jackie, if I were you,' they would say. 'You never know what'll turn up.' They always called her 'Jackie,' rather caressingly, on these occasions, and generally threw in an 'if I were you' – thus betraying, Jackie imagined, a certain superiority and inward mockery of her projects. And although this serene faith in something turning up was assumed with a great show of indifference, Jackie was on more than one occasion led to suspect that some remote forestalling and assisting of the capricious gods was demonstrating itself in the form of various Brothers of persons, not to say Male Cousins, Old Friends, and similar eligibles, with whom she was casually thrown and left from time to time.

Now in order to have any proper understanding of Jackie, and the step she was led to take at this time, it must be taken for granted that she was, on the whole, a complete fool, who was not even compensated with any of that impressionability and flaccidity which might have protected her from her own folly. There was, on the other hand, a certain stamina, interpreted by others (and in some measure justly) as self-will, which marked Jackie from the first. When Jackie said that she intended to do a thing, and underlined the word, it might have been as tremulous an emphasis as you liked, but she was going to do it for all that, you were surprised to discover. You were surprised because rather in the same way as you were mystically unable to credit that Jackie was really capable of carrying anything, of any weight, so you could not believe that she could ever maintain, by direct action, her own theories against those of her advisers. You were mistaken in either case. In this business of a Match, for instance, Jackie was a very depressing subject from the outset, and no amount of eligible reinforcement could bear her down. She had, in fact, quite different views.

When it was made clear to her friends that Jackie's object was to go up to London there was some disapproval, but much less disapproval than when it was understood that she was not going to stay there with the Langham family – a family with an artist father and two daughters who were Jackie's closest friends – as had been taken for granted, but going on her own to live by herself in rooms which were to be let to her by her old nurse and housekeeper, Mrs Lover.

Mrs Lover was a good-looking woman of about forty, who had married well and settled in West Kensington, three years ago, and who had known Jackie a great deal longer than anyone else in the world. And although it seemed to every one else the height of imprudence, it was to Jackie a perfect solution to all her problems. It was this Mrs Lover who had in the first place Put Ideas into Miss Jackie's head, and who had ever since been her closest and most sympathetic confidant on matters which Jackie had been able to share with no one else – her father included. Jackie's admirers, indeed, who formed, in general, a section of the community divided against itself, had cause to be unanimous in the placating and propitiating of Mrs Lover, in whom they sensed a power behind the throne, and rightly. It was Mrs Lover who, with her brown sympathetic eyes and assumption of infinite experience, had sheltered and guided Jackie through all the intricacies of her twilight experiences. It was Mrs Lover who could guess exactly why he had said that, who had told you he would begin that sort of thing, and who insisted that you should be firm now, or there was no telling what you would be getting into. It was Mrs Lover who knew to a fine shade whether you should put Yours sincerely, Jackie, or Yours affectionately, Jacqueline Mortimer, or just Yours gratefully, J., and write it again and cut out one of the 'dears' in the middle so as to tone it down a bit. And the confidence was mutual. For when, in the course of time, the elder was in her turn confronted by the vexed problem of Lover himself, and was herself reduced to a baffling condition of indecision and lack of faith in her own precepts, it was Jackie who took on the sober wisdom of intelligent experience, and gave inflexible rulings and decisions on each turn of the affair. 'But do you *want* to marry him?' Jackie would ask again and again, and 'Do you *Love* him?' – thus getting a little of her own back ...

There was every sympathy to be expected from this quarter, then, and apart from that, it will be understood that in the mere imprudence and slight abandon of setting up on her own there were attractions for Jackie. Not only, after her father's death, did she tell herself that she wanted to get away from Brighton and its memories for ever, but also her whole life had lost its old values since that event, and the gesture, the symbol, of complete transplantation was, she felt, necessary for her in starting again. It may be said, in fact, that Jackie by this time had an almost passionate impulse to burn her ships.

Jackie did not of course come to this resolution all at once. It began as a dim supposition and possible ultimate refuge: it grew in suggestiveness as the days went by and the realities of her position were brought home to her: and at last it flooded in upon her as an inspiration. And by the time she had made her intentions known, there was no moving her at all. And although there was at first much dissent, it is possible that people were not a little relieved at getting Jackie once and for all off their shoulders and away in London. The first gush of hospitality and commiseration had died down into little more than a trickle of friendly sympathy, and apart from Lady Perrin, who was becoming a rather vague, aged and bewildered old person, there was not the same interest, and rash generosity at Jackie's command. Accordingly, when the thing was accepted, all her friends found it easy enough to work themselves up into another climax over Jackie, and to send her off amid the acclamations of a roseate popularity. It was in some way regarded as a purely temporary parting, and she was to write, and to be written to, and doubtless to be met, and shown over the Town, and to come down again, and to visit, and heaven knew what, when she got up there. One of her friends might come and share rooms with her, indeed, if things shaped themselves as was hoped; and there was, altogether, quite a St Martin's Summer of fame and adulation for Jackie. It is true that still very little mention was made of the Stage – nothing but continued slurrings in fact, save in one instance – but Jackie had her own ideas on the subject and rather enjoyed keeping them to herself.

That one instance was provided by the younger Langham girl, Iris, whom Jackie had promised to visit at Wimbledon when she came to London and who claimed to have at her command a Friend, of the name of Gladys Weston, who was closely concerned with the theatre and could be relied upon to give any introductions necessary. It is eloquent of Jackie's general attitude at this time that a Friend of the name of Gladys Weston figured not in her imagination as an individual of any value to her at all. Indeed she was rather offended and chilled by the idea of a Friend of the name of Gladys Weston. It is impossible to say how Jackie conceived that she was going to enter this business without some at least figurative Friend of the name of Gladys Weston, but she did do so. As she walked along the Brighton front, the night before she left for London, she was Going upon the Stage, and the matter ended there.

It may be mentioned in passing that Jackie was very willing to begin with small parts.

4

As Jackie walked along the Brighton front, it became more and more her own Brighton front, and at last it seemed that there was no one there at all to share her striding and buoyant possession of it. At the same time the wind grew higher, bawling violently into Jackie's ears, and the rain came with it, spitting itself into millions of little ardent sharp triangles on the slimy, streaming paving under the lamps. And the sea, which a little while before had been crashing measuredly away (as though it had really rather forgotten what it *was* aiming at, after all the nonsensical centuries it had been at the business), suddenly seemed to awake, and as good as said it had had enough of this tom-foolery, and now the coast should listen, come what might! And that was what Jackie was wanting really, some sort of challenge like that, to nerve her and brace her and give her a sense of immediate and impending battle. And in the sound and rush of the storm about her, in the unquenched but fearful sputtering of the yellow-green lamps, in the wash and thunder of the war-like and long-prepared coast (which had taken the sea at its word and also wanted a row), Jackie planned for herself a very gallant and hand-to-hand and triumphing battle with life indeed. But wherever her dreamings and schemings took her, and whatever heights she scaled, all was concentrated upon, and at last reduced to the clear fact that Jackie intended, stage-struck or no, talented or untalented, mocked or applauded, to Go upon the Stage.

And this is the last that will be seen of Jackie in quite this striding and ineffable frame of mind. She did not so much touch a summit to-night, as she walked along with the little thunders of her mackintosh and her eyes distantly agleam with the blaze of her ships already in flames: rather did she symbolize the whole ingenuous expectancy and glad preparedness for fate which had marked her auspicious youth. She will never again, after to-night so trustingly, so anxiously even, seek to impale herself upon life. This was a farewell to something more than the places of her youth.

It would, therefore, be well to capture Jackie, as she strode along, vanishing and appearing in the light of lamp after lamp, which stood like gaunt sentinels to do honour to her meditations. For when, on reaching the confines of Portslade, where the wind and rain alike seemed suddenly to cease, as though they had done their duty by her and she should now go back to bed, Jackie, rather chilled, and deserted, and damp, turned homewards – and when, after reaching First Avenue again, she had let herself in with her key, and crept up the stairs to her room and lit her candle, and hurriedly and with midnight clandestinity undressed, and climbed into bed, and sat up for a few peaceful and pencil-scrawling moments with a Brobdingnagian Boots' Diary, in which she put on placid record for all time the romantic fact that she was 'writing this at half-past one a.m.,' together with the accurate asseveration that this was her 'last day in this house,' and that 'nothing much happened excepting a theatre and a long walk all along the front at night,' and that she 'wondered what to-morrow' would 'bring forth' – when all this had been in due order accomplished, and Jackie had snuffed out the candle, and turned over, and wriggled herself, with a single wriggle, into the cool arms of Morpheus – she had left behind her, if she but knew it, the whole kindly phase of her early existence.

Book One

THE ASPIRANT

Chapter One

TRAVEL

1

That covertly unpropitious something hovering around Jackie's departure next day, made its presence felt from the moment of her waking. To begin with, the malevolent assault made on her sleep-hazed mind by the crashing fusillade of her Venetian blind being drawn up by Ada, the maid, at half-past eight, left her with nothing to contemplate but a dank, dripping fog which had risen in the night from the sea. This moping wraith thinned itself out somewhat while she dressed, but in doing so only revealed a hushed, dull, gleaming earth which had every appearance of having been submerged all night, up to its slates and chimneypots, by a silent ocean which had amazingly receded to the beach again. Then, on going down to breakfast, she learnt that

Lady Perrin was in bed with a severe attack of neuralgia, and intending to stay there: which threw out all Jackie's unconsciously preconceived ideas of the place and circumstances of the farewell. Then, in the course of breakfast, for which was provided a lukewarm haddock and a boiled egg – foods which she found savourless – she, with no discernible occasion for it, discovered herself to be trembling, and could eat nothing more. Then, shortly after this, when she had settled down on a stool in front of the fire to look at the pictures and cartoon in *The Daily Mirror*, her contemplative frame of mind was disturbed first by Ada, who bounced in apologetically to ask whether she minded the Men setting in upon the Windows, as they had Come; and immediately afterwards by the sight of a red ladder trembling under energetic (but quite impenitent) legs, and the sound of tirelessly ferocious rubbings and squeakings, punctuated by intermittent pail-clankings, all of which eventually culminated in a window being thrown open, an inrush of sea air, an unseemly intrusion on privacy, and a large amount of self-consciousness on both sides. Jackie left the dining-room and went upstairs to put the final polish on her packing. But here, also, there was the same unsettled and unfriendly air about everything. Her room, with its window wide open and the clothes stripped from the bed and removed, seemed to know that she was going and to have given up all interest in her. Moreover, the two servants, as they brushed the stairs and landings outside, were giggling unintermittently over some abstruse drollery of their own; and the world, on the whole, and particularly as exemplified by these two and the brusque polisher beneath, was most depressingly looking after its own business and taking it for granted that she would look after hers. The world, in fact, had no sympathetic recognition for aspirants and adventurers whatever.

She was sorry now that her train did not go until 3.15, and on finding that a coat which had been sent to the cleaners had not yet returned, she decided to go out now and fetch it herself with some sense of relief. Her way took her along the Brighton front as far as West Street.

Now Jackie had intended on this walk to have a last glimpse of her sea; but she had not intended to pay her final respects to it in the condition in which she now found it. She had not intended, that is, to find it a grey, full, mist-lost inanity, purring with feeble and invalid regularity at the brim, as though, even if it could recall that affair last night, it was sick to death of the whole subject and would not allude to it again. She found that she was not prepared, as she walked hurriedly along, for this sluggish, obtuse, workaday forgetfulness of the suggestions of the night before. She felt indeed, though scarcely knowing it, that she was being let down by the sea, and the same slightly treacherous air of disenchantment was over everything to be met out of doors. As she passed the Bedford, Preston Street, and the West Pier, there was no faint God-speed – nothing save surly interest or disinterest – on the damp faces of those that passed her. And by the time she had reached the

Metropole, outside which the baggage of certain young, female, and very much more confident and matter-of-fact travellers than she would be that day was being hauled by obsequious porters on to a taxi, Jackie was aware that, she was seriously out of tune with the day already . . .

As expected, Lady Perrin was not down to lunch, her neuralgia having advanced with the hours, so that the old lady was now sitting up, with a rigidly immovable countenance, and in a dark, curtained atmosphere of eau-de-Cologne, whence her voice emerged like that of an oracle in the first solemn phases of prophecy. She would not hear of the doctor being called in, and she would not hear of Jackie postponing her departure, and Jackie was of course to come up and see her again before she went . . .

Jackie took no pleasure in her lunch, being alone in a dining-room with inexpressibly clean windows, which, in their very immaculate pellucidity, added to the unfamiliar and slightly hostile attitude this house had developed against her: and after lunch she could hardly contain herself with impatience and ennui – the sound of a passing taxi scaring her out of her wits, as her time drew nigh. Also the problems of What you Gave Ada, and If you gave Godfrey the Same or a little less because after all he'd done nothing to speak of, and Should you Give Mrs Baskomb Anything, caused her the acutest anguish, with the clock ticking away the last moments in which she could decide. And even when all this was fixed upon, and she had intrepidly seen through those soft and shamefaced passages with the objects of her largesse, there were harassed surmises on exactly how Pleased she was, and firm self-assurances and dubious convictions on the subject of Enough (all considered).

The taxi, however, came five minutes before its time, and all at once Jackie found herself flying down the stairs (after a flushed farewell with her benefactor), on the principle that, however much time there was at one's disposal, a taxi, of all things in this universe, must not be kept waiting.

The taxi man, although quite kindly, was not sympathetic, and sensing Jackie's defencelessness at once, entered into a vague conspiracy of winks and genial condescension with Ada, so casting an air of light derision over the whole venture. Also, having beer inside him, he took humorous exception to the amount and size of Jackie's luggage, asking, as a satirist, whether This was a Trip to the Continent or What. He shouldered it, however, with some skill, and then curtly slammed the taxi door upon her. And before she knew what had happened, the thing was snarling up the Avenue with her inside, as it had been engaged to do indeed, but not quite as she could have wished, in view of the fact that these were her last moments in the places of her youth. Similarly, as she flew giddily through the crowded Western Road, which seemed itself to be, somehow, giddily engaged in its everyday occupations, she had a feeling that all this had come upon her before she was ready for it, that she had done something irretrievable which she had only half intended to do. She passed the thronged Clock Tower and shot up Queen Street at a furious pace.

Nor did Brighton Station reassure her flagging spirits. Rather did it – with the *judj-judj-judj*ing of its fitful
engines, with its tremulous whistles and bangs and giant
hissings, its penny-flinging and paper-snatching bookstall,
its echoing voices from nowhere, its air of being one vast
improvisation in which all was temporary and unsettled,
save the large clock above which, with its unmoving yet
miraculously advancing hands, testified greyly to the eternal
and irrevocable factors of the universe – rather did it subtly
steal from Jackie the last remains of her confidence in being
in any way the mistress of her own fate, or indeed anything
but an entity drifting impotently on tides of unfathomable
circumstance in a drab and disinterested world. Nor did
the porter, whom she at last enlisted into her service, possess any scintillating or suggestive character wherewith to
relieve the situation – trundling dumbly ahead of her, as he
did, and from time to time inconsequently deserting her, at
apparently crucial moments. But he did finally guide her,
with a certain oafish omniscience, to the train she needed;
walking endlessly up the platform to his own idea of the
proper thing in the way of third-class compartments, and
flinging her suitcase under the seat with his first comment
on the matter – 'There-Yarmiss!' Whereupon Jackie began
to fumble piteously, and like a wild thing, in her bag, while
her porter stood by and observed the ups and downs of the
battle with melancholic detachment. All of which eventually terminated in Eightpence – together with a Halfpenny
(which was dropped) – and a brusque 'Thank *you*' from

the recipient, who laid great stress on his '*you*,' for reasons unknown, unless it was that, in view of Eightpence (an outrageous sum) he was fearful of allowing any attention to be drawn to his 'Thank' – in which case she might have had some small justification in hoping that he had, before passing out of her life, forgiven her. That Jackie winced under his treatment, this porter was aware, but being a cruel and vain porter, whose pride was touched, he walked unrelentingly away, and left the girl to seek absolution where she could find it.

2

Jackie had five-and-twenty minutes in which to compose herself for the journey in front of her, and she was glad of it. This was all but her first experience of third-class travelling, and she told herself that the hardships of the penurious genteel – a class to which she now emphatically and rather pleasurably belonged – had been grossly exaggerated. It was true, certainly, that the company betrayed some sense of catering for the indistinguishable herd. It provided, for example, no pleasant leather arms for the indulgence of individuality or squeamishness: and it provided no pleasant leather straps, at the corner seats, wherewith the opulent might relax their jaded wrists: and it provided upholstery resembling a dusty carpet, in place of the dark blue button-pressed paddedness it provided for those who could run to the extra four and twopence. It was dealing with cattle, in fact, and the frigid statement, printed under the rack, that this compartment could contain Ten, was revealing of its callous and numerical attitude. But these affronts troubled Jackie not at all, and she actually came to the conclusion, by some very obscure process of reasoning, that it was all Just as Nice.

For about ten minutes or so Jackie was left unmolested in her corner seat: but by that time a thickening crowd of travellers was dreamily hastening up to the higher parts of the train, and Jackie had undergone several curious examinations by prospective persons framing themselves in the window, and after meeting her eyes and thinking the matter well out, deciding against her. She was at last risked, however, by an old lady with a suitcase, who took the corner seat farthest away from her, and sat up perkily and spent her time in arduously not looking at her. The spell being now broken, there entered another old lady – which at once caused Jackie and the first old lady, who were previously divided, to unite in critical glances and mild resentment against the suitcases, fussings, and general appearance and character of the second old lady – such being the normally inimical nature of railway relationships. Then, two minutes afterwards, the three of them forgot old differences in a common cause against yet another new-comer, who was a young girl of not more than sixteen, dressed in black from head to foot, and carrying a basket containing a kitten. She bore a bereaved look, and for some reason did not take a corner seat. There then entered a well-dressed young man, who sat directly opposite Jackie.

This young man entered with great decision, did not look at anybody, snatched a book out of his attaché-case, on which were engraven the initials R. G., and commenced at once to read. He had dominated the compartment, and entered Jackie's life, and was reading unconcernedly, before any of them had time to mobilize their critical forces against him. On second thoughts, this young man was not a young man, Jackie decided, but nevertheless he was nothing else: for not by any stretch of the imagination could he be styled an old man, or even a middle-aged man, so what were you to do? Perhaps you could only say that he was no longer a boy – no longer a youth – for he had that air of brown virility and reserved strength which is impossible of acquisition until past the actual prime of life. Thirty-six, thought Jackie, and a lot of sorrow at that. Not trouble, or worry, but sorrow was the word Jackie fixed upon; and by this dramatization she betrayed, if she but knew it, something of her quickly awakening interest in him. In fact she at last awarded him a Great Sorrow, in the singular, and the greater the sorrow the more she fancied him. This was rather the type of young man who would Go out into the Night, thought Jackie. He would fix up the whole affair for the happy couple, and go out into the night. She was, alas, reading his character ill. For although her railway companion had doubtless been out into his Night with the best, in his day, a keener observer would have recognized that that was not his line nowadays.

His face was the most interesting face she had ever seen; and it was unique in this, that it was attractive without giving the slightest offence by its attractiveness. You did not understand, at a first glance, that you were looking at anything out of the way; it was only slowly that you observed, with a feeling of personal and exclusive discovery, that there was a great deal more to it than anyone but you would imagine. Jackie was convinced that she alone could see the extreme charm of this face, and she had a desire to defend its beauty against a world of disparagers. And here again Jackie was as much in error over his powers of attraction as she had been over his dramatic self-negations – as time was to show.

With ruminations of this kind Jackie, who had brought no book or paper, spun out the time before the train started. She also looked about her at her other fellow-travellers. No one else having entered to rearrange the present clash and interchange of personality amongst these, a state of mutual tolerance, almost amicability, obtained. The status of each was clearly defined. Jackie, having been the first to arrive, had the prestige, as it were, of a pioneer and oldest settler, and so might have been regarded as the genius, the familiar spirit of the compartment. The two old ladies, as successful marauders, had an equal and solid standing of their own. The young girl in black was of no consequence, and an object of mere commiseration. As for the young man who had arrived last, he, by the sheer force of his character, businesslike attaché-case-snapping and unconcerned reading, was a kind of Conqueror, who had dominated all save the original founder, Jackie, whose sanctions he could not obliterate, but only share, as an Alexander might have flirted on equal terms with the gods and mysteries of Egypt. Whether this young man, who was now rapidly reading the Life of Francis Place, was aware that he had thus swept all but one before him and come to hold this position, is doubtful. Probably, indeed, he had no idea that he was in this train at all. Possibly none of the others had, either. But these fine shades of personality and prestige were existent, nevertheless.

A very pleasant calm had settled upon this gathering, then, and it appeared that – in spite of the numerous and now rather more apprehensive countenances that bobbed themselves with panic-stricken explorative glances into the window frame – that these five were going to have it to themselves. Doubtless, in fact, they were already preening themselves upon their good fortune at the very moment at which fate singled them out for the vicious trap it had in store for them.

However that may have been, it was within one minute before the train departed, that, with the suddenness of an accident, and with Jovian uproar, there entered a thick smell of gin, and a stamping of feet, and a great lurching and shouting and plunging and throaty growling – all creating a mist of terror and surprise, which, after a moment, cleared away, and revealed to the sight but two individuals of a low class of life engaged in argument and thick verbosity.

And the first and loudest of these individuals was a thin, seedy object of about thirty, wearing a decaying blue suit and begrimed collar and shirt. And the second and softer of these individuals was a grey-bearded and stupefied old gentleman of about sixty, wearing a decayed rain-coat which reached his ankles and no collar at all (though an excellent brass stud). And the first of these individuals was smoking a yellowed tenth of a cigarette (which was in the process of choking him), and addressed the second individual, with not very filial jocosity, as 'Dad': and the second of these individuals was carrying a newspaper-wrapped bundle under his arm, and addressed the first individual, with dreamy paternal sentiment, as 'Son.'

From what depths of the sea-side town these individuals had arisen, and to what depths of the metropolis for which they were so buoyantly bound, they would again descend, are unanswerable questions; but they manifestly had the better of dull care so far as the immediate journey and interim were concerned. Son, in fact, was at this moment standing up in the centre of the compartment and entreating the other, whom he named his 'Pore Old Parent', to Kiss him Good-night – which was a silly, maudlin, and (it is to be feared) revealing thing to be doing at such a time of day in a railway compartment. Nor did the deep and insecure embrace that followed speak any better of their mutual condition – in spite of a weak protest from Dad to the effect that his offshoot was Acting like one of They Frogs – by which he, in his sturdy Englishry, intended to cast disparagement upon the French.

It is impossible to say whether poor Jackie at first realized what was the original inspiration of the joy elevating this couple at the moment, but from the beginning she sensed dimly that there was something overstressed in their jocularity – that there was something, in fact, 'the matter' with these two. It was not, however, until she had observed one of the old ladies, in the corner farthest from her, suddenly to arise, seize her suitcase, and vanish precipitately, that the full truth struck home.

Now it has been demonstrated how foolish a girl Jackie was, how unhabituated to the experiences of this world, after only nineteen years spent in it: and so you will be well able to understand how, when the word struck home (and she had only one reeling, ghastly word for it) – how her face went to ashes and her spirit was shocked.

Drunk! It was as though you had given Jackie a lash across the cheek with a mule-whip. To Jackie it was something abhorrent, like madness, as leering and unthinkable.

You will be well able to understand how she sat there with thought and movement paralysed, how she looked illy around at the others – at the young girl in black, who was most amazingly, and gravely, unperturbed; at the other old lady, who was moving her head from left to right and fidgeting horridly; at the young man opposite her, who was reading the Life of Francis Place as rapidly as ever – how she looked down at her suitcase, which was under the heels of Dad, who was now seated; how she wondered if she might yet escape, and say 'May I have my suitcase, please?' and smile; and how she at last half rose to do so, and met the eyes of the young man opposite, and fell weakly back again . . . And by this time the train was moving . . .

3

Dad began it. Son was engaged in rolling a cigarette. For a few moments, indeed, there had seemed a possibility that there was not going to be much trouble now that the train was off: but Dad began it. This watery-eyed old gentleman, who for a little while had been content, in a sudden access of somewhat pathetic dreaminess, to sit looking out of the window, all at once, and as though in continuance of a previous conversation, put his hand out on to the knee of the young girl all in black, and leering forward, spoke in tones of husky condolence.

''As yer Auntie died then, dear?' asked Dad.

To which there was no reply.

'I expect yer Auntie's died, ain't she, dearie?' asked Dad, who had, apparently, an *idée fixe* on the actual form his fellow-traveller's bereavement had taken.

'Don't you talk such nonsense, Dad,' shouted Son,

suddenly bursting in. 'Of *course* 'er Auntie ain't died. Never 'eard of such a thing. You'll be sayin' *my* Auntie's died next.'

'Well, she's all in black, ain't she?'

Son said that So was Christmas too. This was a perfectly inaccurate and really quite irrelevant argument, but some obscure logic latent in it appeared to satisfy his parent, and there was a lull. Then Son began to sing.

Son was an exceptionally foolish singer, pronouncing all his words not as it was natural for such a common man to pronounce them, but in such a manner as he conceived one who had been benefited by an 'Oxford Education' would have brought them out. It was indeed one of his boasts, when in liquor (as now), that he himself had been elevated by this type of education, as will be shown. He also beat his breast a great deal.

'Ef yew WAH the oanLAY *gel* in the WARLD,' sang Son. 'And Ai wah the OAN LAY BOY!'

Son now turned jauntily to Jackie, as though to paint the prospect for her.

> 'NOTHin' – ELSe'd – MATTAH – INthe –
>   WARLD TOO DAY!
> WEEKood – go on – LOVin' – in the –
>   SAME *OLD WAY*.'

By the way Son stressed the 'same old way,' it was clear that Jackie was committed in the past.

'A garDEN – of EeDEN – just built for TEW,
Dah-dah-dee, dah-dah, DAH DAY! (This very
    shrewdly.)
Ef yew WAH the oanLAY *gel* in the WARLD,
And Ai WAH the *Oan LAY BOY*!'

Concluding which, with a heavenward flourish and a smile of bliss at the giddy supposition, Son at once came back to earth; and feeling his duties as the life of the party, immediately flung out a little green packet under the face of the old lady next to him, and courteously begged her to take a Wood – by which Son intended Woodbine (his own favourites) – but was quietly rebuffed. He was in no way wounded, however, and at once expressed his sociability by the same method to the young girl in black opposite him, who also resisted the temptation. He then stated that he was a Regular Woodbine Willie, he was, and made the same offer to Jackie, which was similarly abortive. Nothin' Abashed, though (as he himself put it), he turned to the young man in the corner, who, to the surprise of all, thanked him and accepted. He then offered one to his father, but expressed his doubts as to the propriety of so doing, on the theory that the old man 'doubtless 'ad 'is Turkish on 'im' – thereby imputing the elder with a certain snobbishness and effeminacy – but this unjustifiably. After which he leant back and remarked, apropos of nothing, and of no previously mentioned lady, that 'She Reclined on 'er Ottoman languidly smokin' 'er 'Ookah,' and fell into silence and contemplation.

There was, in fact, a large and long silence which promised well for all. But promised unfaithfully, as Dad, after looking dreamily out of the window again for two minutes or so, softly demonstrated. It was plain that Dad had the thing on his conscience. He put out another sympathetic hand.

''As yer Auntie died then, dear?' asked Dad.

There was again no answer to this; but this time Son was a little irritated by the pursuing of this so fruitless subject.

'Nah then, Dad, you leave that alone,' he said. 'If you don't interfere with 'er Auntie, she won't interfere wiv *yours.*'

'Well, *I* says she's all in black,' said Dad, defending himself.

'And *I* says so's Christmas too!' retorted Son, becoming heated.

And as this once more placed the matter beyond controversy, and silenced his father utterly, Son did not add to the reproach, and as though to show that there was no ill feeling, relapsed into further irrelevances.

'And 'e THOUGHT of 'is *Deer* Old MOTHAH!' said Son. It is impossible to say what Son intended to convey by this (just as it is impossible to fathom his earlier allusion to the Ottoman); and from what ballad (if any) he was actually citing, is not known; but it was uttered with strong sentiment and in the spirit of the utmost good-fellowship, and it served to change the subject well, even if, in the silence that followed, his listeners were left in the dark as to the inner purport of the declaration.

'Well,' said Son, producing a pack of cards, and commencing to shuffle them with some verve and brilliance. 'What about a little game, then? Solo Whist? Aukshun? Berzeek? Peekay? Or Cabbage? I *beg* your pardon,' amended Son quickly, and with an air of one having made a great *faux fas* (though he was only joking really). '*Cribbaige.*'

Jackie, by this time, was far from comfortable, but the colour had come back into her cheeks, and she felt that she was under some kind of subtle protection from the young man who was not a young man opposite her, who had by now put his book away, smiled once, sadly rather than knowingly, at her, and was watching the invaders in an easy attitude and with his hands very reassuringly in his pockets. Now there could have been no more welcome suggestion than that of a little game, Jackie thought, as it would serve, possibly, to subdue and engross them for the rest of the journey. She therefore waited for Dad's answer with some eagerness. But Dad's thoughts, unfortunately, were running upon other, and by now familiar, lines, and there was much strife yet to come.

'Didn't she leave yer nothin' in 'er Will, then?' asked Dad.

There was a short pause after this, and then the storm broke.

'Now '*ow* many times 'ave I spoke to you about that, Dad?' cried Son, putting out his forefinger and speaking very sharply. 'Don't let me 'ear no more now, you old dog.'

Now this was unfilial, not to say anti-tribal, in Son, and incurred very natural family resentment.

'Oo you bleedin' well talkin' to?' asked Dad.

'Now then, Dad, you keep your talk clean,' said Son, becoming very fierce, and shifting the argument to grounds of piety. 'There 'appens to be ladies present.'

''Ere. You a Churchgoer?'

'No, I ain't no Churchgoer, but you keep your talk clean.'

'You a Churchgoer?' repeated Dad, screwing up his eyes.

'No, *I* ain't no Churchgoer, but you keep your talk clean.'

'Well. I thought you was,' said Dad, and then (it is to be feared) lost control of himself – commencing, as he did, a throaty and threatening growl, and all at once uplifting his newspaper bundle and balancing it augustly in the air, with the object of dealing instant and grandiose retribution on the head of the upstart should his defiance proceed. Whereupon Son jumped to his feet, thrust forth his chin, with a caustic air of welcome, and invited his fate with derisive and challenging words.

'*Will* you, then, *will* you?' asked Son. '*Will* you?'

'Will I what?' Dad was a trifle abashed.

'*Will* you, then? *Will* you just? *Will* you? *Will* you? ... *Will* you?'

''Ere. You startin a Roughahse?' (Dad meant Roughhouse by this.)

'No. I ain't startin' no Roughahse, but you keep your talk clean.'

'You *ain't* startin' a Roughahse?'

'No. I ain't startin' no Roughahse, but you keep your talk clean.'

'You *ain't* startin' a Roughahse?'

'No.'

''Cos you'll tell me if you was, won't you?' said Dad, and sat down again.

And now Son revealed once more his extreme versatility. For after looking into his father's eyes for several lurching moments with diminishing rage and increasing amicability, 'My Pore Old PA!' he said, with sincere and quavering emotion. 'Was I ROUGH with yer?'

'You get along,' said Dad.

> 'And 'e said 'is PRAIRS at 'is mother's KNEE
> Each night at SIX o'clock!'

said Son. Which was very possibly extempore, but was beyond question conceived in a general spirit of remorse.

But this was not lasting, either; for catching sight of Jackie, and for the first time apprehending the homage her beauty demanded, Son without difficulty made the transition to gallantry.

'But Pardon me,' said Son, and bowed. 'Was I treadin' on your pretty little toe?'

Jackie lost all her colour again and made no effort to answer.

'You don't mind my Addressin' you, do you?'

Jackie must have here seemed to have implied that she didn't, for 'A Mere Bagatelle,' said Son, as though speaking on her own behalf, and so forgiving himself. 'But what is this? She Blushes. She Reddens! She Pales! Or am I mistook? The Vapours, methinks!'

Son was far from being mistaken in any of these staccato surmises, and it is fearful to think of what Jackie might or might not have succumbed to, had she not at this moment observed the young man opposite taking a last puff at his cigarette, and extinguishing it with the air of one at last getting down to business. This young man was now her one rock of salvation in quicksands of terror and revulsion, and he was not to fail her.

Son now went down upon one knee, as in the mode of an earlier and more florid epoch, and came at once to the point.

'My dear,' entreated Son. 'Take me for what I am! Take me for what I am!'

At this moment the foot of the young man opposite, who had his hands in his pockets again, came slowly out and rested on the seat just beside Jackie, thus causing a long, strong, firm, tweed leg to remain as a valiant barrier between herself and her suitor. But Son did not at first observe this.

'Bad as I am, I *love* you,' chanted Son. 'So take me for what I am! Come, my dear. I've 'ad an Oxford Education, you know. I 'ail from Bawllyol. I've 'ad an Oxford Education, you know. I'm a Bacheldore of Arts, I am. Come, wilt thou not imprint a kiss on this fair brow?'

At this Son put forth his head in anticipation, and rested his hand upon Jackie's knee: but at the same time the leg gave a little kick, which displaced that hand, and Son came down to earth.

''Ere,' said Son. 'Ooz Limb?'

The young man did not reply.

'Was you aware that you was intruding upon me?' asked Son, and the young man this time replied in a pleasant and very well-controlled voice.

'Now then, get up,' he said. 'And don't make an ass of yourself.'

'Is you aware,' said Son, getting up and brushing his knees, 'that I come from Bawllyol. Was you apprised that I been educated at Oxford?'

'Well, I have too,' said the young man. 'So I'm just as clever.'

'Oh, you 'ave, 'ave you?' Son paused. 'Let me see, now. You wasn't by any chance the Oxford Don, was you, now?' (This with infinite irony.)

'I really didn't know there was such a thing.'

'Nor yet the Senior Wrangler?'

'No.'

'Then would it perchance shock you to 'ear what I think of you?'

'It's impossible to say.'

'Oh, it is, is it? Well.' Son was rather at a loss. 'Well, I says she's a swell skirt, that's all.'

'You can't *be* a swell skirt, you know,' said the young man, with sweet reasonableness. 'You can *have* a swell skirt, or *wear* a swell skirt, but you can't *be* a swell skirt, really.'

'Oh, can't you? Reely?' rejoined Son. 'Well, *I can*.'

There was a silence after this crushing personal testimony, and Son again turned to Jackie. But the barrier was still up, and the young man spoke.

'What about this game we were going to have? Aren't we going to start?'

'What game's that?'

'Come on. We'll have this corner.' He looked at Jackie and smiled. 'Will you shove up the other side?'

Jackie, who was now in perfect command of herself, smiled and rose. The young man then asked her if they might use her suitcase, and smiled, with some sweetness, again, and she said 'Oh yes. Certainly,' and smiled. He then asked the young girl in black, with a smile, alas, as sweet as any he had yet bestowed, whether she would move to the other side of the old gentleman, so that they could have one half of the compartment to themselves. A triumph of organization indeed, and within one minute the whole atmosphere was changed and everything was mobilized for play – with the important exception, that is, of Dad, who at this point was discovered to be sleeping – not in the comfortable and reclining posture fitting to the action, but leaning forward in a stertorous coma which threatened at any moment to level both himself and his bundle with the floor.

Son himself was already considerably subdued. Not subdued, of course, but comparatively so.

'You're a good sport, you are,' he said to the young man.

'I ain't got nothin' against you. Come along, Dad. Come off it. Nah then. Wake up, you Old Snorter.'

Whereat Son shook his slothful and remiss parent violently, and the old man awoke murmuring a senile 'Whassser? . . .'

'Nah then, Dad. Never mind messin' abaht. You come over 'ere.' He lifted his father and dumped him down next to him. And after a short discussion on the game to be played, and a rather longer discussion on the stakes to be lain, and a few more inapposite remarks from Dad, such as :—

'Doewa'e'ay' (I do not want to play),

'Karzordir'e' (The cards are all dirty),

'Wobuie-e-ooig' (What the bloody hell are you doing?), the cards were dealt skilfully by the young man, and a game of Nap began. The storm was passed.

4

The train, all this time, had been advancing in its own inexorable and puffingly detached way into a fog which grew denser and denser every mile and filled the compartment with a garish light, which was the colour of mud, and from which glowed the mournful but steadily window-gazing eyes of the young girl in black, in a manner which struck the heart chill, and overclouded the soul. And as the train advanced further into this yellowing pall, it was compelled to surrender something of its earlier decision and grasp of its immediate object in life – which was to take Jackie to London – and to become more diffident, not only from time to time slowing warily down, and stopping dead with a jerk and deep silence, but also occasionally capitulating to an inconsequent tendency to go back to Brighton again. This it did very slyly, of course, and very tentatively, but it was obvious that it had got into a bit of a funk about the matter and thought another day would be better, if you didn't mind ... The passengers within accepted these manifestations with the patient and trusting stolidity common to passengers – being apprised, by various remote gravel-scrunchings, men's voices, fog-bangs, whistlings, and so forth, in the dark mist outside, that the poor, weak-spirited thing was being coaxed as far as the company's servants were able. Nevertheless, this spirit of morose vacillation soon transferred itself to Jackie, who had imagined she was going to be in the spring-morning of life this afternoon, but was now more damply wretched than she could ever remember having been. In the space of half an hour, the joyous and exulting relief which the matured young man (whom she intended to thank royally, when she had the chance) had brought about by his tact, firmness and management, had all worn away; and she looked over at that side of the compartment without any true satisfaction or self-congratulatory thoughts on what might have been but for him.

As for Dad and Son, they were now behaving, with

minor exceptions, as gentlemen should behave. Dad, it is true, was frequently dropping his cards in a nerveless and disorderly manner, and making very rash calls without anything to substantiate them (for which errors he was being continually brought to book by Son): and it is true that the fumes of alcohol had not yet entirely dispersed in the head of Son himself, who was winning all the time, and who, in his felicity, every now and again leant right over to Jackie either winkingly to reveal the beauty of his hand, or to make such neighbourly but perplexing remarks as 'You mustn't mind my Dad, you know. 'E's been to the Races.' (This in view of the fact that the races this day were at Doncaster, being an euphemism of what he considered the most delicate description.) Or, 'I'll meet you at the Stage Door if you like, my dear.' (This with the air of a hardened and knowledgeable roué.) Or merely, 'She's SOMEBODY'S mother, you know,' in a reversion to that maternal obsession, one might almost say neurosis, with which his spirit was tormented. But in each of these lapses he himself was called to order by the matured young man, and he was extremely placable. There was, in fact, no disturbance of any kind in the whole dragging, despondent journey to Croydon, where this couple left the train.

There was a certain resurrection of high spirits on their departure, both the old lady and the young girl in black leaving here as well, and after several exuberant and redundant farewells, it was found that Dad, in the excitement of the moment, had deserted his bundle. Wherefore the young man seized this bundle, and put his head out of the window.

'Old Gentleman!' he cried.

In a few moments Dad came growling back again.

'Your Bundle.'

Whereupon the young man fell at once back into his seat, reopened his attaché-case, re-embarked upon the Life of Francis Place, and was alone with Jackie as the train slid out on its last lap to Victoria.

5

So here Jackie was! So here she was, on her day of adventure and high aspiration, sitting in the foggy compartment of a sluggardly train, alone with an absorbed young man who had been her salvation but had now nothing whatever to say to her. Life, she felt, had bettered her in this first encounter. It had employed irrelevant and senseless weapons wherewith to knock the courage out of her, and had contrived a foggy day in which to do it.

Her immediate business, though (she told herself), was to thank this young man. That she also yearningly desired to talk to anybody, on any excuse, was true enough; but she did sincerely wish to thank this young man, and had observed that neither the old lady nor the young girl in black had made any attempt to do so. It was plainly up to her. Nevertheless, he did not appear to be the type of young man who would give much response, as far as sentiment was concerned, and her task was not easy. Her soul, in fact, began to palpitate, and her face began to lose its colour again, in the most extraordinary manner, as she framed phrases to start with, and wondered whether she ought to Leave it or not, and what he would Say. And what made matters doubly difficult was the fact that she was now in the corner seat farthest away from him. It was out of the question to commence from such a distance, she told herself.

Eventually, and very suddenly, it was another voice, coming from some mechanical source within her, that was feebly uttering:

'I think that we ought to have thanked you for getting that couple to play that game like that.'

Jackie's first sickening impression, on hearing this voice, was that it had committed itself to several too many million 'that's' and that its owner would spend the rest of her days in unending torments and self-reproach for having allowed it to do so. But the next moment she was pulling round under a very stimulating smile, which very possibly sensed a 'that' or two too much somewhere, but which fully and freely forgave it.

'Yes. It was jolly lucky he mentioned it.'

'But I can't think how you got them to do it.'

'Oh, they weren't really troublesome. I've seen people lots worse than that.'

'Well, I think you were wonderful,' said Jackie. Whereat

Jackie blushed, without a moment's hesitation, for it was not correct to say that *he* was wonderful. It, alone, might be wonderful. He did not reply. He would plainly never forgive her this time.

And now, in the madness of the moment, she plunged even farther into the mire.

'I think I'll come back to my corner seat,' she said, smiling, and the next moment she was sitting opposite him. He smiled at this, but again did not reply. And because he did not reply, and because she had cast away, in her missish gaucherie, the last poor shreds of her self-respect, and because he had smiled civilly and made no effort to rescue them, she now felt rising in her bosom a great hatred for this complacent and self-controlled young man – a hatred which cancelled all other sensations for the time being, and caused her to look out of the window with great disinterestedness and superiority. He also was looking out of the window, but not like that.

'"And he thought of his dear old mother,"' he said amiably, ruminating, and before he had smiled at her, she knew that in some subtle way he had saved the situation again. And she began to adore him again.

'Weren't they terrible?' she said.

'Yes. They were rather ghastly.'

'How awful it must be to get like that.'

'Well,' he said. 'They found it rather nice, I expect.'

Queer, and rather perverse individual, this, thought Jackie.

'Yes. But how *beastly*, I mean.'

'Oh, I don't know. I expect they were rather dears if you only knew them and got used to them.'

A curious conception of dears, thought Jackie, but *she* was not going to argue the point. He was still looking out of the window, with his book open on his knees, and she thought it best to let him go on reading. She therefore picked up a newspaper, which the old lady had left behind, and lightly cast her eyes over it, opening it wide at last, and giving an excellent impersonation of a young girl all at once spotting something of great interest to herself at the bottom of a column. She at once sensed that he had gone back to his Francis Place, and experienced a slight annoyance at this. She then commenced a laborious process of the deftest paper-lowering, and most cunning eye-raising, with the object of seeing him without being caught at it – which took nearly a minute to accomplish, but which was rendered a waste of time and energy by his calm but absolute absorption in his book. This she did several times, with the same result each time. It was clear that she had no longer any existence for him, and that he would not reopen the conversation ever again.

And the fog was worse still, and now they were getting very near to their destination – Victoria. And the realization of this gave another sudden shock to Jackie – she scarcely knew why. She had forgotten there was an end to this, that she would soon have go get out and grapple again with existence. Victoria! The mere decayed, ponderous sound of that irrevocable terminus, where she would have to shift for herself, filled her with apprehension. And at this point the train, with a sudden clattering laughter at her, dashed over Vauxhall Bridge, under which dimly flowed the sluggish and unwelcoming Thames, and panted deeply onwards to the dreaded appointment.

Then came the slowing down, which was the slowing down of Jackie's pulses as well. Uncanny gliding moments of enforced patience and chill eagerness – hoardings, and brick, and dead, disused trains, and the submissive bump of hitherto buoyant rails beneath. And then at last, and suddenly, the Station itself! It was not apprehension that Jackie felt, as the train puffed with funereal and exhausted grandeur under this giant, looming roof; it was fear. It was a child's fear of the dark, the half-dark – of evil noises and nightmare transactions. It was the mouth of some gaunt hell: it was Destination. The roar of the porter's trucks might have been the roar of lions, to whom she and her fellow-travellers were to be delivered, and all the shoutings might have been instructions for the rough-and-ready handling of this grim cargo. The young man flicked open the door: there was a sudden expansion and particularization of noise; and Jackie stood up and mistily pretended to busy herself with her suitcase. By the time she looked round the young man had vanished. 'Well, now for it,' said Jackie, and stepped on to the platform.

Her next object was her luggage, at the back of the train. She made for this in a thick crowd streaming against her, and had some relief in espying the young man, bobbing up ahead, at the same thing. This left her with one straw to keep her from submergence under the massive indifference of her fellow-creatures; and she quickened her pace to get nearer him. The train was of enormous length, and under that glimmering, smoky roof, where, it seemed, lingered all the sorrows and all the terrors of all journeyings since the beginning of time, Jackie chased a bobbing head.

Was her luggage in that van? Was there anything save ticketed perambulators, kit-bags, fishing-rods, hold-alls, packing cases, other people's gloriously initialled trunks and bicycles? Was there (should she ever be lucky enough to see her poor belongings again) the likelihood of ever impressing one of those callous porters with the need of getting them to the cloak-room? No, there was not. But the young man was standing by, with the same patience, though he showed no signs of speaking to her. He had no sense of beauty in distress, had this young man.

A moment came when Jackie could stand this no longer, and she went up to him.

'Can one get a porter here, do you think?'

'Well. I think you can. Yes,' he replied. This was uttered with just a trace of sarcasm, but he immediately rectified it. 'I think I've got one. Will you come on me?'

'I can't see mine here ... Oh yes, there they are. The two of them. All the time.'

'Which? The J.M's?'

'Yes.'

'And the two J.M's please, porter. Over there . . . '

('Thanks awfully' . . . said Jackie.)

But the young man was not listening. 'No. Not the A.D.C.F.'s please. The J.M's.'

'The J.M's, sir?'

'Yes. The J.M's.'

They were walking down the platform, behind the man, in silence.

'Julia Marsden?' suggested the young man, by way of conversation.

'No,' said Jackie. 'Mortimer.'

'Janet?'

'No,' said Jackie. 'Jacqueline.'

'Jacqueline Mortimer, in fact?'

'Yes.' There was a silence.

'Any more?'

'Yes. A beastly one. Rose.'

He seemed to think about that. 'Yes. I don't like that,' he said.

This cross-examination was stimulating her beyond measure, and it was with the utmost misery that she drew nearer to the barrier, where he would for certain leave her, and where she would be cast alone again into the outer world.

'Do you know where one can get some tea here?' she asked.

'Yes. We'll have it together, shall we?'

'Oh yes. Let's,' said Jackie, and if there were not tears

of gratitude in her eyes as she looked up at him, there were in her voice.

6

It was after they had each received checks for their luggage at the Cloak Room, and were walking back across the station again at a rapid pace (set by the elder), she holding his little case and he grasping her suitcase, that he altered her existence again, and set her heart throbbing with joyous, trembling potentialities. He had asked her where she was going in London, and she had replied, 'West Kensington.'

'Oh, West Kensington?' he said. 'I'm coming over that way on Monday.'

'Oh – are you?'

'Yes. I'm playing at the King's.'

Jackie did not quite understand this allusion at first, but something of its awe-inspiring implications crept into her soul as she answered vaguely: 'The King's?'

'Yes,' he said, and looked at her. 'Hammersmith,' he added, as though to make himself clear.

'Oh,' said Jackie, and then the truth filled her. The man was an actor, and all her troubles were at an end. That she would have not the slightest difficulty in using this man for her own ends, that she had found her protector, that all her problems had been solved by the calm will of Providence, and that nothing remained to be done save the exquisite preliminaries and fixing of the details of her immediate attack, Jackie was brimmingly confident. And he was coming to West Kensington! This all was, in fact, too felicitous to bear thought, and with joy she decided to eke it out, as it were, and put it away from her until tea, when she would pick it up again and handle it slowly and luxuriously. She therefore changed the subject.

He took her to a little tea-shop nestling high in a building overlooking the thronged thoroughfares outside the station. A crow's nest of a tea-shop, in fact, above a roaring yellow ocean of traffic – climbed up to by endless wooden stairs, and enlivened by blue-curtained windows and blue neat waitresses, and as warm and grateful to the senses as the sparkling tea and oozing toast provided were to the taste. And here, after a little (and very noticeably thawed) conversation, Jackie lingered deftly, but at last led round to the subject nearest her heart.

'Did you say you were coming to West Kensington next week?' she asked.

'That's right.'

'Did you say you were Playing somewhere there, or something?' asked Jackie, finding this not quite so easy as she had thought it would be.

'Yes. "The Devil's Disciple." The King's. Why?'

'Oh,' said Jackie, as though this had just struck her. 'So you're a—' There was a pause.

'Nactor?' he suggested.

'Yes.'

'Well, I suppose I am. Why, though? Are you?'

'Oh no; *I'm* not. I just thought how interesting, that's all.'

'How, exactly,' said her friend, who appeared to take everything at its face value, 'interesting?'

'Oh, just interesting. That's all.'

He did not reply to this, but busied himself with pouring out the tea. And in the long silence that followed Jackie knew that she was up against it, and must speak now or never.

'Tell me,' she said. 'What would one do if one wanted to become one?'

Her manner of saying this implied much more detachment than personal interest, but there was sufficient of the latter quality to cause her companion's eyes to come up and meet hers with some seriousness.

''Tor or 'Tress?' he asked.

''Tress,' she said, and laughed.

'Do *you* want to become one, then?'

'Yes.' Jackie laughed again.

'I'm very sorry to hear that, Miss Mortimer.'

Now Jackie had been prepared for some sort of rebuff like this. She had sufficient shrewdness to recognize and allow for the mystery-mongering and priest-hood of a professional, and although she had hoped for better things from this young man, she was not surprised. Nevertheless, she liked him less.

'Why?' she said softly.

'Well, I don't think you'd be at all happy.'

'Oh – but I'm prepared for that. I know the hardships.'

There was a silence.

'How do you know *them*?' he asked.

'Oh,' said Jackie, 'I *know* them.'

'But how?'

'I can *imagine* them, then,' protested Jackie, quietly.

At this point he offered her a cigarette, which she took, and he lit a match. His hand was firm as he held it out for her, but her lips were not.

'And the hardships are a sort of added attraction?' he suggested.

Now this was the truth. But Jackie would not let him see that. 'Of course not,' she said. These soft, slightly constrained, cigarette-lighting moments, Jackie did not find unpleasant, and she was confident of getting all she wanted from him before she was through. But he apparently was aware of the dangers of intercourse of this kind, and he changed its tone.

'I say,' he said abruptly. 'Where on earth are you going to-day?'

'I'm going to West Kensington. I'm going to stay with an old nurse there.'

'An Old Nurse?'

'Yes. An Old Nurse.'

'A Holiday with an Old Nurse?'

'Well – sort of. I might go on to stay with friends later. But I'm wanting to set up on my own, if I can. You see, I'm by myself. My father's died, you see, and I've got to do *something*.'

'Do you mean you've got to earn your living?'

'Well – yes. You see, that's why I want to do – what I told you about.'

'Oh. I see.'

'I say,' said Jackie, who after a fairly serious 'I see' like that thought she had better play her best card and win hands down. 'Will you help me?'

'With all the pleasure in the world,' he said, with great sincerity, but she detected something mocking in this glib assurance.

'I mean over That?'

'But that wouldn't be helping you.'

'Oh yes, it would,' said Jackie, softly leading back to the quietudes of discourse.

'Why don't you learn to type or something? Secretary and that sort of thing. You'd do just as well, and work less, probably.'

'I *can* type, as a matter of fact. I've only just learnt. But that's nothing in itself. And I'm not going to spend all my time in a stuffy office.'

'How do you know it'd be stuffy? They might be fresh-air fiends.'

'Oh – it *would*,' said Jackie.

'It's not proved, anyway. But if you could do it at home, would you?'

'Yes. I rather love typing, as a matter of fact. But who's going to give me typing to do?'

'I'll give you some, if you like. I've got a book.'

'Really? What sort? . . . '

'A Book by Me.'

'Really?' Jackie was shocked out of her own preoccupa-
tions by this. 'Do you write, then?'

'Yes.'

'I mean, do you – publish them?' Jackie blushed.

'Yes.'

'How frightfully interesting. What sort of books are
they?' Jackie was still blushing.

'Sort of books on Sociology.'

'Really?'

'The kind of things in which the Italics are always being
Mine,' he said. Jackie laughed.

'And Sincerest Thanks are due to Tireless Energies of
people, in forewords,' he added. There was a silence.

'What's your name, then?'

'Gissing.'

'Gissing ? No relation to—'

'*The?*'

'Yes.'

'No.'

'What's your first name?'

'Richard,' he said firmly, and looked at his watch. 'I say,
I ought to be going soon.'

'Oh – must you?'

'Is there any special time you want to arrive at West
Kensington?'

'No. You see, I said I probably wouldn't be there till

about seven. I meant to have a sort of look round in London before going on. I didn't think of a fog and all that. I thought I might have a jolly afternoon by myself.'

'Oh dear. Well, I'll tell you what. I've a date in Piccadilly. Let's walk across Buckingham Palace way. The fog's not so bad, and you'll get your look round after all. Then I'll see you to your train.'

'Oh yes. Let's.'

'And you're going to have your luggage sent for tomorrow?'

'Yes,' said Jackie. 'That'll be all right – won't it?'

'Yes,' he said. 'It will.'

In a few moments they were out in the street. Mr Gissing walked at the same rapid pace as before, and there was the same arrangement with respect to the suitcase and attaché-case. They talked about nothing in particular for some time, and then another surprise came.

'Have you never been up here before?' he asked.

'Yes. I have been up once. My father brought me up for a week. He was always coming up and down. He was an artist.' Jackie brought out this last fact with some small pride, and as a measure of minor self-defence against the talents and achievements of her companion; and she watched the results in his face.

'An artist?' he said.

'Yes,' said Jackie.

'*Punch*,' added Jackie ...

'Oh! I see light,' said Mr Gissing. '*Your* father was *Gerald* Mortimer.'

'Why? Have you heard of him?'

'Yes. Rather. I remember him well.'

'Why? Did you know him?'

'No. Not really. I met him at a dinner once, that's all: and we walked most of the way home together.'

'Good Heavens,' said Jackie . . .

The prestige which he had now acquired in her eyes was boundless. For if he was not old enough to be her father, he was old enough to have known her father, on equal terms, and yet young enough, if so he wished, to be her own lover, though the thought only entered her mind to be dismissed. And the blending of these two things, like the blending of youth and sorrow in his face, captured her imagination marvellously.

They walked on for some time in foggy silence after this, and soon he told her (they were entering Pall Mall) that they weren't far now. And at this news Jackie, who was becoming extremely breathless (for he walked very fast), became also extremely nervous, and wondered what she could say to him before he departed. For that he would immediately depart, and mercilessly at that, on reaching the point he had fixed upon, she already knew enough of his character to appreciate. She, of course, was all for observations on the Smallnesses of the World, after all; and coincidences, and funninesses, and who-would-have-thoughts. But there was something steady in his grey eye, and purposeful, if not vindictive, in his walk, which forbade the slightest indulgence in sentiment of this kind

before it was uttered. She therefore said nothing, and tremblingly trusted that he himself would open the subject of
their next meeting. This he did.

'Well, when do I see you again?' he asked. Not a scrap
of 'may' about it. Pure 'when'. And yet Jackie took this all
in the course of things, and was content – delighted. At
any other time Jackie would have very possibly resented
such treatment – she did indeed resent it when thinking it
over in bed that night – but he overbore her at the moment.
Moreover, in the space of a few minutes, he was about
to drop her in the middle of a vast, thronged, unknown,
hooting, electric-lit, dark-rumbling metropolis, and leave
her to shift for herself; and this fact naturally blunted the
finer points of her pride. It is revealing of her state of mind
that until this moment she had been utterly unaware and
forgetful of her surroundings, and her business in them. It
was with a sudden shock that she remembered where she
was – London – and the mystery of her presence there. And
fear of this mystery, and also his ever more hurrying stride,
emboldened her reply.

'Well, as a matter of fact,' she said, 'I've a sort of idea.'

'Yes?'

'You're coming to Hammersmith next week, aren't you?'

'Yes.'

'Are you staying anywhere? You said you'd have to
get rooms.'

'Yes. I know a place in Brook Green.'

'Well, why don't you come and stay where I am? She lets

rooms, you see; because somebody's being sort of turned out because of me. And I know it'd be all right.'

He did not stop in his stride, for he was now reaching a kind of crescendo of hurrying, but he seemed to be very pleased by the idea, and in a hundred yards' time he had her address and the whole thing was arranged. Unless she wrote to him, he would arrive on Monday at three o'clock, and she might be in, or she might not be in, to welcome him.

'And when I see you again,' said Jackie, smiling, 'I'll talk to you about That.'

He smiled back but made no rejoinder. They now plunged into a crowded arcade, which she recognized as Piccadilly Underground Station, and he was making for the booking office.

'After all,' said Jackie, 'if you say that acting's such a beastly business, why do you do it yourself?'

'West Kensington, please ... Oh, well; I don't know ... Now, listen.' He led her towards the lifts. 'You go in one of these lifts, you see.'

'And you go Down, naturally.'

'Yes.'

'Well, when Down, you see a thing saying To the Trains. And you walk along a thing like the inside of a toothpaste tube, and then you see a thing pointing to Westbound or Eastbound. You take Westbound.'

'Yes.'

'Well, you get in a train which takes you to *Earl's Court*.

And when you're at *Earl's Court*, you get out and follow the others into a *lift*, which takes you Up. When Up, you look about for other things, but probably ask a Porter, or Man, for West Kensington, please.'

'Yes.'

'Well, he'll tell you to go down some stairs for an *Ealing* or *Richmond* train. And it's the very next station.'

'Thanks ever so much,' said Jackie.

'Well, good-bye,' he said, and smiling faintly, he offered his hand, 'You've got it clear?'

'Yes. Good-bye,' said Jackie. 'And thanks so much.'

She turned, and commenced to walk away.

Now whether at this moment this more than hard-hearted individual caught something of the unthinking obedience and pathetic trembling optimism of the figure departing into an unknown city, is not known. But something must have stolen over his conscience momentarily, for he called her back.

'I say.'

'Yes.'

'You won't be lost or anything, will you?'

'No. I'm all right,' said Jackie, smiling. 'Goodbye.'

'Good-bye.'

And when she reached the lift, he was standing there to be waved to.

Chapter Two

GLIMPSES

1

Talgarth Road, West Kensington ... Talgarth Road, commencing to wind away, like a decayed crescent moon, at a point belonging to a baker and directly opposite the Underground Station; and lying in West Kensington ... West Kensington – grey area of rot, and caretaking, and cat-slinking basements. West Kensington – drab asylum for the driven and cast-off genteel! Penitentiary for misused existences; distressed haven for the house-agent-ridden, the servant-harassed! Land of geysers; rusty baths; gramophones; landladies; breakfasts in bed; meals in kitchens; dark hall-ways; dank, seeded gardens; buses; Belgian refugees; coal carts; Chinese nurse-maids; barbers' shops; West End prostitutes; cripples in Bath chairs; modish youths; chorus girls; barrel-organs, street singers, flautists, harpists (ineffectual and conflicting assuagers of the public grief!) ... West Kensington – grotesque erection on stone pavements quavering to the iron roar of the District trains beneath, which curved crashing out westwards, or went moaning eastwards, in an eternal blunt hurry to get away ... West Kensington – represented not by its District Station, around which its humanity thronged in endless flux and hurry, nor yet by its one gaunt Church, wherein the sight of humanity seemed all but a thing unknown, and from the grimy back-street railings of which humanity appeared to recede, as from its allegoric stagnation and superannuation – but by its Steam Pressing, Dyeing, and Cleaning establishment, to which the whole population shamefacedly and fortnightly repaired for the sly promotion of its deteriorating carriage before the world. It was here, in a foetid atmosphere of steam and dangling overcoats, that all of spiritual courage and earthly rejuvenation to be hoped for, was dispensed. Here was Confession, indeed; and here, for the sum of two shillings upwards, was new birth, of a shoddy and impermanent kind. That thickly padded and vaporous machine, as it hissed down on its meretricious labours, was the obscure symbol of the whole neighbourhood's aspiration; and the spotty young woman at the counter was the tacit, imperturbable storehouse of more mute confidences and hopeless avowals than ever authorized man of God was called upon to receive.

And yet, with all this, it could have been arguable that

West Kensington was some sort of island of struggling gentility set amidst even darker blemishes around. For you would not care to exchange it for the slums of Fulham, nor yet for the welter of Hammersmith: and some might see very little to choose between it and the more green and spacious territories of Baron's Court. For St Paul's School sprawled there, stretching wide and dominating all, and Heaven knew what pernicious impositions of mediaeval learning and close superstition upon the callow and sensual offspring of London tradesmen were in progress behind those red-brick and seemingly pleasant walls. Certainly no susceptible spirit could abide there to endure daily the spectacle of a pimpled but gladiatorial generation (which would one day take over the business of the world) cackling through the streets, or drilling or strolling in the grounds, or tearing at each other's necks and hurtling themselves at each other's feet and ripping up each other's knickers in the abandonment of their stertorous afternoon sport. From West Kensington into Baron's Court was, in fact, for some, merely from the frying-pan into the fire of squalidity.

2

It was twilight at four o'clock on Monday afternoon – a grey, lowering, windy afternoon, big with the threatening and grandiose mischief of the running elements above – and Jackie was standing at the window of her quite pleasant front room in Talgarth Road, West Kensington, and waiting, with an expectancy momentarily more perturbed, and a trust swiftly vanishing, for the arrival of Mr Gissing.

The grey, drab, naked, flat, scythe-like sweep of the road before her eyes was all but entirely deserted – as though people had read the signs of the god-like frolics about to commence overhead, and had dashed to shelter to wait in suspense. And apart from the milkman on his round, who, like some demented walker in a city awaiting destruction, emitted bedlamite yodelling sounds: and apart from his truck, which crashed crazily and spasmodically on its way, there was no person or thing to break the sighing uniformity of the wind-swept street. Mr Gissing was now three-quarters of an hour late.

The room grew darker and darker every tingling minute, and the fire within, with one large flame, flapping like a wind-tugged flag, leapt up to illuminate the room. If Mr Gissing did not come at all (and when it was quite dark she would resign herself) she had her course of action more or less consciously resolved upon. She would go up to her dark bedroom, lie upon her bed, cry until she was exhausted and satisfied, spend two more weeks in London going to every theatre, every day, that she cared to go to; and then return, to Lady Perrin and be married as soon as it could possibly be negotiated. For if Mr Gissing proved false to her (Jackie was now reduced to confessing to herself) she had come to the end of her spiritual resources.

For it had been raining continuously since the night of her arrival, three days ago; and apart from one ineffectual little morning trip to the West End (when it simply pelted and she very nearly lost herself), West Kensington had been all that a desolate Jackie, cast upon herself, had seen of her London so far: and some cause for her dark and tearful frame of mind, as she stood at this window, may be discerned.

Some cause, also, for her bounding sense of deliverance from nameless despairs, of her lightning transition to glad expectancy, may be imagined, as a taxi came wheeling round and snarling up from the station end of the road, and she herself rushed out to open the door and welcome him in.

And when, a few minutes later, he was sitting in the flapping firelight with his overcoat on, and his hat in his hand, and very much at his ease altogether as he smiled up at her, she was an emancipated creature – emancipated from all West Kensingtons, and demented milkmen, and desires to cry – and simply a young girl resident in a twilight city of adventure at the outset of her career.

3

Everything was perfect from the first moment. There was first of all the introduction to Mrs Lover, in which Mrs Lover was, as usual, very shy, and in which even he showed an amiable kind of diffidence – (not knowing in quite what spirit one was to take Old Nurses). And then he was shown his room, which was a rather nervous moment for Jackie, as she listened to their bumpings and conversation overhead, and wondered what he was Thinking of it. And then it was decided to tackle his trunk at once; and he, on his part, took what he described as the Worst End, and Mrs Lover, on her part, took what was by deduction the Best End, of the thing – the enormous size of which he apologized breathlessly for, to Mrs Lover, and the obtruding wooden banisters defeating the advancement of which Mrs Lover apologized, breathlessly for, to him: and then they came down into the hall again (where Jackie was standing) for his suitcase, and here Mrs Lover mentioned Tea.

Whereat there was much silence, and 'Well'-ing, and glances each to each, during which a ghostly vision of a deliriously intimate, not to say dual Tea, hovered in the air, waiting for an earthly medium to express it vocally, and champion its translation into fact. And Mr Gissing said that he rather favoured, if the thing was negotiable at such, short notice, a High one, as he had to play to-night and had had no lunch to speak of. At which Mrs Lover made several tentative efforts to gauge the precise gastronomic dizzinesses conceived by her new lodger, and was at last humbly, assured that he aspired no further than buttered (if possible) toast, and maybe poached (if he did not exceed the limits of audacity) eggs. Which Mrs Lover amicably and virtually 'Pooh-poohed' as a High Tea, as one having awaited a demand for Woolworth Buildings and received an order for Peacehaven Bungalows. And then she asked, About what time? 'Well, I should say about an hour,' said Mr Gissing, and then Jackie cut courageously in. 'Would you like to have it with me?' she asked, and 'Rather,' said Mr Gissing, and it was settled.

'Are you going anywhere particular to-night?' he asked, stopping on his way up the stairs to his room.

'No,' said Jackie, knowing perfectly where this question was leading to, but hiding that knowledge from her elevated self, as well as from him. 'Why?'

'I wondered if you'd like to come to the King's?'

'Oh, I should love to,' said Jackie. 'It'd be ripping.'

'Then you'll come round with me?'

'Yes. Rather,' said Jackie. 'Will *you* be acting, then?'

'Well,' confessed Mr Gissing, 'I will . . .'

'In a manner of speaking,' he qualified, and looked at her not without the remotest traces of that faint sarcasm he had employed with her before now.

'Good Lord,' said Jackie, softly, but why she said this it is impossible to say. Mr Gissing went on upstairs, and Jackie went back to her sitting-room.

Here Mrs Lover had already lit the gas and drawn down the blinds jealously against the benighted world outside. And here the fire was poked, and Jackie sat down in front of it for a quarter of an hour's knee-clasping Nirvana, lulled by the eager flames, which might have been so many ecstatic prospects of the evening in front of her. But this was a mere preliminary, a scented bath of bliss prior to active participation, and soon enough she jumped up, and ran upstairs to change and prepare herself.

And there had never been quite such a changing and preparing of herself in all her life. A violently cupboard-opening, a contemptuously clothes-flinging, a fiercely shoe-polishing, an inconsequently mind-changing, a giddily in-front-of-the-mirror-whirling, a hurried, detailed, insane and chaotic changing it was, and if ever she stopped to listen, there came a leisurely and friendly bump from the light of her existence unpacking in the next room, as much as to say, 'All right. Remember we have the whole evening in front of us.' And thirty-five minutes did this changing take, inclusive of finishing touches, which consumed ten (for however much one Liked him, one naturally had an instinct to Show him, as it were); and then she ran downstairs.

And here the air was ripe with agreeable sounds of cooking – a much Higher tea than ever was bargained for being obviously in preparation – and here she was soon joined by Mrs Lover, who came to lay the table. And Mrs Lover did not at first speak, feeling that it was up to Jackie to fire the first shot of appraisement: and Jackie at last, after much light humming, and a great deal of detached stocking-ladder-examining, asked straight out what she thought of him. And Mrs Lover, it may at once be said (though she herself took some time in coming to the point), described him as Decidedly Handsome. And, 'You *do* think <u>him</u> handsome?' asked Jackie, as though that would not have been the exact epithet she herself would have selected. And Nice, also, did Mrs Lover vote him; and, 'Yes, he is *nice*,' said a fair-minded Jackie, as though that quality in him atoned for certain obscure charges that obtained in the back of her mind against him. Older than one had imagined, too, thought Mrs Lover; and, 'Yes, he *is* Older,' admitted Jackie, and added that that, really, was what made him so Nice, somehow, if Mrs Lover knew what she meant. And Mrs Lover was very quick in picking up the subtleties of this proposition, and said, in fact, that that was the very thing *she* had thought herself. They then both agreed that it was Strange, that they should both have struck upon the same idea, and they were both rather more emotional and glad-eyed about this circumstance than the thing actually warranted.

The High tea went with a bang from the commencement, and although it would be an overstatement to say that the point of actual flirtatiousness was at any moment touched, there was certainly an altogether different and more human flavour in their discourse than had ever obtained before. This was nothing very strong, of course: but there was, nevertheless, an amount of free-and-easy puttings in of lumps of sugar, a quantity of most cheeky Finger-excusing with respect to the cake, and a whole lot of brilliantly casual Askings-for-more and grudging admissions of Enough, which all testified in their way to a new and unconstrainedly humorous intimacy which you could have hardly believed possible half an hour ago. Indeed, by the time they had finished their high tea, and had rushed upstairs for their hats and coats, and had helped each other on with them in the narrow hall-way: and by the time they were walking briskly down the star-lit, frosty streets to the theatre, Jackie had awakened not only to the exhilarating consciousness that the world was at her feet again, but also to the calm pride of foreknowledge that her friend might be relied upon to make love to her at any moment in the near future ... For many had loved Jackie, and she had learnt to read the signs. She was too familiar with these sudden leaping intimacies, these infectious, inexplicable ebulliences of spirit between two strangers, not to know their eventual outcome.

Jackie never forgot that walk to the theatre; and the evening went on from thrill to thrill. And when, as they approached the theatre, they saw a little queue of early-door enthusiasts dismally sheltering themselves from the wind; and when, as they entered the rosy, lit, and yet hushed and unpopulated foyer, he went to the box office and employed his magic professional influence on her behalf; and when, as they emerged again, she stopped before a poster of the play (which was 'The Devil's Disciple,' by George Bernard Shaw) and observed that his name, Richard Gissing, led all the rest – it was as though the portals of fame were swinging back before her. Or, better still, it was as though she were being let into fame by some intimate side-entrance;

and the little wistful queue, standing mutely by, formed the first chain of captives under the yoke of her aspiration.

They then walked down to the stage-door, and there she left him (having arranged to call for him there afterwards), and decided to go for a little walk before going in.

But there was too great a restlessness upon her, too full a symphony of glee beating somewhere in the deeps of her spirit, for mere walking, or the thick sights and roarings of Hammersmith to relieve; and she soon came back to the theatre, where she was with the first dozen or so who took their seats in the stalls.

4

It was a strange and enchanted half-hour which she then spent before the rising of the curtain; and she sat there peacefully reading her programme from cover to cover and back again.

Until at last the house was full, and the conductor bobbed up, like the apex and unifying spirit of the will of the house, and the overture commenced.

And the footlights blazed forth, like opening flowers of light; and there ensued a few minutes of elevated pulsating expectancy, of delicious irretrievability, in which every one tried to cough their last coughs, and make their final adjustments.

Then the house-lights succumbed: a murmurous

darkness descended: the overture died down: a quaint, prolonged pause intervened, as though some hitch had taken place: and then the curtain rumbled, slowly and with a sort of unsteady steadiness, upwards. Not a soul spoke; and the tense old gods of make-believe sat vigilant in the breathless house.

As for Jackie, she sat there alone, with an odd foretaste of stage-fright on behalf of her friend, and watching every movement on the stage as though her existence hung upon it. Even after the first few minutes she was responding with her whole spirit and intelligence to the Satanic melodrama; but when at last Dick Dudgeon appeared, the devil's advocate himself, the deliverer, the champion of the oppressed, the mocker of debased godliness, the hero and protagonist of courage and righteousness – and when Dick Dudgeon was observed, for all his make-up, to be none other than Richard Gissing; and when this individual did, with his loose, swashbuckling carriage, his emancipating wit and genial causticity, his depth and control of voice, which could break where it willed, yearn without querulousness, and hit every inflexion with an inevitability and surety of aim which left the soul released and happy – when, from the first moment, her own rescuer was to be witnessed evoking roars of laughing applause, and giggles of suspended delight, like a great wind over the rustling dark wheat of his audience; or caressing them into uncanny silences, like the threat of rain, which was the threat of tears, Jackie really did not know where she was or what she was doing at all. And when, at the end of the first act of this play, Dick Dudgeon drove forth his enemies and took their crying child-victim Essie under his wing; and when Essie began to cry, and he took her to himself and told her softly that she might cry that way if she liked, poor Jackie, as the curtain came down on that consummate moment, was in a fearful state of not knowing whether to let one's tears roll one after another down one's face, or to betray oneself equally by trying to smear them away. For she had by that time given up all her ambition of Going upon the Stage, all ambition of anything indeed, and had no object or fancy in life but as some eternal Essie to some eternal Dick Dudgeon in an eternal atmosphere of crying consolations.

And the remainder of the play was merely an endorsement of this cardinal point. There were no more emotional heights to be scaled. Indeed, by the time the play was over, and she came out into the air, she had quite cooled down.

5

It was with a curious blending of pride and trepidation that Jackie went round to the Stage Door afterwards, and asked of its guardian for Mr Gissing. Her inquiry was handled with deferential suspicion, and in the few silent moments that she was kept waiting she was granted her first authentic impression of Stage Doors and the stone and brick passages leading therefrom – which was an impression of

something distantly underhand, of business being trans-
acted in a quiet and slightly furtive way, as from a distant
consciousness of sin – which furtiveness was tempered by a
certain humming jollity and ebullience whenever a human
being passed across its background ... But this was but a
fleeting and transitory impression, washed away in a variety of other more emphatic ones, by the time she had been
transported to the door of Mr Gissing's dressing-room, and
her conductor was knocking upon it.

'Hullo!' Mr Gissing was heard shouting, and the door
was opened by Mr Gissing's slightly hostile dresser,
through the defensive arms of whom Jackie peered through
at Mr Gissing, and Mr Gissing peered through at Jackie.

'Come in, come in, come in!' cried Mr Gissing, three
times exactly, as dressing actors have done since the first
dressing actor. 'I shan't be long now.'

Jackie entered smilingly, and the dresser went out,
apparently in a temper.

Mr Gissing's face was glistening with grease; Mr Gissing
was without coat and waistcoat, and wore no collar, and
he was rubbing maliciously away at his face with a towel.
You could have imagined that the labours of the evening
had only just begun, to watch him rubbing. He rubbingly
offered her a chair, and continued to rub, looking all
the time into the mirror, as though in a wild endeavour
to emulate the insane frictional antics of the individual
therein reflected. His dressing-table, which was a long
wooden shelf, was covered with a towel, which was stained

luxuriously with carmine (Marat's bath-towel might have looked rather like this one) and spread with stumps and assortments of grease-paints number five and nine, and blue pencil. An inconceivably vast powder-puff lay to one side, together with a pot of cream (which was the size of a gas reservoir), and Dick Dudgeon's hair. In other parts of the blinding little room lay Dick Dudgeon's overcoat, Dick Dudgeon's top-boots, Dick Dudgeon's hat, and other Dick Dudgeon parts, all lying anywhere, rather as though Dick Dudgeon had been the victim of spontaneous combustion (after all his trials) – as indeed, in some sense, he had – no trace of his character remaining in his earthly medium, who was an actor rubbing away with a keen eye upon his supper.

'Enjoy yourself?' asked Mr Gissing, peering keenly forward to simulate his model in the mirror, who was at that moment engaged in placing delicate slabs of grease along his eye-brows.

'Terribly,' said Jackie, and there was a silence of contentment.

'Saw *you*,' said Mr Gissing.

'Oh, did you? Can one see people from there, then?'

'Well. I knew where you were.'

Here's fame, if you like, thought Jackie. Here am I, with Dick Dudgeon – the chosen one out of all those four hundred odd who are now going benightedly home – sitting behind the scenes in easy colloquy with the figure whom they rapturously applauded, and from whom the whole evening has emanated. Here's fame, if only a vicarious fame, if you like, thought Jackie. Or at least this is what Jackie, who always liked to get the best out of every moment, tried to think. Actually, and for some obscure reason, it didn't seem to work. She found herself obtaining little or no pleasure from the fact.

They talked for about five minutes, during which the dresser returned, and having silently collected all outstanding parts of Dick Dudgeon, with a view to his resurrection tomorrow night, quietly received his dismissal. And then there came a knock at the door.

The new-comer, whose knock was a formality, was a gentleman of about the same age as Mr Gissing, and swiftly identifiable as the gentleman who had played the parson. He wore a thick overcoat which was loose about the collar and rather too large for him, and kid-gloves upon his hands, the left palm of which he punched methodically and genially with his right fist, on and off during the greater part of his discourse. He assumed a bantering tone from the commencement.

'Here he is, here he is, here he is!' he said. 'The last as usual! The last as usual!' (Punch. Punch.)

'Ah, Mr Grayson,' said Mr Gissing. 'This is Miss Mortimer. Miss Mortimer, this is Mr Grayson.'

'How d'you do,' said Jackie, smiling from her chair, and 'Good evening, Miss Mortimer,' said Mr Grayson, bowing mockingly, as much as to imply that you couldn't fool him that she was the genuine Miss Mortimer. A rather rude man, Jackie thought.

There followed a slightly difficult silence, relieved in no
manner by the dull smack of Mr Grayson's gloves.

'Well, and how are we to-night, Mr Gissing?'

'I'm very well, thank you,' said Mr Gissing, fixing his tie.
Punch . . . Punch.

'The Great British Public in a curious mood this evening,
I think?' hazarded Mr Grayson.

'Really?'

'Or do I malign the Great British Public?'

'I thought they were rather sweet.'

'Yes. *You* would. Poor old Dobell, though. He nearly
passed out about his round. It's the first time the dear old
thing's missed it since we opened.'

This was evidently a round of applause, thought Jackie.

'I got mine all right,' said Mr Gissing.

'Oh yes, *you* would,' said Mr Grayson, with great mean-
ing, and there was a silence in which Mr Grayson, punching
mildly, watched Mr Gissing buttoning his waistcoat.

'Of course, how they *get* the jobs I don't know,' said Mr
Grayson, manifestly poking fun at Mr Gissing for Jackie's
benefit. 'It's beyond me. I mean to say, look at the fellow.
Look at him. I ask you.'

Here some voice softly whispered into Jackie's ear,
'Actor's Jokes', and she answered that prompting with a
genial smile until such time as the pleasantry might exhaust
itself. If Jackie had known how many wearied times, in the
career ahead of her, she would be called upon to assume
that dread, fixed, receptive smile for like occasions, it

is possible that she would have had more difficulty in responding now.

'I mean, *look* at him, I mean,' said Mr Grayson. 'I ask you, I mean. I mean – *look*!

'I mean, have you *ever*? *Did* you ever?

'I mean, I could understand it if there was any *talent* ...

'Or any looks even,' said Mr Grayson. 'It must be influence, that's all. What do you think, Miss Mortimer?'

'Yes. I expect it's influence,' said Jackie, and laughed.

There was another awkward, if bland, silence, the conclusion that it was Influence seeming to have brought us to something of a cul-de-sac conversationally, and the jesters having nothing to do but gaze at the silent object of their attack with a kind of paternal mockery. Happily there came a knock at the door. 'Can I come in?' came a man's voice.

'Don't ask *me*. Don't ask *me*.' Mr Grayson would take no responsibility, as a head was put round the door. 'I shouldn't *think* you could. Star's dressing-room, you know.'

There entered a very tall gentleman with a long nose and a diffident air, who was readily recognizable as the gentleman who had impersonated General Burgoyne. His hair was greying and thin, his face nervous and emaciated, and his voice supercilious but submissive. He had the appearance of a legal adviser in a dread of getting flustered, and looked, in general, as though he should have had his cup of cocoa and been under the sheets two hours ago at least. This was Mr Dobell, and Jackie took to him at once.

'I came to ask if it's true there's a Call, to-morrow,' he said.

'*Call*!' ejaculated both Mr Grayson and Mr Gissing.

'Well, our A.S.M. was saying something about it.'

'Well, we've been told nothing,' said Mr Gissing. 'This is Miss Mortimer, Dobell – Miss Mortimer, Mr Dobell.'

'Good evening,' said Mr Dobell, and Jackie all at once found herself being saluted with a long thin hand, reinforced by a long thin smile, both of which vanished as suddenly as they had come.

'Well, then, it's a false alarm, I expect,' said Mr Dobell. 'But he certainly said something as I was coming off.'

'Oh, that boy'll come to a bad end,' said Mr Grayson. 'By the way, did you know Ernest was in front to-night?'

'*Was* he! ...' About three minutes' conversation now ensued on the topic of Ernest; during which another gentleman, apparently the Stage Manager, entered brightly with, 'Well, well, well – what are we all up to? ... Call? No. No call ... Only understudies' – and during which, in the general hubbub, Jackie found herself cornered by Mr Dobell.

'Are you in this business, Miss Mortimer?' asked Mr Dobell.

'No, I'm not, really,' said Jackie.

'Dreadful business,' said Mr Dobell, ruminating, but he did not tell her why.

'Yes,' said Jackie, with the same vagueness. 'I suppose it is.'

'Were you in front to-night?'

'Yes. It was fearfully good, wasn't it?'

'Yes. It plays very well, doesn't it?'

'Yes. I thought *you* were wonderful,' said Jackie.

'Well, it's a wonderful *Part*, isn't it?' said a fair-minded Mr Dobell, but he was a little breathless and flushed over the compliment for all that. 'You can't go wrong. It plays itself.'

'Oh. I don't know ...'

'Gissing's immense, isn't he?'

'Yes, he is wonderful, isn't he?'

By this time Mr Gissing was ready, and a move was being made for the door. Mr Gissing smiled upon Jackie and went ahead with Mr Grayson, and Mr Dobell and Jackie brought up the rear, meekly discussing the weather. On emerging into the fresh air, Mr Grayson immediately began hissing through his teeth and punching with violent regularity, as though he had been wound up afresh: a stoutish woman had materialized, evidently the puncher's choice in life, to whom Jackie was not introduced, and who was apparently oblivious, through usage, to the padded warfare eternally raging in the person of her domestic idol: they all stood there, swaying slightly in the wind, and valedictorily conversational, until such time as some intrepid spirit might say 'Well,' and let them go home; which pioneer work Mr Gissing undertook (Mr Grayson supporting him, with an even more resounding smack than usual): and then they dispersed. Mr Dobell raised his hat and smiled very particularly at Jackie, and the next moment she was walking home under the twinkling stars at the usual rapid pace tacitly exacted by her deliverer.

6

They were passing St. Paul's School, and she began it with 'Oh, by the way,' as people do when broaching subjects upon which their lives hang by threads. And from the first moment he threw up a stolid fort of resistance. But that she did not mind, so long as it was acknowledged that she might storm it, so long as the argument was in the open and they might contradict each other flat without incivility.

'I won't,' said Mr Gissing, looking down at her. 'Honestly.'

'Perhaps,' said Jackie, 'you don't think I could Act?'

'That's irrelevant, anyway,' said Mr Gissing.

'But *do* you think I could?' asked Jackie.

'How on earth should I know? I shouldn't think so.'

'You *wouldn't?*' said Jackie, with a rather mixed air of detachment.

'No.'

'Perhaps you think I'm not decent-looking enough?'

'On the contrary, I think you're extremely pretty.'

'You *do?*' said Jackie, also with a very insecure detachment.

'At times overbearingly so,' added Mr Gissing.

'Well, then ...' said Jackie, but he remained silent. She herself wanted this silence, to think about 'overbearingly so', but she brought herself back to business.

'I say,' said Jackie. 'Won't you?'

'What do you want me to do, anyway?'

'To introduce me to some one, or give me some advice.'

'All right. I Advise you to go to an agent.'

'Yes, but won't you help me?'

'No, I won't. If there was the slightest possibility of ever forgiving myself if I did – I might ... Anyway, the best I could do would be to get you some rotten understudy on tour.'

'Well, that'd be something. But I want, really, to start at the beginning, and learn, and get Experience, and all that. I really am serious, I mean. I'm not one of those who think they can jump into it.'

'Oh, I see. You're one of the I-started-at-the-bottom-Sound-Training-on-the-Road-Nothing-like-it-old-boy school? Then you should start with a fit-up.'

'What's a fit-up?'

'A Fit,' said Mr Gissing, after a pause. 'Up.'

There was another pause.

'But you must *have* Experience, mustn't you?'

'Why?'

'Oh – don't be silly.'

'I wouldn't start on Experience. If you go on with this, you'll have enough Experience rammed down your throat without going out to seek it.'

'Yes – but you must *have* Experience. I bet you've had lots of it, anyway.'

'Oh, *I* have, yes. That's why I'm so full of mannerisms. I was a much better actor ten years ago.'

'Besides, I've got to earn my living . . . And by the way, if it's such a rotten profession, why are you in it?'

Mr Gissing paused before replying to this.

'Well,' he said at last. 'I suppose it's because I'm never really happy except when I *am* acting.'

That struck Jackie as being very good. When the time came, she resolved, *she* would never be happy, except while *she* was acting. That was very nice.

'Well, I think you might help me,' said Jackie.

'That's what I'm trying to do,' said Mr Gissing, and so the argument went on and on, and round and round. They argued all the way back to their lodgings; they argued on the step, letting themselves in; they asked a rather shocked Mrs Lover if they could have supper together, so that there should be no pause in their argument; they argued waiting for, consuming, and digesting their supper, until the clock above the ash-strewn fireplace pointed to five-and-twenty past twelve, at which magic moment Mr Gissing made a concession. This he did not do with the air of a man making a concession, but as one maintaining his own argument: but it was a concession for all that.

'I don't mind 'phoning up and making an appointment with an agent for you to-morrow,' he said, and Jackie nailed him to it like lightning.

'You *will*?' she said, smiling.

'Yes.'

'Oh, thanks awfully . . . I'm sorry to have gone on so, but you've no idea what it means . . . Of course, I don't want you to if you don't really want to,' said Jackie, who only wished now that they could both win the day.

'Very well, then – I won't,' said Mr Gissing.

'What time'll you do it? Shall I be able to see some one to-morrow?'

'I imagine so.'

'Thanks awfully,' repeated Jackie, softly, and, 'It's jolly nice of you, and thanks terribly,' she added.

But Mr Gissing was not going to kiss and make-up like that. He looked severely at her, and rose to go to bed.

Chapter Three

A DAY IN THE THEATRE

1

He came down to an extremely restive and rather scared Jackie at ten o'clock next morning, to ask her if she still felt the same, and five minutes later they left the house.

With very few words they walked down the cold, sunny street, and he guided her mechanically to the post office.

'This is where we 'phone Mr Lee,' he said, and went into a box. She waited outside and watched him through the glass. It took about four minutes.

'Well?' said Jackie.

'A quarter to eleven,' he said. 'I can see you round there.'

'Do you think there's any chance of anything?'

'Yes. He thinks he might slip you in unnoticed with Linell. Stephen Linell.'

'Who's he?'

'Shakespeare. You'll be jolly lucky if you can get it. He's going out for fifteen weeks.'

'On tour?'

Mr Gissing glanced at Jackie.

'Yes.'

There was a pause.

'I hope I can get it,' said Jackie.

They embarked together on the District, and got out at Piccadilly, and walked towards Leicester Square.

'Does one just go in,' asked Jackie, 'and ask for Mr Lee?'

'I think that's just the thing, really,' said Mr Gissing.

There was a silence.

'I'm very sorry to see you so frightened, Jackie,' he said. 'Because all this business is made up of going in and asking for Mr Lees.'

She was too busy pulling round from the 'Jackie' to answer at once.

'It's only the first time,' she said.

'Well, here we are. You go up there, and it's on the right. Will you join me at lunch?'

'Oh yes,' said Jackie.

'Will you meet me at this corner, then, at a quarter past one?'

'Yes. Rather.'

'If you're not here, I'll know that something's happened. Good-bye.'

'Good-bye.'

She was walking up the street to her career.

2

Her career began with a not very impertinent young woman of middling attractions in an outer room. Her career was then suspended for half an hour, which deteriorated her morale at the outset, and during which other submissive individuals intermittently came in and softly tackled the not very impertinent young woman of middling attractions on the subject of their own careers. But at last a giddy moment came when she was running up the stairs; and then she was alone in a room with Mr Carson Lee.

Mr Lee – a large, dark, heavily moustached and abundantly virile man of about forty-five – was at the telephone: and it was clear, at the moment that Jackie caught him, that the entire business of the theatre had reached a crisis from which it was not likely to pull through. But Mr Lee was happily in charge, and he was sitting at the machine, like an admiral who had ruthlessly snatched the wireless from the operator, and was issuing his commands and smelling out the position with awe-inspiring rapidity and efficiency.

In these circumstances, he was just able to concede to Jackie a curt and unsmiling nod, as though he knew that *she* had come with news of the fleet in the North (which

95

had doubtless been sunk by now): but otherwise he did not attend to her.

'What? ... *What?* ... Out of the question! ... Wipe it out. Wipe it out ... What? ... What? ... Well, he must come and see *me* ... What? ... *Good.*'

On this last word, which was pronounced with the minimum of satisfaction (and the maximum of finality), he thrust the instrument from him, and came over to shake Jackie's hand.

'Good morning, Miss Mortimer. Glad to see you here. Mr Gissing 'phoned up about you, didn't he?'

'Yes,' said Jackie. 'That's right.' But at this moment there was a buzzing at the machine. Mr Lee whirled himself back into the thick of the battle.

'Hullo-hullo ... Hullo ... Yes ... HulLO ... Yes ... WHAT! ... Never ... No. Certainly not. *Never!*'

And the receiver smashed down on that leonine negative. The whole theatre had obviously combined against Mr Lee, but he was taking a firm stand. Or rather the naval odds were numerically too much for the distressed admiral, but he was going down with flying colours.

'Let me see now,' said Mr Lee, again rising. 'You've hardly had any experience at all now, have you?'

'No – I haven't, really.'

Mr Lee paced over to the blazing fire, and commenced to warm his back with a kind of expert lasciviousness and a gentle swaying motion.

'Well, I rather think I may have the thing for you.

Richard Linell. If you could get in with him you'd get a fine all-round training, and a real start. And of course he's wanting beginners. (Salary wouldn't be up to much, of course.) Let me see now . . .'

He flashed over to the telephone, lifted the receiver, shouted 'Get me Mr Brewster, please,' and paused . . .

'Let me see now, how old *are* you, Miss – Hullo. Hullo. Mr Brewster there, please? . . . Oh . . . Well, do you know where Mr Linell's rehearsing to-day? . . . Oh . . . Then what time'll Mr *Brewster* be back? . . . Ah . . . Ah . . . Thank you.'

He snatched a bit of paper from a partition in his desk, and commenced scribbling upon it. He rose and handed it to Jackie.

'Now if you'll take that round to Mr Brewster, in Glasshouse Street, you'll probably catch him; and you may see Linell this morning. Of course, I don't know whether he's filled up, but I should think you'd stand a very good chance. You've got the right kind of voice and looks, and you couldn't get a better training anywhere. Benson, Greet or any of 'em. Of course there's nothing to speak of in the way of salary. In fact, it generally means a premium as often as not. But then—'

Mr Lee was summoned to the telephone.

'Hullo . . . Yes . . . Yes . . . Oh yes . . . What! Good God, man, do they think I don't know my own business? (The Government itself had evidently turned against him now.) 'What! . . . Well, tell 'em I take complete

responsibility – *complete* ... Yes ... Good-bye ... Yes ...
Good-bye ... No ... No ... Good-bye.'

He returned to the fire. 'Well. Yes. That ought to be all
right, then. It's a chance in a hundred, really – placed as
you are. Do you know Glasshouse Street?'

'No,' said Jackie. 'I'm afraid I don't.'

He directed her to Glasshouse Street, with some care,
and the interview was closed.

'Bosh!' was the last word she heard Mr Lee (who had
returned to the telephone) using, as she ran down the stairs
and out into the sunny street.

She walked from the comparative quietude of Leicester
Square into the seething vortex of Piccadilly, and was shot
out again into the comparatively quiet and seedy environs of
Snow's chop-house and the Regent Palace, and found her way
to the address she wanted. This address rather awkwardly
coincided with a fishmonger's address, but an assistant with
a glistening dank blush upon his hands directed her to a
narrow entrance next door, and after climbing a very great
quantity of wooden stairs, she achieved an office.

Here there was another young woman who was sitting
in another outer room at her typing. She said that Mr
Brewster might soon be back, and gave Jackie a chair. Then
she sat again at her typing. Jackie watched her with interest
for an hour and five minutes ...

At the end of which period a gentleman came clattering
busily upon the wooden stairs, and entered the room.

This gentleman — a short, greying, clean-shaven man in pince-nez and a bowler hat — glanced in passing at Jackie, and went to the other end of the room to take off his overcoat.

'Parry been?'

'No; Mr Rodd 'phoned, though.'

'All serene?'

'Yes.'

Mr Brewster hovered over Jackie and took her note. He adjusted his pince-nez, and read it. 'Ah, yes,' he said. 'I'm rather afraid you've come a bit too late, though. I think he's all fixed up by now. You might try, though. He's rehearsing at the Lester Halls, Jackson Street, off Tottenham Court Road. If I were you I'd go round. He's wanting people like you. And if it's too late now you might fix up for the Spring. He's going out again, then. Do you know how to get there?'

'No,' said Jackie. 'I'm afraid I don't.'

He directed her with some care. 'And tell him I sent you round, will you?' added Mr Brewster, becoming modestly omnipotent.

'Thank you very much,' said Jackie. 'I'll go straight round there now.'

'Good morning.'

'Good morning.'

Jackie was half-way down the stairs, when a voice recalled her.

'I say!'

'Yes,' said Jackie.

99

'You'll have to hurry. I'm not sure he doesn't leave off rehearsing early this morning.'

'Thanks,' said Jackie. 'I will. Good morning.'

'Good-bye.'

(A little uncanny, all this, thought Jackie, as she jumped hastily off one bus on to another at Oxford Circus, and jogged along above the tumultuous tide of Oxford Street. Strange forces at work in herself – these forces that had suddenly snatched her from her ordinary life, and sent her chasing madly about the whirl and roar of London streets, as though she had no longer any will of her own, but was a mere puppet in the mysterious and thunderous drama of the metropolis about her. She could not remember how it had all started . . . She had imagined that she was to stoop in order to conquer this morning; but here she was rushing about from one address to another in order to conquer, and it wasn't the same thing . . .)

3

She branched off from Tottenham Court Road into an area of wide squares formed by various new and imposing Institutes of various kinds, and she had no difficulty in finding the Lester Halls.

Which Halls reared a very magnificent frontage before the stare of the world, but were sadly lacking in one minute but (to the weak-minded) vital accessory – to wit, a Bell. Now if Jackie had been a strong and decisive character, she would undoubtedly have laughed at Bells and walked straight in (the door was open) to demand guidance: but being a feeble and timorous being (as has been clearly indicated), and accustomed to announcing herself to strangers solely by tentative and wretched tinkling sounds, she was now reduced to walking palely up and down outside the Lester Halls, and wondering what was going to happen next. Happily though, after about ten minutes of this, the undoubtedly official bucket-clanker and floor-scourer of the Lester Halls came out to practise her violent pursuit on the front-steps, and was able to give Jackie the desired information.

A long, dark passage was pointed at, with a dripping brush, and down this passage Jackie went. It grew darker still as she went along, but her doubts as to the propriety of taking this passage were soon assuaged by a voice coming from behind a door at the far end.

This voice was the loudest and deepest voice that Jackie had ever heard, or could conceive hearing, in her life, and belonged, she naturally assumed, to an ogre who had at that very instant been robbed of his supper. If one elaborated this image by conceiving this ogre as one whose supper (previous to his privation) had been composed of the most delicate little children's thumbs he had ever before witnessed, let alone tasted; and if, further, one conceived this ogre as one suffering temporarily from twinges of a giant gout; and if, further still, one conceived this ogre as having been on the boards in his day, probably in Shakespeare, and undoubtedly at the Lyceum (or its equivalent at the top of the beanstalk), where they always shoved him into the heavy parts – some pale notion may be formulated of the voice that greeted Jackie from the other side of this door, and some cause may be discerned for the fact that her piteous knocking with a little gloved knuckle upon the panel of this door elicited no response or invitation from within. Indeed, Jackie was at last compelled to take the handle and walk in unasked.

She entered what appeared to be a large ball-room, with a slippery floor, a piano, chairs all round, and a balcony above. This was peopled, she was surprised to find, almost exclusively by children of her own age (from eighteen, that is, to twenty-three): and in the centre, by the piano, was a selection of chairs so arranged as to symbolize various entrances, seats, trees, tables and such-like, around which the drama (which was 'Twelfth Night') was to be played.

The voice, she was even more surprised to find, was fulminating up from the chest of an untidy, fair, and excessively curly-haired young man (rather like a grammar-school prefect), who was bent practically double in the exertions attaching to an impersonation of Sir Toby Belch – which character had undoubtedly, all the Illyrian morning, been inviting an infinite quantity of Plagues (and their like) to fall upon the heads of his opponents; and alluding to galliards, corantos, coystrils, sink-a-paces, or similar unknown objects or abstractions, with great gusto and familiarity, as was his wont.

The rest of the company, which was about twenty in number, were sitting around, or standing about, or talking softly, or looking on.

Jackie, who felt like a little girl on her first day at school, excited many vague stares, and adopted a kind of arduously mouse-like and timidly observant attitude pending cross-examination. Unhappily, though, she found that she was unable to cancel the natural functioning of the human body with respect to Creaking – and creak she did, to the consternation of all. But at last a young man, older than the rest (as though he were their usher), came forth, and she gave him her note. He gave her a chair in return, and told her to wait.

During this the rehearsal had been in progress without stoppage, and in the next half-hour she was given ample opportunity to remark the leading principles upon which the Stephen Linell Shakespearian Company founded its interpretation of the master. Which principles, Jackie decided, after some consideration, were almost exclusively Village-Hampden principles. That is to say, each young man, having once passed between the two chairs representing the central entrance, automatically assumed an armour of deep-chested and impenetrable defiance, and having, in the space of time allotted to him, strutted towards, bellowed upon, paced around, thrown metaphorical gauntlets at, and generally held the five-barred gate against his fellows (who were similarly engrossed), would walk off with a magnificent sweep and a cocky air of having delivered a snub to Tyranny, from which it would be very lucky if it again lifted its head. Such was the main principle at work, thought Jackie. There were many subsidiary principles, of which the moaning or expiring principle (for lovers), and the 'La, Sir!' wave-hands-about-with-shrill-chatter principle (for serving women) were the most easily discerned, but these acted merely as set-offs to the prevailing convention of aggression.

Over the ravings of this infantile troupe, the actor-manager, Mr Stephen Linell – a slim, dark man of about forty with longish hair, a bow-tie, and features which seemed to be yearning languorously for a medallion where-with they might be perpetuated – ruled with the suavity of a head master taking a lower form. A lower form wherein his birch was needless as a weapon of coercion (his mere person and presence being enough), and wherein he could, therefore, indulge an easy urbanity, or, at moments, a del-icate whimsicality even, without fear of accident.

His ushers, of which there was one other beside the one who had spoken to Jackie, were, as ushers ever have been, in greater fear of the great man than his pupils, but at the same time upborne by the grave bliss of office. To these Mr Linell occasionally deferred, lowering his ear, with a munificent soft drooping of his own grandeur, to their opinions or remarks, and never failing to agree with them. For disagreement would have implied equality on common ground, and the mere prospect of argument would have been fatal to the medallion.

To his pupils themselves, though, he employed a different mode of self-protection. Here his urbanity was even more extreme, however much it might have been a sheep's-clothing over the wolf of his wisdom and authority. Hence it was that his suggestions seemed to come less as commands than as reminders of divine and immutable laws. 'No, I think we do it this way, don't we?' Mr Linell would ask, coming forward to demonstrate, or, 'Yes, but it'd be better like this, I think, wouldn't it?' or, 'Yes, but that's not how we want it, is it?' There was but one absolute way of doing the thing, and that was Mr Linell's way, and Mr Linell had merely to appeal to reason. And even if his pupils dared take inward exception to any of his dictums, they would hardly have dared acknowledge it, even to themselves. For (Jackie noticed) there was an uncanny smell of Premiums impressing itself elusively, faintly, and yet withal sensibly upon this atmosphere, and a disagreement with Mr Linell's technique might have been the confession of a bad bargain ...

Not that Mr Linell could keep his temper at all times. Indeed towards the end of this rehearsal he very nearly lost it. This was occasioned, or rather forced upon him, by the slow coming into being of certain soft, but irritating whisperings, not to say *sotto voce* arguments, not to say audacious conversations on the part of those not at the moment rehearsing: which sounds, increasing in volume, and being taken up all round-the room in defiance of the mild shushings of the ushers (which but served to increase the din), at last infuriated an otherwise conciliatory actor-manager into a betrayal of feeling.

In fact, 'Would you people mind keeping silence!' shouted Mr Linell. 'We're not here for Pleasure, you know.' And with that stern negation of a conceivable fundamental and communal purpose at work in this room, Jackie threw over all hope of interpreting the ranting spectacle before her eyes. Pleasure, indeed – Pleasure of an original and very possibly misdirected kind – but Pleasure, of some sort, for all that – had been her final obscure hope of explanation, her one last resort in her analysis of the scene. With the denial of Pleasure the abyss opened, and she was face to face with Bedlam.

Shortly after this the rehearsal concluded, and Mr Linell, after a short pause, and a state of dreamy expectancy all round, proceeded to set a kind of Thespian prep. He was tolerably contented, he said, with their general results so far as the work was concerned, but he could expand indefinitely upon their remissness with respect to These Words. Mr Linell meant to *say* – really. He had *never*. He *had* never. Quite literally, he meant to say, never. They opened in a week's time, and with the exception of Sir Toby, not *one* of them knew *one single* thing about their lines. Now all this, he meant to say, had to be altered, and if they could not come up on Thursday Word Perfect, he meant to say, they might as well not trouble to come up at all, and he might as well write and cancel the dates before it was too late.

Having said this, or at least having meant to say this, Mr Linell paused heavily and said it all over again, in a different order. He then said that those whom it concerned should try to get down to Nathan's before rehearsal this afternoon, which would begin at three, *Sharp*, and which would be devoted to the Dream. By which Mr Linell meant 'A Midsummer Night's Dream' by William Shakespeare.

He then dismissed the class, by turning away; and walked straight over to Jackie. He came over with the decisiveness of one who should have demolished her before this, and took her note in silence.

'Ah, yes,' he said. 'Well, I'm glad you've come up, because you're the sort of thing we're wanting, really; even if it is too late this time. Let me see, now' – he turned to a lingering usher – 'have we heard from Miss Simmons yet, Mr Clodd?'

'No, Mr Linell, but we ought to hear this evening.'

'Oh yes . . . Well, I'm afraid I can't say anything definite until we've heard from her. You see, I don't know whether she's joining us or not. But if you'll give Mr Clodd your address, we ought to be able to let you know in the morning. I should very much like to have you with us myself . . . Yes . . . Well – I must be going.' He smiled vaguely, shook hands, accepted her thanks, and went.

Her address was laboriously inscribed upon an usher's private envelope, and she came out again into the air.

4

She was ten minutes late, and he was there at the corner.
He guided her mechanically to an apparently agreed destination, and she told him her news. She said that she Liked
Mr Linell, and he said that he liked him, too. Indeed,
added Mr Gissing, but for Mr Linell's lately increasing,
and, in his (Mr Gissing's) opinion, unjustifiable confusion
of himself with God Almighty, he knew few better than
Mr Linell in the profession. But the latter error made for a
certain assurance, a certain self-esteem even, in the man,
which might easily, at times, cause ranklings in the breasts
of his more conscious inferiors. Such was the gist of Mr
Gissing's opinion of Mr Linell. Jackie asked if he knew him
well. Yes, very well. They had been with Benson together,
hundreds and hundreds of years ago.

At this they arrived at a small restaurant, named Line's,
which was in a side-street off the Strand, specialized in lob-
ster, and exuded the rather oppressive, manager-pampered
cosiness common to such resorts. They took a corner table
on the ground floor, and here they were joined by Miss
Marion Lealy.

She came up laughingly and quite suddenly – was introduced to Jackie; and the next minute was invited to lunch
and sitting down and sipping a cock-tail and mocking at
Mr Gissing.

Miss Marion Lealy, whose fame as an actress had been
in Jackie's ears ever since she had left school, was at this

time at the height of her success – or at least at one of the
heights of notoriety to which she invariably leapt every
other year or so – the popular and ineffable ballad, with
the refrain ending:

> 'Marion, darlin',
> Darlin' Marion,
> Darlin' Marion Lealy!'

having only lately (after igniting two continents), reached
the barrel-organ and errand-boy stage wherein it would
finally expire. She was an exceptionally beautiful young
woman of about thirty, and, as a beauty, was known in
roughly three capacities. There was Marion Lealy the
Scientist: there was Marion Lealy the Philanthropist:
and there was Marion Lealy the Actress. Under the first
heading (that of Scientist) came her well-known exertions
in the Press, wherein, from altruistic medical heights, she
held out unflinchingly for a neat lemon before breakfast
every morning, water between (and not during) meals,
and in general discussed, with sprightly scholarliness, the
workings of both the exteriors and interiors of her read-
ers – though insisting, all the time that the Primary Cause
of ill health was Worry, which she alluded to as the Bane of
Modern Life (and of which you were cured by her cunning
expedient of Avoiding it). In her second capacity (that of
Philanthropist) she was timidly but short-skirtedly and rav-
ishingly present at the first phases of an infinite quantity of

bazaars, dog-homes, orphanages or Association Football matches. And in her last capacity (that of Actress) she was to be seen for about nine months of every year playing Revue either at the Palace, or the Pavilion, or at any theatrical point in a Shaftesbury Avenue line drawn between those two foundations of gaiety. And indeed as an Actress (though she was of course a public character and Force for Good first, and only an actress second) she was very versatile and very bright.

She spoke with a strong Canadian accent, and on being introduced to Jackie, said, 'Verrer pleased to meet you, Jackie,' and smiled charmingly upon her. She then entered upon a five-minutes' breathless narration of a minor brawl she had had with a taxi-man just before coming in here; and she took Jackie's breath away as much by the aura of her fame as by the fact of her familiarity with Mr Gissing. With Mr Gissing, indeed, she was intensely familiar, and before the hors-d'oeuvres were over, she was ruffling his hair and pulling out his tie, on the plea that she Jes' Loved Rilin' him (though Mr Gissing, so far from appearing riled, was smoothing his hair and putting back his tie with the equanimity of one knowing these to be the common and inevitable features of discourse with her), and appealing to Jackie to support her in her mockery.

'Have you known him larng, Jackie, then?' she asked, with that glee inseparable from her hurrying voice and temperament.

No, Jackie hadn't. Only a week, really.

'A *week*! My word! I've known little Dickie ever since he was a boy. D'y'know, I'se *so* in love with him at one time! I was, truly. You'd never believe it. I guess I've never been in love like that since. Isn't that so, Dickie?'

'Certainly,' said Mr Gissing.

'Say,' said Miss Lealy, changing the subject like lightning, after her habit. 'I had a dose of *your* friends the other night.'

'My friends?'

'Your little Ox Ford and Cambridge boys. Say – that's the last Boat Race night I stand for! Did you see the pictures of me rowin' on those chairs?'

'Yes. I saw. But they're not my friends.'

'Well, I hope not. D'y'know, I was *that* near walkin' out on them all?' She turned her lovely, grave face towards Jackie. 'I *was*, y'know.'

Jackie returned a serious glance.

'Well, Dickie,' said Miss Lealy, in a lighter tone. 'How's the books going?'

'Very well, thank you, Marion.'

'Did y'know he writes books, Jackie?'

Jackie had heard that he did.

'Did y'ever hear him lecture, too? I did, once. With a lot of old grey-beards all about, like Bernard Shaw.'

'Really?' said Jackie. 'He never told me he lectured.'

'Ye-e-es!' Miss Lealy made another transition to gravity. 'All about those factory people, in the old days, y'know. You know, when they all worked in mills, and factories,

and all that. The poor little kiddies, and all those, all havin'
to work sixteen hours a day. I jes' can't bear to think o'
those poor little kiddies.'

'Terrible,' said Jackie. 'I know.'

'An' talkin' of Mister Burr Nard Shaw,' said Miss Lealy,
switching off again. 'I saw him the other day. But isn't he
jest a *lovely* old man? That *clean* and *spotless*! An' his
smile! My word! Did y'ever see him, Jackie?'

No, Jackie had never seen him.

'Oh, yorter! I like him better than you, Richard,' added
Miss Lealy, softly.

'I don't care,' said Mr Gissing.

'D'ye think he'd like me?' asked Miss Lealy, again serious.

'I should think he'd hate you,' said Mr Gissing.

'Not if I went round to Adelphi Terrace?'

'I don't think that would make any difference.'

'An' pulled his beard?'

'I should think that that would go against you, Marion,'
said Mr Gissing . . .

In this manner the conversation proceeded throughout
lunch. Miss Lealy did all the talking, and Jackie had no difficulty in discerning the secret of her success in life. There
was a brimming mixture of simplicity, soft-heartedness,
unscrupulousness, imbecility, joyous gravity, and, above
all, assured and radiant vitality, which carried all before
it. No one in the world could, or could wish to resist it.
And at any moment there would be a sudden lull, and she

would be fixing her lovely eyes upon you, and speaking softly of 'poor little kiddies'. Towards these transitions Mr Gissing preserved one steady and non-committal attitude, but Jackie, of course, as a stranger, was compelled to follow breathlessly behind, and to mimic the emotion of each phase with the lightning rapidity of a reflection in a mirror.

Miss Lealy now went off into a panting description of her early school-days in Wilkesbarre (her Home Town), which lasted well into the entrée, and then into even earlier days in a convent, which brought her to the subject of religion. At this she at once accused Mr Gissing of being Wicked, and an Atheist, and asked Jackie if she was a Catholic. On finding that she was not, she at once urged her to become one, without delay; because, after all, Martin Luther, who started all the trouble, only did it because he wanted to marry a silly old nun, didn't he? To which summary theology Jackie could not but assent, with the nod of one convinced, and would clearly be in the confession-box before an hour was over. Whereat Mr Gissing said that if Miss Marion Lealy wanted converts she shouldn't be divorced so much (which was rather unfair, because she had only done it twice); and Miss Lealy, who took all remarks from him as coming from the promptings of the Foe, refuted him with the explanation that *she* was not a *Good* Catholic.

There was then a long pause, which Miss Lealy broke with a benign 'Well, *you're* a verrer pretty little girl, Jackie,' and by asking her if she was in her own profession. Jackie smiled, and Mr Gissing answered for her.

'No,' he said. 'But she's trying to be.'

'Have you done anything, Jackie?'

'No. Nothing,' said Jackie, weakly.

'I guess you can dants, an' sing, an' all that?'

Jackie put forward her accomplishments in these directions.

'Why don't you come out in 'Little Girl' with us, then, Jackie?' asked Miss Lealy.

This was a difficult question to answer. At a first glance it would have appeared that there were innumerable, and even obvious, reasons why she should not join Miss Lealy in 'Little Girl'.

'We don't begin rehearsin' till to-morrow, and if I spoke to Mr Ronaldon I'm sure I could get you in.'

'Could you really?' asked Jackie, very eager, when Mr Gissing cut in:

'Now, be careful, Marion. She can't do that, you know.'

'Why not, pray?'

'She can't. You don't want to be a chorus-girl, do you, Jackie?'

'I should love to be one,' said Jackie.

'Whart's wrong with a chorus-girl, anyway? *I* got started as one, anyway, an' you've got to get Ex Perience. Don't you listen to him, Jackie.'

'I forbid it,' said Mr Gissing.

'Who'se you to forbid? Will you come in "Little Girl", Jackie, if I can get you in?'

'*Rather*,' said Jackie.

'You don't understand, Marion. It's not her line. She's not used to it. She's Alone in the Great City, and it'd be a crime. Who's going to look after her?'

'Waal, she'll be in my show, won't she, and I'll be there? An' d'you think she's goaner be seduced or something? You don't know your chorus-girl if you think that.'

'I know my chorus-girl lots better than you, and I tell you I forbid it. Besides, it's a foul life, and you know it.'

'Would you really like to come, Jackie? An' you're not' scared?'

'Yes. I *really* would,' said Jackie. 'And I'd love it.'

'Well, I'm goaner 'phone,' said Miss Lealy, and left the table.

There was a silence.

'I wouldn't do it, honestly,' he said. 'You'd hate it. You'd be far happier with Linell. And you'd have to go on tour with this, just the same. They're going to Manchester and God knows where, before it comes to Town. Don't do it, please.'

'But why not? I've got to get experience; and here I'd be starting from the very beginning, wouldn't I? You don't realize how terribly badly I want to succeed. And I won't *stay* a chorus-girl, after all, will I?' pleaded Jackie.

'I wish to Heaven I'd never brought you here.'

Miss Lealy returned. 'I've fixed up to take you round to Mr Ronaldon at three,' she said.

'Oh, thanks awfully,' said Jackie.

Mr Gissing continued to plead with Jackie and to revile Miss Lealy, but without result.

'And what about Mr Linell's post-card, to-morrow, saying that he *can* have you?' he asked, as they got up to leave.

'Oh, I forgot that, really,' said Jackie. 'But I don't expect he will. Do you?'

'And, anyway,' said Miss Lealy, decisively, 'it's no use startin' off all scrupulous like *that*.'

5

Mr Gissing left them outside, vaguely saying that he would see Jackie in the evening, and within an hour of that the whole thing was settled. She was taken in a taxi by Miss Lealy to the large offices of Messrs. Ronaldon, Maxwell & Co., in Soho: she was introduced to a middle-aged man who said that he was pleased to see her, but did not substantiate that asseveration by speaking to her again throughout the interview: and she was then taken by Miss Lealy, in another taxi, to the Empress Theatre, Shaftesbury Avenue. Here she was led, trembling, on to a grey, large, bare and dismantled stage, in the front of which, up against the fire-curtain, a small but imposing gentleman was standing at a table in converse with one who appeared to be an assistant. To this gentleman Miss Lealy introduced Jackie with 'This is Miss Mortimer, Mr Crossley.'

Now this small but imposing gentleman, who had been in telephonic communication with his superiors, was fully aware of Jackie's identity a few moments before the actual introduction, and knew that he had little choice in the matter of approving her. But there are different ways of doing these things (it must be remembered), and one way is to look rather jumpy at having your conversation broken into, glance at you vaguely, suddenly shout out something to an assistant the other side of the stage, and walk mistily away muttering 'She'll do, she'll do, she'll do,' from the unutterable depths of an omniscient and omnipotent detachment. This way is a rather good way – being presumably the way that Julius Caesar (just after a triumphal entry into Rome) would have employed when answering off-hand a question about the new Aquilifer; and Mr Crossley (who, by the way, bore a seedy but close personal resemblance to that conqueror) employed this way himself. It was, of course, a method which stole the confidence of the aspirant, generating, in him or her, a degrading desire to throw broken and jagged ends of bottles, or such-like, into the face of its serene exponent; but it was effective enough in getting you three pounds ten a week and a chance of evening employment for months to come; so you couldn't really grumble. Jackie didn't, anyway.

Chapter Four

REHEARSAL

1

It was some three weeks later, on the bare stage of the Clarence Theatre, Shaftesbury Avenue, that Jackie had a nightmare. She kept on thinking that she was going to wake up from this nightmare, but she never did. She dreamed that she was on the bare stage of the Clarence Theatre, Shaftesbury Avenue. The time was half-past twelve in the morning: the curtain was up, revealing the deserted stalls, and the dusky echoing tiers of circle and gallery, which loomed semi-circularly in the feeble light gleaned from the half-lit stage; and she was deliberately facing this inhuman (and yet somehow critical) wilderness of dumb seats, and she was supported on each side, as though being carried away after an accident, by two long rows of scented, exceptionally solid, insouciant, rather surly and rhythmically shuffling feminine flesh.

And after every five steps or so to the right, Jackie, along with her rows of supporters, gave a large kick (in a spirit of invitation rather than ejection) out at the stolid wilderness in front; and after every five steps or so to the left, she did the same in that direction. And each kick was a kind of culmination or punctuation. The mind waited for it, as for a promise, teasingly, humorously, and yet withal deliciously withheld.

And after each five kicks or so she would leave off stepping and kicking, and commence marking time, like an effeminate little soldier – not emphatically, but with a faintly collapsing right knee, followed by a faintly collapsing left knee – an equal amount of times on each – a devout balance and mathematic exactitude being the *sine qua non* of this type of performance.

And when she had done this for some time, she did a little more stepping and kicking, and then all at once cast off her support, as though suddenly cured of her accident, and turned right round, to reveal her back (which was another climax), and came back to the old position, fitting in again, and entwining her arms, with the slick perfection of a mechanism.

The whole row then moved a little way backwards, and commenced to sway – going right over from left to right, and from right to left, like a lot of inverted pendulums of girls.

Which was taken up in a minor key a few moments later by a process of affectionate (if slightly accelerated) Nodding, in which each girl rested her pretty head first on the shoulder of her right neighbour, and then on the shoulder of her left neighbour, without favour to either, for something over a minute.

And so on and so forth – all in the strictest obedience to the dictates of a not very well behaved, but exceedingly well-shaved (though still blue-cheeked) little person, not at the moment in the theatre to witness the enactment of his ingenuity.

2

Jackie, in fact, was at her art.

Or at least at the rehearsal of her art, and giving her small share to the chorus rendering of that most hopeful number in 'Little Girl' – *'Tea Time in Florida'*.

Which was (it may be added) also:

> 'My baby's *knee* time in Florida,
> Oui-oui-oui-*oui*-time in Florida,
> and
> Just you and *me* time in Florida,'

into the bargain, and was an exotic time of day altogether.

And in some dark and obscure way, the Noddings

above-mentioned, together with the swayings, the turnings, the shufflings, the time-markings, and the kickings, were expressive, were cumulatively expressive, of tea-time in Florida.

Dark and obscure to the uninitiated alone, who might chase eagerly some elusive relationship, some artistic mystery or subtlety just beyond their ken. But to the initiated as clear as day.

For tea-time in Florida involves a little maid, a whole host of little maids in fact, to serve the tea. And a whole host of little maids involves a whole host of little uniforms, with the pleasantest little skirts up to the knee, and the most ravishing little pinafores in front, and the pinkest and most delightful of frail underwear beneath. And when once you have reached that, your kickings, at least, explain themselves. As do also your sudden turnings, which cause the air to achieve the same effect. And as for your swayings, and your noddings, and your side-steppings, they are merely your rhythmic vehicle, your delicious delayings and lingerings over the essential glory. In fact, the not very well behaved, but exceedingly well-shaved (though still blue-cheeked) little person, knows what he is after, and deserves his cigar. And Jackie knows what he is after too, and can conceive without difficulty her uniform when the great night arrives: and she is not enjoying her art at all. In fact, she would far rather try some other art (Brick-laying, for instance), any day. And that is why it is all like a nightmare, from which she is momentarily hoping to wake up, but from which she cannot succeed in waking up.

3

There was, at the moment, no music coming from the piano at the right of the stage, the time being given by a middle-aged little gentleman, with the appearance of a nagging hen, and a nagging hen's outlook on life, who beat the air excitedly, and who occasionally came forth to some member of the row to shout 'ONEtwothree, ONEtwothree, ONEtwothree' at her face for some time, before looking mollified and becoming general again.

And in the absence of the piano, the click-shuffling noise set up by the exertions of this pulsating line, together with the little rustle of skirt with skirt and bare arm with arm, and yet another impalpable disturbance of the air wrought half by breathlessness, half by sheer vitality – were the only noises to be heard. And they were quiet but very terrible noises in Jackie's ears.

There was, indeed, something deadly about rehearsal without music – something deadly about rehearsal altogether. And much as Jackie dreaded the actuality and the first night, the thought of it did not cast the same shame upon her soul as she felt now. For with a certain musical abandonment and spontaneity (which would probably obtain on the first night), the thing might be carried off without degradation. But this rehearsing – this cool, exacting preparation, this steady making-ready, this eager subservience, was too much for her.

Eager subservience to whom? As Jackie looked out at the darkened auditorium, and the dumb stiff seats arrayed therein, she could already visualize the soul and appearance of that many-headed provincial overlord (in a plush seat) for whom this organized Pride of Flesh was in such detailed preparation. Like some patient, couching tarantula, the ghost of this monster was waiting out there in the darkened stalls – waiting for her self-esteem. And yet still she shuffled on, and kicked, and turned about, and still she did not wake ...

The long line supporting Jackie reached a distinguishable climax of effort, and all at once ran off to the right, like beads sliding off a suddenly broken thread. Whereat the hen became querulous, and the chickens, breaking into groups, put their hands on their hips and sneered very prettily, or stared into the distance, or were silently pert. Jackie attended illy and dumbly. They then reassembled, and started it all over again, but this time with music. Also they sang the words this time – a thin, tinny, and far from pleasurable piping sound, just prevailing over the hammering of the piano and the shuffling of feet. And at this point Jackie, as she always did where she could, began to cheat – not contributing to the noise, but moving her lips and humming softly in a base counterfeiting of her duty.

The names of the individuals of this energetic team were,

reading from left to right: — Miss Janie Dunstan, Miss Royal Fayre, Miss Honour Lang, Miss Effie Byng, Miss Betty Hamilton, Miss Dolly True, Miss Dot Knowle, Miss Lalla True, Miss Biddy Maxwell, Miss Jackie Mortimer, Miss Dot Delane, Miss Belle Hawke, Miss Mary Deare, Miss Elsie Rutland, Miss 'Lovey' Shiel, Miss Hazel Parry, Miss Pinkie Dove, Miss Cherry Lambert, Miss Alice Crewe, and Miss Lizzie Snell.

Chapter Five

THE OTHER GIRLS

1

The process of becoming acquainted with the Misses
Dunstan, Fayre, Lang, Byng, Hamilton, True, Knowle,
True, Maxwell, Delane, Hawke, Deare, Rutland, Shiel,
Parry, Dove, Lambert, Crewe and Snell, had been a far
from engaging process for Jackie, and at once an abrupt
and laborious process. Abrupt, in that she had been thrown
upon them and amongst them (on a wet Wednesday morning following the Tuesday afternoon of her acceptance),
without a moment in which to collect herself or adjust her
ideas towards them, in a little room for dressing next to
a rehearsal room in Soho: laborious, in that Jackie, who
was the friendliest and most accommodating creature as
a whole, found from the first that there was something

ineradicably antagonistic towards her, and even something ineradicably antagonistic in herself, which was going to render even common intercourse far from easy.

Her Occidental and Edwardian training, indeed, could not but rebel at her inclusion in this querulous harem of aromatic, coarse-tongued, and supercilious competitors – this assembly of brides sacred, and in training, to some sensuous consummation – this band of foul-mouthed yet ingenuous nymphs. And her first few moments in that dressing-room were very possibly the most hideous moments of her existence so far.

It was as though she had been thrown amongst a different, a more aggressive and vital, type – a type of Amazons as it were: and amid this flaunted meretriciousness, these swayers and swingers of the flesh, she was revealed as an inferior. Her delicacy and fastidiousness would be of no more avail to her, in such a circle, than the same qualities in a Greek slave would have availed him in the days of Roman ascendancy – rather less, in fact. In a society of this kind she had no place, and was plainly too weak to survive for long.

On a drizzling Wednesday morning, then, and in a little room above a public-house in Soho, Jackie received her first impression of her fellow-professionals: and in a large room next door, containing a piano and some wooden chairs, she faced the ordeal of her first rehearsals. The actual stage at the disposal of the company was, of course, during these preliminary days, made over exclusively to the stars, who would rehearse for some weeks in lofty secrecy before

taking their place before their chorus under the final production of Julius Caesar. And up here in this room, though
everything was a little more personal, it was also a little
less terrifying, and, under the supervision of an alert and
affable little Frenchman, who was held in great derision
by the Amazons, but who treated Jackie with the utmost
patience and consideration, she just managed to scramble
through her first steps. (All this was taking place, of course,
in the days before chorus-work had commenced its more
positive intrusion in the sphere of acrobatics.)

Not that Jackie, who was naturally the least experienced
there, escaped disgrace entirely. For her little Frenchman
was not her only instructor, and many a time was the long
chain broken, and a silence made, while the faulty little
link Jackie was blown into a red heat to be forged again.

From 11 a.m. to 1 p.m., and from 2.30 p.m. to 5.30
p.m. – these were Jackie's working hours. And in several
lunch intervals, of course, she had to go to Bond Street or
Regent Street for fittings – fittings from which she emerged
neither satisfied nor happy, being overborne by the cunning
and energy of her companions, and compelled to snatch at
what cast-off bones of millinery at their sartorial banquet
she could procure. She had lunch, as a rule, at the Lyons
Corner House, in Coventry Street, and was quite happy
in there with the bright lights, and the orchestra, and her
book. (For she had stuck to her book bravely against the
combined hostility and mimical stares of the nymphs, who
were of a Dionysian rather than Apollonian temper.)

And with the passing of these first few weeks, of course, she was able to develop and particularize her first impressions of that highly individualistic troupe, referred to, in their own daily speech, as the Other Girls. She learnt soon to identify individual face-formations in a mass of (at first) almost indistinguishable confectionery. And it was not long before she was alive to specific character, even – of which there should have been a large diversity, nearly all ages from the ages of sixteen to thirty-five being represented in this chorus. But actually there was little diversity of character and habit, and the simplest method of differentiation, Jackie found, was either by the costliness or quantity of their finery, or by the costliness (and maybe quantity) of their Boys – and most particularly the latter. Boys, indeed, were axiomatic – the requisite complement of this community, which could actually not be conceived as existing without them. Chorus-girl presupposed Boy – as effect presupposes cause. Boys were therefore less their prey than their natural nourishment. The Boys ... My Boy ... Their Boys ... Her Boy ... Our Boys ... Boys ... Boys ... Boys – they ran through their possessive feminine discourse unceasingly. And some of them had Nice Boys, and some of them had Horrid Boys, and some of them had Funny Boys, or Naughty Boys, while some of them even had Lovely Boys. But Jackie (who had positively no Boy) took some time to adjust herself to this calm outlook upon Boys – though she had plenty of opportunities, on leaving the rehearsal room at the lunch hour (when there were quantities of Boys in patient attendance), of observing by what measures one qualified as a Boy, and won the spurs of Adolescence. Which measures, it appeared, consisted principally in being anything over the age of forty, with all traces of a possibly once-existing boyhood permanently eradicated from one's features and soul, and also by other measures – such as the sporting of long aluminium cars; the blending of blue suits, blue cheeks, and blue-striped shirts with the blue smoke of cigars; the adoption of a shrewd, sleek, and acquisitive expression; or the embellishment of one's hands with signet rings – Boys being, in general, a bedecked, if quiet crew, and particularly ready with swift means of transport.

Not that there was not, on the other hand, a certain variety of admittedly (and even vaingloriously) Homely Boys, celebrated for common sense and integrity rather than parts, who (it was understood) were in the habit of taking no nonsense from the respective apples of their eyes and pearls beyond price, and gazed with glowing aversion upon the bedecked, whom they threatened to demolish, at any manifestation of indecency, with blows. These, in fact, maintained a heavy and nosy suspiciousness towards the Footlights, as objects favouring a libertine atmosphere, and clearly the little things would one day have to choose between these insecure gaieties and the nobler (if less effervescent) conditions imposed by his suburb.

And so week followed week (there were five and a half weeks of rehearsal altogether), and they came down on to

the stage, and rehearsed there along with the stars. This constellation consisted (in order of merit) of Mr Jack Laddon,
whose business it was to be funny – Miss Beryl Joy, whose
business also was to be funny – Mr Lew Craik, whose business also was to be funny (but in a broader style and with
a rather redder nose) – Miss Jean Lowe, whose business it
was to be dainty and coy (and who was a great adept with
ribbon-swung hats and crinolines) – Miss Lotty Brockwell,
whose business it was to be vulgar – Mr Dick Flower, whose
business it was to be vulgarer – Miss Janet Lidell, whose
forte was lingerie – and a few more comedian-feeders who,
like the last three mentioned, appeared as maids, butlers,
beauties, policemen, landladies, etc., in the countless little
irrelevant sketches punctuating this costly pageant. Miss
Marion Lealy, it will be observed, had thrown over her
part, which had now fallen upon the shoulders of bewitch-
ing Miss Jean Lowe. Miss Lealy had done this for various
reasons – among others a strong distaste conceived for and
a subterranean quarrel directed against one Mr Tom Crewe,
who was also in the cast, and reflected her aversion. This
young man, whose business it was to succumb in public to
Miss Lowe, came from America and was a charmer of the
first order. His simple, nonchalant, cigarette-smoking talent
was occasionally defeated, if not distantly travestied, in
this production, by the necessity of appearing as a Sheik, a
Chinese Emperor, a Pharaoh or similar potentates of slightly
imbecile demeanour; but he was a pleasant young man in
private life, and very kind to Jackie when he had the chance.

The relations existing between this constellation and its chorus were roughly the relations between Above-stairs and Below-stairs – but as though in a very large establishment where there was much condescension on the part of the employers, and much familiarity on the part of the servants, and where the young gentlemen of the house were decided rakes as regards the maids.

It was not until the last week before opening that the floats went up on the stage, a sense of imminence prevailed, and Julius Caesar, whose appearances and interferences had been growing daily more frequent and provocative, came down into the front and produced in earnest. It was then realized by all that they had let themselves in for this business, and that there was no backing out. Hitherto the possibility of the first night at Manchester, like the possibility of death to human nature, had been remote – but now there was a knocking at the gate. They awoke to find themselves committed; all fooling had to cease, and Julius Csesar, glowing from the darkened stalls amid his patrons and right-hand men, was like some heavy-handed marshal (newly appointed in place of one recalled) who was to deal with the crisis. Chorus-girls were best seen and not heard at these times – had best flit like pale obedient spirits around the mighty workings of authority. Ineffectual were their sneers, and insignificant their flauntings, and not until the show commenced might they resume their sway. And in the new state of affairs Jackie, of course, was the least significant of all, and escaped notice almost as much as she desired to do so.

Not that she escaped notice altogether. On the third day before opening, indeed, and in that most promising and Asiatic of numbers 'Old Man Wong', who, it may be noted, was herein celebrated as much for his Silly Old Song as for his almost incessant performances upon a Gong, in the district of Hong-Kong (where the next-door neighbours didn't seem to mind, maintaining that such an enchanting, if infantile, old person could not possibly Go Wrong) – in this number Jackie came into direct contact with Julius Caesar, and was picked out to sustain the arrows of his disapprobation by herself.

'What,' cried Julius Caesar, from the darkness, 'does that girl on the sixth from the right think she's doing?'

There being no available answer to this conundrum, nor any answer expected; nor yet any means of ascertaining whether Julius Caesar was referring (imperially) to his own right, or (sympathetically) to the right of the stage, there was no reply but a kind of obedient all-round wonderment along with him. What *did* the girl on the sixth from the right think she was doing? You couldn't tell. But not what that girl on the sixth from the right *ought* to be thinking she was doing, they were quite sure . . .

An eager fluttering and murmuring of assistants ensued in the darkness – a murmuring in which the word 'name' was to be sensed rather than distinguished – and then the voice of the stage-manager rang out.

'Miss Mortimer!' cried the stage-manager, half in reproach, half as identification.

There was a silence.

'Do you think we've come here for a funeral, Miss Mortimer?' asked Julius Caesar.

Jackie looked blushingly on to the floor, as though she hadn't been quite sure about it previously, but now saw her mistake.

There was then another silence. Julius Caesar, who always got the best out of everything, delighted in silences of this sort.

'Because we haven't, you know,' he added.

Clearly we had not.

'It's not something congenital, is it? You are able to smile, aren't you?'

Jackie acquiesced with a queer little smile at once.

There was then another very long and punitive silence, in which Julius Caesar gazed with enormous interest at her, as at a queerly behaved animal, and then, 'Now then, please——' he said, and led on to other matters.

And, moreover, in so far as there were positively no broken bottles, kettles of scalding water, consignments of vitriol, or the like, at that moment upon the stage, and in so far as Jackie could hardly have reached him, at that distance, even if there had been, the incautious gentleman continued his activities in security.

Chapter Six

HIGHMINDEDNESS

1

It is half-past four o'clock on Sunday evening, and the train is on the last lap of its journey to Manchester — streaming blindly but resolutely through the falling and enveloping night.

It is the fifth hour of the journey, and the windows sweat a grey patchy dew, and reflect the compartment. This contains, in all, eight of her fellow-professionals. And none of these speak a word; but all are sprawling or lying back in varying attitudes of resentful lethargy — militant lethargy even, for they are Amazons even in repose and defeat, and they grudge every moment of this forced submissiveness. Indeed the Stygian light falling down on them from the sickly little bulb above, reveals lines of ill-temper and determination which, could they be seen and recalled, would cast an interesting aspect over the winning warm smiles and delectable kickings which will divert a northern city to-morrow night. But to-morrow night is now unspeakably remote . . .

Jackie has a corner seat, and opposite Jackie is Miss Stella Hawke, who is the eldest girl of the entire garden of girls. She is a girl of forty years, in fact, and she is a formidable girl. With her history, Jackie, along with others, is acquainted – that history being simple and consisting of the notorious fact that Miss Hawke is one who has been (in the existing phraseology) 'sent back to the chorus'. Which means that Miss Hawke, at some period in the past, has sunned herself in the especial favour of the Sultan, and, having at last worn out her charms in that service, is now the object of a merciful and entirely matter-of-fact system of, as it were, half-pay. So long as her lost master lives she will remain in his choruses, though, with increasing age, she may not keep her hold in the No. 1 companies. She has, indeed, little to look forward to: but she is at present a lusty and unrepentant old pensioner, and has from the beginning struck a chill into the heart of Jackie, to whom she has never addressed a word, and to whom she will, as a point of pride, never address a word so long as they are thrown together.

But for all that she is not uninterested in Jackie, and, if Jackie but knew it, she has summed Jackie up and disposed of her in her own strange, hard, and perhaps even kindly way. But although she has summed Jackie up and disposed of her, there is something in Jackie which causes her to be recurringly not quite satisfied with the summing-up and disposing, and from this fact certain difficulties are at this very moment arising.

For Miss Hawke (who is naturally a deceptive creature), while at this moment feigning to be asleep, is actually opening her eyes, every half-minute or so, with a sudden pop, and drinking in as much of her junior's face and demeanour as it is humanly possible to do in the time and in conjunction with ostensible oblivion. And Jackie is also fast asleep, but is also popping. And a quantity of simultaneous poppings are taking place which are proving ruinous to the peace of mind of both parties. But neither of them is able to leave off ...

And so the train streams on, or slows down, or stops hissingly for ghostly joinings, and conversation is reopened, and fades out, and begins again, and excludes Jackie (whatever else it does), and the Stygian light burns on ...

And all at once she begins thinking about him again. And foolishly imagining things ...

If, for instance, by some miracle, he was there to meet her, at the other end ...

Standing there to meet her – in front of them all ...

And if, miraculously, he put her into a taxi and told her that this had got to Stop ...

And if she asked him what had got to Stop ... And if he said that she knew what he meant ... And if she said she didn't ...

And if he said he loved her – beyond everything in this world – loved her and loved her and loved her ...

And if she said she always had, from the beginning ...

She wonders what he is doing at this moment. Touring the country, like herself – probably in a train ...

She will write to him when she gets to her room this evening. Sit up in bed and write to him ...

Or if this wasn't a train going to Manchester at all, but a train going to Dover (like the train she went on when she went to Switzerland) – and if they were together ... And if she held his arm, as they left the train, and the sea was ahead ...

If the sea was ahead for their venturing – a calm sea, and yet just flecked with foam – and stars overhead, and a wind, and a moon half hidden ... The old, dark sea ahead, for their venturing ...

And if she smelt the sea ... And if she smelt the sea! ...

2

Jackie's landlady at Manchester was Jackie's first taste of theatrical landladies, and a bustling woman of about forty named Mrs Grounds. Grounds was alive, though seldom in evidence, and a Character. His affectionate wife, indeed, had constant occasion to allude to him as a Puzzle, a Problem, a Customer, a Proposition, a Desert Sphinx if you Like, a Facer, a One, or, fractionally, a One and a Half or Not Half a One – mystery and monosyllables being the leading traits of this Character. Jackie was of the private belief, in her very slight acquaintance of this individual, that he was, if the truth were known, a mere bundle of affectation; but she was alone in Manchester and had no choice but to adopt the more mysterious and adulatory interpretation of his manners. Also his wife took pleasure in recording, firstly, that he would Do Anything for you if you only Tackled him on the Right Side, and did not Cross, Rub Up, or Brook him; secondly, that a large amount of his apparent surliness was to be palliated by his own arrogant confession that he had been Brought Up in a Hard School; and lastly, that whatever he did it was Only his Way. And with these assurances Jackie had to be content.

3

It was a very successful first night, and an experience of panic which Jackie never forgot. From the moment of entering the harem, at seven o'clock, there was an air of hurry which nearly sent her out of her mind. It was as though the Sultan, while having given the date of his return, had arrived six hours before he was expected and thrown everything and everybody into scampering terror.

Jackie never forgot the dressing-room, where she found herself with seven or eight others; she never forgot the blazing electric bulbs, lighting the red-ochre walls, and reflected by blazing little mirrors on the wooden shelf all round; she never forgot the mad disorder of everything; the smarm and smell of greasepaint – Number 9 – Number 5 – Number 2½ – carmine – blue pencil – the clouds of powder and the scent of flesh. She never forgot the torrents of strident and lewd imprecation pouring forth around her with the monotony of a solemn, set incantation. She never forgot the call-boy's raps upon the door, his buoyant '*Arfnar Peas*!' at the half-hour – his sinister '*Quartnar Peas*!' at the quarter. She never forgot the savage over-emphasis and over-colouring and intensification of trembling beauty when all were made up – the scarlet and blue and pink and white – as though all had been dipped in some sickly rainbow essence . . .

She never forgot the running down the cold stone stairs – the first clashings of the orchestra – the lining up for the opening chorus – the flowing murmur, talkative and genteelly zealous, of the stalls and circle – the stir and more callous expectancy of the high, packed gallery . . .

She never forgot how the curtain softly and suddenly arose amid the noise – how its rising gave the same breathless, irrevocable and utterly elusive sensation as a diver might feel in mid-air – how, for a moment after its rising, all consciousness was lost, and the body functioned like another body altogether, which, by some infinitely happy chance, knew the business in hand . . .

And then all at once she had run off the stage, and was in the semi-darkness amid the electricians, and the stage-manager, and his assistants, and shifters of various kinds, and a very pale and trembling comedian who had not yet gone on ...

4

Jackie had imagined that all except the most mechanical exertion would cease after that first night, but here she was mistaken.

The fact that the reception in the press next morning was decidedly lukewarm and mixed gave Jackie some sly pleasure, of course (for she had a grudge against her employers and employment which no appeal to her pity could ever placate). But when, at the call next morning, she found herself, with the rest, being held personally impeachable for this, she was less pleased. There was, in fact, on the part of her superiors, an atmosphere of authoritative scolding – a self-important air of calm in a crisis – and an amount of talk about Saving the Day, Working Together, and Pulling this fantastic and offensive balderdash Round, which she found incredibly nauseating. The more so in that it was indulged in principally by the constellation, to whom it was obviously all part of the fun. Jackie soon discovered, indeed, that in such circles a crisis of some sort was little short of indispensable, for if you haven't a crisis there is absolutely no means in this world of setting in and being Absolutely Frank, and (after all) having Nothing but the

Interests of the Show at Heart, and Laying all your Cards upon the Table, and Only wanting to Do what's Right, and only Wishing you could See it as they did, and so forth, and at last explaining everything beautifully, and kissing and making up, and going out in a large and large-hearted manner to the bars ... And after all, if you can't be Absolutely Frank, and have Nothing but Interests of Shows at heart, and Lay Cards (at the right moment) upon Tables, what is the use of being this type of actor?

The tragedy with Jackie and her chorus girls was that they were given the scolding but deprived of the highmindedness. And inasmuch as to spread yourself out in every branch of austerity, altruism, benevolence and brotherly attachment is the cardinal prerogative of their profession, they were conscious of being deprived of something essential to their spiritual welfare, and suffered accordingly.

Indeed they were at last compelled to look for some crisis in their own ranks.

This they could do with some assurance of success, knowing that the unwritten law which had held in check the hostile ranklings obtaining all throughout rehearsals, was automatically repealed with the first night of the show, after which all vendettas might confess themselves and proceed in the open. And in this instance, sure enough, they had, ready to hand, the case of Miss Royal Fayre and Miss Pinkie Dove, who, having nourished, each against the other, the secret viper of scorn, hatred, and conscious superiority for the last five weeks, on Tuesday night were led into what they both querulously and simultaneously declared they had no intention of being led into – namely, a Scene.

The finer details of this Scene – although it was enacted in a public passage shortly after the finale, and witnessed by both Miss Cherry Lambert and Miss Dot Delane – never came to light. But it appeared that Miss Pinkie Dove, acting under the belief (true or false it is not known) that her opponent had Passed a Remark about her while she (Miss Dove) was leaving the stage, confronted Miss Royal Fayre at the next opportunity to ask her (as a Simple Question) whether she had done so or not.

To which Miss Royal Fayre, shirking the issue, had retorted that in so far as she (Miss Fayre) had not Started Interfering with no one, no one need not Start Interfering with her.

To which Miss Dove had rejoined that she was merely asking a Simple Question.

They then both began that violent and inharmonious disclaiming of any personal participation in a Scene. Which gave way at last to a sudden dreadful lull, and a certain amount of fatal muttering. Which was followed, all at once, by a lightning blow across the cheek, delivered by Miss Royal Fayre upon Miss Pinkie Dove.

One of the Assistant Stage Managers coming along at this moment – a Mr Wicks, who prided himself greatly upon his tact with the Girls – found both antagonists staring at each other in an entranced manner, and Miss Royal Fayre heatedly absolving herself for her unladylike, her

almost Scenic act, with the plea that Miss Pinkie Dove had
called her a Name. It was plain that Miss Fayre had been
called many things, but never, in the entire course of her
career, a Name. But Miss Dove offered to call her a Name
again. As for Mr Wicks, he thought that one shouldn't
worry about Names, embraced both girls round the shoulders, alluding to them as Pinkie and Royal, and told them
to Come Along – as though he were a kind of mild policeman of the passions and was making a gentle arrest. Where
they were to Come Along to he neither said nor knew, and
his limp authority was treated with the neglect it deserved.
Similarly he failed to cajole them with the dictum that we
should all Live and let Live. It was not, indeed, until Miss
Cherry Lambert and Miss Dot Delane came forward to
support him, that the parties were separated and dragged
to their respective rooms, where the affronted Named one,
on the one hand, took to tears, and the bestower of the
affront, on the other, examined her slapped cheek in the
glass and paced dramatically up and down, threatening to
Teach her assailant any amount of things—

Where she Got Off,
To try it on again,
Her place in the gutter,

or merely What For, being but the more outstanding items
on that ghastly scholastic schedule.

This was all over the theatre in a trice, and the

highmindedness at once began. Impartiality being the leading characteristic of highmindedness, there were no factions caused, but all were united in a fanatical desire to see the adversaries Shake Hands. The perfect efficacy of this ritual was treated as axiomatic, and the actual spiritual reconciliation of the couple was either implicit or of no account – what Pinkie and Royal had to do was to Shake Hands. It was the battle-cry of the altruists. 'Come along, Pinkie, Shake Hands,' urged Miss Cherry Lambert, and 'Now then, Royal,' urged Miss Effie Byng, 'aren't you going to Shake Hands?'

And 'Now then, you're going to Shake Somebody's Hand, aren't you?' persuaded Miss 'Lovey' Shiel.

'What those two girls ought to do,' said Mr Wicks, 'is to Shake Hands.'

But neither of the girls would commit themselves to this symbol, and the argument proceeded for four days and nights, no possible solution to the situation being found until Thursday night, when Miss Pinkie Dove gallantly conceded that if Miss Royal Fayre would only apologize to *her*, she would be the *first* to apologize to Miss Royal Fayre, and Miss Royal Fayre gallantly conceded that if Miss Pinkie Dove would only apologize to *her*, she would be the *first* to apologize to Miss Pinkie Dove. Which was no solution at all, but a complete dead-lock, and very abstruse. The only escape on such lines, indeed, would have been to have had some kind of Simultaneous Apology, in which some one held a watch and a pistol, and it was 'One-to-be-ready, two-to-be-steady, three-to-be – BANG! *Apology!*' – and all honour satisfied in a fair start. But this was not suggested, and the final solution was at last afforded on Friday night by Miss Pinkie Dove, who, in a moment of tenderness (not impossibly traceable to the receipt of her salary envelope), Took Back the Name. Which withdrawal was instantly communicated to Miss Royal Fayre, who allowed that she herself, anyway, Kind of Reckoned she had Forgot herself. If she had merely confessed to having forgotten herself, this concession would have lost much of its power; but to have Kind of Reckoned she had forgotten herself introduced, by some magic verbal process, the orthodox flavour of diffident repentance, and there remained nothing but the actual meeting and reconciliation. This took place in the interval, under the auspices of Mr Wicks (who had little trouble in making his arrests), and was carried through with simplicity, but not without sentiment, and consisted solely of Royal taking Pinkie's hand with 'Sorry, Pinkie,' and Pinkie taking Royal's hand with 'Sorry, Royal,' and nothing more. Which was deemed impressive. Any super-fluous Reckoning was left to Mr Wicks, and he Reckoned it had all been about nothing. The matter was closed.

5

On Thursday of this week Jackie received an invitation, along with the majority of her companions, to a supper given by Mr Ronaldon to the company. This took place, after the show, at one of the largest hotels in the place, two high spacious chambers of which were hired for the purpose.

All but the entire company was present, as well as various gentlemen on the business side (little seen hitherto) and one or two of the backers – pale, stumpy, shrewd, moustached little gentlemen from the north, much given to cigars – which cigars were possibly giving them very little pleasure, but which were stoutly persisted in, it being manifestly impossible to Back without cigars. There was also much champagne, which induced an early state of that blurred fatuousness essential to the making and hearing of speeches, which were, from first to last, great successes – each orator sitting down to enormous applause and with a highly satisfied grin – which grin would grow broader and broader but sicklier and sicklier as the evening wore on, and everybody else made much better speeches, and you had to show how free from jealousy you were ... But every one had to have their say, and, indeed, it was not until a whole row of green grins lit the long table with their garish light that this torture ceased. The last speech was made (on behalf of the chorus) by Miss Hazel Parry, who had a great reputation for Cleverness (not to say scholarship), and it was rated, though in a rather patronizing way, as successful as any. After which there was some dancing, and manifestations of drunkenness – a strong tendency to Chase arising in the less important males, and a corresponding willingness to Flee betraying itself in the nymphs – the whole being carried through in the highest spirit of the Classics, and culminating in the breaking of a chair. Also in one of the more breathless Daphnes slipping up and straining her ankle, for which she received the most ardent consolation from her humorous oppressors, and massaging of a sentimental and lingering nature.

While these exciting pleasures were in progress among the sprightly, others, of a more deliberate nature, were already indulging in what Jackie described to herself as Corners. One of the rooms had been partially darkened for this.

As for Jackie, who was unfitted for both Chasing and Corners alike, she stood against a wall in all the misery of one friendless in public (which is so much a sharper misery than the same thing in private), and it is impossible to say what would have happened to Jackie, had she not at last been spoken to by Mr Merril Marsden.

Mr Merril Marsden was connected with the business side of 'Little Girl', and Jackie had had a few words with him before now. Mr Marsden was a pasty gentleman of about forty-five, with a slight (and possibly affected) stoop of the shoulders, jaded features, thin greying hair smarmed backwards, a black bow-tie which went twice around his collar, and an irritable monocle under the supervision of a black ribbon. He had fights with his monocle the whole day long – the poor round thing having from the beginning decided to stay Out of his eye, and the harassed gentleman having from the beginning decided to have it In. It was plain that the spirit of neither would ever be permanently broken; but, for all that, it served Mr Marsden well in the battle of existence, enabling him to assume a detachment with respect to human emotions denied to most of us. In that, whatever the quandary that faced him, he had but to hunch his shoulders and lift the thing slowly to his eye, to give out an air of impersonal and purely scientific research upon the matter in hand, but no committal of himself to either side. Where others had to attack life direct, he was privileged permanently to spy upon it from behind his monocle. Otherwise he was not a distinguished man – but credited himself with being so. He came from Caius College, Cambridge, and had translated, and had seen performed in London, a not very suggestive French play dealing with the unfaithfulness of a wife. He was also a producer and an actor – for both of which activities the monocle again came in useful. But he did not confess to being an actor, alluding solely, and stiffly, to the Theatre, which, he confessed, at weak moments, was his God. And there is a great difference between an actor and a disinterested gentleman whose God is the Theatre. On the same principle he alluded to his fellow-actors as Actor Fellows. To emphasize these distinctions he played Cricket and he played Golf, very badly, but very hard, and he dressed for dinner very hard, and he had a Man. Most particularly did Mr Marsden excel in his Man. This Man was in reality replacing, in Mr Marsden's unpretentious flat, Mr

Marsden's ordinary servants, but Mr Marsden's large and feudal references to has Man presupposed Cook and an entire ménage and Mr Marsden's status was elevated.

He spoke to Jackie this evening partially because he had heard that she was the daughter of Gerald Mortimer, whom he had met some years ago, and partially because he was intoxicated. Jackie did not respond favourably to Mr Marsden's character, but she was glad of any attention at the moment, and they entered into a long discussion which Mr Marsden afterwards described as a discussion on Art – a discussion on Art consisting of rather maliciously throwing at each other's heads as many names of popular and bygone painters as could be thrown in the time – which was about half a dozen a minute.

At the end of the bombardment he bore her no ill-will, however, and on their being joined by a third party, also drunk, he introduced her (you will be happy to hear) as the *First* Intellectual Chorus Girl – presumably of his acquaintance, but possibly of Europe, so enthusiastically did he speak. He also asked her out to lunch to-morrow – which she accepted. And then she mentioned Mr Gissing, of whom they spoke for some time, and whom he vaguely (Jackie found) disparaged.

'Something of an eccentric, really,' said Mr Marsden.

Jackie agreed.

By this time the party was beginning to disperse, and Mr Marsden, spying another friend, courteously took his leave.

Whereat the First Intellectual Chorus Girl fetched her cloak and, with a view to quiet departure, entered the lift. Which lift was a small and dark lift, and contained, besides the First Intellectual Chorus Girl, the attendant and a departing Backer. Which Backer, now divorced from his cigar, did, when the descent was but half accomplished, all at once plunge his bald and moustached head into the breast of the First Intellectual Chorus Girl, and commence a variety of snorting noises indicative of passion. Which behaviour the First Intellectual Chorus Girl was at first prompted to resent as abnormal, if not indecent behaviour. But it was all so quick, and she had had so many new experiences within the last few weeks, that she could not but feel that this was, in some obscure way, in order – that a Backer, in a lift of this kind, had natural privileges with his Backed – and that she should consider herself uninformed rather than outraged. So the First Intellectual Chorus Girl made no comment, and when, as they reached the ground floor, the gate was swung back and they emerged, each went their way with a quiet and pleasant sense of having capably fulfilled a minor item of daily routine.

6

But after this Thursday night Jackie began to feel a little more at home with the company of 'Little Girl'. She had got the hang of it by now, and was beginning to find her own niche. And indeed Jackie did have a niche to herself, and one recognized by the rest. And in this niche she existed, consciously, and at last conscientiously, as a 'funny little thing'. And as a 'funny little thing' she was treated with tolerance, if not, at times, a certain amount of awe. In fact:

'She's the Little Lady of the company,' Mr Wicks (a man of discrimination) had remarked, and the others felt that he had hit upon a truth.

Distinctions and classifications of this kind, indeed, were popular amongst the chorus – and just as Hazel Parry was ungrudgingly allowed to be the Clever Girl, and Biddy Maxwell held to be the Funny one, and Janie Dunstan the Cheeky-one, and Lalla True unanimously voted the Tease – so Jackie Mortimer was honoured as the Little Lady of the company. For in this hard and coarse-mouthed society, there was a substratum of the utmost simplicity and sincere ingenuousness. Indeed the transitions between that coarseness and that ingenuousness were at times baffling to Jackie. It seemed as though, in their vitality, they knew no mean between the two.

And just as Jackie was beginning to feel more at home with the company, so the company was beginning to feel more at home with itself. It had resolved itself into its final social attitudes, and Jackie was able to review it as a whole – from Miss Beryl Joy, the star of stars and comic genius of the show, down to the palest and least emphasized of the chorus men. And the various contacts in progress between these two extremes Jackie was able to observe.

There was the contact between Miss Beryl Joy and her immediate male supporters, upon whose knees she sat facetiously during rehearsals, with threats of smackings; there was the contact between Miss Beryl Joy and the smaller parts, which was one of light patronage on the one hand, and adulation on the other; there was the contact between Miss Beryl Joy and the two comedians, which was one of camaraderie. There was the contact between the smaller parts and the two comedians, which was one of adulation on the one hand, and barely concealed scorn and loftiness on the other. There was the contact between the first comedian and the second, which was one of open nonchalance and secret backbiting. There was the contact between Miss Beryl Joy and her chorus, which was one of aloof disregard tempered by an occasional chat with a favourite. There was the contact between the smaller parts and the chorus, which was one of humour and chaffing on the one hand, and sprightliness on the other. And there was, lastly, the contact between the two comedians and the chorus, which was the most interesting and well-defined contact of all. And this contact was neither a furtive contact, nor yet quite an open-handed one, and consisted of diverse fawnlike encounters (on the stage behind the set, or in public passages) between Mr Jack Laddon, or Mr Lew Craik, and any member or members of the chorus who desired such things – encounters which were subsequently related in detail in the girls' dressing-rooms, where there was much laughter, and where Mr Jack Laddon and Mr Lew Craik were revealed (not unaffectionately) as Awful ... And it appeared, from these narrations, that in these encounters Jack and Lew manifested their high spirits in all manner of ways, but perhaps most particularly in the matter of lingerie, concerning which (it seemed) they feigned a pure, scholastic, and disinterested curiosity, inquiring, and even suggesting, the names, colours, trimmings, and various unfathomable feminine uses of same in the most exquisitely tickling (though of course outrageous) manner. Indeed, kind of serials used to take place in this connection (as far as Jackie could see) – the irresponsible and Rabelaisian pupils coming up every night to inquire what variations had taken place since the night before, and leaving with the presumption that this all-absorbing topic would be resumed in a next instalment. And all this was the cause of deep amusement, as were also the occasional very much more audacious insolences on the part of the libertine pair.

Such were the different contacts and relationships, as Jackie saw them, after the first week of the show's run. And all the time she had been a little puzzled as to what exact relationship those surrendered creatures, the chorus men, bore to all this. From the first they did not seem to fit, and she at last had to decide that they bore no relationship. They formed, rather, a gaunt background of pallid, weakly parasitic, and insecurely sexed stragglers – a netherworld of the defeated. They seemed seldom in evidence, and an air of quiet hung about their dressing-rooms, where, doubtless, some kind of life of their own was in progress – whence, even, the sound of half-hearted cheer or laughter might occasionally emerge – whence glimpses of yellow drinks in dirty tumblers might be obtained – whence some white and stricken individual might at any time come forth into the passage, and giving you an inoffensive time of day, pass vaguely on – but for the rest they seemed an unsheltered lot, incapable of creating any atmosphere of their own wherewith to defend themselves.

With the band of nymphs opposite they had little or no communication. They were, indeed, treated by these with direct or implicit hauteur – and not unlike some cast-off and expiring swains were they, with respect to these, as opposed to the full-blooded and satyr-like qualities of the two comedians, who carried all before them. The finer, the successful type prevailed, and lingerie-serials were only for supermen.

But Jackie, who had no taste for lingerie-serials either, if it came to that, was not so fastidious, and could not differentiate so sharply. And so Jackie's heart rather went out to the chorus men. And because her heart went out she was able to concede certain minute civilities, when the occasion arose, which it was not difficult, but was not usual, to concede. And so it came about, it is believed, that the rumour that Jackie was the Little Lady of the company, was a rumour prevalent in the men's dressing-room, as well.

Chapter Seven

THE GIFT

1

It is half-past six on Saturday evening, and Jackie, after a pleasant high tea supplied by Mrs Grounds, is returning to the theatre. She is still, despite her tea and a short rest, a little giddy from the labour and stress of the matinée behind her, but she is gently reviving under the influence of the brisk, lit Saturday streets (which have revived Saturday-evening actors and actresses in the same way since the beginning of play-going), and she tells herself that she is, taken all in all, very happy and contented.

And she tells herself that she is an actress now, and that she can look back upon a clear achievement. And she is getting experience, she tells herself, and this cannot last so very long. And in so far as she has won out in this, her first and most arduous step – surely that is in itself some demonstration of her power to succeed throughout, and surely the heights are still for her victorious ascension.

And Jackie leaves the lighted shops, and takes to the quieter streets, and faces the stage door again, and walks quickly and confidently through.

But here she is arrested by the stage-door-keeper, who after banging at his glass cage in an uncivil and excited manner, comes out and asks her if she is Miss Mortimer.

She confesses, not without some trepidation, to being this, and he hands her a parcel. This he does with a defiant and punitive air, and testily retires.

Jackie goes very white on receiving this, and does not appear to know what to do, for she does not know what it contains, but she knows from whom it comes, and is almost trembling in her eagerness to open it. And at last, after making for the stairs, she turns back again and goes out into the street, to open it, if not in privacy, at least without interruption.

And she walks two hundred yards before she takes the thrilling plunge.

And it is a volume of Shelley's poems (apparently quite impulsive, for she cannot imagine why) and a letter.

And '*My dear Jackie,*' says this letter. '*Thank you for your letter. Got this for you yesterday. Hope to meet you some time if we're anywhere near each other. Let me hear your dates and addresses. Yours ever, R. G.*'

And it is in a very elated and serene frame of mind that she returns to the theatre again, and goes in.

And what a different going-in is this, with her book under her arm! It is as though he has given her his own strength, as though he has joined forces with her, and that little volume is a little sword wherewith she may meet and do battle with all that may come her way. She feels no longer quite defenceless, and no longer quite alone.

But she is five minutes late already, and as she climbs the stairs she can hear a thick flow of talk, behind shut doors, from the packed dressing-rooms – a thick bubbling flow relieved every other moment by the sound of high cackling laughter, or strident challenge, or off-hand imprecation. And she opens the door of her own room and goes in.

And in this room are the Misses Cherry Lambert, and Honour Lang, and Effie Byng, and Biddy Maxwell, and Hazel Parry, and Dolly True, and Belle Hawke, and Dot Delane. All are present, in fact, and all are in the best of spirits, and all are in an advanced stage of undress – with the exception, that is, of Miss Biddy Maxwell, who is by the door, and whose existence is temporarily suspended, and vision temporarily blinded, by her dress, which she is hauling over head, with athletic motions, for the purposes of removal.

And Jackie's opening of the door seems to waft out into the passage, for one swift moment, the pungent air of flexible and sensuous femininity that is within – but she closes the door at once, and the secret is intact. And from the other side of the door it may still appear to be a secret – and a very tantalizing and enthralling secret at that – but once in here, and there is no mystery whatever. No ascetic, having entrance here, need fear for his poise – only the rake might flee in horror from the immediate destruction of his cherished beliefs. For from here the breath of languor is expelled, and all feminine blandishment replaced by a vitality and overbearing practicality that does not challenge, but implicitly refutes illusion. This is a place of flesh, and blood, and sinew, and human need. This is not Revelation; it is letting the cat out of the bag. And if the door is shut fast (as of course it is), it is surely so shut as a protection less from the ardours than from the instant despondence of man, who could enter here (and such invasions are not unknown), as eunuchs might have entered a harem of old – disenchanted, liberated, as by magic, from his normal instincts.

There is quite a chorus of welcome as Jackie comes in – an ironic 'Hooray!' in the friendliest of spirits, and much surprise that Jackie, of all persons, should be late. And 'She's got a Book, too,' says Miss Biddy Maxwell, coming into the world again. And Jackie is putting her book down on the shelf and commencing to undress.

There is a kind of energetic rustling all around her, and for a moment no one is speaking. But this is broken by Miss Cherry Lambert, a frivolous girl of about twenty-eight, who is highly interested in Jackie's peculiarities and temperament, and who now, to Jackie's horror (since all are listening), addresses her.

'Well, Jackie, been ———?' asks Miss Lambert, whose remarks are frequently, and for long stretches, unprintable.

'Been what?' asks Jackie, to whom Miss Lambert's remarks are not unprintable, since they are not understood.

There are glances from each to each amongst the girls, and here Miss Delane cuts in.

'Don't you know what a ——— is, Jackie?' asks Miss Delane.

'No,' says Jackie, blushing.

'"No," said she, blushing,' says Miss Biddy Maxwell, who is given to reporting her friends' speeches and mannerisms in this way, being of a derisive turn of mind, and far from friendly towards Jackie.

Miss Delane elucidates the mystery.

'Oh,' says Jackie.

'"Oh," said she,' says Miss Biddy Maxwell.

There is a silence.

'Then you haven't been doing *nothing* since we saw you last, Jackie,' affirms Miss Lambert, in friendly tones.

'No,' says Jackie.

'Nothing will Come of Nothing,' says Miss Dot Delane. 'Ain't that so?'

'Sure,' says Miss Effie Byng, and it appears that a great truth has been hit upon.

'That's Shakespeare, ain't it, Jackie?' asks Miss Delane, plainly appealing to an expert.

'*I* don't know,' says Jackie.

'Oh, I thought you knew all about Shakespeare,' says Miss Delane.

'Why should I?' asks Jackie.

'What? – *don't* you, Jackie?' asks Miss Dolly True, who is next to Jackie at the dressing-shelf, and who speaks with some concern. 'I thought you was a Reader.'

'Well, I may read a bit,' says Jackie. 'But I don't know anything about Shakespeare.'

'Said she,' caps Miss Biddy Maxwell, who considers this eminently and exquisitely worthy of report.

'Shakespeare? Hooz Shakespeare?' asks Miss Belle Hawke, in her thick, heavy, ageing voice, from the end of the room.

No one enlightens Miss Hawke.

'You can *'ave* the old bastard,' adds Miss Hawke, bestowing the dramatist with less magnanimity than vindictiveness upon her neighbours. She also adds that she will Shake his Something Else (in a moment).

There is a silence. They are now all facing their mirrors and smarming in their number five.

'The Tragedy of King Lear,' says Miss Hawke, with great significance ...

'I read Shakespeare at our school,' offers Miss Dolly True. 'We acted "The Merchant of Venice".'

('With Nobs On,' says Miss Biddy Maxwell quietly, but as one who would depreciate the achievement.)

'The Dark Lady of the Sonnets,' says Miss Hawke, again

irrelevantly, but with the same air of implacable grudge against this author . . .

There is another long, greasy silence.

'Mr William Bloody Shakespeare,' murmurs Miss Hawke, in the middle of this greasy silence.

'What's your book, Jackie?' asks Miss Cherry Lambert, in an off-hand way. This young woman's enormous curiosity with respect to Jackie and her quiet, mysterious ways, seldom leaves her alone for long.

'Well . . .' says Jackie, and does not know what to say. 'I don't know, really . . . It was sent me . . .' Happily Miss Biddy Maxwell here cuts in.

'Well, I got many things in my time,' says she. 'But I never got books.'

'No,' says Miss Lambert, '————.' Not Miss Lambert's words, but rather her ideas, are unprintable.

The girls laugh.

Suddenly, 'Come on, what's 'er book?' cries Miss True, and snatches at it, and begins to read.

'Oh, my word!' announces Miss True. 'It's Poetry!'

'Jesus wept!' cries Miss Delane, genuinely overpowered.

'Poetry?' cries Miss Hawke. '*I* know some *Poetry*!' And Miss Hawke says this with the utmost bitterness and rancour, and it is clear that it is a very different kind of Poetry that she knows.

'Percy – Buysher – Shelley,' reads Miss True. 'My word!'

'Oh, Perssaye!' cries Miss Hawke, who is becoming positively querulous.

'But I expect he's a fine poet, though, ain't he, Jackie?' asks Miss True, with some deference.

(Miss Maxwell adds Nobs to *this* conception, as well.)

'Yes. I think he is rather good,' says Jackie.

Here Miss Hawke again arrogantly reveals herself as no woman of letters, by remarking that she (if given Five Minutes for the purpose) would take some of the Shell out of him.

'Sure. I guess he's one of the greatest,' says Miss Hazel Parry, who has hardly spoken before. And because Miss Parry speaks quietly, and because Miss Parry has hardly spoken before, and because Miss Parry has the reputation of being the Clever Girl in this company, this remark carries great weight, and there is a silence.

The breath of scholarship, indeed, is for the moment chilling.

But at this moment Miss Delane comes forward, and having the flimsiest of clothes upon her person, strikes a mock-athletic attitude, and offers to Wrestle some one.

Which challenge is taken up by Miss Biddy Maxwell, who is similarly clothed, and who takes some pride in her strength.

'Come on, then,' says Miss Maxwell. 'I'll Wrestle you.'

'All right, I'll Wrestle you,' says Miss Delane.

But although both ladies assume Japanese positions, and declare with great firmness that they will Wrestle each other – neither of the two ladies give, at present, any manifestations of being about to close.

'I'll Wrestle you,' says Miss Delane.

'Come on, I'll Wrestle you, then,' says Miss Maxwell.

'Go on, Wrestle, you two,' urges Miss True.

'Wrestle her, Biddy,' urges Miss Lambert.

'All right, then,' says Miss Delane. 'I'll Wrestle her.' And she seizes her friend with diffident antagonism around the neck.

Whereat both ladies begin to pant very hard, and to push very hard, and to look very amiable very hard, and to grit their teeth and strain. And Miss Dot Delane, who is clearly Losing, grants a magnanimous 'My, ain't she strong!' and Miss Biddy Maxwell, who is clearly Winning, repeats, with humorous vindictiveness, that she will Wrestle her. And both young ladies are smiling the wrong side of their faces. And 'Go on, *Wrestle* her, Dot!' cry Miss Delane's supporters, and 'Go on, *Wrestle* her, Biddy!' cry Miss Maxwell's supporters, while Miss Hawke makes technical but rather caustic allusions to Half Nelsons. And at last there is a sudden withdrawal of strength, and both fall on to the floor with a heavy bump. But Miss Biddy Maxwell is well on top, and Miss Dot Delane is seen to be frowning and quiet – Hurt, in fact.

'Did I Hurt you, Dot?' asks Miss Maxwell.

'No – you're too Rough,' says Miss Delane, and it is clear that she is upset.

'You're Hurt, aren't you, Dot?' asks Miss True.

'Oh no, I'm not Hurt. She's too Rough, though.'

'Well, it was only Fun,' says Miss Maxwell. 'Sorry if I hurt you though, Dot.'

'Oh, I guess that's all right.'

There is a sharp double bang upon the door. 'Quartnar Peas!' cries the call-boy. And recedingly down the passage he does the same. 'Quartnar Peas! ... Quartnar Peas! ... Quartnar Peas! ...'

'Lord, there's the quarter,' says Miss Delane, returning to her place. And she has now quite recovered and is a little jealous of her prestige. 'I guess I fell the wrong way, then, Biddy,' she adds lightly. 'We'll have another go some other time.'

And 'Yes,' says Miss Dolly True, coming to her aid. 'You're a good match, you two.'

And for one passing moment it occurs to Jackie, who has watched this little episode from the beginning, that she has, perhaps, judged harshly of these – that each of these individuals is, if she but knew, the same solitary, defensive, defeated, striving creature as herself ... But the moment is a passing one.

There is now little time, and the conversation succumbs to the exertions of dressing. After ten minutes the call-boy returns to bellow 'Oavtewer Peas!' at them, and they go in couples, or alone, down on to the stage, which is strongly lit in the set, but dark behind (where Jack and Lew, as impudent as ever, are already engaged in serials).

Jackie has brought her book down with her, and all through the show she is hugging it to herself, and glimpsing slyly at its pages, and putting it down, when she has to perform, on a little property table in the dark, and coming back immediately afterwards to embrace it again.

And this causes a certain amount of comment and hostility amongst the company (to whom Belles Lettres are anathema), but she does not mind that. Indeed she is intensely proud of the book, and it is as though she is telling them that she has a friend of her own now, and doesn't care a hang for anybody.

And shortly after the interval she has a long time off the stage, and she takes it into the o.p. corner, and hugs it to herself, perfectly content, and watches the show. A Swiss scene is in progress at the moment, and Mr Jack Laddon is causing great amusement with an alpenstock. He is also Yodelling with great skill, and receiving, with great inconsequence, ventriloquial slaps in the face from Miss Beryl Joy, who plainly considers him revolting ... And Jackie watches this dreamily, and listens dreamily, to the great hoarse roars of laughter that each movement of Mr Laddon evokes in this Saturday multitude ...

And in this corner she is quietly joined, after a little, by Miss Cherry Lambert and Mr Lew Craik, who also want a glimpse. And these two have evidently been having some conversation before, for Miss Lambert comes up saying, 'Oh, Lew, but you gave me a shock, then, you really did,' and Mr Craik comes up saying that he will smack her backside for her in a moment – as though Miss Lambert is in the regular habit of chastising herself, and he is merely displaying practical and active sympathy with the disciplinary principle. And Miss Lambert replies, 'Oh, will you, Lew?' very intrigued; and then, 'Hullo, here's Jackie. Still got your book?'

'Yes,' says Jackie.

'She's always reading, Lew – this little girl,' says Miss Lambert.

'Oh – thasso?' says Mr Craik, without looking at Jackie, and with some asperity, for this little girl is not at all the type of little girl with whom Mr Craik has sympathy. But Miss Lambert has a kinder heart.

'I used to read Poetry at one time, Jackie,' she says.

'Did you?' says Jackie, smiling encouragingly ...

There is a long pause.

'Used to read Carlyle, too,' adds Miss Lambert, and there is another pause ...

And all three stand there, with painted, blanched faces, watching the show ... And Miss Lambert used to read Carlyle ... And an even greater roar of laughter goes up, and with it, simultaneously, the music begins. And a lightning and exquisite reconciliation takes place between Mr Jack Laddon and Miss Beryl Joy, and they take hands, and face the audience, and dance together along the floor. And still the three look on, in the blare of the band – Mr Craik dreamy and sophisticated, Miss Lambert dreamy and vague, and Jackie very dreamy, but very contented, and with a little eager thoughtful look behind her dreaminess. And under her arm her present of Shelley ...

Chapter Eight

DESOLATION

1

It was in the seventh week of her association with 'Little Girl', and when she was at Liverpool, and on her twentieth birthday, that Jackie had news of the death of Lady Perrin. She had been corresponding with the old lady a week before this, and it was a great blow, and sickened her very much.

From Lady Perrin's death she received the sum of seven hundred and eighty pounds; and she was, at first, delighted and intrigued by this amount, which she played about with mentally and brooded and speculated deliciously on every kind of imaginary expenditure. Ultimately, however, it was this bequest which brought her to an understanding of her true situation, and caused her to take stock of her affairs.

For with the death of Lady Perrin her last ship had been burnt, and she had herself and her own exertions alone to rely upon. There was now no turning back. And in some measure she was scared by this, and in some measure she was braced.

For although Jackie had undergone multitudinous and varying emotions since she had left Brighton, her primary ambition remained as clear as it ever had been. She still held that to endeavour to rise to the utmost heights of the profession she had chosen was a self-evidently noble and splendid aspiration: and she was still convinced of her talents and perfect capabilities in this direction. As for the vulgar and alien society in which she was now moving, and the slow grey depression of the northern towns through which she was now passing – she took them on sufferance, and regarded them as purely temporary inflictions. She would come properly into touch with her profession soon.

And to all this there was one solution, she told herself. There was one clear, too simple solution. Too absurdly simple and too absurdly beautiful. And because it was that, by now she had begun to put it away from herself, half in fear. It was a thing beyond her, and no purpose could be served by contemplating it. 'This has got to stop,' said Jackie, very firmly, one night in Newcastle; and she had succeeded since then in divorcing it from her (as it were) practical emotions. It lay somewhere apart, where it need no longer trouble her.

2

And yet when (and she was at Sheffield when this occurred) she had one night a wire from him saying that he was coming to spend the day with her, she might have known, from the pure glad gaiety and sudden unreasoning happiness that she took in the news, how far she had been deceiving herself in thinking that she could detach this thing from her existence.

It was almost like a reprieve – the prospect of seeing him again. And even if the sentence were passed anew, when he had gone – she could not trouble to think about that . . .

It was a very pleasant meeting at the station – on a cold, biting, cloudy Sheffield afternoon. And from the first moment there was a kind of new intimacy established, a reasonless and champagne-like affability, such as had, inexplicably, never been before between them. And to Jackie, at least (though she felt somehow sure that it was the same with him), the lowering sky over this sombre city, in which the first evening lights were peeping out, was dashed with all the beauty, and all the mystery and romance, in the world. She could not think of the future. This was enough.

And they walked round about for a long while, in no particular direction, until at last the sky had cleared to deep, bitter blue, and the stars had come out: and then they went into a quiet, rather deserted hotel, near the station, and had tea.

And here they were all alone, in a high narrow room, with a single and attentive waiter, and a very old gentleman at another table (who made very unique grunting noises, but subsequently departed). And their cheeks were red from contact with the thin, cold air; and the fire near by was blazing red. And the night was falling, and the tea was more than gratifying. And they talked, in low tones, unceasingly – talked until they knew nothing but the tune of their own low voices along the high, narrow room.

Until at last, the night outside looming more and more mysterious, and the red fire within blazing ever more ardently from the dark, and the waiter having deserted them, and left them altogether alone – a sudden feeling of oppression and nervousness seemed to steal upon them both, and they looked out of the window, and there was a long silence ... It was, indeed, for a moment, as though they were suddenly face to face with something, and had nothing to say. As though their talk and ebullience had been obviously leading up to something, and then fallen dead.

And it was more than a sense of oppression with Jackie: it was a fear, almost – a fear of the night ahead and outside, of the theatre to which she must return, of the chillness of life itself – an aching longing for him to gladden and reassure her now, to say the word, and make her exalted. But he did not speak, and they looked out of the window, and were silent ...

'Then where have you come from to-day?' asked Jackie, at last. 'You haven't told me yet.'

'Come from? London. Why?'

'London?' said Jackie, in surprise.

'Why – what's the matter?'

'Are you on business up here, then?' asked Jackie.

'No. I came to see you.'

'*Me!*' cried Jackie, smiling, and sitting up and pointing at herself.

'Yes. What did you think?'

'Good Lord,' said Jackie ...

And there was another very long and very heavy, and very complimentary and embarrassed silence ...

'And are you going to perform in anything again soon?' asked Jackie.

'No. I've retired, I think. Anyway, I shan't go back unless I have to. I've got this book on hand now, and I've got to concentrate on that for about six months.'

'What book's that?' asked Jackie.

'Oh – the usual stuff ...'

And there was another pause.

'Do you – sort of,' asked Jackie, 'make money from that?'

'No. Not a penny.' He was looking at her now. 'And with a wife to support and one thing and another, that's where I'm always getting into a mess. You see, I'd cut out this acting business altogether if I could only—'

'Oh, are you married, then?' said Jackie, suddenly, but she did not hear herself saying this. And she scarcely knew where she was or what she was doing. She only knew that she wanted to run away into the night, and cry, and forget – cry and forget. She could forget, she was sure, if you gave her the time. And she wanted to think. She wanted to think.

And outside a large car, with two glaring headlights, like some irresistible monster, snarled slowly up to the door of the hotel. And she was watching this car, and thinking of nothing at all.

He had replied that he was married.

'I thought you must have been,' said Jackie. And he did not reply to this.

And then the waiter came in and lit the gas.

And all at once there was no more night, and no more mystery, and sinister red fire, and trembling, romantic desolation. They were two rather wearied, and jaded, and commonplace earthlings, sitting opposite each other in the muddy gas-light of a hotel dining-room in Sheffield. And there was cigarette-ash sprinkled messily over the cups and table-cloth, and it was time to go to the theatre.

'Oh, well,' he said, and clumsily affected a yawn, with his knuckle on his mouth.

'Oh, well,' said Jackie, and sat straight up.

'Will you have your bill, sir?'

'Yes, please.'

There was a scribbling silence.

'The lady had two cakes, sir?'

'Two cakes … Did you have two cakes, Jackie?'

'Two cakes? Let's see, now. Yes. Two cakes. That's right.'

'Two cakes, sir? ... Thankyousir ... Thankyousir ... '

'All right.'

'Thankyouverymuchsir. Thankyousir.'

He was helping her on with her coat.

They were out in the cold night air.

'Well, what happens now?' asked Jackie. 'Are you going back, or what?'

'Well, shall we go and look up the trains?'

'Right you are ... Isn't it cold?'

'Yes. Foul up here.'

The life had gone out of both of them.

'Will you wait here?' he said. 'And I'll go and ask.'

He was gone nearly five minutes, and she waited alone, tremblingly cold, amid the noise of engines and station cries. She might never see him again, she reflected, after this.

'Well, there's one in ten minutes, really,' he said, and stood above her, looking down on her.

'Oh,' said Jackie, and looked about her.

There was a pause. His face was strained. He also seemed to feel the cold.

'Of course, I shall stay the night here in a minute ... '

She giggled feebly, as though that was a very idle thing to have suggested, and there was another pause.

'Come on, Jackie.' He took her arm and began to lead her away. 'I'll stay here the night, and see you down to the theatre. I can't face a journey now.'

'But how can you ? You haven't got any things ... '

'Doesn't matter. I'll buy them.'

'Oh, don't be silly. How *can* you?'

'Come along. We'll buy them now. We've got three quarters of an hour before you need go in, and then I'll meet you after the show, and we'll have supper.'

Supper ... It was not all over yet ...

And because of this sudden reprieve, the cloud and chill which had fallen upon them seemed suddenly and unreasoningly to be lifted. And he took her arm, and they walked snugly away into the cold wind as though there had been no interruption.

But she forced herself to ask him, in a conversational way, some more about the subject which had so upset her. And it transpired that he was not living with her, and had not done so for four years. And he described it as having been a very foolish business altogether. And this, too, made her feel a little happier ...

And indeed a kind of sad gaiety, a mutual agreement to be gay, came upon them both. And the shopping that followed was a very delightful shopping – in which they were two humorous conspirators against the servile grandiosity of the shops. And in the Men's Department of the big store they entered he was very amusing about his pyjamas, implacably insisting upon wide stripes, and vacillating, with great earnestness, and constant appeals to her, between mauves and reds. And it was even more fun in the chemist's over the way, where he held out tenaciously for green as the sole decent shade in tooth-brushes, sneering at innumerable whites (as being full of integrity but without sensuous appeal), and at last coming round to Jackie's notions, which had been from the beginning in favour of a mild pink. And when they came out of this there were the most delightful arguments on the subject of Carrying, in which she said she would not go any farther unless she did, and was at last granted the tooth-brush, which she bore with great courage and intrepidity from then on. And equally delightful was a subsequent debate upon Shaving, in which he wondered whether he could Go for a day, and submitted to her decision, while she, in an exquisite little surge of possessiveness, examined his face in the light of a shop-window, and at last, on her own responsibility, allowed that he might. And at last they came to the Stage Door, where it was arranged that she should keep the Pyjamas, as well as the Tooth-brush, because she easily could, and because he was meeting her after the show, and could give them to him then. And he was going in front, and would probably be round in the interval.

And in the interval there he was, with his hands in his pockets, and his hat and coat off, talking fluently yet languidly to Julius Caesar, at the back of the stage. And he was talking thus to Julius Caesar, but he had come up from London to see *her*. And he was excusing himself from Julius Caesar, with a polite smile, and coming over to her. And he was smiling at her, as only he could smile, and they were saying 'Hullo' softly, and standing together without a word, but with perfect cognizance of mutual happiness and harmony in their silence. And they were joined by Miss Biddy Maxwell.

'Hul*lo-o-o*, Richard!' said Miss Maxwell. 'What do you think you're doing up here?'

'Hullo, Miss Maxwell,' he replied, and they had a little conversation, and she passed on.

Everybody seemed to know him, thought Jackie, and everybody seemed to love him, as she did. How unintelligent and irrational had she been in thinking she could have had this individual, this patently attractive and desirable and unique individual, to herself.

'Hullo!' said Miss Cherry Lambert. 'You here, Mr Gissing?'

'Rather.'

This was getting too much for her.

After a short conversation, including a hint that she should be entertained by him to-night (which was courteously rebuffed), Miss Lambert passed on.

'You seem to know everybody,' said Jackie.

'Yes,' he said. 'I do seem to. Misspent youth, I suppose . . . '

'Hullo, Gissing,' said Mr Jack Laddon. 'I heard you were in front to-night. How's things?'

'Very well, thanks, Mr Laddon. And how are you?'

'Oh, not so bad. What are we like from the front?'

'Very good indeed.'

'What are you up for, then?'

'I came up to see Miss Mortimer.'

'Oh,' said Mr Laddon, glancing at Jackie, and rather at a loss. And 'Ah-ha,' he added, encouragingly . . .

There was something about Mr Gissing which seemed to steal from Mr Laddon his natural easy arrogance. 'Well – so long.'

'Good-bye.' There was a pause.

'How do you get on with Mr Laddon, Jackie?'

'Well, I don't see much of him. I don't like him very much, though.'

'Yes. Isn't he foul?'

And at this point Jackie herself had to go, and he returned to the front.

In the dressing-room, at the end of the show, Miss Maxwell, ruminatively cutting her toe-nails, brought the subject up.

'Richard Gissing's been in front to-night,' she said, to the room at large.

'I know,' said Miss Lambert. 'I spoke to him.'

'So did I,' said Miss Maxwell, not without slight haughtiness. 'I spoke to him a lot.'

'He's a Real Good Sort, is Dick Gissing,' said Miss Lambert, who was never above a little sentiment. 'And I have Reason to Know.'

'Oh yes,' said Miss Maxwell. 'He's a Terrible Gentleman.'

By which Miss Maxwell meant, not that Mr Gissing was a terrible gentleman, but that he was, to a very advanced degree, a gentleman.

'He acts in Shaw a whole lot, doesn't he?' asked Miss True.

'Yes, that's right,' said Miss Lambert. 'I've seen him once. How'd you come to know him, Jackie?'

'Oh, I just met him,' said Jackie . . .

'It was from him, really,' added Jackie, softly, 'that I got that book.'

And a long and heavy silence fell over the whole dressing-room.

'Well,' said Miss Lambert, at last. 'I'm sure you couldn't do much Better.'

For Miss Lambert was in a moral mood to-night.

3

The rest of the evening passed off very simply and quietly.

He met her, as arranged, in the front of the house, and they walked together, not speaking very much, through the deserted streets – where it was already snowing and the pavements wore a thin bright carpet of deadening white – straight to his hotel.

Here he gave her a supper such as she had not had for a very long while, and which, after a long period in rooms, reminded her rather unpleasantly of the warmer things of life she had forsaken: and here he told her a lot about himself, and here she too described much of her early life, and her present circumstances and feelings.

And they lingered a long while over their coffee, the room becoming more and more deserted, and themselves becoming more and more mute.

And the hour grew very late, but they sat on ...

And then, with extraordinary suddenness, he got up, and said that he must see her home. But because he had confessed, a little while before, to having a very bad sore throat, she said that she would not let him see her home, and that he must go straight to bed. And as she seemed to be in earnest, he sat down again, and there followed, a rather sickening and dull argument about it, and it was at last decided that he should put her into a taxi.

After some difficulty a taxi was found, and he came out with her into the snow, which was now about half an inch thick, to see her into it. (She was too tired and weak to protest against this.)

And she took her place on a cold black leather seat, and he slammed the door on her, and gave inaudible instructions to the man in front. And 'This *is* paid for!' he shouted through the window, and 'Good-bye!' And 'Good-bye,' said Jackie, and smiled and waved her hand. And he smiled and went inside.

He was a long time starting, was this taxi-man, and wasn't at all sure about his doors being fastened properly, and had to get out twice to wind himself up again.

But he did get going at last, and the hotel swept slowly out of sight.

And she was alone, with the glistening snow, and the taxi-man's heavy back, and the snarl of changing gears, and the mystery and coldness of her own existence.

Chapter Nine

LUNCHES

Three weeks later 'Little Girl' came into Town. The first night passed off with Mafeking applause: the Press next morning was moderate in its acclamation: and it settled down immediately into a steady run.

Jackie, of course, returned to West Kensington: but she did not spend all the time she had apart from the theatre in this district. On the contrary, being now, in a quiet way, enormously popular in the chorus, she was receiving constant nightly invitations on all sides. These were, of course, often of a rather wholesale nature – consignments of The Girls being requisitioned in a very callous if palatial manner by some flaunting Croesus desirous of entertaining his friends; and at these Jackie's pride naturally took offence. But there were others, including one or two suppers and dances on the stage, given by the management, and in the nature of command ceremonies, which she accepted.

And she was taken out a good deal by Mr Tom Rocket and Mr Merril Marsden.

Mr Tom Rocket was a slightly competent young comedian of thirty, who played a small part (that of a clergyman) in 'Little Girl', and who had, at a quite early stage of the tour, betrayed a preference for Jackie. He was a young man with an ill face, thwarted aspirations, a common manner, but a character of strong sentiment and principle. Indeed he had first been drawn towards Jackie on account of her moral integrity and as one in possession of what he termed her sex's Most Precious Jewel – to wit, chastity, which he took for granted (by the way) on quite insufficient evidence.

He had, in fact, conceived a slow admiration for her which had become daily more obvious and had at last culminated in his confessing his love for her. Upon which a flood-gate of metaphor had been loosed upon the situation, the principal and most recurrent comparison being that of Jackie to God's Snows – which she was (he said) as White as – if not as Cold – (which he sometimes thought her). He also sometimes made more particularized references to Mont Blanc, which foreign summit he had not personally visited, but credited with the utmost detachment, purity, and chill.

Jackie, who had from the first assumed a passive, and if possible dampening rôle in this affair, at once said (according to a stale formula) that she was Very Sorry. She apologized, in fact, for being as White as God's Snows, but made it clear how difficult it was for her ... There was really no solution to the situation. He, however (and perhaps sympathizing with her difficulty), laid no blame upon her shoulders, and was not exacting. Further to being as White as God's Snows nothing was expected of her.

A kind of mutual agreement therefore arose, that she should go out to lunch, take walks, or visit the pictures with him – merely Being, within the time allotted, as White as God's Snows, and considering her part of the business fulfilled. What satisfaction to either party there was in this, she left to him; but he appeared to be perfectly satisfied. The two facts – first, that he had a wife in London (understood to be of a far from Alpine nature) – second, that he himself was a confirmed drunkard – while leading Mr Rocket into constant metaphorical beatings of the breast and declarations that he was not Good Enough for her, and could Never Come to her with Clean Hands – never succeeded in striking him as adequate causes for breaking the attachment. And when Jackie begged (as she so often did) that he would forget the matter and say no more, the instant threats, on his part, not only of self-destruction, but of Going Berserk (which was obviously much worse) caused her to conciliate him with the promise to remain that Something Worth Living For which he so emphatically declared she was. For although Jackie had been threatened with the self-destruction of her suitors ever since the age of thirteen, the whole manifestations of their devotions to her had been so utterly incomprehensible to her, that she still had a lurking fear that her imagination was lacking somewhere, and that they might. Also in this case there was a question of drink, wherein she thought, perhaps, she should not fail him.

All this did not pass by unnoticed by the company of 'Little Girl', even while yet on tour; and soon the two names were coupled and it was rumoured around on all sides that the key to the situation was to be found in whether Mr Tom Rocket could, or whether Mr Tom Rocket could not, Keep off the Whisky. An opportunity for highmindedness being immediately scented out, as well as for reconciliation and disinterested altruism, the thing grew at an intensive rate, until at last it came back to Jackie, who was told, quietly but firmly one night, by a mutual acquaintance, that Mr Rocket was the best fellow in the world, but what Jackie had to do was to Keep Mr Rocket off the Whisky. Now in so far as Jackie had not entered the theatrical business (as was partially suggested) to keep her associates off the Whisky, and in so far as she sincerely felt that Mr Rocket's Whisky was, fundamentally, his own problem, she took some offence at this friendly caution. She was also angered by the coupling of her name with Mr Rocket, and decided in future to treat him with greater coolness. This, however, in face of his too subservient infatuation, not to say further threats of Norse behaviour, she was not able properly to do, and the thing dragged on until they came to London.

Here, however, and on the third night of the show,

he succumbed entirely to liquor, and passing Jackie in a passage, assumed a misty kind of appraising attitude, and affirmed, in a thick voice, not that Jackie was as White as God's Snows, but Wizegossnose – which was an ill-timed, if not definitely frivolous abbreviation of the familiar sentiment. Jackie passed by with an unfeigned look of disgust, and the next evening, intending not to speak to him again, very obviously avoided him and hoped that the thing was now at an end.

But shortly after the interval she was arrested in a corner of the stage by one Mr Phillip Genaro, a young Italian singer who had a number to himself and was as high-minded as any, who asked her what she had been Doing with Poor Tom.

Having expressed complete innocence, she was informed that the gentleman was at that very moment having to be Held Down, and kept away at all costs from dressing-room Razors, which he was glancing at in a sinister fashion. Jackie again expressed innocence and indifference, but Mr Genaro, taking this to be mere hauteur, recommended tolerance as a motto in life, and begged that they would Patch it Up. This presumption of a relationship again angered Jackie extremely; but seeing Mr Rocket, a few minutes later, gazing at her from a corner in apparently genuine desolation, dutifully went over to him and reinstated the old conditions.

It was thus that apart from her work at the theatre she was seeing something of Mr Rocket at this time: and she was also seeing something of Mr Merril Marsden, the gentleman who had spoken to her at the dinner in Manchester. Mr Marsden, in fact, was by now in the habit of asking her to lunch at least once every week, and that with apparently disinterested motives. She attended these meals solely in her capacity of First Intellectual Chorus Girl, and no reference was made either to her character or beauty. Indeed, the purely scholastic atmosphere obtaining on these occasions would have tired Jackie a great deal, had she not been alive to the compliment of his invitations: for whereas, in her dealings with Mr Tom Rocket, the sole topic of absorbing interest was Jackie herself, in her dealings with Mr Marsden the sole topic of absorbing interest was Mr Marsden himself. Mr Marsden was interested in himself to a degree far beyond spasmodic egotism. He had reached, rather, a phase wherein he could (and did without cessation) treat himself academically, being quite willing to have new lights thrown upon him, fresh data collected about him, or unusual schools of thoughts rising about him; and remaining admirably broadminded, even if, in the last resort, dogmatic concerning himself. In fact Jackie's meetings with him (in which he did nearly all the talking) at last resolved themselves into little else but laboured and sober debates upon himself.

From the first few meetings the thing was detached, and a First Intellectual Chorus Girl's interest in the matter implicit. 'Of course, I happen to be *born* that way,' Mr Marsden would explain in these early stages. Or, 'Of course, That is *Me* (all over).' Or, 'Of course, I can't help it, but that Simply Happens to be My Way of Looking at things.' Or, 'I have no doubt I may be wrong, but I simply cannot *help* it.' There was but the lightest disparagement of differently disposed individuals: he was merely giving Jackie an elementary schooling in the mysteries of his character. Later he became more detailed, and a quantity of other axioms and immutable laws of his personality transpired. It transpired, for instance, that Mr Marsden was not Easily Roused, but when so, an implacable and even dangerous opponent. It transpired that Mr Marsden was Extremely Sensitive, though he showed (for such was his character) Little of this. It transpired that Mr Marsden was (though he said it himself) an Artist to his Finger Tips. It transpired that Mr Marsden was of course (and this perhaps was his most significant characteristic) Incurably Frivolous. It transpired that he was Very Sorry for this, but it could not be helped. He was, in fact, Cursed with a Sense of Humour. At least Mr Marsden said that he was cursed by this. But as he also spent a great part of his time Thanking God that he had been Blessed with a Sense of Humour (at least), one didn't quite know where one was. Also one waited for manifestations of his affliction (or good fortune) without result.

With this Sense of Humour – and in the same way as Mr Rocket had taken Jackie's spotlessness for granted – Mr Marsden immediately credited Jackie. Indeed this was where, he explained, they were in such sympathy; and their lunches together generally ended in their sitting dreamily over their coffee rather morosely thanking God that they had been cursed with a sense of Humour.

Jackie, to whom all this meant little, and whose sincere secret conviction was that Mr Marsden was a damned fool, nevertheless entered, in an apparently whole-hearted spirit, into these debates; and was always ready at hand to come up and consider his character in a new light. And apart from the compliment he paid her by seeking her suggestions, he invariably gave her what appeared to her to be an extremely good lunch, promised her his paternal protection, and (what was of graver import) spoke of a play in which he was interested, and in which there was a part, he said, suited to her, which he might get for her. He also promised her many introductions to influential persons without keeping his promise.

Chapter Ten

THE THREE WEEKS

1

Thus it was, with 'Little Girl', and Mr Rocket, and Mr Marsden, and Mrs Lover at West Kensington, and a ticket at Mudie's, that Jackie occupied herself throughout the winter. And 'Little Girl' moved to two different theatres, and the cast and various numbers were altered, and it still did steady business.

And one morning, suddenly, the sun was yellow and quiet in a hushed Talgarth Road, West Kensington, and the spring had come ...

And with that yellowness and quietness, and that poignantly frail air upon everything, that puzzling sad hopefulness which made itself felt even in this distressed neighbourhood, Jackie's heart, which had numbed itself throughout the winter with a dull sense of loss and unhappiness, now responded seekingly and achingly to the promise of the season.

She had heard from Richard, as she now called him, only once since that night in Sheffield. He had written from Brittany, telling her something about himself, but talking of no further meeting when he returned to England.

At times Jackie could not help wondering – and Jackie, being what she was, conceived herself at such moments as one verging on abysses of thought – she could not help wondering why Richard was now away in Brittany and the whole thing was so out of the question. She put this to herself as a thing which she would not allow to enter her calculations, but at times she was enormously interested in it hypothetically.

Jackie, indeed (but this only at sleepless midnight, when the great moral tide of her twenty years was at its lowest ebb), could really not see why people couldn't get Divorces ... She did not know much about these things, had never dreamed of them as anything ever touching herself, and the mere word had a sort of base practicality about it which chilled her. But, for all that, when people were really unhappy ...

But, of course, in that case, people would have to be absolutely terribly in love with people ...

Well, she could do that all right, on her side ...

2

And then, suddenly, and again by telegram, he announced that he had returned, and was coming to see her. And he arrived one evening, two hours before the show, she meeting him at the station on a hot, crowded, dizzying summer's day.

And he saw her round to the show, and had supper with her afterwards, at Lines'. And he told her that he had come to London about his book, and was going to stay in London for about three weeks.

And sitting there, after the show, in the warm pink-shaded lights, at half-past eleven – but with the night, somehow, still young, and wild, and soft, and mysterious – it seemed to Jackie as though a sudden paradise had been opened before her eyes – as though another reprieve had come – yet another – and she could glory in it. And they talked and talked. And as they talked, and the black bent waiters hovered about, as though in half-leering but eagerly conspiratorial possession of their secret, she looked at his warm yet clear-cut face, which was now so infinitely dear to her, and let her whole soul recline upon the three weeks ahead.

And those three weeks contained no disappointment for Jackie. Indeed they ever afterwards stood out as perhaps the most precious weeks in her existence. They were days of dustiness and blazing London sunshine; and he met her every day, and took her everywhere. And every evening, when the skies were red, behind London house-tops, and the air was cool, he was softly escorting her round to the theatre. That one moment of departure was as dear to her as any other, with its sweet surety of return. She never forgot those red cool skies, and those soft escortings to the stage-door ...

And the days themselves, and the trips they had ... Hampstead – Maidenhead – Richmond – Cookham – Shepperton – Hindhead – Virginia Water ... And sunshine always, and green and cool places, and water ... And lunches ... Innumerable lunches ... And teas ... teas by the river ... languorous but cool teas by the river, with cress and bread and butter ... And the railway ... always by railway ... first class – alone ... or with unknowing and foolish people of whom fun might be made ... And always the fear of being late for the theatre ... and always the taxi just in time ... and always the red, cool sky at the end. The red cool sky, behind the house-tops, after the full green joyous day.

And nothing ever said, nothing ever admitted. And sometimes, because of this, a sadness and melancholy on Jackie's part, in so far as it was possible to be sad, so long as he was there ...

And the whole thing so manifest and very simple ... Jackie, on the one hand, a normal human being, striving frailly and unprotectedly to live to the full, to spread herself emotionally, and fulfil her instincts. And seeing in him her chance to do so, her chance to throw down all barriers, to devote herself to one sufficient and beauteous object, to have and give protection, and warm herself for ever ...

And he, on the other hand, a less normal and more aggressive and knowledgeable individual – but recognizing in her that warm, transparent, inner life of hers – that inner life working itself out behind her grave, clear, foolish, and to him extraordinarily beautiful face. And yearning to deliver and console that inner life; and knowing, with too great a conviction, of his power to do so ...

That inner spiritual life which Jackie always carried about with her, like a burden ... that inner life only to be caught at work occasionally, and unawares, in a thoughtful, unconscious glance ... that contemplative, optimistic, puzzled, striving and never confessed inner life ... to which everything he might say was quietly referred, for sober meditation, and from which all her speech sprung automatically, and all her too artless tones and self-betraying looks ...

The charm of Jackie, indeed, was overwhelming.

And because the whole thing was so obvious and ingenuous, it hardly needed confession, and they knew this. It was simply with them ... It was with them in the roar and tumult of London traffic, with only five minutes to get there, as much as it was with them on the quiet lawn of Skindle's, with the river calm below, and the quiet, cushioned, vulgar punts floating lazily by ... It was with them as much in the tender invitation of the Waldorf band (with which they sometimes supped), as it was with them on the summit of the Sussex Downs, with nothing but the sky and the wind, and the brown sunlight scudding over a hazed and map-like county beneath. It was with them at all stations – at journey's end or journey's beginning, that is – either at the rural and earnest quietude of the Hassocks halting-place, or under the gaunt blackened roof, and sense of fear and hurry, of the Victoria terminus. And what was going to be done about it neither of them had any idea, and (quite genuinely) neither of them cared.

And nothing was done about it. One week slipped by, and she still had two weeks to recline upon – two weeks slipped by and she still had one week to recline upon – and the last week slipped by (and there was never any suggestion that the time should be prolonged) until there were but two days left. And then there was a last, sad, brilliant day; followed by a pale, nervous, anti-climactic morning, upon which the senseless sun blazed as brightly as ever. And she had lunch with him, and spent the afternoon with him, and had tea with him, and at last saw him off at the station to Brighton. He was going there to stay with his brother.

It was a swift moment, that of the parting – under the clock. A vast engine was hissing near by, and they were shouting at each other like sailors giving orders before being submerged in a sea of noise: and at one moment he was there, and at the next he was gone, and she was looking vaguely at the three-and-sixpenny novels on the bookstall ...

It was always at Stations, wasn't it, she thought, as she walked away ...

And having nothing to do, and nowhere to go, she walked across Green Park, where she sat down for a little by the water, in mute contemplation: and on to Piccadilly, from whence she walked up and down Regent Street for some time: and then she went into Shaftesbury Avenue, and turning up a side street, unescorted, entered the theatre. Here the stage was wrapped in complete darkness and deathly silence, and she appeared to be the first to have arrived.

And she went up the stairs, and entered the deserted dressing-room. And the casement window of this looked out upon a crowded Soho back-street, and the same, always the same, red, cool sky. And everything was very unfamiliar in the dying light of day, since she had never before seen a dressing-room other than in a blaze of light and noise.

And she sat down in the dusk, amid the lifeless glimmer of cast-off clothes, the lurid smear of greasepaint and carmine, the towels and littered cosmetics of the virile and absent feminine; and she looked out of the window at the red, cool sky – the red, cool, unknowing, incurious sky – and she wondered where he was now.

And she desolately imagined him arriving somewhere, in some far, remote, sunset distance. Somewhere a train was carrying him away – after all the warmth and eagerness and inexpressible consolation of these three weeks – carrying him unrelentingly away. And the subdued roar of the traffic, all around, was like the roar of the unappeasable world which had taken him.

And as the dusk fell deeper, and as she looked down at the street below, where the lamps were already glowing emerald upon the dead fruity litter of the vending and beautiless humanity that thronged this quarter, Jackie felt that she could not bear another parting like this.

Chapter Eleven

CRICKET

1

Jackie had learnt a good deal about Richard, and Richard's past life, in those three weeks. But it was not his habit to speak much about himself, unless urged to do so, and concerning one subject particularly, that of his brother – a subject in which she was very greatly interested, since she could not conceive, and rather trembled at the conception of, anything in the same stamp as himself – she still remained very much in the dark. She had heard, indeed, that he was an elder brother, that he lived quietly on his own estate in Sussex, and that he was on terms of perfect accordance with Richard: but this was all. The three facts combined had awakened in her a certain trepidation, together with a certain grudge and antagonism, which engendered in its turn a very strong desire to meet this individual and win him over to her side. She doubted whether this would be easy, but reminded herself that she was lucky in having but one relation (and that a male) to contend with.

So little, however, had she learnt from Richard concerning him, that it was Miss Cherry Lambert from whom she first got the news, one Saturday about a month later, firstly that Charles Gissing was an amateur cricketer in the Sussex eleven, secondly that he was at this time playing at Lord's. Miss Lambert claimed to have met him, and described him as charming. This was a great blow to Miss Biddy Maxwell, who disputed every inch of Gissing-ground with her friend; but she retorted quickly, if a trifle inapplicably, with Tate, whose autograph she claimed to have, and offered to produce. She also said that she thought it very Snobbish having Gentlemen and Players like that, as the players were just as much gentlemen as the gentlemen, and it ought to be altered, and it was very Snobbish. Which was also a One (in a subsidiary way) in Miss Lambert's Eye. There followed a discussion on Oxford and Cambridge, both of which were deprecated. Jackie, however, had decided to go to Lord's.

2

On Monday morning, therefore, she found herself at eleven o'clock on a hazed blue summer's day, queueing up, with a rather agreeable sensation of excitement and espionage, outside the ground. The unusualness of this procedure, together with an unalterable conviction that she was doing something slightly underhand, provided her with a thrill from the beginning, though she had no idea how thrilled she was actually to be.

This was not, of course, her first experience of this summer game. At Hove, indeed, and when her father was alive, Jackie had had free entrance to the member's pavilion of the County Ground, where she had spent many of her happiest though most languid days – from her earliest youth, when, for mysterious purposes of her own, it was her habit, for absorbed hours on end, to keep the score; down to the latest period before the war, when she attended for more social and less interested reasons. She was thus far from deficient in knowledge of the game, and as she now strolled over the lazy arena, after all these years, she felt stealing over her a melancholy and pleasurable reminiscence of the unhurrying life that had once been hers. The theatre seemed very distant on this sunny, green, quiet, hot day.

Hearing in the distance the quick *pock-pock, pock-pock* of the practising in the nets – a sound infinitely more excited and eager than anything the rest of the day or the actual game would provide – she strolled over there in the vague hope of seeing and being able to recognize the one she had come expressly to observe. But here, although she made several attempts, she was unable to select anyone, and shortly afterwards she bought a card, upon which his name was printed as number five, and found a high seat on a sunny terrace, and prepared to watch.

It was almost like a call, this – a sunny call to the life she had left ... She remembered it all so well. The rolling of the pitch, the clanging of the bells, the slow dispersing of the crowd from the field, the emergence of the umpires – the whole semi-official but leisured and warm-hearted routine. And Middlesex still batting, with three wickets to fall. And Hendren still in, with his score at eighty-seven. And the emergence of the players, to mechanical applause, and the placing of the field, and the digging in, and the looking round, and the first maiden over, and the slow settling down to one of those mornings-after-the-night-before of cricket, which Jackie knew so well, but which she now found inexpressibly delightful. Indeed, by the time Hendren had reached his century, and the three figures on the black and white board whirled giddily and exultingly up amid a swelling storm of applause, Jackie was quite overcome with pleasure.

Hendren was bowled at a hundred and five, and ten minutes later the innings ended.

She had thought that perhaps she would not see this brother before the lunch-interval, but in the slow hour that followed three Sussex wickets fell, and he was fifth upon the card. The ground, meanwhile, had been growing very full for this always most popular London match, and the sun on the terraces had been growing very much more hot;

and an air of seething expectancy was over all. And then the fourth wicket went down.

The last player vanished – there was a pause – a portentous silence from the crowded members' pavilion – and then a flash of white against and amid those stolid rows, and he was out on the green – raising his cap to that more emphasized applause commonly accorded to a new amateur, and walking at an easy pace to the wicket . . .

She couldn't see . . . but much browner . . . and possibly larger . . . and kindly . . . shoulders built for kindliness alone . . . and brown . . . extraordinarily brown . . . and smiling brownly at Hendren . . . and Hendren smiling back, as only that enchanting professional was able to smile . . . and taking his stand . . . and looking around . . . and cutting his first ball off Durston for a single, and running up the pitch to a soft swelling burst of applause . . .

He made twenty-four before lunch.

Jackie's lunch-hour, by which time the sky had become grey, and for which she had been provided with very luscious egg-sandwiches by Mrs Lover, was like a curious dream . . . That this individual was not out – that the whole game, that the whole crowd, clustering and pacing in a released manner over the field, was thus suspended and as it were dependent upon him; that this was Richard's brother; that Richard loved her; that she loved Richard; that she might never have Richard; that she might have Richard for ever; that no one in this schoolboyish, plebeian or supercilious crowd was remotely aware of these tragic but exquisite complications ... it was all so quaint. But there was also a pure detached thrill about it which she could not resist. And she sat there munching her sandwiches, and spilling the crumbs, and brushing them off, and saying No this seat was not engaged (so far as she knew) and going on munching – surely the most singular and singularly involved figure that ever watched a day's cricket in the history of Lord's.

The sky was even greyer still by the time the game recommenced, and he came out looking stronger, and browner, and cooler than ever. And he had another little humorous passage with Hendren (for whom Jackie had by now conceived an adoration) and he settled down with his partner to a very slow game indeed. But he scraped his way up to fifty at last, and the huge pea-in-box roar of applause that arose was, for some reason, very sweet in Jackie's ears ...

He then settled down again, with the slow intent of one aiming at his century: and at sixty-four, with a suddenness so great as momentarily almost to divert the mind from the catastrophe, his stumps were in a mess and he was walking away ...

But even then the day was not quite over. For the Sussex wickets fell very quickly after this, and an hour after the tea interval Middlesex were batting again. And the last hour of the day was as happy as any to Jackie, with the plunging and deepening-yellow sun shining blindingly in her face, and the glowing green grass and white glowing figures in front ...

And for a long period, when he was in the long-field, the most astonishing proximity ... Practically invisible, because of the sun, but not more than twenty yards away ... His back turned, his eyes shaded with his hand, and the creak of his cricket boots, and the aura of his energy as he paced up and down or ran ...

And then, all at once, a vast thundercloud looming up, darkening the field and daubing the sky with sharply defined and outlandish rays. And a chill wind rising ... and shiverings ... and the slow-rising streams of the first departures ... And enchantment gone, and a coldness at heart ...

And then a few rain-drops, and an umbrella raised hysterically in the distance, and a general stir and disturbance ... And only five minutes to go in any case ... And a sudden snatching of stumps and a rushing in ...

But not raining properly yet, and Jackie, very cold, and very desolate, in the thick, dusty crowd on her way to the gates ... Very cold and desolate, and the scrunch, scrunch, scrunch of feet on the ashen-white gravel ...

But a glorious day, for all that – an unforgettable day. A sunny and quite unforgettable day ...

And Richard at the main gate – as though waiting for her.

3

'Hullo, Jackie,' he said. He spoke sadly and quietly, and looked down at her without apparent surprise.

He had a newspaper, screwed up like a baton, in his hand, and his collar was a little disordered, and his face and hands a little grubby from a day obviously spent at Lord's. And Jackie observed all these things and observed none of them. And she had a terrible sense of having been caught – trapped irrevocably – and she read his sadness and quietude as his scorn. And she heard herself saying, in a frightened mist, 'Hullo, what on earth are you doing up here?'

And at this moment a roll of thunder – like the piano-shifting of some evil-minded tenant in the gaunt grey above – broke upon their ears. And they looked into each other's eyes, in a fascinated way, and ignored it, Consciously and deliberately, and until it had expended itself, they ignored it, saying nothing.

'I've been here all day, Jackie,' he said.

There was a pause.

'You know, I didn't mean you to see me,' said Jackie, attempting a smile, which he returned.

'I did see you though, Jackie. I saw you having lunch.'

'No. *Not* my sandwiches?' pleaded Jackie.

'Yes. Sandwiches and all. And I was so hideously fascinated I simply couldn't spoil it. Otherwise I might have given you a decent one.'

'Jolly glad you didn't ...' said Jackie, vaguely, and there was a pause.

'I've sent you a wire to-day.'

'Have you? What about?'

'Well, what are you doing now?' Here a departing gentleman collided with Mr Gissing.

'I beg your pardon, sir,' said the departing gentleman.

'All right.'

'Well,' said Jackie. 'I was just going over to the theatre, really.'

Large spattering drops of rain commenced to fall. Deliberately and consciously they ignored these drops of rain.

'Theatre. Yes. Well, I've got to be somewhere at eight. What shall we do?'

A flash of pink lightning – a snarl exploding in a crash – a darkening and a panic, and a straight-falling torrent of rain. Every-one was rushing for shelter.

'Damn!' He took her arm.

And she was no longer afraid of his scorn, or ashamed of herself. She was forgiven (if there was any forgiving), and all was as before. She was in a thunderstorm at Lord's Cricket Ground with the man she loved. And she relied upon him. And it was very strange, and very uncomfortable, and entirely beautiful.

'Taxi,' he murmured, and led her into the middle of the road. Here he stopped a machine, and opened the door. She got in.

'Where to, Jackie?' he cried.

'Where to? I don't know. Where?'

'Swiss Cottage,' he shouted to the driver. 'What? . . . Oh, the station . . . and back again!'

He was in beside her and sitting opposite her. The taxi was moving away.

His clothes were dabbed with wet, and his newspaper baton was limp. She had never before seen him so grubby and untidy, and found him more than usually attractive in this state. Also it was the first time she had ever seen him truly nervous and ill at ease. He was like a small boy impatient under pain. He kept on jabbing his knee with his paper, and looking meaninglessly out of the window as he spoke.

'Look here, Jackie. I've got on to a job for you. That's what the wire was about. You'll find it at the theatre. You know "Little Girl"'s coming off in three weeks?'

'No!'

'Yes. Well, this thing I've got is a chance for stack. Just the thing you want, really. You won't get paid much, and there's a certain amount of work, but you'll get all the experience you want. Walter Carters – the man who owns the Old Strand. He's taking a show round the London halls, and then he's going down to the King's, at Brighton, to do some repertory – a month or two. Awful trash, but just the thing you're wanting. And I want you to go along and see him, to-morrow.'

'I say – how ripping,' said Jackie, who had no idea what she was saying. 'Do you think I'll get it?'

'Bound to. You see, when they get to Brighton I'm going to play the leads.'

'You!'

'Yes – you see – and we can be in it together.'

The skies crashed above: the rain threshed the roof and spat at the window: and in the garish dusk of this strange chamber he looked over at her, in a strained way, and jabbed his knee with his paper. And the taxi was speeding up by the long wall of Lord's on its way to Swiss Cottage.

And the other side of that wall, she suddenly and inconsequently reflected, was the brother of this distressed and lovable being. Probably changing now, in that receding but still visible pavilion ... And it was a very wet day, and this was a curious connection she had developed with the cricketing world ...

4

'I say, where *are* we going?' she said.

'God knows. He'll take us round, I suppose.' He looked at his watch. 'We'll go in this to the theatre, and I'll leave you there. It'll be all right.' He was calmer now. 'Well, Jackie, what have you been doing all this time?' He leant forward.

'Oh – nothing much.' She lay back, as though weary, and smiled. 'Just the same.'

He looked out of the window.

'It's all so sudden,' said Jackie. 'I'd no idea "Little Girl" was coming off. It's wonderful of you to have got me this, though.'

'Oh, while we're at it,' he said, and he gave her instructions as to what she was to do, and where she was to go to-morrow. And how she was to give notice to her management at the end of the week. There was then a very long silence. For quite three minutes they had nothing to say.

He leant out of the window, shouted orders to the man, and sat down again. He left the window open.

Through the muddy London streets the taxi jolted on, and still they said nothing. It rained unceasingly and the streets were practically deserted. They came to Baker Street station, and whirred down Baker Street.

'Are you up here just for the day, then?' asked Jackie.

'Yes. I came up to see my brother.'

She was looking at him, but he would not look at her.

'He was wonderful, wasn't he? I was terribly disappointed when he didn't get his century.'

'Yes. So was I.'

'He's not like you, is he?' said Jackie.

'No.'

He was still peering out of the window, and now she raised herself to do the same. The draught was coming in full upon her, and she was trembling and cold.

'Is this Selfridge's?' said Jackie.

'Yes. Selfridge's.'

'Not far now.'

'No.'

'You'll write to me, I suppose?'

'Be up to see you, I expect. Damn this weather.'

'Yes. Isn't it awful?'

She was clenching her teeth to keep them from chattering. She was freezed to the bone, and she wished she was dead. It might have been raining since the beginning of the world.

He brought the window up with a bang.

'Oh, Jackie,' he said. 'What *are* we going to do?'

She saw him looking at her, in an agonized way, and she looked away. She looked in front of her and could not speak. She could not trust herself to speak. She was like a little ashamed child, about to be ill.

'Well, Jackie?'

'I don't know,' said Jackie . . .

But now he had his hand upon hers, and she watched this. She observed its warmth and its brownness, and the way it was fondling hers. And this fondling was a curious, timeless, and inexplicable event – something which might be watched in a detached way – something which might never have begun, and which might never end . . . 'God,' he said. 'Here we are.'

He withdrew his hand. The taxi stopped, and she looked up at him. He was opening the door, and stepping out into the rain. She followed him, and he took her hand.

'Well, good-bye, Jackie. If I don't come up, I'll write.'

'Right you are,' said Jackie, and went inside.

Chapter Twelve

THE UNDERWORLD

1

The next day Jackie saw Mr Walter Carters at the Old Strand Theatre in the Strand. She was kept waiting for two hours, in which she had two cups of coffee on two separate floors of a neighbouring A.B.C. establishment – the stage-doorkeeper having no notions concerning, nor any apparent interest in, Mr Carters' whereabouts. At her fourth inquiry, however, she encountered Mr Carters in the doorway, and he asked her if she was wanting him. She showed her letter of introduction from Mr Gissing, and he murmured 'Oh, yes,' and asked her to follow him. He took her up the stairs into a small dressing-room, where he switched on the light. The room was bare save for some red-bound and decayed scripts on the shelf, a disused whiskey-bottle, pen and ink, and Mr Carters' overcoat on a property basket. He read the letter through in a difficult silence.

Mr Reginald Carters was an untidy, thickly built, sunburnt, listless little man of forty-five, with a small moustache and very blue and innocent eyes. He had been, actively concerned in this business for forty years, and was indeed something of a landmark and rock in his profession. His theatre, the Old Strand, which he had inherited from his father and now shared with his sister, had reached a legendary status – and from this legend he had made no attempt to break away. The titles of the plays and revivals with which he had, for the last twenty years, had almost exclusive connection, were revealing of this tendency. Such titles as 'Alone in the City' – 'Just a Girl' – 'Married for Money' – 'A Girl's Best Friend' – 'A Soul for Sale' – 'Three Lasses from Blackpool' – 'Tried and True' – 'Masters of the Turf' – 'Merely the Drudge' – 'White All Through' – 'Only a Working Girl' – 'Waifs from the Workhouse' – 'For God, King, and Country' – or 'Sweet Seventeen' were representative and immediately identifiable titles. The plots of these melodramas accorded with these titles, and were similarly identifiable – dealing, as they did, exclusively and traditionally with infamously monocled scoundrels, pathetically credulous young women, oily-mannered (but black-hearted) solicitors, young men vaguely on His Majesty's Service (but with plenty of time for white flannels, father-defying, and yachting caps), Generals (given to plumes, adamance, and remorse), aged but benign priests (with a benediction habit), youthful and moth-like clergymen, temptresses for same, hirelings of the monocle (abiding in taverns), a sprinkling of female Spies, and a red-nosed postman, or a red-nosed publican, or a red-nosed bookmaker, who, in imbecile partnership with his wife (who would behave in a captious and querulous manner), afforded light refreshment in an otherwise unrelieved emotional essay in high piety and moral integrity. The action took place in England and abroad, and amounted, in the long run, to little. Abroad there was a War, which people came back from (after many years), and found things lamentably altered: at home there was free and incessant criticism of motives, under the nervous wear-and-tear of which somebody at last got up and Struck some one, and there was a great to-do. The whole was presented in from sixteen to twenty scenes, with ample use of front-cloths, which were, in their two-dimensional placidity, unconvincing, and, in their frequently exercised ability to deal facetious but savage blows upon the comedian's back, supernatural. There were introduced on the stage as many trains, battles, live racehorses, shipwrecks and the like, as could be afforded or negotiated.

With these plays revived, or with new attempts in the same model, Mr Walter Carters was now almost exclusively associated – the 'Old Strand', having one of the largest stages in London, being admirably suited to this type of thing. He was able to work with a minimum of cost, having a vast theatrical stores (another family legacy) down at Wimbledon, whence came not only a great part of the costumes and scenery of his productions, but also much of his printing. Hence, and in the nineteen-twenties, large posters depicting corseted young women with a multitude of petticoats standing challengingly and temptingly on tables, or red-coated soldiers strutting forth with their padded and chess-queen-shaped 'gals', or a straw-hatted nobility going floridly down on its knees before skirt-sweeping and hair-crowned suseeptibles, or black-moustached landlords ejecting ancients (and their daughters) from honey-suckled but mortgaged property – directly defied a modern period, and added to the general historical flavour of the whole. Mr Carters was, in fact, more of an artistic excavator of the past than a modern producer; and those vast dusty stores at Wimbledon, at which he spent so much of his time, could furnish an instructive tale of bygone melodramatic decades and rantings long ago.

At this time Mr Carters had two shows in the provinces – one of which, 'The Loves of an Empress', had left the Old Strand some months ago and was paying him extremely well – the other of which, 'The Girl from Somewhere', was losing him from fifty to two hundred pounds weekly. He was withdrawing this and replacing it with a play called 'A Man of Steel' – a revival from nineteen-eight, which he was giving an experimental run on the London Halls. He was also the owner of the King's Theatre, Brighton, where he proposed finally to take 'A Man of Steel', and afterwards commence a repertory of the old dramas.

Mr Carters' professional manner was innocence, slight confusion, kindliness, slow speech, slightly wounded simplicity, and a general air of being on the verge of

bankruptcy, but carrying on for others' benefit alone. He
was, indeed, a genius at evasion, as he was also a genius in
his own line, and he had a wide reputation for being grasping. He knew, however, how to handle actors and actresses.

'Yes,' said Mr Carters, naïvely. 'I think I might have a
Part for you.'

'Oh, do you think you might?' said Jackie.

'You haven't had very much Experience, have you?'

'No,' said Jackie. 'I'm in "Little Girl" now . . .'

'Very good show, that . . .'

'Yes,' said Jackie, 'it is . . .'

There was a pause.

'Well,' said Mr Carters, taking up his manuscripts and
making a sudden move to the door. 'I can't say anything
definite just Now. But I think I'll have something for you,
and I'll let you know. Of course we can't Pay you very much
here . . .'

'No,' said Jackie, following him out . . .

'But you've got the right voice-and looks, haven't you?
And I think I could find something for you . . . Well, I'll let
you know in a few days' time, shall I?'

'Will you?' said Jackie. 'Thanks very much.'

The next morning she received a thin, tattered part,
bound in brown paper, and a letter agreeing to employ her
at two pounds ten shillings a week. She was therefore able to
get her blow in first with the management of 'Little Girl' –
which was a very trifling and barely observable revenge – but
one giving her enormous satisfaction for all that.

2

And so it was that three weeks later, at eleven o'clock on a grey morning in July, Jackie found herself in the Strand, walking to the theatre for her first rehearsal. In her bag she had a printed rehearsal-call card, as well as her part (which she had intended, but for some reason unknown still neglected to have learnt by heart), and she was very nervous indeed.

There were signs of professional life outside the Old Strand Stage Door (which opened on a spacious side-street) but no signs of participation in theatrical transactions. That is to say, there were several little groups of two or three, standing chatting out on the pavement, or lurking in the doorway; but all appeared perfectly content to remain chatting there, with a complacency which surprised and puzzled Jackie, whose call was for eleven and who was accustomed to the strictest discipline. There was an air of something portentous occurring inside, which did not at present affect those out here.

She therefore walked up and down, or stayed self-consciously still, surveying her new associates, who all appeared to have some acquaintance with each other, and who in turn surveyed her with cold and peering interest (on the part of the women) or grave detachment (on the part of the men).

The women were all much older than herself, and extremely dowdy. This caused Jackie some vexation

PATRICK HAMILTON

with respect to her own coat and skirt, which she had arranged to wear for the first time to-day, and which she knew became her well. Nor did their glances spare her. The men also were all much older than herself, and their glances did not spare her either. In two of the groups there were children; and there was, in fact, a heavy, marital and almost boastfully domestic atmosphere over the greater part of those assembled here, which Jackie found displeasing. She was unable to explain this displeasure. Apart, that is, from a vague feeling that individuals with responsibilities in this world had no business with this kind of tomfoolery, and should not be hanging idly about stage doors at eleven o'clock in the morning. But then she had not as yet consciously and deliberately identified it as tomfoolery ...

There were one or two very old men, who talked ponderously and gazed miserably ahead; and there was one old man, in an old hat whose hair was white and whose eyebrows were painted thick black. Very crudely and foolishly and naïvely painted black. There was one short young woman of about thirty, who was fairly good-looking, and better dressed, and more aggressive. And there were four or five curious males, who wore rough suits and cow-boy hats, and had an air of familiarity with starvation and lassoes. ('A Man of Steel' was a Western drama.) At one o'clock these would be observed hanging outside Jones' Restaurant in Leicester Square, conferring either with their own kind or with stout yet waisted gentlemen with

216

abnormally peach-like complexions ... Not all these were to appear in the present show – many having come solely on the chance of seeing Mr Carters with a view to the future. The rumour, flying like fire down Garrick Street and St Martin's Lane, that Reggie, or (as he was sometimes even more colloquially and intimately termed) 'Rej ', was taking out a new show, invariably inspired assemblies of this sort. Jackie felt that she was nearing abysses in the theatrical profession.

Mr Carters came bustling at last, however, with scripts under his arm, and after various waylayings and swift conversations outside, vanished within. And then the rest slowly filtered in after him – Jackie amongst them – down the stone steps and on to the vast, bare, historic stage of the Old Strand, where the curtain was down, and the groups reassembled, and a low running murmur of brooding talk floated echoingly up to the grid. But it was dark, and cosier in here.

3

Jackie once caught the roving eye of Mr Carters (who looked diplomatically away), but otherwise no notice was taken of her.

There was an old wooden table up against the curtain, and at this there were two chairs upon which Mr Carters and a pale, hook-nosed young man were seated. There were also one or two chairs placed, with apparent plan, about the stage. The rehearsal began, amidst the mumbling, almost before anyone was aware of it.

The plot of 'A Man of Steel' involved eight or nine leading characters in one Saloon scene, and one Ranch scene in Kansas, and it was a simple plot. The characters, also, were simply conceived.

The only character of importance, however, was *Jack Lawson* (sometimes termed Honest Jack Lawson, which was deserved), who was first the owner of the Lazy Z Ranch, and later a peer of the British Realm, where he had suffered singularly in youth from a false charge of embezzlement. He was a disillusioned man, and his relationships with *Sadie Hicks* (a saloon dancer of low repute) – with *Big Jim Granger* (a foreman with a taciturn but honest nature) – with *Lady Gwendolyn Power* (an English Rose) – with *Two-Gun MacFerran* (an outlaw from Western society, upon which he revenged himself with curses, Indian-flogging and revolvers) – with the *Hon. John Power* (a gentleman who had the monocle, moustache, and gait of an embezzler, and was one) – with *Mr Hardbite* (a lawyer and inheritance-announcer) – and with *The Boys* (a crowd which hardly ever opened its mouth except to cheer its Boss) – need not be described. It is enough to say that these relationships would have broken any other man of steel, but could not break this one.

Jackie's part, which was that of *Lady Joan Hope* (the English Rose's dearest woman friend), ran to three pages:

1

LADY JOAN HOPE

Act II. Scene II.

......and I'm going to do it now!
   (ENTERS with others. Stands R.)
...... if it isn't Joan!
   Why, Jack, how long is it since I saw you last?(Takes
Jack's hand)
...... a little girl in short frocks. You haven't changed. You're just the same
as ever.
...... and both of us were sent to bed.
   And that was all your fault, Jack, and you know
it. Always up to mischief. Always in boyish scrapes. And,
what a memory you have, to be sure.
...... and nothing when we got there.
   (Laughs)
...... and perhaps he won't!
   (Follows others out)
...... don't want a row just now.
   (ENTERS)
...... if you'll pardon me, ma'am.
   I'm afraid that I don't quite understand what you

2

mean.

...... never try it on again, I assure you.

...... (ENTERS chatting with others)

...... And I too!
          And I too!
              (Exits)

...... is in the hands of the gods.

...... and let me think. Let me think.
          (Lawson goes out. Pause. Enters softly R.) Why,
Gwen? You still here?

...... that would be funny, wouldn't it?
          But --

..... . and it'll be my last!
          You poor, poor thing! (Kisses her) Now, Gwen,
you're coming straight along with me, and I'll put you to
bed. And you're not to think about it again until tomorrow.
Come along.

...... have said it, unless it were true.
          (Thoughtfully) Isn't that a little unfair to
Jack?

..... but never means it.
          (Pause. Walks up R.) Not always, Gwen, surely.

...... never, never, never!
          Now, will you come along. (Takes her arm)
Please, Gwen. (Leads her out)

3

Act.III. Scene.II.

...... the last, my God, the last!
...... (Runs on excitedly with others)
       for ever and ever. Amen.
       Amen.

This, to Jackie, was at once simple and obscure. She trusted that she would be able to endow it with life, and give a satisfactory rendering of character.

4

The rehearsal began very quietly, with a burly gentleman putting his foot upon a chair, adjusting his pince-nez, leaning over to look at his part, and commencing a conversation, first by Reckoning that his companion was just about Right, and then by endorsing categorically every one of his own and his companion's previous statements. This he did with the utmost innocence, but the utmost thoroughness, establishing his disinterest by naming his drinks, lighting a cigarette, and similar airy business. It was very lucky to have caught him at such a moment, for he explained a great deal.

He was soon out of the way, however, never again to return, and the rehearsal continued quietly until twelve o'clock, when Jackie made her appearance. There was little production. The hook-nosed young man, with his eyes glued to the script, occasionally edged forward to explain positions and interpret difficulties in an amiable way; and Mr Carters – strolling ruminatively about and having odd little chats with his employees (who all attempted to catch him) – himself made occasional suggestions, which were treated with great deference, and gave final judgments in appeals. And this was all there was of production. Mr Carters was alluded to, in general, as the 'Guv'nor'.

Jackie had become very tired from standing all this time, and she had at last ventured to seat herself upon a property chest. She was beginning to wonder whether she would be called upon to perform this morning, and if not, why she had been brought here, when the hook-nosed young man, with his eyes still glued to the script, sidled over to her and advised her to Stand By. This, he said, was where she came on.

Whereat Jackie rose, with her heart pounding of its own accord, like some steady and intelligent instrument, and stood at the edge of a group of three, which also appeared to be about to perform. Unhappily, though, at this point the last five pages were taken again ('Better have that, once more,' said Mr Carters), and ten minutes passed before they were back again at the same place. She then very cleverly recognized her cue, which was given by Mr Derek Anderson, a handsome if somewhat portly gentleman who impersonated Honest Jack. She moved forward with the other three, and gazed at her part in horrified concentration and complete suspension of her reasoning powers. She heard voices about her, she was aware of Mr Carters looking at her, but she was otherwise without consciousness . . .

She was then aware of a silence that in some mystic, swift, and hideous way was surrounding and bearing in upon herself.

'Miss Mortimer?' said the hook-nosed young man.

'Yes?' said Jackie, looking first at the hook-nosed young man, and then at Mr Anderson.

'Why, and God bless my soul,' said Mr Anderson, strongly but mechanically (for he was repeating himself), 'if it isn't Joan!'

'Oh,' said Jackie. 'Sorry, Er—' There was a pause.

'Why, and God bless my soul,' said Mr Anderson, 'if it isn't Joan!'

He held his hand out with great cordiality, and Jackie, swiftly removing her part from her right hand to her left, accepted it. She was now, however, unable to see her part.

'Why, and God bless my soul,' said Mr Anderson, 'if it isn't Joan!'

'Sorry,' said Jackie, and he freed her hand. 'Why, Jack,' added the wretched girl, in a very feeble, indeed in a barely audible tone, 'how long is it since I saw you last?' She blushed.

'How long?' cried Mr Anderson with renewed gusto. 'Why—' But here Mr Carters cut in.

'Speak up there, dear,' said Mr Carters. 'Don't be afraid to speak up.'

'No,' said Jackie ...

There was a silence.

'Why, and God bless my soul,' said Mr Anderson, 'if it isn't Joan!'

'Why, Jack,' said Jackie. 'How long is it since I last saw you?'

('Saw *you* last,' amended the hook-nosed young man.

'Saw *you* last,' said Jackie, and looked at her part.)

'How long?' cried Mr Anderson. 'Why, it must be twelve years at the least. When I was running about in knickers, and you were a little girl in short frocks.'

'Well, you haven't changed. You're just the same as ever,' said Jackie, but she was not fully alive to the cordiality of this reunion.

'Bring it right out, dear,' said Mr Carters. 'Don't be afraid to bring it right out. "*You're just the same as ever.*"'

'*You're just the same as ever,*' said Jackie.

'Don't be afraid to bring it out,' said Mr Carters.

'No, I won't,' said Jackie . . .

'Have that again, shall we?' said Mr Carters.

At a quarter to two the rehearsal ended.

'I think you're going to be very good in that part, Miss Mortimer,' said Mr Carters, in his usual slow style of speech, as he met her in the passage on her way out.

'Oh,' said Jackie. 'I—'

'You won't be afraid to speak out, will you?'

'No. I must try,' said Jackie . . . 'I'm afraid I was awful to-day.'

'No. I think you're going to be Very Good,' repeated Mr Carters, firmly, as he entered his doorway.

'Hope so,' murmured Jackie.

'And you'll *look* very nice – too,' added Mr Carters . . .

Who had a heart of gold.

Chapter Thirteen

DATES

1

The first night of 'A Man of Steel' passed off on a close, heat-mazed night at the Shoreditch Hippodrome with a minimum of fuss and to moderate acclamation. There were no telegrams, no alarms, and no suggestions of suppers upon the stage afterwards. The actors and actresses came in, told each other how they had got there (a penny tram from Liverpool Street was the thing), changed, made-up, performed 'A Man of Steel' through twice, changed again, and vanished into the as yet tram-thundering night for their beer and cheese or cocoa in unknown but presumably rather squalid destinations. Nor were there any serious hitches in those first two performances themselves. It is true that the introduction of a singularly white and beautiful horse (upon which Jack Lawson rode, in a slightly circumscribed fashion, into Town) was the cause of the acutest spiritual agony during the four climactic (though slippery) minutes in which the noble creature disported itself on the stage: but a firm (if quite superstitious) belief that Providence had, in its ineffable wisdom, obscurely arranged that one should *not* be trampled to death on the stage of the Shoreditch Hippodrome; together with an ineradicable faith that the curtain would (owing to some magical dispensation) *not* at any moment fall upon a shrieking populace and scenes of gore, stretchers, and death agony – saw even this predicament through with creditable calm, though a certain amount of furtive and rather ill-balanced backing ... It is true, also, that a certain wagon in the third act – supposed to be attached to two mules, but actually attached to nothing of the sort, the stage manager and his burly assistants having charge of the matter out of sight – it is true that this wagon did, on commencing to remove itself with its load of cheering Boys, also commence to remove the entire out-houses of the Lazy Z Ranch – which outhouses had become entangled, and which no amount of cheering would disentangle. But here also, after a short interval in which a sense of an impasse was experienced, Jack Lawson, with extreme presence of mind, came forward and quietly unhooked the Lazy Z Ranch (which was after all his own), and so allowed the drama to proceed. And otherwise – apart from a minor hitch brought about by a small automatic pistol wielded by

Two-Gun MacFerran, which misfired three times before behaving, so keeping his victim in a state of interesting suspense (not to say amazing forbearance) – there were hardly any hitches.

2

Shoreditch, Islington, Camden Town, Poplar, Woolwich, and Portsmouth and Liverpool – these were Jackie's dates. And always at the music-hall of these districts, where their printing replaced either that of Variety or No. 2 Review, and always twice nightly, from six o'clock to half-past ten. And every night Jackie went on, in a blue frock and with a very foolish parasol (which was an Aristocratic touch Mr Carters had insisted upon) and told Jack Lawson that he had not changed at all. Which piece of information was received with deadly silence, but apparent satisfaction, by those dark blurred patient ones who had paid their money expressly to react to enlightenment of this sort.

And if she was not performing, and if she was not sitting in her dressing-room (sewing with her more matured friends, who drank stout and sewed incessantly), then she was on the stage, sitting down, hanging about, or patting the Horse (which was a champingly acquiescent Horse when not performing, and susceptible, though rolling-eyed and thankless, in the matter of sugar-lumps). Jackie, indeed, never failed weakly to pat this Horse, half to express her sympathy for it in the twice-nightly quarrel, and half to curry its favour in future skirmishes. This was not, of course, the proper way to treat a horse, as the numerous histrio-equine experts, who surrounded it at all times of the evening, clearly demonstrated – the proper way being to wallop its side, and punch its nose, and say 'Grrr!' and '*Would* you!' But Jackie could never get any further than her weak pat, and though conscious of making very little impression upon the beast, remained content.

3

With the members of the company Jackie had very little sympathy. She knew very little of them apart from the theatre and out of costume, and she was almost consistently ignored. She dressed with two others – Mrs Leeson and Mrs Grover – middle-aged ladies, with middle-aged husbands who brought the beer into their dressing-room and were chaffingly domestic. But since these four had apparently known each other and been in the business since the beginning of their days she knew herself out of place. And she had very little liking for any of the rest – handsome Mr Anderson himself, who went about in strong breeches, a blue shirt, and a self-conscious obliviousness of her existence – Mr Lindsey (Big Bill Granger) who sometimes said 'Good evening' on the stairs, but mostly conferred with Miss Jean Crewe (Sadie Hicks), who ignored Jackie

without any self-consciousness whatever – Mr Lovat, the
assistant stage manager, who flapped about in cow-boy
costume and was civil – Mr Brough, the hook-nosed stage
manager, who gave her incessant hook-nosed advice in
tactful corners on the subject of Speaking Up (she became
Much Better after a time) – Mr Crabbe, a large man who,
in the black suit and silver star of the Sheriff, threatened all
the ladies vulgarly with smackings, but particularly Miss
Jean Crewe, whom, amid gigglings and screams from her
room, he was once heard actually to smack – Mr John
Clayton (Two-Gun MacFerran), who would have smacked
as well, had he not been burdened by a wife (which necessarily precludes smacking) – Little Joan Newte (Little Bill
Lawson), who was thirteen and a petted and precocious
little girl, but no friend to Jackie, who was not much
good at that style of thing – with all these Jackie had very
little sympathy.

Nor did she have any greater sympathy with the Boys
themselves – the supers. These strange creatures she would
observe, from her dressing-room window during the interval, trundling over in all their costumes and paint to the
nearest public-house over the way, where they would spend
ten minutes and return, to the astonishment of the public
at large, but with manifest pride in their vocation. She also
heard a great deal of them in their dressing-rooms, where
they appeared to be arguing incessantly. On the stage
they let her pass first, and called her 'Miss', or (if drunk)
'Madam', when they generally begged to be Pardoned.

And when she had passed they commenced to titter and make worldly soft comment. Indeed, they appeared to have a permanent little joke on, when it came to Jackie – this being their indirect way of demonstrating their admiration for her attributes – which was extreme.

Shoreditch ... Poplar ... Woolwich ... Islington ... Camden Town ... And Portsmouth and Liverpool ahead ... And not a line from Richard, and the weeks flying by ... And every night a train-ride home, with a tired powdered face, and tired aching limbs, and a blue advertisement of Bovril opposite, and the roar, roar, roar of the rails – the incessant roar of the rails, and a blue advertisement of Bovril ... Life was reduced to that.

Chapter Fourteen

LIVERPOOL

1

At half-past three one morning, in a downy and extremely large double-bed, which was in a small room feebly glimmering in the light of a lamp in the street outside, which was concealed somewhere in the slums of Portsmouth – Jackie lay awake having an imaginary conversation with Miss Iris Langham, her old school-friend at Brighton. This conversation was conceived as taking place at an imaginary five years hence, at the Bedford Hotel, Brighton; and Miss Langham's eyes were conceived as being affectionate but deferent.

'And seeing you like this,' Miss Langham was saying, 'I sometimes think I wish I'd tried to do the same, Jackie. Do you remember how we used to talk about it all?'

'Yes. I remember, all right,' said Jackie. 'But you ought to think yourself jolly lucky that you didn't – honestly, Iris. You don't know – you can never *understand* – what one has to go *through* . . .'

'Yes. I dare say,' said Miss Langham.

'Just because I *happen* to have got to the top,' said Jackie . . .

'And you've done that all right, Jackie.'

'Oh, I don't know . . .'

'It's getting simply funny. I don't seem to be able to ever pick up a *paper* without seeing your name somewhere.'

'Yes,' said Jackie, who wished only to be fair-minded. 'I know all that. But I still *say* – that all things taken into *consideration* – it's not *worth* it. You don't know the sufferings – I can't tell you the *humiliations*. I literally wouldn't advise anybody, however talented, to try to go through with it. And that's what I *do* say, of course,' added Jackie, 'when they *do* come along . . .'

Miss Langham was gazing intently at her.

'You're wonderful, you know, Jackie,' said Miss Langham. 'All that you've done.'

There was a smiling and difficult pause.

'Oh, not wonderful,' said Jackie. 'Just not being discouraged, and sticking to it . . .'

And it was profitless to say anything further . . .

She returned to Portsmouth, looked at her wrist-watch, and went to sleep.

2

And after Portsmouth, Liverpool again. Jackie arrived at Liverpool at half-past five on a freezing summer's evening, made her way to the bleak drab heights where the Hippodrome lay, and found rooms near by. Here she was given a cup of tea by the landlady. She was to be given thirty-nine cups of tea before leaving the town – her landlady (a black-eyed, black-haired, drudging little Italian woman) having no other way of expressing her goodwill than by a taciturn but incessant supply of this stimulant. And that it was a gesture of goodwill, and that this floundering little woman, in whose eyes still sometimes flashed the lost sunny lands whence she came, was attempting to manifest her unhappy kinship with Jackie in this cold and God-forsaken domain, Jackie had no doubt. Indeed, her heart was so touched that, apart from a futile little episode in which Jackie endeavoured to tempt a geranium with tea, she accepted the lot without demur, and praised it highly.

The Hippodrome was within fifty yards of her bed- and sitting-room, and as it was raining all day long all the time, her day was spent almost exclusively between the two – a queer figure, in a queer latitude of the world, and engaged in rather queer business altogether. But she was now numbed to its queerness, as she was numbed to all else.

'A Man of Steel' played to very poor business at the Hippodrome, and the fact that the auditorium and stage of this theatre were quite twice the size of those of any of the

London halls they had come from, added to the bleakness of its reception. There was no mass, no collective will, in those sparsely scattered blobs which were faces; and there was a feeling, on both sides, of a formal rather than vital function. Nor did the numerous photographs of Mr Anderson – in rancher's, apache, costermonger's, priestly, or ordinary costume – which littered the shabby front of the house, have the same impressive effect as they had in London or Portsmouth. 'A Man of Steel', in fact, was to Liverpool less of an event than a vague and slightly inexplicable and sordid incident. The actors, however, were able to keep their courage up in the dressing-rooms behind, where there was as much beer, sewing, and smacking as heretofore.

And then, one night, the clash of Mr Anderson's spurred boots along the stone passage outside, and the sound of Mr Anderson's deep voice:

'HulLO, Gissing!'

'Hullo, Anderson.'

The boots clanged down the passage and no more was heard.

'Sounds welcoming, doesn't it?' said Mrs Grover.

'That's Mr Gissing,' said Mrs Leeson. 'He's taking over the part next week.'

'What? At Brighton?'

'Yes. Johnnie's just told me. Our Mr Anderson's got a job in Town.' Mrs Leeson introduced a 'My, we *are* becoming, great!' flavour into this latter statement.

'And *we'll* have to *rehearse*, I suppose.' Mrs Grover spoke bitterly.

'Yes. To-morrow. Eleven-thirty, my dear.' Mrs Leeson was acidly resigned.

'You're running it close, aren't you, Lady Joan?' asked Mrs Grover.

'Yes. I must fly,' said Jackie.

Trembling so that she could hardly see, she left the room, and ran along the passage to where he was standing. His hands were in his pockets, he had no hat or overcoat, and, as he stood there talking to Mr Anderson, he seemed very much at home already.

'Hullo,' she said weakly. 'I've got to fly on now. See you afterwards.'

She ran down the stairs before he could reply.

Ten minutes later she returned. He was standing in the same place, but alone.

'Hullo,' she said.

'Hullo?' He was taken by surprise. He looked involuntarily down, for a lightning moment, at her forefinger. This forefinger was horrifyingly, and with ludicrous trembling exactitude, prodding the middle button of his waistcoat. She withdrew it in mad haste, clasped her wrist and looked up at him.

'Well, how are you?' she asked, and smiled.

'I'm all right.' He smiled back. 'We're in the same show now, Jackie, aren't we?'

'I know,' said Jackie . . .

Jackie looked vacantly down the passage. The loose change in his pocket set up a hideous din. He looked vacantly down the passage.

3

The next morning, which was Saturday morning, Mr Gissing ran hastily through his part with the company on the Hippodrome stage. He did not fail for a word – though he beat his forehead with his knuckle, every now and again, and begged not to be told. He ran through his long speeches with enormous rapidity, and was clearly going to play with less emphasis than Mr Anderson had employed. As he was on nearly all the time, he hardly spoke to Jackie at all. And he was compelled to have lunch with Mr Carters.

There was a matinée in the afternoon, which (with the two performances after it) meant that Jackie, with a short interval for tea, remained in the theatre from two till twelve. (Twelve instead of half-past eleven, because it was Saturday night, which involved packing.) At about a quarter-past seven in the evening you had practically forgotten all your previous existence, and had difficulty in imagining any future. You were a painted part of the painted scenery, in the glare of which you moved about with blind, unconscious instinct, as a mite would move in cheese, hardly differentiable from the substance. And if you were asked whether this was the first, second, or third show, you would have had to go back and work things out before replying.

He spent his time between the stage and the front, and she occasionally spoke to him. At the end he came to her dressing-room, and saw her to her lodgings. But these were only fifty yards away, and it was raining very hard. Also she had a serious headache, and told him as much.

Chapter Fifteen

THE RETURN

1

The train-call being for seven, Jackie had had only four hours' sleep when the sympathetic little emigrant stole in with the last cup of tea she was destined to give Jackie on this earth, and touched her arm softly and told her the time. This was five forty-five, and at twenty-past six Jackie was outside the front of the Hippodrome waiting for a tram. The town was hidden in a raw, wet Sunday mist, and was an evil, gleaming, sodden old town, with very few wayfarers. The tram contained two women (who wore shawls over their heads) and was a clanging, bumpy tram. Lime Street Station contained various porters and trucks (which seemed to clatter about more in the roof than down below) and was deserted in appearance. Then one began to encounter odd actors and actresses, who walked briskly about, and were nervously cheerful.

Five third-class compartments of the train were labelled 'Reserved', in red letters, and at the bottom of each label was inscribed, in pencil and a very scrawling hand, 'Man of Steel Co.'. Jackie got a corner seat with her back to the engine, and watched the rest arriving. They were not long in doing this. The actual men of steel came last, one each side of Mr Carters, and they went into a first-class compartment by themselves. One of the men of steel was clearly not listening to Mr Carters, as he came up the platform, but scanning the train in search of a friend, at whom he smiled gaily. That smile had to last a day's journeying, and succeeded in doing so, though the journey was dull.

The men went apart from the women, and remained apart. They were soon, indeed, unapproachable, and very male indeed. They were never at a loss for conversation (as could be dimly heard from next door) – an inexhaustible stream of theatrical reminiscence, army reminiscence, and smut (reminiscent or inventive) buoying up their spirits all the way to Euston. Occasionally one of them came and stood in the ladies' doorway, conversing, with the Siegfriedian glow of his manhood upon him, for ten minutes or so; but this was a favour and a condescension. Only at the end, when Johnnie broke his back trouser-button, and came in for what he named a Delicate Little Surgical Operation at the hands of his wife, was there any general intercourse. And then there was great amusement. Johnnie could only expect to get Pricked if he didn't sit still, and Johnnie could not sit still while they were all standing there drying him up like that ... There! ... The men were unanimously dismissed as Big Babies.

After a rushed two hours in London, in which Jackie made a flying visit to West Kensington to get some clothes, she boarded the train for Brighton at Victoria. In this there were no corridors, and no reservations, and she escaped from her fellow-professionals. She travelled down with two commercial travellers and an old lady, and they were very pleasant and restful to the eyes. Also the ears.

At Brighton Station she put up her suitcases at the cloak-room, and with a few addresses in her bag, walked forth into the town in search of rooms, for which she had neglected to write. It was a windy, grey-and-yellow, show-ery summer's day, and from Queen Street she had a glimpse and scent of her old Brighton sea. This was flecked with foam and of a rough muddied azure colour. The sight of it depressed her. It had no air of having noticed her absence, and had no welcome for her now. Moreover, this was a curious return to the town of her birth ...

She found a room in Over Street, which was a rather dreamy slum a few hundred yards from the King's Theatre. She had not sufficient spirit to go further, though she was far from satisfied by the size and appearance of the apartments revealed to her. Also the landlady promised her an immediate cup of tea, and said that Dad would go to the station and fetch her bags. This settled it. Tea was brought: a cipher-like and subservient head of the family clicked the front door behind him as he went off to the station; and Mrs Gribble had a long conversation with Jackie as she sat and drank. They discussed Mrs Gribble's little daughter. Mrs Gribble's little daughter had a keen knowledge of the French tongue (which was more than her parents had), could play the piano (but here she took after her mother), and was having dancing lessons twice a week. She was, in fact, a clever little girl – That clever. Jackie went further – from what she could hear she thought her prodigious. Mrs Gribble admitted that she was Surprised, sometimes. Only the other day, for instance, when Dad saw her getting out her books when she came back from school, he spoke to her. 'You're always reading at them books, Eileen,' he said. 'Don't you ever want to go out and play with the other children?' What did Mrs Gribble's little daughter reply? Jackie could not guess. The answer was astonishing. '*Ah*,' replied Mrs Gribble's little daughter, 'when *I* grow up I *want to be able to help my Mum and Dad.*' Nothing very much, but there you were. Then only yesterday Mrs Gribble herself had spoken to her. 'Do you want to go on the Stage when you're grown up, Eileen?' she had asked. Mrs Gribble's little daughter had thought about that for the moment, like. 'Well,' said Mrs Gribble's little daughter at last. '*I don't want to go on the Stage unless it helps my Mummie.*' Now how was one to read that? Nothing much in it, perhaps, but Mrs Gribble meant that it wasn't All children that spoke like that now, was it? She meant that it wasn't quite Usual, was it? Jackie, by numerous affirmatives and nods, made it quite clear that it was NOT. 'Ah, well – Queer little things – children,' proclaimed Mrs Gribble. But this was too modest. Queer little things *perhaps*, was the effect of Jackie's rejoinder – but how about CLEVER little things? – how about little geniuses in the family? – how about infant prodigies? Jackie had obviously alighted in a house of destiny. 'Oh, well, she certainly is different,' said Mrs Gribble, and left her lodger on the best of terms.

Jackie's bedroom was at the back, looking out on to a yard which was two yards square. In the house on her immediate right there lived a couple with five children, whose heads were intermittently and audibly banged by the aforesaid couple (which caused them to cry); and in the house to her left were two prostitutes, who did not rise from bed until the evening, and who were the quietest and least assuming lodgers in an aggressive and banging neighbourhood. Jackie did not like the neighbourhood at all, silent as it was on Sunday, and after tea she took a walk.

She walked out to Hove in a purple sunset over a dove-grey sea, and she glimpsed her old house in First Avenue.

The fact that this was occupied by strangers amused her fancy. She had an unalterable impression that those strangers were pitiable amateurs and pretenders as regards that house. Fancy thinking it was their own! What did they know about it? She was so ashamed for their presumption and innocence that she felt quite agreeably disposed towards them. It was, after all, not their fault.

The King's Gardens, too, seemed to wear an almost pitiable presumption ... For there were many new faces along those lawns and in those shelters – those lawns where she had spent a decade and more. She could afford to feel lofty ... She had been a success along those lawns – a legend, almost ... But there were many old faces, she observed, as well; and she could not feel so lofty towards these gardens as she had felt towards her house. There was just a touch of the expelled angel, here ...

But she was glad she was here no longer. She was sure she was glad. There was something blank and unawakened about that life of leisure, she decided. And if she had not met Richard! To have dwelt unknowingly here, and not to have met Richard. How pitiable would she herself have been then!

In this purple sunset over this dove-grey sea, existence was strangely softened. She walked back to Brighton and had a meal at Booth's. Here none of the waiters recognized her – though none were changed since the days her father used to bring her here. She was glad they did not. She had fish, and an ice, and coffee, and sat in a far corner where she excited little comment. It was dark and raining when she came out, and the sea was up. On reaching her slum she encountered the two prostitutes next door (who looked at her strangely): and from her front room she heard the sound of the piano, which was being vigorously played. She rattled her key in the door, and there was a sound of scampering. She was struck by the innocence and wickedness of life – the ingenuousness and rat-like pleasures of the poor.

She refused all offers of supper and went straight to bed. The poor did at least comprehend the laws of a comfortable bed – they probably had need to do so. She was dreamily, downily and exquisitely comforted. The last thing she heard was the crash of the sea in the dark.

2

There was another rehearsal for Richard next morning, on the stage of the King's. This stage was quaintly small – almost doll-like after that of the Liverpool Hippodrome, but it was for all that a stage of normal size. In the middle of the rehearsal he came over to her.

'I say,' he said, as though slightly aggrieved. 'Aren't you coming over to Southshore?'

'How do you mean?' asked Jackie. 'I'll come over if you like.'

'I mean to stay,' he said.

'Stay?' said Jackie . . . She met his eyes in a startled pause.

'Mr Gissing!' cried the hook-nosed young man, and 'One moment,' he said, and left her to perform.

In a quarter of an hour he returned.

'Well?' he said.

'But how could I?' asked Jackie.

'Easily, Jackie. I'm very sorry. This is me.'

In half an hour he returned.

'All fixed?'

'But how *can* I? I can't.'

'What's your address?'

She told him.

'You, Mr Gissing!' cried the hook-nosed young man.

'I'll call for you,' he said, and departed.

When the rehearsal ended he retired upstairs under the superintendence of Mr Carters, the hook-nosed young man and a lady identified as the wardrobe mistress, and it was clear that he was seeing about his clothes for the evening. She did not see how she could wait about, and she went back to her rooms for lunch.

She could eat little of her lunch – which was a pungent stew. She wondered whether she was to stay in all the afternoon, in case he arrived.

He arrived before she had finished eating.

'A gentleman come to see you,' said Mrs Gribble, agreeably, and tactfully vanished. He looked around the room with sarcasm.

'What *do* you think you're doing, Jackie?'

'What's the matter?'

'How on earth did you get this? Why didn't you come to me? I've got dozens of addresses.' He sat down on the sofa.

'Have you had your lunch?' asked Jackie.

'No. Can I have some?'

'I should think so,' said Jackie, looking vaguely at him.

'Shall I go – or you?'

'You go,' said Jackie ...

'What's her name?'

'Gribble.'

'Mrs?'

'Yes.'

He strode fearlessly outside.

'Mrs Gribble!' he cried. She came thudding up the basement stairs. 'Got any lunch?'

'No more stew, sir. Got some tongue, sir.'

'Can I have some tongue?'

'Certainly, sir.'

She felt that he was being a little cruel with Mrs Gribble. Poor Mrs Gribble was only a landlady now, and the genius of her little daughter seemed to have shot down at a hideous rate – almost to normality. She was conscious of betraying Mrs Gribble. When the tongue was brought, Mrs Gribble was openly betrayed.

'I'm taking Miss Mortimer over to Southshore to-night, Mrs Gribble,' he said. 'Will that be all right – if she pays for the week's rooms, and the meals she's had?'

'Yes, sir. That'll be very nice, thank you, sir.'

'But I can't,' said Jackie, when Mrs Gribble had left the room. 'Who's going to be there?'

'Only my brother.'

'But I can't. Really I can't.'

There was a pause.

'Seduction?' he asked. He was helping himself to tongue.

'No. Not seduction. But I can't. Is there no one else there?'

'There's a housekeeper, and two sort of wenches, and a gardener. And me. Besides, he's got everything ready for you.'

'Is he expecting me?'

'Of course he is.'

Twenty minutes later they were on their way to the station. Jackie was to call back for her bags that evening, after the show. Mrs Gribble, if she called at the theatre that night, would find three tickets waiting for her. The third one (Jackie expressed the hope in parting) would be for the phenomenon.

3

Southshore Station was a countrified little station from three to four miles from Brighton, and about a mile from the beach, which was fringed with a colony of bungalows. For these bungalows the village was celebrated, and in these bungalows were gramophones, gaiety, and insecure domesticities: but otherwise it was a sleepy village, lulled by the flat hills behind. These hills belonged to Charles Gissing.

Silence was a thing which could almost be touched with the hand as Jackie and Richard emerged from the thudding little waiting-room and the hissing of the engine, and made their way, under his mute guidance, to Knottley Lodge.

She had forgotten this silence of villages. And she had forgotten green, sun-dappled lanes; and she had forgotten curates on bicycles, and labourers with implements, and local grandees with walking-sticks – she had forgotten the whole thing. Or at least she had not properly apprehended their existence. She had always been such a creature of the town. Richard seemed to take it all very much for granted. They spoke little on their way. She felt very peaceful.

She became very scared when they reached the house, which was behind a high old wall in one of the aforesaid shady lanes, and which they entered by a high, green back-gate. They entered an old stable-yard in which there was a motorcycle, a fair-sized car, much spilt and multi-coloured oil, and one chicken. This chicken he seized, without a tremor, and placed it in its proper sphere, which was in a chicken-run behind – which was at the edge of the large field, which contained two remarkably lifeless cows in the distance. He then took her back again, and through another gate, into a kitchen-garden. Here there was an aged gardener with a grey beard, bending over his work. With this gardener Richard now entered upon a discussion of strawberries. This gardener was deaf. Just because he was deaf, this gardener had no reason for thinking everybody else was deaf as well; but he did do so. He bellowed at his employer's brother, like Jove, whom he would have closely resembled if he had only been a bit larger and cleaner. Unhappily he had no roof to his mouth, either. Just because he had no roof to his mouth he had no reason for thinking that the noises he made could be interpreted by those accustomed to noises made with roofs; but he did think this, too. He was, in fact, a shameless gardener. Jackie was sure he could be heard all over Sussex. It also struck her that he was being deaf on purpose; for he had little wads of cotton-wool in his ears, as though he had made up his contrary mind not to hear, from the beginning. Jackie was not sure that she liked him until, at the end of the discussion, she found him mysteriously, but with the utmost goodwill, smiling upon her. She returned the smile, and breathed enormous relief. He was on her side after all. And in this peaceful countryside, and amid these technical discussions on strawberries in private kitchen-gardens, to have the fearful force of this senile personality on one's own side, was half the battle . . . They smiled again before they parted – diffidently, enchanted – an incomprehensible sympathy and understanding filling the soul of each. There was no longer any seriousness in strawberries. Then they left him, and passing through a door in the wall of the kitchen-garden, came out on to a narrow, sloping lawn with a quantity of trees and a great deal of roses and forget-me-nots. The roses increased in profuseness as they got nearer the house, which was white and low, and with a rose-covered veranda. Jackie's soul hesitated before plunging into this wealth of beauty. That would come later, when she had time. At present Brother filled and weighed down the warm air to the exclusion of all else. They came to the front-door, which was wide open, and like all such

front-doors – honeysuckle and incredibly dusty old pull-
bell. They were in the dining-room. 'I'll go and find him,'
said Richard; but at that moment they heard a scrunching
on the gravel path outside, and he was with them.

'Hullo, Charles. This is Jackie.'

'Howd'youdo.'

'Howd'youdo.'

It was very awkward. 'You're coming to stay with us,
aren't you?' he said. He bore little resemblance to Richard.
His clean-shaven features were thinner, harder, than
Richard's, and he was brown – almost alarmingly brown –
as brown as a Red Indian. This made his teeth whiter and
his eyes more blue. In the teeth and eyes one noticed what
there was of resemblance. He wore breeches and a very
old coat. Remembering Lord's, she remembered she was in
the presence of genius, and felt this unassuming costume
to be fitting. Genius, she knew, was pre-eminently unassuming. His hands were, at the moment, very dirty, but he
was a very clean person. He was very slow in his speech
and gestures.

After a little talk they wandered out into the garden.
There was an unexpressed but mutual feeling that she was
being shown round. She walked between them, and they
towered above her, each side. Their hands were in their
pockets, and she was awed and enraptured by their height.
Also by their quietude and friendliness. Charles offered
her a cigarette, which she took. He lit it for her, and they
walked on. For the moment it seemed that they were both

equally charming in their eyes. As brothers they seemed to be on the friendliest and easiest terms, making several leisurely allusions to local and garden matters, which they never failed to explain to her. Such things formed the staple of the conversation. Then, after about half an hour, at the conclusion of which they warmed up considerably in a humorous discussion of the horse which Richard had that night to ride upon the stage, they went in to tea.

The tea was served in the drawing-room, and there were strawberries and cream for tea. They gorged themselves upon these without restraint – Jackie, in an ostensibly diffident but actually methodical way, winning by a clear dozen. After tea they wandered out again, in the best of spirits. Then Richard, suddenly crying 'Mrs Gribble's seats!' dashed into the house to telephone. They smiled at each other and walked on in silence.

'Of course I've seen you before now,' she said.

'Really?' He put little interest into the answer, and she was momentarily annoyed by his slowness. Through tea she had flattered this slowness as a brown steadiness, but there were limits. Was he an antagonist after all?

'At Lord's,' she said.

'What? Were you at Lord's? The last time?'

'Yes. Rather. I saw you batting.'

'Sixty-four?'

'That's right. It was wonderful ...'

'Well,' he said, as though this was really good news, 'I never knew *you* were there.'

There was a pause. He was the most enchanting creature on earth.

'I saw you fielding, too. You were just near me, but I
couldn't see you properly because of the sun.'

'Did I get in your way?'

She laughed.

'But you've got to get in somebody's way,' he said. 'If
you stand still.'

'I suppose you have,' said Jackie. His simplicity, also,
was ravishing.

He led the way mechanically through to the
kitchen-garden.

'Richard show you this?'

'Yes. He brought me through this way.'

'Let's look at the chickens,' he said.

On their way to the chickens they encountered two
dogs, and one cat, all of whom betrayed curt recognition
of their owner: and after the chickens themselves they met
a pony, who came stamping towards them as they stood at
the edge of the field, and for whom he had a lump of sugar
from the depths of his pocket. The pony munched this,
and went immediately away. All these animals had that
unique preoccupation and detachment of dumb things – a
detachment which was partially a welcome, though – and
although he did not speak to them, the understanding was
perfect. She was all at once alive to the mystery of animals,
and knew she was with a priest of these mysteries. And in
the yellowing sunlight she was very happy.

Richard was waiting for them when they reached the house again. He was, for the first time in his life, rather pathetic, she thought, standing there ...

She was introduced to the housekeeper, Mrs Bradley, who was extremely welcoming and reassuringly stout, and who showed her her room. After this she had a cocktail with Charles and Richard in the dining-room, where a blurred but ineffable frame of mind intervened: and the next thing she knew she was sitting in the front of a car, which Charles was cranking up, and which Richard was going to drive into Brighton. In Brighton the public awaited him ... They were already late.

They bumped down the lanes, hooted through Southshore, and whizzed along the open road by the sea. The air was fresh, her shoulder touched his vibrating shoulder, and they did not speak. She was lost in adoration of life and of him – the two were mystically blended.

Chapter Sixteen

CHARLES

1

At the time that Jackie first met him, Charles Gissing was thirty-five years of age — one year, that is, older than his brother. Their father had died ten years ago, and he had thus, at the age of twenty-five, come into his property. This comprised the greater part of the downs for several miles around, was severely mortgaged, and in a very low condition altogether. Knottley Lodge was the Dower-house, the family place having been let, at some profit. The last ten years of Charles' life had been given over to the steady improvement of his estate — and the results had been astonishingly good. So much so that he was now esteemed luckier than his brother, Richard, who, as a younger son, had taken an income from his father's investments and been cast adrift.

Charles was a very different character from his father, though strongly allied to him in temperament. His father had been a slow but indisputably benign old gentleman, who trundled about all day in the saddle advising his farmers on their crops – and who, at the age of seventy, had had a seizure in his rose-garden, at the time of sunset, and was taken into the room in which Jackie now slept, where, giving lingering, incoherent, but still loving instructions for the bringing home of the harvest, he died. The sunset was appropriate. He was said to have been one of the last of the squires. Much was said to have died with him, but actually there expired little more than the old style of entertainment at Knottley Lodge, and the practice of curtseying in the village of Old Southshore. It was from the first found impracticable to curtsey to a public-school tie. One or two of the very much older feminine generation did, as it happened, when Charles entered the village, still manage to achieve this fluttering drop, and he tolerated it as something affording recognizable pleasure to the giver: but this was becoming very rare. The younger feminine generation was not a generation of curtseyers. It was a rather touchy younger generation, on the other hand, and its forte lay, rather, in the pillion – which involved cosmetics, knees, and an air of tart superiority to one and all. A young squire might now even be expected to provide the pillion – such indeed was the case with the three young sons of the Graysing family, whose estate adjoined Charles'. Charles, however, being from the first a young man of intensely and serenely independent character, had kept his pillion to himself. He had no more taste for knees than he had for the go-up-to-London-to-see-the-Queen atmosphere they had superseded. Hence it was that, despite his leisured amiability to all, he had no great popularity in the neighbourhood, and from what remained of the local society he was permanently, though not openly, estranged. His political opinions (of which he had none) were suspicious, and although he did his hereditary duty in the way of local bazaars, and fêtes, and committees for Ex-Service-men's clubs, etc., he could not be prevailed upon to have any dealings with the fast-rising local Fascist organizations. At Knottley Lodge he hardly ever entertained, except to tea, at which his strawberries were famous. Occasionally he shot rooks with his neighbours, but he did not hunt. He was, on the contrary, a confirmed enemy of the fox, having made himself conspicuous in a much-discussed encounter with one of these creatures, which, having entered Charles' chicken-house one pitch-dark morning at half-past one, was discovered by an awakened and suspicious Charles at half-past three. There were seven chickens in all, two of which were consumed – the rest in a loathsome state of wreckage. An uncanny two hours. Not one had escaped, and the red animal had lost its sprightliness when found by Charles, who, in a moment of calm hatred of the bloody scene, fired two bullets from his Webley revolver into its head. This, in the opinion of his neighbours, and in view of the scarcity of the fox, was held to be an unprecedented and impermissible course of action to have adopted.

Thus it was that Charles was voluntarily out of touch with both the modern and the elder set around Southshore. Nor did his alliance with his brother, an actor and a writer and a manifestly heretical character, improve matters here. Together they were too formidable.

He was a quiet figure – very. He spoke little and slowly, as his father had done, and he had the appearance of having little to do throughout the day. This was partly because he rose at half-past five and got through all his correspondence and estate business before breakfast, and partly because combined slowness and skill gave an appearance of idleness. In the last few years he had been continually absent in the summer on account of his cricket. He appeared to take this talent very much for granted, but actually it was his one passion in existence. It was only lately that he had struck an odd streak of form in batting, and he was now included whenever available. Before the war he had had some notoriety as a promising young bowler, but had subsequently failed completely in that line. But he still bowled a little, and was one of the finest fields in the country.

His response to Jackie had been immediate. He had not been with her five minutes before clearly and unemotionally apprehending that he desired to have her for his own. That this was out of the question did not perturb him. He merely recorded the fact. He was aware that, had she not had the moral weight of his brother's approval behind her, it would have taken him much longer to realize this; but with that approval she was immediately and obviously flawless.

As they walked in the garden he experienced no tremor – no disappointment – no envy. As she stood patting the pony's head he looked at her and listened to her friendly speech. Every line of her face, every word she spoke, the colour of her hair, her eyes, her mouth – all conformed to his precise ideal. But this was not adoration – it was calm identification. His brother deserved no praise for discernment. The thing was patent.

2

She awoke at seven o'clock to a washed blue sky and the tops of wet green trees, and a cup of tea brought her by Mrs Bradley. And all the world was in a green conspiracy of quietude, and she was neither happy nor unhappy, but a part of that quietude around her. What the day held in store for her she could not imagine, but she was to have him the entire day.

She was out in the garden by eight o'clock, and amongst the roses – drunk amongst the roses. She had never seen so many roses in her life.

It had been wet and stormy in the night, and their petals were scattered everywhere in the dew. They were roses that had had a pillow-fight overnight, and spilt their water-jugs, and distracted their sheets, and flung themselves about, and then suddenly and inconsequently gone to sleep ... Debauched roses – overblown but luscious young harlots of roses – regardless of their mess ... Jackie could have cried.

And up above in the house, various signs of life. Charles and Richard, just returned from a bathe in the sea, calling in swimmers' voices to each other from their rooms – a girl laying the table in the dining-room – a dog in the front doorway, already prone and winking in the amber sun-light. And then the sight of a hurrying Mrs Bradley, and the welcoming prolonged tinkling of a gong ... Every one was contented in a silent, brisk routine – a routine which came to her like a memory, and thrilled her, after a year in rooms. Particularly was she pleased by the dog. That old dog had lain winking in that light, of a morning, without her knowing it, year in and year out. He knew how to live, did that dog, but took it all for granted. This atmosphere was his. She revelled in her sudden participation in his amber secrets and wisdom.

And the smell of bacon, and silver dishes again, and a sideboard. How could she ever face rooms and tragedies again? And two powerful young or youngish men, who, while remaining quite civil, were of the united opinion that they were in the presence of the most perfect young woman on earth. And Jackie reciprocating the sentiment, though also remaining herself. As for her love for Richard, she felt for the moment that that could wait.

And after breakfast they strolled for a long while in the

garden, seeing some more of the chickens, and some more of the pony, to whom Jackie this time (in a rather frightening moment, but it was all right if you held your hand right out flat) gave a lump of sugar – and after that they got the car, and pottered about on Charles' business in the town of Southshore. And after that they went for a drive to Worthing, via Lancing, and then came back to lunch.

And after lunch Richard had to go into Brighton to see Mr Carters, and she was left alone with Charles. And they talked about books for some time (they were in perfect agreement with each other), and he showed her his collection of Richard's books, which were seven in number and of a technical nature, and then they had another stroll, which again ended laughingly in Pony, to whom Jackie gave another lump, this time with the utmost confidence and intrepidity. And then Richard returned and they had tea, at which there were again strawberries, and at which Jackie made the same rather revolting pig of herself. And after tea they had a game of cricket.

Charles had a nice pitch and a large net for this, at the end of one of his fields, and a very pleasant hour was had. Charles batted, and Richard bowled with a hard ball, as became a man, and Jackie bowled with a soft one, as became a woman. And Richard's balls were treated with brusque respect, and Jackie's balls were treated with courteous solemnity – which was rather difficult to keep up, as they were aimed at his head. For Jackie was an underhand bowler, who took great pride in her pace. After this Jackie batted herself for ten minutes or so. But as Jackie's principles for striking the ball were to stand on one leg, close both eyes, clench thirty-two teeth, and swing the bat round violently to the sky; or, failing that, and when completely baffled by a ball, to wabble about insecurely but earnestly on a high heel, and then collapse in a defeated heap upon the ground – the play lost in pace what it gained in good nature. After this Richard batted, and she went behind the net to Watch. She enjoyed that most of all.

And after this there was the large feeling wrought by exercise, consummated by cocktails: and then she was against the vibrating shoulder, flying back on the straight sea road to Brighton. If she had never lived in the past and would never live again, she was living now. She did not speak to him.

Chapter Seventeen

'FOR GOD, KING, AND COUNTRY'

1

On Wednesday morning belated rehearsals were begun for
'For God, King, and Country', and work (as it was called)
commenced in earnest. They were now, for five weeks, a
stock company at the King's, putting on a new show every
week, rehearsing every morning, and playing twice nightly
with one Thursday matinée. Jackie was unable to flatter the
act of moonily lolling about on a half-lit stage from ten to
two every morning with the name of work. It was, rather,
a kind of deliberate and intensified form of idleness . . . But,
taken in conjunction with the nightly performances, it was
the most laborious undertaking she was ever to experience
in her career, and during the day she was only out of the
theatre for four hours in the afternoon. These she spent in

Brighton, either at the pictures, or with Charles, who came over expressly to entertain her. Richard was far too busy.

For he, at the request of Mr Carters (who was constantly absent), was undertaking the production of 'For God, King, and Country', and he was down on the stage or up in the office the entire day. He was also partially stage-managing, in conjunction with the hook-nosed young man, and filling the General's uniform in the drama. He was, as far as Jackie could see, enjoying himself immensely, and having acquired the habit of ordering and talking, never left off talking, and at midnight supper at Knottley Lodge gobbled his food at a hideous rate.

Jackie had the juvenile lead. She played it neither well nor ill (it being quite impossible to do either) and she gave satisfaction. Large posters in the slummier parts of the town depicted Jackie, in a dress belonging to nineteen-hundred and the arms of an officer (Mr Grover) whose uniform was of the same period. Her first taste of fame. If she had only been playing at the Royal, she would have looked up the Langhams.

There was no dress-rehearsal for 'For God, King, and Country': nor was there any seriousness or alarm on the first night. There never was, in Mr Carters' companies. Each actor was left pretty well to shift for himself, and, buoyed up with the pervading spirit of religion and patriotism, the thing was easy. Religious patriotism, and the swagger thereof, atoned for lines, which were very poor. Richard's slogan during production was apt. 'When in doubt, say "Never!" and wait to be prompted.' This was quite safe, the entire play consisting of people swearing they would Never, under any circumstances, or the acutest torture, and taking an enormous bloated pride in the grandiose refusal.

The cast of 'For God, King, and Country' was not the same as that of the Western play preceding it, though many, like Jackie, stayed on. The cowboy supers were dismissed back to Jones' corner and the under-agent-world, where some of them got crowd-work on the films, some of them starved, some of them took to window-cleaning or bar-tending, and others lived by running away from their rooms. These were replaced by a quantity of young fishermen in the Brighton sea, who worked for ninepence a performance, whose naïveté was refreshing, and who, with the historic impressionability of toilers on the deep, took the most pious interest in their parts, which were military and constabulary. These, in conjunction with a military band from Lewes, made up the number of forty, and formed one of the most impressive scenes of the play. This took place in Whitehall, the curtain rising upon two mounted guardsmen in their glorious red array. Which received, for reasons obscure to the mind, storm after storm of applause. Whether it was Whitehall which had made the hit, or whether it was the two men, it was quite impossible to say. Neither gave the secret away. Whitehall wabbled flimsily in the draught: the two men remained as stiff as stone, and it was clear that the country was saved.

When this was over the comedian arrived with his wife, who made a great fuss of him in his new uniform, and beat the villain, who came on coarsely to disparage the celebrations, with her umbrella. Without, however, creating a scene in this ministerial thoroughfare, for no one else arrived until the arrival of the band, which marched on to the tune of 'Colonel Bogey', lined up on the pavement, filled the theatre with its scarlet noises, and received rather more applause than Whitehall. There was then a great stir, and the General appeared in a plumed hat, saluting vigorously. A curious crowd might now have been expected to have assembled for this portentous not to say national spectacle, but this was manifestly not the case. Firstly because the comedian was making rude faces and derisive gestures behind the General's back (which the populace could barely have tolerated in so solemn a scene), and secondly because there was no sign of a crowd. The only solution was that some surging mass, out of the picture, was somewhere being held back by a cordon of police. This would also account for the absence of traffic, which would have otherwise cramped a General's style when pacing into the middle of the road to make his speech. His speech was addressed to the buildings opposite (the windows of which were doubtless thronged), and was a pleasant blending of private and public sentiment.

'Ah – could I have been wrong,' he began, 'in thus letting my son leave for the front – without a word – without letting him know that he is already forgiven in my heart?

Could I have been wrong?' He evidently rather thought he had. He paced up and down, and clasped his hands behind his back, as one who says 'Tut-tut'. The army, however, in the meanwhile, had an air of being kept waiting, and so he became more general. All differences, he said, were now sunk in common cause against the enemy. Every gallant lad had answered the trumpet-call of Duty, and filed up in his country's ranks. The General was proud – yes, proud – of them all. He was proud – proud – proud . . . He was prouder than he would have been if he had not forgotten his lines at this point (which he invariably did), but he was proud in any case. He expanded on the subject at great length, clearly carried away by these thoughts, which did not seem to have occurred to him before. He continued for some four minutes – every now and then, with a sweep of his arm, including the army, which possibly thought all this was very much to the point but which was looking stiffly ahead and slyly licking its lips in preparation for the brassy tune it would march off to. This, on the cue 'God, King, and COUNTRY!', it did; and the scene would have ended significantly did not the audience at this juncture imperiously demand an encore. This it marched back to give, with the enforced approval of the General, who put the soldier away and revealed the connoisseur, joining his hands behind his back and lifting his head in benign appraisement, as much as to say, 'We're a musical country, and should have more of this kind of thing'. It was, however, a difficult moment for him. It was clear that his authority, though not yet defied,

was being ignored. Furthermore, the War had developed
into a concert, which it should not have done. The others
on the stage – the comedian, his wife, the villain, and various subsidiary ladies – having no claim to authority were
not in the same difficulty. They could simply look on with
the rather proud pleasure of those having wangled a pass
through the cordon. An astonishing spectacle altogether,
only to be equalled by the spectacle which followed three
scenes later. This was of a more gruesome nature, being
enacted at the Front. Where this Front was it was not easy
to discern (the precise War itself not being specified); but
it was in a red twilight, and the villain was present, pretending like anything to be a Correspondent, but actually
being a Spy (and behaving like one), and the comedian
was there, and so was the General (necessarily), and the
question immediately harassing this General was, Could
our Lads Get Through? It was doubtful. A battle decided
this. This took place on the stage, commencing with a
succession of violent bangs, and a sudden glorious inrush
(R.) of the army, which, flinging itself upon its belly, or
taking up statuesque positions on one knee, proceeded to
defend itself (prior to Getting Through) from a hypothetical enemy of obscure nationality but great redoubtability
L. This army was composed of fifteen Boys, four of whom
were supplied with blank cartridges, which made a great
deal of noise and pink fire, and carried off the scene. The
rest were forced to content themselves with dummy rifles
and inspired military gestures – such as taking off one's

cap and cheering, pointing madly ahead as much as to say 'Look at that one. Watch me get him!', shouting 'Bang!', pretending to be wounded, or, in privileged cases, dying. Dying, indeed, was obviously the particular treat; and the Boys were difficult to control in this matter. 'We can't *all* die, you know,' Richard had weakly pleaded, during the short rehearsal given the Boys on Monday afternoon. But he was overruled by the incontrollable sentiment of his performers. Some, indeed, he expressly forbade to die, but all those escaping this stricture succeeded, when the heated moment came, not only in dying, but in dying several times a minute – having a miraculous faculty for abruptly surviving purely in order to experience once more the luxuries of heroic extinction. The fact that in these brief moments of renewed existence they invariably allowed themselves another shot or two must have been as discouraging to the enemy as it was outrageous to a sense of fair play. There were, however, at least thirty fatalities among fifteen men in the four minutes allotted to this battle. To supplement the din supplied by the blank cartridges, the hook-nosed stage-manager dropped an enormous quantity of scenery weights and braces time and again on to the wooden floor behind; and overlooking the battle, in a tactical and Ney-like position on a mound, stood the General (who was Richard Gissing) gazing steadily and at length through a handsome pair of opera glasses at Jackie Mortimer, who was dressed in Red Cross costume for the next scene, and who never failed to come round into the wings at this time to undergo this remarkable scrutiny. At the end of the four minutes there was a sudden cheer from the ranks at the arrival of a gun on wheels. Which gun was rushed on at a victorious pace, and was useful less as a weapon of destruction (being composed entirely of wood) than as some curb upon the popularity of dying – inasmuch as both the quick and the dead instantly arose and fought for places in wheeling it, with exulting cries, off Left – which was much more natural behaviour. The scene was now at an end. The Boys returned, cheering with their caps upon their bayonets: the hook-nosed young man indulged in a final orgy of dropping behind: and the General, deserting his mound, paced down-stage to encounter another General, whose congratulatory hand he warmly shook. The Boys, without moving an inch, had Got Through, and this was a manifestly historic reunion between two Generals. They held it, and the curtain fell.

Of such stuff was 'For God, King, and Country'. There being no seats in the house above two shillings, a rough-and-ready money's worth was being given, and there was no possibility of complaint. The whole was, moreover, to those who had the wit to see it and make it so, as subtle and exquisite a piece of fooling as the theatre might provide. But even apart from this point of view, and taking into account the pious gravity with which it was for the most part received, Jackie never had again, in the course of her career, the same assured sense of fulfilling an honest demand. She could look back upon this period with affection.

In the next three productions Richard had no hand. They lost a great deal in spirit and abandon, but he was in each case given the leading part, which he played with a breadth exactly calculated to fit his audience. On Saturday nights he gave a West End performance, and evaded derision, and on Thursday night (the early-closing and most impressionable of nights) he expanded into the Surrey side and carried all before him. Mr Carters was conscious of having found a jewel, and came forward with startling contracts, which were refused. It was a lesson, to Mr Carters, against the employment of cheap labour – a lesson, after years of conservatism, impossible to be learnt.

The juvenile parts were thrown to Jackie, who acquitted herself well. With her accustomed quickness and gravity she learnt enough shallow tricks of voice and gesture (there were only about a score) to carry herself through without disgrace. On this substratum of elementary technique she hoped, when the time came, to build a performance.

And so the time fled by until the last week. It had long been decided that she would not be able to remain at Southshore for the last week, for Charles would then be absent on his cricket. There was talk of her staying on alone with Richard, but it came to nothing. Richard was plainly against it.

Thus it was that one Friday evening, at five o'clock (and without one word said to each other about themselves), she found herself looking out at the sea from the window of a pleasant room in Kemp Town. Richard had found this for her, and had just delivered her. She had one week more down here, and then London awaited her. Her suitcases were on the bed, and she was back again with her rooms and her tragedies ... She could hardly believe she had to face them again.

And then, on Wednesday, which they spent in the country, the thing happened.

Chapter Eighteen

THE RAIN

1

They were to spend the day on the Downs, and he called for her at her rooms, and they caught a bus at Castle Square for Patcham.

It was Thursday. She had not yet lost the sense of release in having her mornings free from rehearsals, and she was bright in the sunshine of the Square, and talkative on the jolting bus.

The conductor's bell pinged away, with automatic and unquestioning merriness: she clasped her sandwiches, and looked at the sky (which was doubtful), and smelt the cold air, and let her spirit slide upon a thin layer of content.

They reached Patcham at eleven o'clock. Here the sky was already grey, and the bus, ranting through the chill, still little village, pulled up amongst the trees, and was quiet.

If it had not ranted so, previously, its sudden quiet would not have been so breathless a quiet, nor would the stamping leisured exodus of the few wayfarers from the top of the bus, and their immediate vague disappearance to dreamy destinations, have struck the heart with something akin to dread. But this is what it did to Jackie. The thin layer of content was sensibly breaking up.

He helped her on with her mackintosh, and she helped him on with his, and speaking of the weather, which was obviously going to be very bad, they took the road that led to the Downs.

'Would you like to go back?' he said.

'No. Rather not,' said Jackie. 'I expect it'll pass.' And then, because she had a sudden ill thought of next week and London, she found herself almost trembling, and she knew that the layer had collapsed.

It was a nightmare – a rain-grey nightmare on a white dusty road. The idea of going back to Brighton was horrifying. The whole idea of existence was horrifying – greyly, coldly desolate. She could just keep in touch with it, just survive, so long as she walked with him along this road. She could never do anything else . . . This must be infinitely prolonged.

They walked on, in a seldom broken silence, for about ten minutes, and then he said they might as well put their sandwiches in his pocket: he thought there was room.

She gave him the package, and he commenced to try to do so . . .

'I'll do it,' she said, and he succumbed without a word. The moment of contact was dreadful. He lifted his hand weakly as she stuffed them in. He was a weak, trembling, inefficient, inadequate thing, like herself . . .

They walked on again. The rain still held off, and they came to Clayton Hill. The road lay between two steep embankments. Here he said that he thought he saw some blackberries, up above, and she looked upwards languidly with him. And then left him, and climbed up to get some, with a kind of numbed despair, and found a great deal. 'There are lots up here,' she cried, and 'Are there?' he said, but would not climb up to join her. She picked a handful. He watched her from below . . . A car rushed by, and he said nothing, and looked at her . . . Then she climbed down, warily, and with the awkward grace of her youth. But could not manage the last part, unless she risked a jump, and smiled weakly at her predicament, and took his hand, and managed it. But the blackberries were all crushed in her hand. She showed them to him in her messy fingers, and they stood close together, and he selected the best one for himself. He ate this, and she consumed the rest – one after another – her childish greed for sweet things rising momen-tarily above her sombre mood – blending strangely in with her disconsolate condition . . . They walked on in a dream.

In a dream. At the top of the hill they side-tracked to the right along a rutted clayey road that led to the two windmills of Clayton Hill. The sky grew darker every moment, but still it did not rain. There was a wind up here, though. Far in the distance, and over infinite grey undulations, lay the lead-grey sea. One of the two mills was in motion – steadily creaking in the wind. Creaking above the county, which sang in the gusts beneath. An unearthly sound, heard alone by them. And miles below they discerned a doll-like train, gushing madly ahead to London, like a messenger with vindictive tidings. They could not hear any noise, though they thought they caught a long-drawn whistle ... That silent, gushing train was most dream-like of all.

And then it began to rain.

Hesitantly at first, with sudden dashes of spleen. They put their collars up, and he took her arm, and they made for a tall-treed little wood in a valley to their right. The spleen increased, and all at once it was no longer spleen, but the steady deliberate abuse of intentional downpour ... They cried to each other and commenced to run ... They were racing each other. She half fell once, and he looked back, but she recovered and followed ... They arrived together, hand in hand: and they looked each other gravely in the eyes, and found themselves in each other's arms, and paused, and kissed each other.

It was the rain's doing. It patted down on the roof of leaves, and stormed slantingly in the open. It was ruthlessly responsible.

The rush of noise was amazing. They were the most

quiet of all things on the Downs. After a while she left his face, and put her head on his shoulder.

Then she was lying back, speechless, on the wet turf, and he was leaning over her. And 'Oh, Jackie dear – dear!' he was saying. And she was taking his head in her hands and kissing it – shamelessly, deliberately, and with profound proficiency. She had never done such a thing in her life before, but she was, from some mysterious and beautiful source, an adept. Each contact of her lips was the deliberate signing and sealing of her surrender. She was his for ever, and that was the end of the matter. Then she put him away from her, and they sat up, and began to talk.

The rain still held. Sometimes Jackie left their retreat, and went out to blink at the sky, and hold out her hand, and make unfavourable reports. Sometimes he joined her, and held her hand, while they blinked together. They smiled and laughed continually, and he seldom let go of her hand. At half-past twelve they had their sandwiches. They sat up, munching with smiling stuffed mouths at each other, infinitely charmed by this droll and irrelevant replenishment of their baser selves. But then they were infinitely amused and charmed by everything. And they called each other 'dear' and 'darling'. Tremblingly, exultingly they did this, and giddy with their sudden right to these age-old utterances of cherishment – their sudden admittance into the ranks of lovers.

They saved a few sandwiches providently for Tea (as they called it), stowed them away in his pocket, and as it was now raining very feebly, went out, arm in arm, for a walk. They began to talk about the future after a time, but they soon decided that that might wait for to-morrow. After all, they had the rest of their lives for that, hadn't they? They spoke little. There was nothing but the grey scudding sky, the roar of the wind, the soggy white track, and the rumble and exactly recurring creases of her mackintosh as her body swayed along ... 'Thank God it rained,' she said.

They came into the main road at last, and encountered a poor wet cyclist, wheeling his machine up the hill, and a dismal labourer, who asked them the time. With infinite pains did they endeavour to give the true time to this labourer. In such a way only might they weakly compensate him for his unlovely and loveless condition. They desired to compensate the entire world.

They had a look at the Clayton church, and they had a look at some ducks in a pond near by, and were filled with pity and affection for their perky, splashed, rainbow-coloured, benignant, waddling, silent affairs – an affection communicated to each other solely by the hand, for they had no words for such things. Then they said that they would go home for tea. But by home they meant their old retreat under the trees, and by tea they meant their sandwiches. They climbed the hill by another route. This climbing was marked by a charming event, for, going aside from the road, Richard discovered a nest. And in this nest was a thrush, resting upon its young. It appeared to take no notice of them, but looked ahead, in the quiet, dripping hedge, with shining eyes of angry patience. They were almost horrified by the intensity and stark singleness of purpose in nature. The poor bird, as Richard said, couldn't even read a book: its present object was to sit upon its young, and it had to wait, in utter resigned exclusion from all activity, until that object was fulfilled. Richard took this light-heartedly; but Jackie, as they passed on, was thoughtful and impressed. Under the influence of her love she was a different creature – queerly sensitive to new strange appeals . . .

They found their old place, and they sat down to have their tea. But the sandwiches were all crushed and damp in their greasy paper, and, on their being put down for a moment, two little ants were found running all over them in criss-cross directions. And a beetle was near by, with an air of having had an evil black, bite or two; and they were rather put off. But they did not want their tea, really: they only wanted to sit up, warm and close to each other, and watch the rain, which was now pouring down with all its old liberality, and coming in two fascinating different rains – one slantwise and heavy – the other perpendicular and fine – a clever, enchanted pattern.

And sitting and watching this rain on the humid ground, and with Jackie's little wrist-watch ticking away the last hour they had, and with Jackie's grubby, moist little hand in his, and with Jackie's face and mouth, all stained with blackberries, and in a great mess, lain against his own, they spent the last glowing hour of their day.

And all at once it seemed to Jackie that until this moment she had not understood this thing at all. She felt something stealing in upon her – something which made her cold and frightened, and yet infinitely consoled . . . She remembered that thrush, in all its little fortitude and helplessness and loneliness, and she was suddenly aware of communing with something beyond herself, above herself – of being an ally, even, in some magnificent and pitiless purpose beyond her.

All things conspired to this conclusion – the whole thick, intense, labouring life of the drenched grey summer about her – the lush grotesquerie of it all – birds, trees, ants, spiders, beetles, flies, nettles, weeds – the flora and fauna of a rain-soaked universe, working out their own strange, vivid destinies. She was filled with the uncanniness and stupendous wickedness of nature in this half-light. And yet because she was here with him, because her whole life was now fulfilled by him, she was part of that wickedness, and exulted in that participation. She was in the grasp of nature – and nature, with all its merciless cruelty, was a merciless bestower as well – a bestower for its own ends, and she had been singled out for its loveliest and most terrible of gifts.

And if nature was cruel, thought Jackie, then she, Jackie, also was cruel. And from her eyes glowed all the mysteries of all the cruelties since the world's beginning.

*

His arms were still about her, and she could not move. She could never be parted from him, ever again. She was damp and afraid, but she was safe. So long as he held her, she was safe. It was not her own doing. The earth around her, with its gaunt burden of mist and rain, imprisoning them here, was answerable for it all.

All these thoughts flowed through her, and she wanted to express them to him. She wanted to tell him her revelation, her new, exultant understanding and wisdom. She wanted him to know that she, a poor thing in the rain, was the proudest and most momentous thing on earth; that she was no longer a girl – that he, mystically, had made her a woman. Yes, that was it; he had transformed her into a woman. She was a member of the race: she was uplifted: she was here to further the divine and terrific intrigue of the weeping world around her. It had found her, and she had found herself. And he had done this. He was her own. She looked up at her possession. He was quite a weak thing – a mere implement in the hands of her overflowing and irresistible emotion. And yet her whole soul surged out in a flood of gratitude to him, for having come and awakened her. She could never tell him. She began to cry.

Book Two

THE ACTRESS

Chapter One

DECISIONS

The young woman of racial experience, who, on the next morning of her life, walked briskly along the front at eleven o'clock towards the Hotel Metropole (there to meet and confer coolly with the humble object of her transcendent purposes), was not the type of young woman that is way-lain by any quibblings of any nature. She had a driving singleness of purpose, had this young woman, and on the whole she rather scared him.

The cocktails were a mere formality. These were taken on wicker chairs amongst cages of green parroquets and the sickly atmosphere of morning recuperation. They were as sensitive to this atmosphere as anyone else present, knowing that their own emotional orgy of yesterday exceeded by far any other kind of orgy indulged in by those present. They had, indeed, an emotional 'head', and were anxious to get down to business and justify themselves.

She met all his statements with curt resignation and an implication of their obvious irrelevance to the main issue. To begin with, he said, they could not be married for a very long while indeed. Well, she had expected as much. Two years, he said, at the least. Well, that was nothing. (Jackie was full of rather surly 'Wells'.) If, he added, ever. Here Jackie was quiet for a moment, and looked in front of her, but then she said Well, that would be all right, too. He said that it would be far from all right. He maintained that legality and registration were of much graver portent than a young girl of her tender years and experience might have been led to imagine. She asked him whether he Loved her. The question, he said, was neither here nor there. On the contrary, she replied, it was the entire question. Did she not know her own mind? Did he think her an infant? He did. She was still an infant, legally and virtually. She then brought up in his face every one of his previous opinions on the ethics of marriage, and considered him confounded. He said, however, that it was different. She said that it was not different. It was a perfect case in point. He then told her about his wife.

In this individual Jackie had not the slightest interest. The thing was an error, on Richard's part, made long ago, and long ago repented. It was a part of a vivid but incomprehensible past. It was of a piece with all the other inexplicable events that had filled his early youth – his visits to Russia and America, his books, his flying during the war, his acting. Richard dated from the first moment of his meeting her. All that had gone before did not affect her: whether he had been sullied or not was of no moment. He was what he was now, and the matter ended there.

He had met her, it appeared, in a night club, and married her while on leave during the war, and they had parted after a year. She came from a middle-class family, was a heavy drinker, and a ruthless pursuer of her own inclinations. She was now living alone in Montmartre, where, so far as he could learn, she was mingling with a crowd of others of similar ruthlessness. The life being exacting, her spiritual and physical existence had lost much of its earlier pleasure in itself, and she was now, he understood, fortifying that existence with daily quantities of drugs. She was, however, a devout Catholic, and would not consider divorce. Also, in this connection, she was entirely faithful to her husband, the elevated sensations arising from brandy, ether, and heroin, completely destroying her taste for any coarser delight or indulgence. But the religious scruple was quite sincerely uppermost. These contradictions were unspeakably revolting to Jackie, who barely knew of the existence of such characters. Richard had been hit hard. In a vain and excited moment he had lain himself open to chance, and chance had dealt him its worst. He had attached himself to an imbecile.

The process of ridding himself of this imbecile was now carefully discussed by both of them. It was decided that he should go to Paris at once, there to apprise himself of the exact state of affairs and to seek his freedom. She was to return to Mrs Lover at West Kensington. He could get jobs for her in the meanwhile.

He had no hopes of a successful issue. They alighted upon two years as the farthest limit of time they could grant to these negotiations. If, at the end of that period, he had not brought the thing off, they would be compelled to 'take action'. That was how they put it, and they looked doubtfully at each other as the words were spoken.

They had another cocktail, and then he dived for his hat, and handed her bag to her, and they went out on to the front. They walked towards Booth's, where they intended to lunch.

The front was streaming with rain, and the sea was raging. Life was dull, and swimmingly sad, and swimmingly hopeful.

Chapter Two
THE ACTRESS

Actually it was two years and a half.

In that period Jackie gained the bedrock of her experience, and at the end of that period she came out a professional actress. Not that Jackie ever believed herself to be an actress, or that any play she acted in was a quite genuine play ... She knew she was playing at it (just as she was playing at being twenty-four and grown up), but at the same time she knew that she had achieved the outward signs of this role in life, and the world was taking her at her face value.

She had, in all, six jobs during this period. She gained an exhaustive knowledge of the railway systems of England, and she was acquainted with every leading town. She travelled not less than 20,000 miles in trains. A Sunday earth swept reeling away beneath her feet, and she came to recognize mounds, rivulets, or fields she had passed oh a Sunday six months ago. Sunday England! To the infinite piquancies and horrors of Sunday she was alive: she was part of its drear dreaminess: she partook avidly of its hideous drugs – cocoa, tea, coffee – these at the junctions or termini, or at her rooms immediately, when she arrived late ...

She was unclassed and without fixed abode. One Friday night she would be having a tepid, rusty bath by candlelight in a Cardiff slum – by the midday of Tuesday next she would be buying suede gloves at a granite-built shop in Aberdeen. One Thursday afternoon she would be fighting the rain and wind in Princes Street, Edinburgh – by next Wednesday evening she would be watching the sweet stars break over the seven black hills of Torquay ... And by next Tuesday evening she would be under Peterborough Cathedral, with a new stick of number five in her bag ... Her rock, her ever-recurring and recognizable aid, was Boots Cash Chemists. It was also her library. She read a great deal.

Every morning she went down to the theatre for letters: every morning she held light discourse with her fellows, vanished vaguely, and returned in the evening to report her doings in the town, and listen to their reports. She was on terms of good-natured hatred with all. With various exceptions she hated, and was hated, with such manifest and axiomatic completeness, that genuine good nature was the only possible medium of contact. Jackie did not begin the hating. It merely was that her physical charms, her inexperience, and her undestroyed belief in life were reminders and offences to those who took a certain surly pride in having lost all three ...

Her first engagement in these two and a half years, obtained for her by Richard before he left for France, was with that well-known play, or rather creaking series of forlornly humorous situations, 'Charley's Aunt'. This was played at No. 2 (or, if the district was vile, No. 1) houses all over London, and also in the southern provinces. Dates were precarious, and often they were out for a week or fortnight. These holidays were pleasant enough to Jackie, but to others of the company they bore a more troubled aspect, as Jackie incredulously discovered. But then, with this play, Jackie changed her whole outlook on her fellow-professionals.

There were practically none in the cast under the age of thirty-five, very few under the age of forty, and few of them had been less than fifteen years in their profession. They were a depressed and mechanical crew. They had naturally no belief in their work as an art: they would not dream of so much as inwardly criticizing each other's performances: they were heavily married: they called each other 'dear' incessantly: and the gentlemen drank bitter, and were chaffed for it, and the ladies drank apologetic Guinness. This was to 'pick them up'. Only Guinness – for where Guinness was medicinal, common beer was sin in a woman. They never had More than One, and they never did have more than one. And for the purposes of being picked up they were allowed to follow their men into the Saloon bar, where they sat looking perkily and restlessly around with the firm belief that they could not be mistaken for street-walkers – in which belief they were justified. The sight of one of their own men drunk would have caused heart-failure. They were the public-house ultra-respectables. They helped, advised, and relied on each other. 'Damn' was audacious, if allowable in a wag. Jackie's short skirts and bobbed hair evaded censure in one so young: otherwise she would have been esteemed 'fast'.

They had all the pious superstitions of their domesticity. For whistling in a dressing-room there were exclamations of genuine horror, and you were bustled outside and made to turn round three times before returning. Uttering the last line of a play during rehearsal spelt ruin. Most of them had children at fourth-rate preparatory schools, where they wore green caps, were quite extraordinarily promising all round, brilliant at wireless, and certainly not going to adopt their parents' profession.

They hung about agent-land during the day, and at night they reported progress. The word 'Town' flashed in and out of their discourse like a bird from Paradise across the Hades of their provincialism. 'West End' similarly. Admittedly it was thus. They were without snobbery. 'We shall see you in Town next!' was a common form of raillery. Or, 'These West End Actors – my word!'

It was here that Jackie realized she was up against the

true professional. Their profession was taken so much for granted that they were without response to it. This may not have been so when they had started, fifteen years ago, but it was so now. Any views expressed on the subject of acting would have been fanciful (if quite interesting). Their leading technicalities were appraisements of the weather with respect to business. If it was raining They wouldn't come Out: if it was fine They wouldn't come In . . .

Their humour (of which there was not much) consisted principally of chiding each other for making puns. They would pretend to faint, or collapse, when a pun was made, or to be nauseated beyond all measure. The men in particular. 'Come along! Get on out! Turn him out – *turn* him out!' Or, 'You ARE! . . .' Or, 'Any more of THAT, my boy!' and a very threatening look . . . They felt full of the warmest and most kindly sentiment at these moments. They were a warm and kindly people.

Much less pleasant was Jackie's next engagement, which was with Mr Stephen Linell and his Shakespearian Company. It will be remembered that she paid a visit to this gentleman on her first day in the theatre. Here she was at the other end of the pole, as far as professionalism was concerned, and amongst the young of her own class. This was a great shock to her vanity. That she, in the height of her youthful ambition, should have staked her self-respect in the romantic gesture of fighting her way into this business, was a thing allowed; but the spectacle of over a score of other young romantics, all apparently labouring under the same urge, had a wholesale aspect which revealed unpleasantly the values of her own case. And while barely able to admit that it was vanity in her own case, Jackie was all too alive to the vanity that lay behind this youthful and inefficient crowd forcing itself upon an overstocked profession – with, she noticed, combined ignorance and scorn of the true professional it was succeeding in ousting. The ignorance she forgave (she was ignorant enough herself), but the scorn she could not overlook. For she saw nothing to choose between the urge of vanity which led young persons to spit and fulminate Shakespeare's lines with great heroism and an air of superb artistic achievement, and the urge of circumstances which led elder and much more experienced individuals to revive, with quietude and modesty, a threadbare and foolish farce. Moreover, she was troubled by another observation she made on joining this company – an observation on the subject of Looks. She had often wondered to what extent these entered into the calculations of the aspirant, and she was now horrified to sense, all around her, the enormous weight they must have carried. Indeed, it was all too obvious. Young persons stricken with permanent plums in their mouths, to say nothing of lisps, and inabilities to pronounce 'r' otherwise than as 'w' (with one of which natural errors the majority of this company were smitten), must perforce rely upon Looks in the creation of dramatic beauty. The thing that irritated Jackie (and particularly on the male side) was a patent consciousness of Looks in the placid owners of the same, combined with a suave unconsciousness of Plums ... The more so when the horrors of the latter completely nullified the barely discernible charms of the former, which they quite invariably did ...

It was thus, from reasonings of this nature, that Mr Linell himself commenced to lose whatever attractions he had ever had for Jackie. Indeed, that gentleman's hawk-like medallion of a countenance relapsed entirely from the patrician character it had once seemed to bear, revealing instead (it is to be feared) a disturbing resemblance to the head of a bird of prey. A bird of prey upon the vanity of the young. Or, worse than that, a bird of prey upon the less forgivable vanity of the parents of those young, whose premiums (though repaid in salary) lined his pockets. This impression became ineradicable when one reflected upon the absolute ruthlessness and fullness of his exploitation and capitalization of vanity in general. He had it every way. He began by organizing the foibles of others at enormous profit to himself (his bookings were prodigious): he then gave full rein to his own inclinations by playing all the leading parts and filling the centre of the stage: and then, having taken all the credit for this, swooped down and indulged by far his greatest passion (that for dominion over docile souls) by his Coaching, as it was called, in the rehearsal room. And he took the credit for this, too. He was, in fact, an indisputable genius at eating his cake, and having it too, and then gobbling it up. After which he would swallow it. Jackie might have admired this feat, seeing that she regarded those imposed upon by it (Plums, to wit) as richly deserving of their fate: but there were, unhappily, certain Bathing and Cricket complexes in Mr Linell at which she stuck. Not only did Mr Linell, by the weight of his terrible personality, compel his pupils to chatter their teeth at abominable hours of the morning at all the seaside towns they visited (himself squirming hairily and skinnily over the stones in a very queer pink costume): he also organized cricket matches amongst his pupils, at which he became horribly angry if you got him l.b.w. (which you could easily do), but didn't show it apart from a little muttering about Whole Things being Farces of course ... Things were, in the course of nature, farces, if they defeated Mr Linell's habitual miracle with his cake. And there was also a Briar Pipe complex, which embraced Fresh Air, flannel trousers, sports coats, Wholesomeness, and the idolization of Rudyard Kipling – particularly 'If', which was Mr Linell's life's motto. Mr Linell was a perfect marvel at keeping his head when all about him were losing theirs and blaming it on him. Such a thing happened frequently. Directly Mr Linell began to announce that he was Keeping his Head, you kept as far away as possible, for what Mr Linell really wanted you to do was to Lose yours and Blame it on him – which would not have been a wise course to adopt. But perhaps it was Wholesomeness which Jackie found least acceptable in Mr Linell. For it was on behalf of Wholesomeness that Mr Linell angled for those celebrated Talks with his young men, while on tour. For these he asked them to tea with his wife, and having dismissed the good woman, and begged his victim (whom he would address as Old Man) to Put on a Pipe, proceeded to discourse with all the delicate obscenity of the Clean. The young men came out with the glorious news that their Bodies were Temples. Also that whenever they were in Trouble they had only to come to him. They were pleased to hear this, but had a faint awareness that their trouble would have to be a rather indecent one if it was to get his consideration.

Nor did Jackie have any great belief in Mr Linell's powers either as an actor or as a tutor of that art. This was because she did not believe in teaching young people (who might one day, if they were lucky, become at least cheerful nonentities in the provinces) the village-Hampden principle of defying and stamping and spitting in almost every phase of their performance. Nor did she believe that, in dramatic or tragic moments, young persons should be advised to pronounce such lines as 'Take it away. My heart wants it not' as 'Ték it awé. Merhut wunts it nut!' and to stagger about the stage like a rather serious-minded drunkard. Nor yet, in romantic moments, to pronounce such lines as 'Still let me sleep in dreams of bliss' as 'Steele lett mee sleep in dreams of bleace!' and to give every appearance of being about to float voluptuously in air. She had no doubt that this kind of thing was the kind of thing expected of Mr Linell's productions, but she was aware that it would hate to be unlearnt by those desirous of making their living.

Jackie did not get much further than the playing of wenches and pages during this tour, which lasted eighteen weeks. She understudied heavily, though, and, on the illness of her senior, Miss Lily Danham, played Cordelia in 'King Lear'. The affecting filial proximity to Mr Linell involved by this, revealed rather dirty ears, not to say Lozenges, both of which took her mind off her performance. Mr Linell said nothing about her performance: nor did anyone else in the company: but she was mentioned favourably in the local Press. 'The beautiful Miss Lily Danham,' it was said, 'played throughout with a delicacy and fine restraint.'

The Press received Mr Linell with unvarying adulation. Mr Linell, indeed, was one of those persons who had done More for Shakespeare ... What Shakespeare had done for Mr Linell was not debated. It was assumed automatically that he was a martyr, for he never left off saying how he Backed his Belief in the British Public's Good Taste and Love for Shakespeare, and no one but a martyr did that. Who Said, asked Mr Linell defiantly, that the British Public didn't want the Good Things when it Saw them? Whoever did didn't dare to lift his head, and everyone was pleased. With the exception, perhaps, of the younger members of the various visiting school parties, girl guide parties, etc., who had two and a half hours of life and air and amusement stolen for ever from their lives by the pious exigencies of Mr Linell's Belief. But even they, being children, probably got some fun from the grotesquerie and incomprehensibility of the spectacle.

At the end of this tour, which (she told herself) she would not have survived had she not been seeing a great deal of Richard all the time, Jackie, nothing daunted, sought fresh work. She still had a perfect faith that she would one day succeed in getting in touch with her profession, and that the mechanical imbecilities at which she had so far assisted, valueless in themselves, were serving to equip her for honest work. Her next engagement, however, which raised her hopes by giving her a little foretaste of Town, fulfilled none of these requirements.

This was at the Miniature Theatre in John Street, and her part was that of a maid. This maid opened the play by behaving briskly with a feather mop and a manservant, whose attentions nauseated her. This maid was called Celestine. The plot of this play revealed the self-immolations of a happily married ex-courtesan intent upon placing her son at Sandhurst – military colleges standing for the highest ideals recognized by this play. It ran for two weeks. It was called 'The Greater Love', and the leading part was taken by the far-famed Miss Annette Brill, who had touched her heights between 1901 and 1905 and was now fifty-one years of age. Her method of acting was to punch her nose incessantly with a sodden handkerchief, emit dangerous gurgling noises from an inexhaustible chest, and to fling herself on the floor at the end of acts. She was, indeed, one of the most Handkerchiefy actresses in London, and reputed for these orgies. She also played the piano upon the stage.

'The Greater Love' had been written by the also well-known Mr Andrew Laming, who, on the strength of one vast success in 1903, had since been losing hundreds of pounds annually for his friends. He still had a few more years in which to do this. He also produced (it was one of those 'Annette, dear' and 'Andrew, dear' productions) and Jackie got on very well with him. He said that she was the prettiest thing (of course) that he had ever met.

With Miss Annette Brill she fared worse. It was the habit of this lady, in fact, to Queer her. (Jackie was horrified to find herself using this word, but she had caught herself in many other exhibitions of professionalism by this time.) Jackie had one scene in the second act wherein she was allowed (as Celestines are) thirty seconds of vituperation in the French tongue. This concluded with a very excellent 'C'est infame! C'est infame! C'est infame!', and a round on her exit was pretty secure. The French tongue, however, was a rival to Piano, and Miss Brill laid great store by accomplishments. Therefore Jackie was allowed but ten seconds of those thirty – though this was not demonstrated until the second night – when Miss Brill, whose voice was invincible, adopted the naïve expedient of relieving the drama of two hundred words. There was no appeal.

The rest of the company were not very distinguished. There were one or two elderly women; there was one of those fair-headed young Scotsmen who spread their pantingly earnest incompetence over the London stage; there was a furtive little dark person with curly hair and spectacles who was said to have won prizes for Greek at Oxford; and there was an engaging, untidy, bow-tied young man of short stature but attractive countenance, who edited a musical periodical and had written a life of Mozart. With respect to Greek Prizes, however, the state of mind wrought by them prohibited the wearing of a hat in the street (as it also prohibited friendly human discourse), but it did not prohibit the habit of creeping up behind you as you read a book in a corner, jerking a lightning nose over your taste in literature and retiring with an amused and ineffable expression. And a Life of Mozart had similar social drawbacks, being very affable and courteous until it got you in a dark taxi, when it commenced to handle your knees in an off-hand but experienced manner until rebuffed. Jackie's favourite was the young Scotsman, who read the most refreshingly innocent double meanings into everything she said, and would have fallen head over heels in love with her had he not been scared out of his wits by the appearance of Richard, at which he at once gave her a book of poems and retired.

The epithet for the play employed by the company was Bloody, but 'Annette' was said to be 'perfect'. The Life of Mozart alone rejected this view. He maintained that the latter was, if possible, the bloodier of the two. But this young man had a bristlingly independent type of mind, and abhorred Miss Brill for having taken exception (through the stage-manager) to his whiskers.

Immediately after this, and through the influence of Mr

Laming, Jackie got a job in a sketch for two weeks at the Coliseum. She got five pounds a week for this (her highest yet), and struck up, during the short time she had there, a pleasant acquaintanceship with a gentleman who earned his living by growing any amount of inches while you waited. It became clear, in fact, that Jackie, if she played her cards right, could put herself in a position where she could have one by her who, for the rest of her life, would privately increase or diminish at any time of the day and at her lightest whim. And such a thing was not to be sneered at. But feeling that this phenomenal and charming feat did not truly touch the essentials of life, in the way that, for instance, Richard's attributes did, she repulsed (not without difficulty) his attentions.

And after this Jackie got a one-line part as the daughter of a Duchess at Ascot in a Drury Lane drama – a part which she doubled with a Mill Lass and a waitress and a passenger in a train, and which she found very hard work: and after this she went out for a sixteen weeks' tour with the No. 1 company of 'Barney' – the successful play of the successful novel, which had, in its ten years of existence, reached the status of an institution in touring circles. Here she was amongst, for the most part, rather aged permanent exiles from Town, who had their own recognition in the provinces and were perfectly content in that. They were homely creatures, who lent her a great number of books, took pride in their learning, and involved her in endless circular train discussions upon Spiritualism, Higher Thought, a fourth dimension, or Christian Science. Each one of them harboured a self-defensive belief in being the most unique character in the theatre, and they buoyed themselves up with that Sense of Humour which they did, to a much too self-conscious extent, possess.

Jackie had procured a certain amount of friends during this time – enough, at any rate, to bring her in an average half-dozen wires on her first nights. Her most persistent acquaintance, however, had been Mr Merril Marsden. This gentleman continued to invite her to luncheon debates upon himself – the topic absorbing them more than ever, and reaching various crises which served to maintain the excitement. He would allow, for instance, at moments, of apparent divergence from their academic conceptions, that he was, after all, a Strange Man in Many Respects, and such a confession Was not to be taken lightly. The air surrounding them became sinister with his mystery. There were also, he was beginning to discover, Odd Streaks of Anger in his Character, which Needed Watching. The air shuddered in apprehension. There was, however, a Queer Strain of Pure Nobility in his soul, the existence of which could not be denied, though it was, perhaps, Common to the rest of his Fellows. Jackie, in reply, had to throw great weight on her *Perhaps*. Mr Marsden's pasty features vaguely glowed with a positive Red Indianness of pure nobility, as you watched them.

Jackie sometimes experienced, of course, a certain tedium in all this, but the lunches themselves were pretty all right. For it was by now a stale axiom that whatever Else you Accused Mr Marsden of (and he quite invited you to accuse him of things, if only for the sake of debate), you could not Accuse him of Not Knowing how to Dine. This was proved, if not actually by his choice of food and wines, at least by his manner in the restaurant. Which manner involved the intermittent and testy muttering of French interjections immediately on entering, the utter rejection of at least two dishes, a slight confusion of himself with Voltaire, and the continually reiterated and swaggering asseveration that he would certainly have to End Up by Marrying his Cook. The Irony of such a consummation, he said, Appealed to him Irresistibly.

Unfortunately, towards the end of this period, his paternal instincts towards Jackie assumed a heavier form, and he began to feel in Many Ways Responsible for her . . . Also things began to be Not his Business, which was a bad sign. He said that he had No Business, for instance, to make any inquiries about a certain person, whom he would not mention, but whose name he had heard Connected with hers. But People, he said, were beginning to say things. Jackie was aware, he hoped, of the very shocking scandals attaching to the individual in question. He did not profess to know anything about it, but he trusted that Jackie was not involving herself. He personally disliked and distrusted her friend. He (Mr Marsden) was a man (thank God) of the utmost tolerance and forgiveness for the shortcomings of mankind, but there did happen to be Things. It was the habit of Mr Marsden occasionally to state, with over-bearing reticence and sanctity, that there happened to be things. Things were a nasty subject to tackle Mr Marsden upon. There were Things, for instance, which necessitated Horsewhips, which Mr Marsden was quite capable of Going Down with. (A person always went Down, never Up, with Horsewhips – crashing into bestial depths from an implicit moral eminence.) One could almost sense a distant flick in Mr Marsden's warnings against Richard.

In such a way did this long period pass for Jackie, and she came out of it a wiser, and more jaded, and less happy young woman.

Chapter Three

THE EVENING

1

Jackie had seen a great deal of Richard, and they had not been altogether unhappy. At the end of the first year, indeed, their hopes had run high; but after that they had suffered shame and humiliation.

The humiliation of Richard was complete. He made, in all, five trips to Paris, each time returning with renewed optimism, which was each time destroyed by imbecilic communication from one who, having no longer any mind (and scarcely any memory) of her own, was prepared to defer to Richard in person, but to awake to resentment of his demands in his absence. He told Jackie as little as possible about these negotiations, and she asked little. She had a certain cold hatred for the cause of her own unhappiness – a hatred which developed into a more lively loathing, and something akin to fear, when she learnt that that individual had come to London. But she was only in London three weeks, and the feeling passed. A twenty-four-year-old Jackie, who was allowed to read some of her letters, was struck in a curious way by the references to herself as 'this woman'. After his fifth visit to Paris, Richard definitely gave up hope. Jackie, however, at this time, was away on her tour with 'Barney', and it was not until some months later that they came to their decision.

This was brought about, curiously enough, by another letter from France, which again made them hopeful. It was too much for them. They could bear the burden of resignation, but they found that they could no longer bear the burden of optimism; and the thing happened, very simply one night, in the Garrick Theatre.

It was their habit to go to the theatre when in London together: they found a kind of communion in sitting together at the back row of the stalls, and very often, in the darkness, they held each other's hand.

It was in the middle of the second act. They were both gazing at the stage, and they both appeared to be very interested in the play. But her remark was the most natural one in the world. It sprang as inevitably from the wearied thoughts of both of them as if they had been actually conversing.

'Oh, do take me away somewhere, Richard,' she said, and looked at him wretchedly.

He did not answer her at first, but stared at the stage with his arms folded. Then 'All right,' he said. 'I will.'

A roar of laughter burst out in the auditorium as he said this, but they had no consciousness of it.

'I mean we can't go on,' whispered Jackie. 'Can we?'

'No,' he said. 'We can't.'

It was decided. Three minutes later she found his hand. They watched the play.

2

He found rooms in a little crescent not far from the Edgware Road, and they went in at five o'clock on a Friday afternoon. It was the month of February, and it was raining.

It must not be thought that Jackie and Richard did this under the influence of any emotion. Their behaviour was entirely mechanical. They experienced no love for each other whatever at the time. They merely acted soberly and logically upon the recorded and indisputable fact that they adored each other. Less might a commander, in the height of battle, revert to the ethics of his war, than they should now indulge in that adoration. The actual sensations they had were of a quite different nature.

It would have been all right if it had not rained, and it would have been all right if Richard had not, in an odd (and rather unimaginative) way, attempted to celebrate the occasion. He was, for instance, visited by the freakish idea that they should go to the Metropolitan music-hall in the Edgware Road. This was within walking distance, and when they had unpacked, he said, they could go along there for the first performance, and then come back to supper in their rooms. He wanted to do this, he said, because it was at this theatre that he had played his first part ... There were moments when Jackie thought that Richard had gone a little mad this evening ...

Their unpacking was not a very agreeable operation – smash in and pull out drawers as they might, and call to each other from gay distances, and comment most favourably upon the desirability and suitability (nay, delegability) of their rooms. 'Jolly lucky to have got them,' said Richard. 'We couldn't really have done much better.' And 'No,' said Jackie, 'I don't know how you found them, Richard.' 'Ah – the man's a marvel,' he replied ... There was something misplaced and awkward in this trite retort, and they both knew it. They were silent.

And then their first amiable passages with their very amiable landlady were not very much more agreeable, either. Jackie did not quite know what to think when she heard herself being called 'Mrs Gissing' and 'my wife'. She would not let herself shudder at the callous perpetration of this subterfuge, but she wanted to. She felt for a moment that all her love had been destroyed, that it could not ever bear this contact with reality ... And as the night fell, in the rain outside, she wondered whether she would ever come to hate Richard ...

And when, a little later, they left the house together, quietly arm in arm, she was even more depressed. The combination of 'Mrs Gissing', 'my wife', with this quiet walking out together into a hushed and disinterested street, was too much for her altogether. She could not properly analyse her emotion, but she thought it was partly shame and partly embarrassment at the serene and undramatic ease with which they had accomplished their desires. She felt all the distress of one receiving an over-emphatic apology ... She wanted to apologize herself, but was unable to do so ... Nobody was complaining.

And when they reached the Metropolitan, and were seated in the fifth row of the stalls, the slight sense of reassurance wrought by contact with the crowd soon wore off. And there, amid the clash of the band and the cries and gesticulations of third-rate, over-painted performers, and with all the terrors and mysteries of the evening before her, Jackie hardly knew what to do with herself. Fancy watching a daubed juggler, flicking up balls and cigars and top-hats, to soft music, on one's bridal night!

They came out before the last turn, and found it raining. And they could not find a taxi, and they decided to walk it. They had not a word for each other on the way, though she held his arm ... She would never have believed that Richard could have made such a mess of things ...

But it was not until they had reached their rooms again that she realized what a mess Richard truly had, after all, made of things. For in their sitting-room, on their chilly return, the table was set for two. And on the table, in the green light of the gas, were all manner of delightful cold foods (which he must have purchased himself) and two bottles of champagne. And she had to be surprised! And after they had removed their things, and washed, they came down into this sitting-room, and, still with very few words for each other, faced their meal.

It was the champagne which hurt her the most. The banality of that champagne! The banality and inadequacy of those two bottles, standing with a perky air of celebration, upon the table! And his perfect consciousness of their banality, as he strained at the cork, smiling weakly under her forced approving looks! She was so ashamed for his foolishness she could hardly look at him – let alone talk.

And then the meal. The cheerful criticism of the dishes – the making of the salad – the demanding and the passing of the condiments – the friendly, munching, how-are-you-getting-on atmosphere. And the first sip of the champagne. He lifted his glass first, and she accidentally caught his eyes, and lifted hers. They were caught. 'Well, Jackie—' he said, and they smiled. It was a grim smiling, and a grim toast, and it was a grotesque meal. They were without conversation.

It was half an hour before Jackie began to cry, and she had no knowledge why she began. It happened after another visit from their most amiable landlady, who stayed quite five minutes to chat. She went on to the sofa, and it seemed as though she would never desist. Nothing he or she could do would stop it. It was like a sudden added calamity fallen from the skies. It lasted for a clear half-hour, breaking out again when they thought it had stopped, and playing the devil with them. 'Shall I take you back, Jackie dear?' he pleaded. 'Let me take you back.' But she repulsed him. She repulsed everything he said as being foolish and irrelevant.

But after a while she found herself in his arms, with her head on his breast. And it was quite a happy evening after that.

Not exactly happy, but they found a lot to say, and a lot to do. They exchanged photographs, among other things, running upstairs to hunt in their trunks for them, and coming down again, to the fire, and being warm and jolly before it. And on his photograph he wrote 'For my dear wife', and stuck it on the mantelpiece, and then they held each other and wondered what she could write on hers.

And there was a lot of talk as to what she was to write, and they couldn't come to any conclusion. But at last she took the pencil and scribbled on the back.

'To dear, dear Richard,' she scribbled, 'from his mistress.'

And he did not want her to say that, but she said she wanted to: and very soon she was in his arms again, and weeping.

A curious, nervous evening. Even the landlady, passing their door, and hearing one or two noises, herself felt unaccountably nervous.

Chapter Four

THE TOURING COMPANY

1

Jackie and Richard did not have very much time for idleness after their union: for at this period Richard had found backing for one of his own plays (Richard wrote many plays), and before three weeks had passed they were in rehearsal.

This play (which dealt with murder and detection) was called 'The Knocking at the Gate' and was being financially supported by Mr Gerald Banton. Mr Banton was in debt to Richard for £300 (this sum having been lent him, seven years ago, for the purposes of getting married), and it was now felt that he was making some sort of repayment, or at least reparation. Richard, who suffered unceasingly from the expansiveness of his own early youth, considered himself very lucky. So also did Jackie, who was to have the leading woman's part and a genuine chance in Town.

The play was to have a four weeks' try-out in the southern counties, and then, it was hoped, they would get in at the Coburg. Mr Banton reserved the right to produce this play.

2

Mr Banton was a bustling little man of about forty-five, with pince-nez, untidy clothes, and flowing hair which he ruffled excitedly but gracefully when being a Queer Little Genius. But he was only a Queer Little Genius about three times a day, and he didn't remain one for more than half a minute or so, and his friends could afford to wait in patience until he returned to the detail suspended by these spasms.

He was classed, essentially, as a 'little man'. People would not have done this to him if he had not talked such a lot, for he was not much beneath the average height; but as things were he was garrulously and beyond redemption little. He had offices in John Street, where he was surrounded by caricatures of himself (his one palpable vanity); posters of 'Mr Policeman' (the operetta upon his association with which he had founded his rather precarious reputation as a producer); a telephone apparatus with any number of indicating gadgets (sources of never-failing delight to him); and a typing-and-office girl to whom he made love spasmodically but with success. He drank about a pint and a half of whisky and soda each night, and about half a pint of 'the-hair-of-the-dog-old-boy-you-know' next morning. He had hardly ever been seen the worse for drink, but continually the better. His worst moments were at tea-time, when he became rather greasy and irritable.

Mr Banton had an affectionate nature, a pathetic long-ing for popularity, an inner divination that the greater part of his friends referred to him as 'that foul little swine, Banton': and production, with Mr Banton, was one glo-rious and palpitating make-believe. Make-believe that he was a producer and engaged in a serious and recognized business. 'After all, this is Business, old boy, isn't it?' he would say, very firmly. But the next moment he would be blurting out, 'I say, old boy, what about doing all that scene in black tabs?' and his eyes would be alight with school-boy's awe and wonder at the contemplated lark. 'Not a bad idea, old boy, you know,' he would add, and the hearts of the imaginative would go Out to Mr Banton.

Of all joys in the immeasurable joys of this make-believe, the joy of casting won the day with Mr Banton. This, in the case of 'The Knocking at the Gate', he did in conjunction with Richard, and accomplished it in three days. The first call was on a Tuesday morning at a place known as the Lovat Rehearsal Hall. This was not far from Great Portland Street and had originally been a Methodist chapel. It was run by a young man named Lovat, who got you into corners, handed you his card, and told you how well he was doing. Dancing Lessons and Boy Scouts also occurred at this hall. You were continually finding yourself intruding on the last ebullient phases of Boy Scouts, and perpetually being driven forth by the diffident importunities of Dancing Lessons. Boy Scouts and Dancing Lessons also had some difficulty with each other. In fact the young man named Lovat had an awkward time of it – what with 'The Knocking at the Gate', and Dancing Lessons and Boy Scouts. And he carried on a flirtation with Higher Thought, as well, which very nearly finished him. But he had some knowledge of the vanities of this world.

3

Jackie had a clear sense of restarting her theatrical career as she went by herself (for Richard was as usual with Mr Banton) to the Lovat Rehearsal Hall for her first rehearsal.

She was at last, she thought, in touch with her profession. She was playing in an intelligent and comprehensible play, and with West End actors of established worth and reputation. Her own part was good enough, with scope for creative exertion, and the acting itself would no longer be (as it had been in all her previous engagements) a mere accessory to the undertaking of performance, but the whole object of her endeavours. She was at last (she trusted) to be an artist.

She arrived early at the dusty, bare-boarded little hall, and found there the stage-manager, his assistant, and Miss Bella Starkey. She fell into light conversation with these. She was interested and slightly shocked to meet Miss Starkey, that lady having reached the height of her fame during Jackie's schooldays. Her name had been, indeed, a household word with Jackie: and this middle-aged and unsuccessful woman before her, with the over-blue and watery eyes of the advanced spiritualist, and an extreme affability which was still graciousness to those who remembered her triumphs (but ingratiation to those who had superseded them), chilled Jackie's conceptions of success.

The rest of the company arrived one by one. There was Mr Plaice, a tall, slim, grey-haired, monocled, perfect gentleman of about fifty-one – lately belauded in the Press for his perfect delivery of English – in the habit of walking daily down the Haymarket with an ill countenance but a consciousness of perfection – and getting less famous, but more tall and slim and monocled and perfect, every year. There was Mr Grayson, in whom Jackie recognized the glove-puncher she had met on her first night in any theatrical dressing-room, and who had doubtless been punching his way through the years without stoppage, for he was punching more than ever as he entered. There was Miss Elinor Potts, obscurely related to the famous author, Verril Potts, and resembling a tall and very superior housekeeper of about forty-eight. There was Mr Gerald Gifford, a dark brown, well-equipped and handsome young man, whose first appearance in legitimate drama this was, his activities having been hitherto confined to musical comedy. And there was Mr Manlove, a gentleman of about sixty wearing an auburn toupé which caused much resentment. It caused resentment because toupés invariably awake resentment, never pity, in mankind; and because Mr Manlove's toupé was a rather grubby one.

By the time all these, and a few others, had arrived, a great murmuring noise had been set in flow, Miss Starkey had deserted Jackie with a 'Hullo-o! How are *you*?' to Mr Plaice, chairs were being put shriekingly into position by the A.S.M., and chaos was reigning all round, until, like a rap on the table at a public dinner, Mr Banton arrived with the author, Mr Gissing, and complete silence fell. This slowly rose to a new murmuring as the soul became hardened to the impressiveness of Mr Banton and the author – the former introducing the latter, all round, with considerable pride. 'Here's the fellow we're all going to murder,' he said.

This not inaccurate statement was treated as an excellent piece of fun, and a benign atmosphere fell, until all at once Mr Banton whispered to the stage-manager, who shouted, 'Scene one, act one, please!' Whereat a stern, self-abasing atmosphere fell ... Which was followed by various mumblings on the part of Mr Plaice and Mr Banton – which was followed by Mr Plaice coming forward, with his nose in his part, and speaking the first line of the play. Which was all wrong, and had to be done again ... Which wasn't quite right, either, when you came to think of it, because that chair was all wrong. Also Mr Plaice thought it was the settee. No, no. Not the settee. The armchair. At least it *was* the armchair, wasn't it? Let's have a squint at the script. Here we are. Yes. That was right. Armchair. 'Sorry, Plaice, old boy.' 'No – my fault.' 'Well, let's start again, shall we?' ... '*Damn sorry,* Plaice, old boy – but you're coming in *Right* now. It ought to be left.' 'Well, it's marked "right" here.' 'Well, it shouldn't be.' 'Well, it *is*. Look here.' 'No, it isn't, old boy. There's L. for you.' 'Where's L.? – Oh yes. Sorry.' 'Doesn't matter, old boy. We've just got to work at these positions this morning. Let's shoot.' ... 'No, you mustn't Sit on that, old boy!' '*Not* sit?' 'No – I want you to sit later.' 'He's going to drink standing, then?' 'Yes. You can drink standing, can't you? SORRY, old boy!' 'No, that's all right.' 'Of course, sit if you WANT to, old boy. If you feel it that way.' 'No, that's all right.' 'I mean it's an armchair, after all, old boy, and you've got to get up in a moment.' 'Yes. That's all right. I don't want to sit ...'

At this point Mr Banton observed that the door was open.

'Here! Shut that door!' he shouted. 'Shut that door! Shut that door ! What d'you think you're doing?'

He spoke most sharply to the A.S.M., who scuttered to the door. There was a solemn pause as the door was shut, and the sharpness of Mr Banton's tone was held to be justifiable by all.

This was owing to the large band of hypothetical malignants lingering (without doubt) in the doorway, with the intent of taking down every line and gesture of this play in shorthand, and dashing away with the glorious news.

But they were foiled in time, and the rehearsal proceeded.

4

With Mr Banton, Jackie got on very well. He had been requested by Richard to 'leave her alone', and this, combined with his knowledge that Jackie was not married to Richard, inspired him with an enormous conspiratorial tenderness for her, which served her well.

Mr Banton's technique as a producer was, as with all producers, twofold. There was his dramatic technique and his producer's technique. He had no dramatic technique whatever apart from a vague system of Christy Minstrel grouping, a morbid fear of anybody covering anybody else, and a belief in the efficacy of perpetual little climaxes and falls. And when these climaxes were over you were to 'hold it, old boy, hold it!', and when you had held it long enough you were to 'come in and lift it right up, dear, RIGHT UP!' And while you were holding it, Mr Banton put his head and shoulders down, as though it were a kind of Rugby scrum; and when you had lifted it right up, he lifted himself up too, and was all relief.

His producer's technique was more involved. This was made up partly of 'SORRY, old boy!', partly of witty depreciation of himself, and partly of Queer Little Genius, which was exemplified in the scrum, and caught him unawares. Also he Knew he was Awful, and that covered all he did. 'I know I'm Awful!' he would cry. 'I know I'm Awful!' It was Awful, for instance, when he said 'For heaven's sake let's get ahead with this bloody – oh, AHEM – scene!' Absolutely awful. He had been caught napping. And it was awful, for instance, when he said 'Sorry I'm late. I got talking to a pretty girl – AHEM – I mean our advance man!' Caught again, you see. He gave himself away right and left. And it was awful when he said 'Go on, *kiss* her, old boy. She's not a lump of cold fish!' We meant to say – the vulgarity of the man! But he did get through the work (we heard) in a most Extraordinarily Effective way, and we had nothing to complain about. We tittered missishly at his lapses.

Quarrelling time was not reached until about the tenth day of rehearsal, but then the various duels to the death were carried on more or less in the open. There were three leading duels to the death – Jackie Mortimer *vs.* Miss Bella Starkey and Miss Elinor Potts – Mr Plaice *vs.* Mr Grayson – and Mr Rackett (the stage-manager) *vs.* Mr Gerald Gifford.

The first of these – Mortimer *vs.* Starkey and Potts – arose from a conviction, burdening Miss Potts, and communicated to Miss Starkey (who had always had the conviction), that Miss Starkey should be playing Miss Mortimer's part. This she most certainly should have been doing (as Jackie herself knew); but the news of the sedition, when it reached her ears, taken in conjunction with the manifest lunching, go-back-together-to-rooms alliance of the two ladies (those sinister stage alliances!), and the humiliation already suffered from the obvious slur of being the wife of the author, awoke Jackie's resentment. This was the least emphatic of the three duels, and only made itself noticeable (at its worst) either by Miss Starkey announcing joyously to Mr Banton, with respect to Jackie, and in front of her, that this little girl, of course, was coming on quite too well for words; or by Miss Potts telling Jackie that Miss Starkey was too wonderful, wasn't she, and one could learn More about Acting by simply watching her ... or by Jackie telling Miss Potts that Miss Starkey, if the truth was known, ought to have her (Jackie's) part ... No more blood was spilt than that, though that was quite enough.

The next of these duels – Mr Plaice *vs.* Mr Grayson – was more serious. This arose from a conviction burdening Mr Grayson that Mr Plaice, with his Thousand and One Old Actor's Tricks, was endeavouring to Queer him. But if the actual tricks from which Mr Grayson claimed to be suffering were subtracted from this enormous amount, there would have been precisely one thousand left. For the sole complaint Mr Grayson could succeed in lodging against Mr Plaice, was that infinitely stale grouse against your confrère for keeping (like a cad) up-stage, so that the scene was played to him, instead of keeping (like a gentleman) down-stage, so that the scene was played to you.

These subtleties were the cause of great bitterness, which
culminated in one of the nastiest little scraps (apart from
the quarrel outright) to be seen in the rehearsal room.

This took place in the middle of a long afternoon in the
middle of the second week, and awoke a kind of hell-born
joy in the breasts of those who witnessed it.

MR GRAYSON (*affably*). 'Would you mind coming
    downstage just a bit, old boy? I think it'd
    be better.'

(*Unpleasant pause.*)

MR PLAICE (pulling himself together). 'No. Not at
    all. (Coming down.) Here?'
MR GRAYSON. 'Yes. I'm only thinking of the good
    of the play, old boy.'
MR PLAICE (looking interestedly at his part). 'Yes.
    I'm sure you are.'

(*Singularly unpleasant pause.*)

MR GRAYSON (*appealing to Mr Banton*). 'That's all
    right, isn't it, Jerry?'
MR BANTON (*at a loss*). 'Yes. That's all right. Keep
    it like that.'
MR GRAYSON (*to Mr Plaice*). I'm only thinking of
    the *Scene*, you know, old boy.'

MR PLAICE (*more interested in his part than ever –
positively turning over pages of it*). 'Well, let's
get on with it, shall we?'

(*Quite overbearingly unpleasant and
prolonged pause. Air palpably shuddering.
Singing sensations in ears experienced.*)

MR BANTON. 'Well, let's see ... Where were we? ...
Let's take that again ...'

The third of these duels – Mr Rackett *vs* Mr Gerald
Gifford. – was even more deadly still. It proved fatal, in
fact. Mr Rackett was the aggressor in this case, having
taken a dislike to Mr Gifford for several reasons, uppermost amongst which was the fact that he (Mr Rackett)
had been dismissed, eight months ago, from the stage-
management of a musical show in which Mr Gifford
had appeared with success. Mr Rackett believed that Mr
Gifford had given publicity to this fact. He had. This duel
reached a crisis on the twelfth day of rehearsal, and Mr
Rackett won the day.

It happened in the morning. Mr Banton was absent,
and Mr Rackett, as stage-manager, was holding the script.
Mr Rackett was a heavy, dark man of about forty, with
a long nose which he employed for the purpose of ironic
sniffing. He was a perfect Anatole France in his nose, was
Mr Rackett, being able to put every type of sarcastic dig

into his breath – from a real animal pull (which was his bludgeon) down to a delicate, eighteenth-century perfumed intake (which was his rapier). And he could put his tongue into his cheek, to all sorts of different extents, and suggest a thousand middle shades of withering opinion.

'Do you always keep your hands in your pockets, Mr Gifford?' asked Mr, Rackett.

'No. Why ?' asked Mr Gifford. He blushed.

Mr Rackett said that he thought perhaps he did – that was all ... The smashing irony of this deserved a sniff, and got it.

'This isn't musical comedy we're in now, you know,' added Mr Rackett ...

Mr Gifford said that he hadn't said it was ...

'*Oh*,' said Mr Rackett ...

The rehearsal proceeded.

That night Mr Gifford left the cast. This was not owing to any difference of opinion with Mr Rackett, but merely because he was not Happy in the Part, and would rather Stand Down. A great fuss was made of these sentiments, which were brought to the ears of the company, and the young man departed in an exquisite and roseate glow of Unhappiness ... The conspicuousness of his absence that morning gave scope for just that warm-hearted sympathy (with a dash of highmindedness) so needful to the collective theatrical mind. It was pounced on eagerly, as there hadn't been much highmindedness at present.

Curiously enough, three weeks after these events, the

young man in question committed suicide by leaving on the gas in his room. This, it may be said, was not due to Mr Rackett's irony. But the company was horrified. Miss Potts even went so far as to make references to Mr Rackett's Shoes, in which, she declared, she would not like to be. As for Mr Rackett, he wouldn't have exchanged his Shoes for anyone's. He had the time of his life, and played it heavily and with considerable effect. He was sorry, Genuinely Sorry, he said, that he had Gone Roughly with the boy. He reverted to the thing perpetually in bars of an evening. He was very conceited. He might have committed suicide himself, the way he went on.

5

As the author's wife, and therefore as something of a priestess of the production, Jackie awoke to the slight wistfulness and fundamental disadvantage of actors . . .

Whatever their success and qualifications, they had been out of work at the moment of their present offer, and they were not (she was rather shocked to discover) even above a little Pumping . . .

That Week Out, for instance, after Torquay.

It was strange how the conversation, in her presence, hovered nervously (though all but insensibly) around that Week Out . . .

'I *Take* it there's still nowhere after Torquay,' said

Mr Plaice, one morning, looking at the sky out of the window ...

Well, it was very forgivable, of course. But from Mr Plaice! And to her! Mr Plaice – with his monocle and bow-tie and perfection and immaculate English! ... And to her – a little chit with four years' experience and her present engagement wangled! ...

She felt as though she had caught him stealing.

6

The first date for 'The Knocking at the Gate' was at Ramsgate, and the dress-rehearsal began at a quarter to three on a Sunday at the Ramsgate theatre. It ended at eight.

A pretty deadly time of day, and day of week, and town of England in which to dress-rehearse, and a pretty deadly dress-rehearsal. It was far from pleasant to play to Mr Banton's glinting but unresponsive pince-nez in the tenth row of the stalls: and it was far from pleasant to find yourself, in the glare of the floats, shouting at your friends' chromatically unfamiliar faces into a hollow auditorium, which either made no response to your effects whatever, or filled in your pauses with the rather brusque and unimpressed pail-clankings of an obdurately unshooshable charlady in the gallery ... And it was not pleasant to wait about in the passages and on the cold stage of the Ramsgate theatre during the changing of the

PATRICK HAMILTON

scenes – which changings never took less than twenty
minutes to perform, and were carried through with impre-
cations, bangs, foulings, hammerings, cries and grunts, as
though they were all in a ship which was going down in
the night ... And Mr Banton's notebook, in between the
scenes, was not any more pleasant, either, and his complete
overthrow of courtesy no less distasteful for being allowable and traditional ...

'... And you're the worst of all, Manlove. You've got
to speak up, man. I can't hear a syllable ... And you,
Miss Potts. You're pitched far too high. Simpering. You're
supposed to be grim. You're playing it like an ingénue ...
You've got to stop that wriggling with your hands, Mrs
Gissing; it's getting on one's nerves ... That's very good,
Plaice, but get a bit more speed into that telephone scene.
We're playing years too long already ...'

It was very hard to keep one's temper, but there was only
one dangerous lapse. This was in the second act, when
Mr Plaice, after having been prompted by Mr Rackett,
against his wishes, and quite unnecessarily, but very dramatically and hoarsely, for a long time, all at once arrested
the rehearsal to lift his eyes to God and say 'Thank
you. *So* much.'

That 'Thank you. *So* much' was a sudden flash of lightning illuminating for one sharp moment the ghastly abysses
from which they were all kept only by the Herculean exercise of self-restraint. It may be observed in passing that
actors always say Thank you when they are beginning to

get angry, but for this particular Thank you Mr Rackett never forgave Mr Plaice, reviling his acting and character, in bar conversations, for the rest of his life. Also he more effectively punished him next week, and during the tour, by making him dress with Mr Manlove. (Mr Manlove would otherwise have been thrust upon Mr Grayson.) The dressing-room card, which he personally wrote and vindictively pinned on the door, read:

MR MANLOVE
Mr Plaice

– which was a pretty strong disciplinary measure.

'Er – where am I dressing, please?' asked Mr Plaice.

'In here, Mr Plaice, with Mr Manlove,' said Mr Rackett, sharply opening the door, and went away with a sardonic grin and murmurs about these Blasted West End Actors behaving like Funny Old Women over their dressing-rooms.

That night, after the rehearsal, there was a general invitation to the men at the large hotel where Mr Banton and Jackie and Richard were staying; and, with a corner of the lounge to themselves, an affectionate state of intoxication was reached. It was, in fact, Old Boy this and Old Boy that until midnight.

They had never Heard of such things (Old Boy) in all their careers.

Things (hang it all, Old Boy) weren't worth their whiles, were they (Old Boy)? They Asked them now?

They knew Old Boys would never possibly Credit it, but there you were.

Old Boys could not only credit it, but could quote similar soul-shattering experiences.

And Old Boys Only wanted to Appeal to the Logic of Old Boys. They were impotent. They Meant to Say, Old Boy, *Damn* it.

7

On Monday evening, two hours before the show commenced, there was a call on the dim-lit stage for words in Scene 2, Act 1, and this was united with the Mutual Congratulations (or Highmindedness) Call, which had been tacitly expected of Mr Banton.

The last word was said, and the company began to disperse. 'Oh – just one moment,' said Mr Banton.

The company paused.

'Just one moment. Call that couple back, will you, Rackett?'

'Mr Manlove!' cried Mr Rackett. 'Mr Manlove! Mr Grayson!'

'Hullo!' from the passage.

'Just one moment.'

The couple returned with interested but scared expressions.

'Won't keep you a moment,' said Mr Banton. Mr Banton

quietly lit a cigarette. 'Just want to say something, though. While you're all here.'

An austere silence fell upon all.

'Don't know that there's – much to say,' said Mr Banton, puffing at his cigarette; and silence was more austere than ever. Mr Banton looked at the ground . . .

'I suppose I just want to – thank you – really – for the absolutely – splendid way – in which you've all worked together for the good of the show. Honestly – *honestly* – and I'm not codding – I can *not remember* ever having worked with such a really fine lot – such a fine lot for pulling together. It's been splendid. You've all been splendid.'

At this the company, along with Mr Banton, bowed their heads respectfully to the ground, as those who uncover before a passing coffin.

'We may have had our difficulties – I don't deny we have,' said Mr Banton . . .

The mourners did not deny it.

'*Nobody* would deny that we have,' added Mr Banton, firmly, and as though that was a great point. 'But we've pulled through and really got the thing into excellent shape. I don't care who says we haven't. But what I want to say is, we could never have done what I've done – what we've done – unless I'd had your really fine co-operation. I may not have shown how much I've felt all this during production, but the feeling's been there all the same. All I can say is that the whole thing's been carried through, from beginning to end, in, well – let's say the Real British Spirit – honestly – the Real British Spirit.'

At this there was a decline of the burial service atmosphere, and a kind of mental Union Jack was hoisted, amid mental cheers. Also an extraordinary impression that this play had been written, and was now about to be acted, for God, King and Country (at great personal risk), was to be gained from the faces of the company. Instead, however, of expanding upon Outposts of Empire, and Hands Across the Sea, as Mr Banton's statesmanlike and defiant stance suggested he was going to do, he struck a humorous note.

'I know I've been awful. I know you must have wanted to throw me out of the window at times (Mr Banton tittered, and the company smiled in a sickly and repudiating manner), but I really think we got on very well on the whole. And I want to thank you, *for* the author, *and* for myself, for the really splendid way in which you've seen it through.'

It was now obvious that Mr Banton desired to thank the company.

'I don't know how they'll treat us to-night,' said Mr Banton, clearly perorating. 'I don't know how they'll treat us in London. That's in the hands of the gods. But all I can say is – that I thank you – really sincerely – for your really fine co-operation. And that's all.'

Whereat a series of appreciative but abortive grunts, and an attempt on Miss Potts's part to say that she was Sure of something (which was left in the dark, but which was undoubtedly very tender), and another attempt, on Mr Manlove's part, to say that he was Sure they All Felt something (which was also kept in the dark, but which was undoubtedly very reciprocative), and the emergence, from mumblings on the part of Mr Plaice, of the single word 'Thank', and the corresponding emergence, from similar mumblings on the part of Miss Starkey, of the words '*You, Mr Banton*' – formed the sole response to Mr Banton's human little endeavour.

Mr Banton then went off, talking to Mr Rackett, and the company dispersed in a silent and slightly shamefaced manner, as though they had all been caught kissing each other in the passages, and Mr Banton had, very rightly, given them a lecture about it.

8

'The Knocking at the Gate' played to £30 (mostly circle) and a good deal of paper that night, and was accorded the automatic ovation of a try-out first night – the curtain rising and falling twelve times at the end, and revealing twelve different groupings of actors, who, in the seven minutes to which the ovation ran, dragged each other on, ran away from each other, assumed charming despair when left alone, and gave a general effect of having a rather nice and nudging game of hide-and-seek in the wings. There were then several cries of 'Thor! Thor!', as well as one or two slightly peculiar (and possibly ironic) cries of 'Honkore! Honkore!' from a slightly drunken man in the gallery . . . Whether this slightly drunken man thought that they were going to do the play again, for him, was not known. (Anyway, such a thing was quite out of the question.) There was then some more applause, after which the author came on and made a speech, which was applauded, and then the curtain fell for the last time. Whereat the orchestra, without hesitation, played:

'God – save – our – *Gray* – shusking!
Long – live – our – *No* – bullking!
    God – Save – Our King-g-g-g-g !
                    (Prum!)'

– which piece of curtailed and abrupt loyalty was neither brought forth in a prayerful spirit, nor very highly relevant to the matter. It served, however, as a kind of 'Come along. All over. Get along out with you' to the audience, and there was soon nothing to hear or see in the front of the theatre save the gentlemen of the orchestra – who wiped their moustaches, coughed, wrapped green things round their instruments, and made murmuring and stamping noises under the stage.

It being a notable if undesirable fact that most phases of ebullience on this planet must perforce conclude with coughs, moustache-wipings, and green things round instruments – or their equivalent.

9

There was, of course, a call next morning, and a certain amount of cards were laid upon the table. The general feeling, though, was one of satisfaction.

There were the most exuberant notices in the local Press, and an excellent notice in the 'Stage' on Thursday, and another good one in the 'Era'. A firm belief that they would Just Get Out all right, uplifted the management – which suffered from that revealing yearning to get Out of every town it has purposely entered common to touring managements. They dropped, however, seventy pounds.

There was, indeed, a marked apathy in this seaside town towards 'The Knocking at the Gate' – an apathy which was not to be shaken by an infinite number of throw-outs, in the shape of a door-knocker, left about in shops and bars and lounges all over the town – nor yet by a large advertisement in the local paper, surrounded by Bicycle advertisements, and reading

HAVE *YOU* HEARD THE KNOCKING AT THE GATE?

and portraying a tense but rather badly printed pair of lovers in the act of catching the terrible sound. Nor was there any spiritual invigoration for the management forthcoming from the innumerable letters received from critics and individuals in the locality. There was, for instance, this type of letter:—

DEAR SIR,—

As a critic, hardened playgoer, and writer for the theatre of some fifteen years' standing, I should like to send a little word of appreciation and thankfulness for the very delightful and enthralling two hours I spent on Tuesday evening. The play, in its line, could hardly be bettered, and I am one who rarely gives praise of that high order. I have seen nothing so good for many moons. Of the author, 'Richard Gissing' (am I right in suspecting that this is the 'nom de plume' of a woman?), I expect to hear a great deal more. She has a true sense of the theatre. There were, however, one or two minor points which struck me and which I think you would be well advised to alter. In Scene II, Act II – the window scene – the most is not got out of this situation. The girl, instead of announcing herself suddenly, should be heard crying excitedly off-stage, and not appear until the father has heard the cry and gone to the window. The old man could thus have some 'business' – a startled look, say, or sudden ejaculation, which would increase the effect of 'nerves' at which you were aiming. Otherwise the play falls off – 'drags' hopelessly at this point. Then again, in the fight for the revolver, this is very badly handled. They should not pounce together like that, but fall wrestling upon the ground, at about a yard's distance from it, and strain slowly, surely towards it – the victor disentangling himself and springing up with a cry of triumph. It also might be a good 'trick', at the end, if the revolver was *not* loaded, after all. This would increase the foolishness of the villain's position, and add an amusing 'twist'. It would, in fact, make a very good 'curtain', though for this you would have to cut out the last five minutes of the scene. I do not think you should have any difficulty in doing this, though, as the last part is quite needless, and, as it stands, falls very flat. I recommend this strongly.

The last act, of course, is poor. This is in some measure unavoidable after the climax in the second, but it could be vastly improved by clever production, and by taking it at least twice as fast. As it is it hangs fire altogether, and the actors seem to have lost interest in their parts and gone to sleep. This is the fault of the first act, too – where a little 'pep' (if I may be allowed the Americanism) would make all the difference.

As for the cast – Gerald Plaice is a fine actor, and does his best, but there has been a bad bit of 'casting' here. He should change places with Mr Grayson. Miss Starkey is an 'old favourite', of course, but is, I fear, 'beyond it' now. The pretty Miss Mortimer, who gives a charming, if inexperienced performance, should be taught what to do with her hands. Miss Potts is much too heavy, and Mr Manlove rants too much. He lacks restraint.

I have already written more than I intended, so I
will not expand upon how you might, with advantage,
dispense with the part of the butler altogether, letting
the maid, with a few alterations, have his lines – or
how you should try to get more mystery into the actual
'knocking', muffling it, perhaps, or hitting a more dead
surface – or how you might get a rain-machine (there
are excellent ones to be had these days) for the storm
scene, and so add to the grim effect. I will simply thank
you again for an evening of unalloyed enjoyment.
Please convey my congratulations to 'Richard Gissing'.

Yours sincerely,

JAMESON BLAYE.

And there was this type of letter:

DEAR SIR,—

In 'The Knocking at the Gate', which I witnessed last
night, there is a strange oversight which I think you must
have overlooked. In act two the clock on the mantelpiece
stands at half-past eight. The curtain is then lowered
to denote the passing of three hours. To my surprise I
noticed that the clock's hands remained precisely where
they were! Time seems to move slowly in theatreland!

Pardon my impertinence in thus pointing out a little
error which may be easily remedied.

Yours faithfully,

RONALD BULL.

And there was, also, this type of letter:

DEAR SIRS,—

Kindely send me a cop. of yr. play quickly as will be
in Wales soon & unable to look at it. i should think
it would be a sucess, what with these modern plays
about Jaz. i dont know what the worlds coming to.
please send me that cop. I hope you will have a good
time, i Enclose two stamps and will not
Yrs
HENRY STACKS.

Chapter Five

LONDON

1

The first night in London of 'The Knocking at the Gate' took place on the 25th evening of a January. This evening did not differ from any other evening as far as the general London public was concerned – the thunderous pageant of returning workers, and the softer excited inrush of adorned pleasure-seekers, enacting themselves in the same manner as usual – but it was, to Richard and Jackie, like the last evening of the world.

The last red glow of the sun, shining through the windows of their rooms upon Richard, as he fixed the stud of his blazing evening shirt, and tied and untied his tie, was the kind of sun that shines upon a condemned man. And the taxi they took together, some time later, was a Black

Maria of a taxi, if the intensity of fear and the solemnity of ordeal in progress between its closed doors (as it moved through the blocked streets of London to Dean Street) could but have been communicated to the people outside.

They dined at a restaurant almost opposite the theatre, amid the everyday (and yet somehow swimming and unnatural) attentions of the waiters, and various cloaked and chattering suburban ladies who were going, that evening, to the same theatre as themselves. Then he took her to the stage door – an unpleasant walk – and left her.

After that it was all a whirring nightmare in the stewing electric light of those underground, dungeon-like cellars so discrepancy coloured, cushioned and carpeted.

She split open her telegrams in a maze of giddiness, she cried 'Come in' to the knocks upon the door, and she exchanged greetings with her limply smiling fellow-professionals. Such greetings are given you just before you take the anaesthetic . . .

And in all the dressing-rooms, all along the passage, the same thing was happening . . . A knock – a cheery 'Can I come in?' – a cry of recognition – and the sound of mumbling and insecure laughter . . .

And the 'Half-hour' was called, and then the 'Quarter'. And dimly, and from afar, upstairs, came the troubling sound of ripple and restlessness from an incoming audience. This sound was to be divined rather than heard, and you did not dare reflect upon what was taking place up there . . . Actually a line of glistening motors was filling the cold street for three hundred yards – doors were slamming briskly, people were entering brightly, and shaking hands, and everything was as cheerful and above-board and social as it was, down here, sinister, palpitating and secretive. The wings of horror beat the air down here, but only by the acceptance of that horror was the pleasure and piquancy of the evening upstairs to be maintained. Such is the marvellous power of mankind for deliberately creating and inflicting thrills and agonies upon itself.

And then a vague, distant atmosphere of bells, and the cry of 'Overture, please!', all along the passage, and then the overture itself. Jackie did not appear until twenty minutes after the commencement, and she was ready too early, and sat mistily looking at herself in the glass. An uncanny, trembling, and beautiful Jackie – with every beauty of hand, and nail, and nose, and eye, and lip over-emphasized and made monstrous by paint – scarcely Jackie at all, and yet Jackie multiplied by herself – a mad magnification of her loveliness. Her eye-lids as blue as the Mediterranean, her lips as red as a soldier of the Queen, her arms like a miller's, and her eye-lashes burdened with little globes of black . . .

And then the high, hysterically supercilious voice of Mr Plaice (who opened the play) as he walked down the passage to his fate . . . And suddenly the end of the overture . . . And a sudden slow rumble (the curtain) . . . And a breathless, pause . . . And then the sound of stamping, and the sound of voices, and the old familiar lines, muffled by distance . . .

And now a great silence in all the dressing-rooms – a

voice and step at the end of the passage, a cough, or a giggle, drawing anguished attention to itself. It was as though some of the operations had already begun, and, if you listened, you could hear the first opiate stirrings and unconscious sighs of the victims. There would be a scream in a moment (you felt), and then quiet again ... And up above, the muffled thudding and voices, continually ...

A bell buzzed. Steps clanged down the passage. A double knock on the door.

'MISS MORTIMER, PLEASE!'

She was the first to be called. 'Coming,' she said. She flew to the mirror, powdered herself again, swung herself round, and rushed out. She passed under the stage, where the boards were positively cracking under Mr Plaice's boots, and where you could almost hear the actors breathing (they were doing it very hard), and she came up on the o.p. side. Here she met Richard, who said 'Hullo', and courteously took her hand. This author had been shaking over a hundred hands since he had seen her last, and he was not in a condition to differentiate. Nor was she.

2

Three minutes later she found herself on the stage.

She was facing Mr Plaice (who was sweating), and

speaking her first lines intelligently to him, and he was speaking intelligently to her. But although he was speaking the lines of the play, and although his facial expressions were apparently appropriate to his speech, his more subtle expression was conveying something quite different to her, and she was conscious of this alone. He was sympathizing with her.

'Here we are, you see,' he seemed to be saying, 'playing on a first night. They're out there, and we're here. And I'm smeared with grease-paint and ever so queer-looking to you, and you look the same to me. And we're both in a sea of horrible, blinding, amber light, and how it all came about it's impossible to say ... But we've got to keep it going – you and I. Of course, I've been on longer than you (that's why I'm sweating so) and I'm getting hardened ... I know all about that foul coughing female in the third row ... And I know all about this family in this box here ... Oh, and I know all about that chair ... It's been miles too far up-stage ever since I came on. I've been trying to shove it down all the time ... And notice the whisky. Burnt sugar and water. Much too pale. And they gave us water at the dress-rehearsal, didn't they? You'll get used to it in time ... '

Such thoughts, which were all her own thoughts, did Jackie read into Mr Plaice's look.

She felt a great oppressed kinship with Mr Plaice. After a time she began to settle down, even going so far, at moments, as to become conscious of what she was saying.

And when the time came to go she had a certain regret at leaving.

3

At the interval there was a bustling and brighter, if still nervous, air over the dressing-rooms – as though one or two of the operations were over, and favourable results had been reported.

It was not until the last five minutes of the play that a new sensation overtook Jackie. She had the stage to herself and a scene where she was left alone in the dark. And all at once she awoke to the fact that this was truly an occasion, that all eyes were concentrated upon her, and that she was able to cope with it. She was a young actress able to cope with a London audience on a first night. She glimpsed the eagerness of chins lying on glowing arms in the gallery, and she sensed the dark and serious watchfulness of the whole house, and she was filled with a true exultation in her achievement, and played with all the knowledge and skill and depth that she had at her command ...

And when, two minutes later, the curtain fell, and she took her call with Mr Plaice, she heard what she had done ...

Jackie never forgot that applause. It snarled up like thunder at her – it took her breath away – it seemed as though it would never cease ... It was like a mad wave carrying her forward, rolling and surrounding and submerging her in unreasoning bliss ... And it was the applause of London! It was an embrace from infinite sources of metropolitan good nature – undreamed of, absurd, abandoned ... She could only bow, and smile up weakly, and listen ...

And there was then a great deal of applause for everybody else. And then again, 'Miss Mortimer and Mr Plaice!' cried the stage-manager, and she walked on with the curtain down. 'Mr Plaice!' cried the stage-manager. '*Mr Plaice!*' But Mr Plaice was not in evidence.

'All right, Miss Mortimer!' shouted the stage-manager, and Jackie had a call to herself.

And again it smashed up at her – as it always will smash up at a single figure – and she heard the sound of cheering – and she saw the audience in that curious, glowing, hat-holding, disintegrated state which invariably overtakes it just at the end – and she bowed and smiled, and looked upwards timidly, and bowed and smiled again ...

And then she was with the others in a row, like a lot of good little girls and boys, and Richard was making a speech ...

Chapter Six

ARRIVAL

1

And so it was that Jackie entered in upon that brief period allotted to her as a West End actress.

She was not asleep until half-past five that night, but at nine o'clock she was sitting up in bed with her heart beating, and a batch of papers, which Richard had brought her, at her side. It was not altogether easy to find mention of the play. For although the greater part of the headings, such as 'PLAY THAT NEARLY SUCCEEDS' – 'TELLING SCENE IN NEW PLAY' – 'THRILLS AT THE COBURG', were readily identifiable, there were, on the other hand, many such as 'GHOSTLY SOUNDS IN DEAN STREET' – 'NEW METHODS OE DETECTION' – 'CRIME AND A DOOR' – 'POSTMAN'S KNOCK'— 'AN EERIE

EVENING', and so forth, which baffled the seeker for a long time.

And when they were found, it was rather a nasty moment as you said 'Here we are', and rattlingly adjusted the paper, and skimmed hastily through the rather naïve distortion of the plot to the mention of yourself. A kind of newspaper giddiness overtook you. But it wasn't so bad to find that you, 'as the beautiful if somewhat icy Paula' acted with 'a shrewd sense of character and a genuine stage sense', or that 'good work' was 'also put in' by you, or that scenes were 'excellently handled' or 'tellingly played' by you, or that your 'personal charms, in themselves, enlivened what threatened, at moments, to be a dull evening'.

Though it was not so gratifying to learn that when you had 'gained technical skill' you should do very nicely, or that you 'decorated rather than improved' the drama, or that you were 'a young and dainty new-comer' who still had 'a great deal to learn'.

You were consoled, however, when you reached the theatre that morning, by the news that all inimical critics, either of yourself or the play, were not in any way worthy of the name of critic – these treacherous malignants having either:

(1) Only looked in for half an hour during the dress-rehearsal.
(2) Arrived blind to the world.
(3) Received, only that night, news from New York that

their own play had been withdrawn after two nights.
(Hence a green and surly attitude.)

Or

(4) Deserted the Coburg (in favour of the Savage Club
and revelry) before the third act.

And you heard of all the distinguished people who had
been in front last night, and they had never seen any play
quite like it.

Jackie was rather horrified, as she entered the theatre
that morning, at half-past eleven, to find the understudies
already and busily rehearsing. It had a curiously depressing
effect upon her sympathetic nature. She thought that she
would destroy herself, if she ever became an understudy.

'NEW YOUNG ACTRESS'

was the headline in the 'Evening Star' notice that evening,
and there was a picture of her. She went to her work eagerly
that night.

2

And so Jackie was established, at the age of twenty-five
and in her fifth year in her profession, as the leading lady
at the Coburg Theatre. She had all the privileges of that
achievement.

The dressing-table of her little blazing underground room was littered with green and white cuttings from Durrant's Press Cutting Agency: she had constant delightful pictures of herself in the daily and weekly papers: compliments from famous producers in front were reported with pleasant regularity: she received £25 a week: young men visited her during matinées with requests to paint miniature portraits of her: she made a little speech to the Gallery First Nighters on a Sunday: she granted bashful interviews for northern newspapers; she could stand gazing at her own name over the live wire in tube stations: she had, in fact, a thousand and one little satisfactions which gave her no satisfaction whatever, and she remained, to the public at large, quite unknown.

Her achievement, also, would reduce itself to this sort of thing:

A knock on the door during the matinée, and the stage doorkeeper's head put round.

'A lady to see you, miss.' He hands her a card.

The name on the card is unknown to her, but on the back, in pencil, is scrawled 'Iris Langham'.

Jackie is enormously gleeful. It is her old school-friend.

'Do tell her to come down,' she says.

She swiftly tidies up the room, and looks at herself in the glass. This is one of her moments. This is better than coming back in her glory to play at Brighton. She is playing, in her glory, in Town.

'HulLO-O-O-O, my dear!' They embrace..

They talk brightly for a little, and then Jackie gives an opening.

'Well, here I am, you see,' says Jackie, standing up and powdering her face. But her friend is looking vaguely about the room. 'My darling, don't you get most frightfully hot in here?'

'Yes, it does get a bit hot sometimes.'

'There doesn't seeing breath of air coming in anywhere, my dear. I should hate it.'

'I know,' says Jackie. 'But you have to get used to worse than that.'

There is a pause.

'Are you going on with this sort of thing, then, Jackie?'

'Go on, dear? How do you mean?' They smile at each other.

'Only whether you're going on. I just wondered . . .'

'Rather,' says Jackie. 'I'm doing all right at present, anyway, aren't I?'

But her friend does not answer this.

'Of course, my dear,' she says, brightly. 'You know I'm married!'

'Married!' cries Jackie. 'No!' She sits down.

'Yes, my dear. Two years now.'

'My dear Iris! Who to?'

'Oh, you've never met him, dear. He's the most marvellous husband, though. Let's me do anything I like.'

'Good lord,' says Jackie, and takes to adjusting her hair.

There is a silence.

'We live down at Maidenhead,' says Iris.

'Oh, yes?' says Jackie.

'And we've just got the most wonderful little car, to bring us up.'

'Really? How ripping.'

There is another silence.

'Oh – and, my dear!' cries Iris. 'The most *wonderful* little dog! A little terrier! I do wish I'd brought him up to-day. You'd've loved to have seen him.'

'Yes. I wish you had.'

'You'd absolutely adore him, my dear. He's got a little black spot, all round his nose!'

Jackie clearly thinks that this is almost too charming a thing for a little dog to have.

'I brought him up the other day. The poor little thing had to have an operation. He was frightfully good. Of course I spoil him most hideously.'

Jackie's smile infers that she can understand it . . .

'Do you come up here often?' asks Jackie.

'Oh, a fair amount. Just for the theatres. But then there're so few decent shows going on nowadays, aren't there?'

'No. There aren't really,' says Jackie . . .

'Good heavens,' says Jackie. 'I must go on! You'll be here all right when I come back?'

'How long will you be?'

'Only about ten minutes.'

'Well, my dear, I think I ought to go. It's getting dark and I swore I'd be back early to-night.'

'Oh.'

They go out into the passage together, and they say 'Goodbye'.

'You must look in again some time,' cries Jackie, at the end of the passage.

'(Yes) and if you're over our way, you'll give us a look up, won't you?' cries Iris.

'Rather!'

Her heart is bitter as she goes on to perform.

3

And during the run of the show Jackie had many invitations to theatrical dances, cabarets, and night-clubs.

She accepted most of them. With the muffled crash and lilt and shuffle of the Merrickian haunts she became familiar, and she was very often having breakfast in Soho at half-past three in the morning.

She inflicted herself with these unimaginative activities partially out of a desire to leave nothing undone in her new role in life, but mostly because she was unable to rebuff the importunities of her (by now) many friends. It took her away from Richard, however, and she began secretly to look forward to the time when 'The Knocking at the Gate' came off. This it did after four and a half months.

Chapter Seven

JACKIE AND RICHARD

1

On the strength of 'The Knocking at the Gate', and 5 per cent on the gross issuing therefrom to Richard, they left their rooms and took a flat in South Kensington.

It was a very desirable flat, at the top of a very high building, and reached by fourscore stairs.

It was possible to confuse yourself with Samson, at the close of a very stiff day at the mill, as you went round and round in endeavouring to reach the summit of these stairs, but it was a very desirable flat when you got there.

They had very sweet hours together – with the world shut out. Jackie did not, by now, have the same feelings towards Richard as she had at first. They were not so poignant and lively, but they were deeper and firmer. He

354

was infinitely charming, and attentive, and indispensable, and, what was much more important, unspeakably dependent. His content, and her power of giving it, were her pride and joy.

When he was with her in public he spoke very little. He was a vague, inscrutable figure at the back of rehearsals, looking lonely and not very interested, and speaking to no one, and watching her. He would make queer little excursions amongst the stage properties, and finger things, and peer at them, and generally end by bringing them down with a crash. He was always wandering off, and muddling about, and bringing something down with a crash. And then he looked foolish. He was like a strange cat in the theatre. A queer noise would be heard, and the rehearsal would stop, and it would be Richard, standing there and trying to look as though he hadn't. He was very lovable to Jackie when he did this sort of thing. It was his silly way of expressing his impatience for her.

2

But he talked enough when he had her alone. Indeed his garrulousness and ebullience, at times, were almost wearing. It was as though he had never had anyone to talk to in his life before. And the more he talked, and the happier he grew, the more pathetic he became. He was an astonishingly pathetic creature sometimes, and at the least likely moments.

And they flirted and were foolish with each other all day long, and they bathed in the glow of their own irresponsibility and a love not needing mention ...

They had their own private idiom and their own private humour, and their behaviour was incomprehensible.

In the morning, after breakfast, for instance, he would come charging into her, as she sat in the front room, and go over to the table in the corner with some papers. He would pretend that he had not seen her, and he would be muttering to himself ...

'Ha!' he would mutter. 'I wonder where *she's* got to ... Can I go on with this much longer? The strain of having to pretend I love her? Is it worth it? Ha, ha! If she only knew!' He would give a devilish chuckle and commence to write. 'What would she think then? What would she think if she knew I married her *purely* for the sake of her *Money*? Eh? What then? Ha, ha! Little does she know! Little does she guess that I engaged her simpering affections *solely* in order that I might obtain a Certain Legacy, left her, I believe, by One Lady Perrin (a Rich Widowed Lady of Brighton, now Deceased) – thus saving myself from exposure and ruin (for I had been embezzling heavily with my firm's money, and was compelled to make up the deficit). It was a Lucky Business for Me! Well – she must not know – yet. The time has not come. Bah! The milk-and-water little fool! How her timid affections nauseate me! When I have what I want, she shall see no more of me! I shall cast her off like an Old Shoe!' At this he would turn round and give a start of recognition. 'Heavens! She is in the room! Could she have heard what I said? No – surely not! . . . But I must go more carefully in the future. Now, I suppose I must lovingly greet her!' He would rise and come over to her.

'Ah – my darling. I did not observe that you had entered the room. I trust that you have enjoyed a pleasant night's repose.'

'Very nice, thank you, Richard.'

'I am glad. But what – what is this? There is an air of restraint – of coolness, almost – about you. I have not offended you, I hope.'

'No, not at all, Richard.'

'Ah – my error, doubtless. And I would not have you so this morning, my pet, for there is a little Business to transact. There are Certain Papers, which I wish you to Sign. They are here. I do not think you need trouble to Read them. Do so, of course, if you wish. But such a pretty little head, I know, cannot be bothered with these dreadful commercial matters—'

'Richard, did you leave the gas on upstairs?'

'Don't think so, darling.'

'I'd better go up and see.' Jackie would rise. 'All right, I'll sign them when I come down,' she would add, and leave the room.

By the time she came down he would have forgotten about his schemes, and be sitting on the sofa reading 'The Daily Mirror'. She would go and sit close to him.

'Richard,' she would ask. 'You didn't *really* marry me for my Money, did you?'

'Yes, I did.'

'No. Not *really*, Richard, did you? Didn't you marry me for anything else?'

'No. I've married you for your Money.'

'No – but, you haven't *really*, Richard,' Jackie would plead, but, 'Yes, yes, yes, I have,' he would maintain. 'I *have*.'

And however much she asked, and pleaded, and embraced him, he would never admit that he hadn't.

Though he might Come to love her, he would sometimes allow.

3

In all their time together they had no disputes. In any crisis he telephoned for help.

He would swing out of the room, and she would hear clicking noises outside.

'Hullo ... Hullo ... I want Earlswood, please – yes, please ... Thank you ... Ah – hullo! Is that Earlswood? ... The Asylum? ... Ah – may I speak to the Director of Raving Lunatics, please? ... What? ... The *Director* of *Raving Lunatics*, please. Thank you ... Hullo. Is that the Director of Raving Lunatics? Ah. Good evening, sir. I've a nasty little case here ... No, a woman, I'm afraid – my

wife ... Oh, yes, beyond question ... A van, did you say?
Naturally. Padded, I hope ... And eight men? Oh – at least.
Thank you. Be as quick as possible, won't you, sir? It's
rather creepy here. Thank you. Good evening.'

'Oh, you are a fool, Richard,' Jackie would say. 'And I'm
not going to.' But it was all over for her.

4

Or on the stage, just as she was about to go on, he would
materialize from a dark corner, and speak gravely to her.

'Ah, Miss Mortimer,' he would say. 'The management
want to know if you will play in Chinese to-night? Will
that be all right?'

'But why Chinese, Richard?'

'I don't really know, Jackie. But I think they think it
would be appropriate.'

'But why appropriate, Richard?'

'Oh – I don't know. Courtesy to an ancient civilization,
you know.'

'Well, I'll do my best, Richard.'

'Thank you. You will have no difficulty, I hope?'

'Well, I was never very good at Chinese, Richard.'

'Never very good at Chinese? What is this? I married you
for your Chinese, kindly remember.'

'Well, I'm sorry to hear that. Because I know next to
nothing about it.'

'Next to nothing about it! What is this, please? Why have I not been told this before?'

'I'm sorry, Richard.'

'How did you think you were going to entertain my friends?'

The logic of this would appeal to Jackie.

'I'm very sorry, Richard,' she would say.

'This, of course, quite Alters the complexion of Everything,' she would hear him muttering, as he went away, and she went on to act. And when she came off again, ten minutes later, she would go up to him.

'Richard, you didn't *really* marry me for my Chinese, did you?'

'Yes, I did.'

'But not *really*, Richard? Chinese doesn't *really* matter, does it?'

'Yes, it does. I married you for your Chinese.'

And whatever she said, and however much she cajoled him, there was no other reply. There *could* be no other reply. He had married her for her Chinese. That's what he had married *her* for.

5

Or else, at midnight in their flat, as they put out the lights, and cried to each other lazily from adjoining rooms, he would meet her in a doorway and take her hands. 'Oh, *how* did I meet you, Jackie darling?' he would cry, and look into her eyes.

'I don't know how it happened at all, Richard,' she would say, and as their eyes met, and they kissed each other, they would both be almost crying.

Then he would say, 'That window's open, dear. Go and shut it. I'll go and turn on your bath.'

And as she went through the dark room to the window, and as she heard the first splash of the water in the jolly bath-room upstairs, and as she glanced down at the street below, with its silent row of taxis in the mauve bare thoroughfare of the almost deserted station – then the mystery and the sadness, and the infinite sweetness and surety of their existence together, would come over her.

Chapter Eight

TENNIS

1

It was in the summer of this year that Jackie was enrolled as a member of the Rockingham Hard Court Tennis Club in South Kensington. This catered almost exclusively for actors and actresses in their leisure hours (of which they had about twelve daily), had sixteen courts, and was productive of as many bandeaux, sweaters with triangular stripes; retired Majors; young men to spring like lightning from wicker chairs when ladies left the table; shower-baths; bridge-markers in the form of bathing girls; copies of 'The Field', 'Vogue', or 'Punch'; or easily familiar and technical allusions to horses, dogs, the army, Kanelagh, Wimbledon, Twickenham, Fearful Outsiders, the peerage, hunting, and India – as the heart of any actor or actress might desire. It is true that there was also, unhappily, a slight sprinkling of blue-shaven cheeks, short stature, huskiness, and diamond rings – to say nothing of one or two thoughtless young men, not only unable to spring (with any abandon) from wicker chairs, but also in the habit, in the hot weather, of putting rather unpleasant white Handkerchiefs over their heads, and fixing them with four very revolting knots (to the impotent horror of the club at large) – but such cases were not prevalent, and were the cause, for the most part, of mere tolerant amusement.

Unhappily, also (as far as Jackie was concerned), the professional atmosphere was in no way smothered by this unprofessional atmosphere. Indeed Jackie had now begun to realize that actors and actresses, however lightly or derisively they might speak of their craft at times, had a certain solemn affection for it which she, if she was to take her place amongst them, would be expected mutely to share.

There was, for instance, that Curious Something about the Smell of the Greasepaint, which rather worried Jackie ... This Something (often classified with that other Something about the Sight of the Floats, or that Something about the Look of a Dressing Room) was an Indefinable Something. But if you were a real Pro. (and who would dare say she was not?) you found that, however much you complained, you Came Back to it every time and knew your destiny in life. This was taken as an axiom, and it cast an air of absolution and romance over any of the irregularities and indignities of theatrical life. There was Something about the Theatre.

Nevertheless Jackie, who, when in the presence of greasepaint, made continued and elaborate sniffing experiments (with the utmost faith and ardour), found that science did not endorse this theory. Or else she was not a Real Pro. – which she would have been loth to admit.

2

At the Rockingham Hard Court Tennis Club Jackie also found that she was not very good at Christian names, either. She did not mind calling people by their Christian names, of course: but when she knew very well-known people by their Christian names, she was unwilling to employ them too often of too ostentatiously, because it seemed (to her doubtless over-sensitive mind) that one might thus put oneself under the suspicion of sunning oneself in, or even trading upon, an intimacy. She did not know whether she was too much, or too little, impressed by fame – but in either case she felt that a little care was needed here.

Christian names, however, were lavishly in evidence at the Rockingham Hard Court Tennis Club. Indeed, what with Gerald, and Godfrey, and Gladys, and Marie, and Madge, and Norah and so forth, you barely knew where you were. They were hardly ever out of the conversation.

And when Jackie heard young men (reclining largely in chairs) say, 'As I was telling Gladys the other day—'

she could not really see how the fact that he had told it to Gladys affected the point at issue. It seemed irrelevant to her. Now, if he had said that Gladys had told it to him: that would have been all right. It would have been the opinion of a famous English beauty, which might have been worth having. Or even if Gladys had said, 'That's very, very true, Mr So-and-so' – there would have been some value in that. But the mere telling of it to Gladys did not touch the argument either way, so far as she could see. You could stand outside Buckingham Palace and tell things to the King, if you tried hard enough, but the ultimate value of your assertions did not rest upon the status of those who listened to them. At least that was how Jackie saw it.

Furthermore, Jackie was a little surprised to observe that – when the actual owners of these Christian names came down to the courts of an afternoon (as they very occasionally did) – the immediate chorus of joyful recognition and acclamation which she had expected to arise, did not arise at all. On the other hand, the news of their arrival at the clubhouse, had a habit of running round those courts like very wild, but very silent fire, as well as bringing into being an extraordinary amount of low-toned, rather uneasy remarks, and quaint little conversations at the net. Also when the innocent cause of all this revealed himself or herself in the open (and on the occasion at which Jackie was most struck by these manifestations it was Gladys herself), there was a strange vagueness of play in the adjoining courts, and there were uncanny prolongments in the act of looking for balls (which were doubtless hiding themselves, and were therefore earnestly looked for, in rather suggestive corners); and young men who had told things so emphatically to Gladys only the other day, rather went off their game.

Not that the Christian name itself was submerged by this atmosphere. On the contrary it took on a slightly hysterical stress such as it did not have at normal times.

'*Gladys* here, I see.' 'Ah-ha. The worthy *Gladys*!' 'Gladys here this afternoon, I observe.' 'My dear boy, be careful. I'm sure you don't want Gladys to see you like that.' 'Now, look your best for Gladys, dear.'

In fact, it was Gladys here and Gladys there, and Gladys everywhere – so no one was really impressed, you see.

No one except Jackie, that is; and she was tremendously impressed.

In fact, it is believed that on one occasion this terrible girl (doubtless unhinged by the awe of the moment) was observed to go over calmly to her partner, point innocently with her racket, and utter, in a simple, clear voice, the mad, the outrageous, the unthinkable word

'COOPER'

– but this is only a rumour.

Such a word had surely never been heard before on the courts of the Rockingham Hard Court Tennis Club, and will (let us very sincerely hope) never be heard again.

Chapter Nine

REPUTATION

1

Jackie, however, in indulging her doubts concerning the more subtle ethics of the Rockingham Hard Court Tennis Club, had not reckoned with any doubts, concerning more obvious ethics, which might arise about herself. Indeed, if she had known in full the reputation she was eventually to gain, she would probably have left this tennis club at an early date.

The history of Jackie's reputation, being a history very similar to the history of a great deal of reputations acquired in this profession, and throwing some light upon the characters of its creators, may be given in some detail.

It may be called the Bath Room reputation, and it was a reputation for abnormality. A reputation for abnormality is easily acquired in theatrical circles – the taste of nearly all single young men being, according to their gossip, far from correct: and the habits of nearly all single, or even married young women being Famous – a tricky but somehow comprehensive word.

With Jackie the thing began, undoubtedly, with Mrs Player. This lady (who was married to an author of situational (but unsuccessful) farces, and had spent her entire latter existence understudying in Town) was sitting on the lawn one afternoon (as Jackie passed), with a young man of the name of Thwaites. Mrs Player was one of your 'And-who-is-the?' type of ladies. If she had not been an 'And-who-is-the?' type of lady, the thing might never have begun. But as things were:—

'And who is the beauteous blonde Who smiles upon us so graciously?' asked Mrs Player.

'Oh, that's Jackie Mortimer,' said Mr Thwaites. 'Up at the Coburg. I was round there last night, having gin and ginger beer with her husband.'

'Ah, yes,' said Mrs Player, languorously. 'And which was more attractive – the gin and ginger, or the leading lady?' (Some people still talk like this.)

'Oh – the gin and ginger, undoubtedly.'

'Perhaps there was a little ginger in the lady too?' suggested Mrs Player. (They talk like this too.)

'Ah, well. Ah, well,' said young Mr Thwaites.

'I know too much about you, I'm afraid, Mr Thwaites.' (*And* like this.)

'There's nothing to know.'

'Oh, but I'm sure there is.'

'Oh – but there's not – really.'

'Oh, yes, there is. You can't deceive *me,* you know . . . '

The topic of Jackie was temporarily forgotten.

2

Jackie was not taken up again until three days later, and then at about a quarter to ten one night in the Smoking Room, where Mrs Player and Mr Thwaites were playing Bridge. The party was slightly drunk.

'Look!' cried Mrs Player, pointing at Mr Thwaites. 'He's getting all flustered! I'm sure he's Dying to rush off. Isn't he, poor thing?'

'Far from it. Far from it.'

'He wants to go and have his drinks with his Jackie Mortimer, doesn't he?'

'Jackie Mortimer? What's all this about Jackie Mortimer? I hardly know her . . . '

'Oh, *no,*' said Mrs Player, with great irony, and here Mr Danham, Mrs Player's partner, cut in.

'What? Does he go and have his drinks with Jackie Mortimer?'

'My *dear,*' said Mrs Player, who was dealing. 'I wouldn't like to tell you . . . '

'Most touching,' added Mrs Player . . . They picked up their cards.

'Of course, that's *just* like Thwaites, isn't it?' said Mr
Danham. 'Always works in the dark. Always something
thoroughly nasty and underhand. Now, who'd've associated him with Jackie Mortimer?'

'But, my dear boy, it's an entire – an en*tyer* – fabrica-
tion!' pleaded young Mr Thwaites.

'Oh, yes – we know all about that. And what do they
drink, Mrs Player?'

'My *dear*!' said Mrs Player. 'Gin ... What else?'

3

It was three days later that Mr Danham was walking from
the club to South Kensington Station with his friend, Mr
Geralds. Mr Geralds was a thin, ageing, strained little
man, who made great hits with his drunken fathers and
drug-takers. Mr Danham was in an expansive and sophisticated mood. They were discussing the Gissings.

'Well, of course, Old Boy,' Mr Danham was saying, 'I
never hit it off with Richard like others seem to, somehow. I
don't know what it is, but there's a sort of Air of Restraint,
Old Boy – you know what I mean? I've got nothing against
the old chap, mind you, but we just don't seem to get any
Further. Of course, the truth is that *I* think him God's
Worst Playwright, and he *knows* I think it. That's the
root of the matter. He's rumbled me. And then, of course,
there's this Brand New Wife of his ... '

'Oh, yes. I've heard of her. What's she like?'

'I honestly don't know her, really, old boy. Only seen her at the club. But just the usual sort of thing, you know. I mean you know the Type, old chap. Drunk parties with Reggie Thwaites at the Coburg, you know – and all that sort of thing. You know – pints of gin and can't act for nuts – the usual dope.'

'Oh – it's that sort of thing – eh?'

'Yes. That's right. They were ragging poor old Reggie about it last night.'

There was a pause.

'And Not – I think – married?' suggested Mr Geralds.

'Not Tonnyer *Life*oleboy,' said Mr Danham with emphasis. 'But then Who is? These days . . . '

'Who, as you say,' said Mr Geralds. 'Is?'

4

It was on the next afternoon, at tea-time, that Mr Geralds, entering the almost deserted club-house for refreshment after a strenuous game, observed three of his friends speaking in low tones at a table in a corner. The trio comprised Miss Ethel Drage, a vivacious young London actress of thirty-five, who had not performed on any stage for eighteen months – Mr Alec Douglas, a young man now playing a large part at the Duke of York's, which part had been obtained (it was widely – though inaccurately – reported) through influences of a scandalous and depraved nature – and Miss Storm Lovat, an extremely good tennis-player of about forty, who had gained some recognition in the theatre as an interpretress of harridans, procuresses and drunken society ladies.

'Well,' said Mr Geralds, approaching. 'Still gossiping?'

'Ah!' cried Miss Drage. 'Mr Geralds! You're the very man! Now come and sit down and tell us. We've been fighting for about five hours, my dear.'

'What's it all about?' said Mr Geralds, and seated himself.

'That's right. Now *who* – Mr Geralds – now *who* – and don't answer this lightly – give it time for ma*tewer* consideration – *who* – now think it out – *who is the biggest drunk in this club?*'

'My dear,' said Mr Geralds. 'What a question!'

'Now don't be silly. Go on. Tell us.'

'No, my dear,' said Miss Lovat. 'We know the biggest drunk. It's the biggest *female* drunk.'

'Yes. The biggest *female* drunk.'

'The biggest female drunk?'

'Yes. Now go on ... I know who he'll say! I know who he'll say!' Miss Drage positively clapped her hands with glee. Mr Geralds, however, was rather at a loss.

'Well,' he said at last, 'I know a lot who can put it away.'

'But who, *who*?'

'Well, that little girl who's just left the room can do her fair share, so I hear.'

'What? That? The Mortimer person? No, she doesn't drink, does she?'

'Well – rumour may be wrong, but I hear that she gets through gallons nightly in her dressing-room at the Coburg.'

'Yes, I thought she must,' said Miss Lovat, but did not say why . . .

'Oh, but, my dear – how thrilling!' said Miss Drage, fixing her bright, eager eyes upon Mr Geralds.

'I say,' said Mr Douglas. 'This scandalizing and gossiping, you know!'

'Oh, shut up, Alec.'

But Alec was not to be shut up. '*You* haven't heard the worst Geralds. They've been going on for hours before you came in. Something terrible.'

'Have they? I'm sure they have. Who's it this time?'

'The Mastersons this time,' said Alec.

'Oh, but Mr Geralds must know all about the Mastersons,' said Miss Drage.

'I don't.'

'Oh, but, my dear! . . . Can we tell him?'

'I shan't blush. What've they been doing?'

'Oh, my dear, it's not what they've been doing . . . Oh, if you don't know, I really can't tell you.'

'Go on – go on. Come along. Get it over.'

Miss Drage lowered her voice, and made her points with her forefinger.

'Well, my dear . . . you see . . . it's like this. They're a very nice married couple, you see, but they have a Bath Room . . .'

'A Bath Room?'

'Yes. A Bath Room. In which, you see, the servants perform their ablutions ...'

Mr Alec Douglas here made snorting noises.

'No, shut up, Alec. And at the top of this Bath Room, you see, which is *his* bedroom, you see, he's made a Little Hole, you see ... And he spends the whole night Peering Down ...'

'Oh, I see I shall have to leave the room,' said Mr Geralds.

'No, my dear! It's *True*! It's an established fact!'

'Of course, *I* don't believe a word of all this,' said Miss Lovat.

'I should hope not,' said Mr Geralds.

'But it's true, my dear! Honestly it is! It's established! They're Famous for it! '

'They? How does *she* come in, then?'

'Oh, my dear, you haven't heard the worst! You see, it was *her idea*, originally. And they sit up there together and Take Turns!'

'Well, I'm going,' said Mr Geralds, but did not go.

'And of course the most amazing scenes take place, my dear,' added Miss Drage. 'I mean to say after *Supper*, for instance, you see, his wife gives him a sort of Nudge, you see, and he gets up, and walks Airily along the passage to the Kitchen, you see ... And he says, "Well, Annie (or whatever the girl's name is, you see), going to have your Bath soon?" And she says, "Yes, sir," you see, very respectfully, and everything's very pleasant, and they all *Rush* upstairs – no, it's no use grinning, my dear. It's an absolute *fact*! . . . It's Common Knowledge . . . '

5

It was three weeks later, and in wicker chairs on the lawn overlooking the courts, that the following conversation took place between a young actor of twenty-five and Miss Lovat.

'Have *you* come across them at all?' asked the young actor of twenty-five, leaning forward on his racket.

'Oh, just casually,' said Miss Lovat, puffing at her cigarette, after a hard game. 'She's at the Coburg now, isn't she?'

'Yes.'

'Aren't they the couple that have a Bath Room?' said Miss Lovat . . .

'Oh, it's THEM, is it?' pounced the young actor of twenty-five. 'I've heard that story, but I couldn't place it.'

'I think it's them. But I've given up listening to these stories that get about. I can't even trouble to sort them out nowadays. This place is getting really too ghastly for scandal.'

'I know,' said the young actor of twenty-five. 'Something deadly.'

6

It was the same evening that the same young actor, behind the scenes on the stage of the Kennington Theatre (after infinite cajolings, and reproaches for having entered in upon something he dared not conclude), related to a young actress of his acquaintance, an amusing trifle concerning a Bath Room and a Hole. 'Oh, no! ... No! ... Shut up! ... No!' ejaculated the young actress, all the time, as she listened.

And at the end of it, just before she went on and said, 'Where is my *Daddy*? *What* have you done to my Daddy? *Where* have you taken him?' – (for she was that type of juvenile actress, and it was that type of play) – 'Well,' she said to her friend. 'I'd've never believed it, my dear. Of course, I knew they both *Drink* – like *Fishes* – *she* does, anyway – but I'd never heard *That* ...'

7

And it was the next morning, that the same young actress, while changing her shoes at the club, was heard to remark, in a loud and decisive voice: 'Well, I don't know how one can *expect* to act, if one does such peculiar things.'

She was putting herself in the position of such a one as Jackie Mortimer. The last-named entered the room at the moment, and heard the remark.

The young actress began to hum.

Also there were various relieved pantings, puttings of hands upon breasts, liftings of eyes to Heavens, when this young actress got outside the room with the friend to whom she had made the remark.

'My *dear*? . . .'

8

The final touch to the thing was not given, however, until about a month later, and then in a conversation between Mrs Player and a certain Mr Goddely. This took place on the identical spot (on the lawn overlooking the courts) at which Mrs Player had herself originated discussion of Jackie.

Mrs Player spent a great deal of her time here with Mr Goddely. Mr Goddely was one of the original founders of the club, a retired army man, and a particular friend of Mrs Player, with whom he discussed India. That is, they did not really discuss India, but they reviled Mrs Besant and hurled names of delightful people who used to be in India at each other's heads for hours on end, and, except when they tried to speak Hindustani to each other, kept their tempers very well. But when they tried to talk Hindustani to each other, they were not at peace: because neither of them could make out one word of what the other was talking about, and they became glassy-eyed. Their combination on the lawn, however, was a credit to the club.

'Then who's the four,' asked Mr Goddely, 'playing up there in the second court from the end?'

'Oh. Them,' said Mrs Player. 'I don't know. One of them's Jackie Mortimer, isn't it?'

'Oh, yes.'

'"The Knocking at the Gate", you know.'

'Oh, yes. I've heard of her.' There was a silence.

'Yes,' said Mrs Player, and there was another, and inviting, silence . . .

Mr Goddely handled it cleverly.

'She's not very popular round here, is she?' asked Mr Goddely.

'No,' said Mrs Player. 'I don't think she is . . .'

It was now up to Mr Goddely . . . But being aware of something being expected of him, he lost his nerve, and remained in silence. The lady had to speak.

'Of course one simply can't believe in *half* these stories,' said Mrs Player . . .

'No, no,' said Mr Goddely . . .

'No,' said Mr Goddely about ten seconds later . . .

'But one does hear such Extremely Unpleasant Things,' said Mrs Player.

Mr Goddely nodded.

'I mean, *doesn't* one?' asked Mrs Player, appealingly.

'Oh, very much so, very much so,' said Mr Goddely.

'And I mean,' said Mrs Player, 'it's obvious that there can't be any Smoke without Fire – can there?'

That was how it had appealed to Mr Goddely.

Chapter Ten

MR MARSDEN PRODUCES

1

In October of this year, the fearful and uncompromising warning 'LAST WEEKS' was pasted hysterically across the posters of 'The Knocking at the Gate': you had a vision of an improvident London populace scampering in Gadarene-like haste to the Coburg Theatre: and in a fortnight the play was off. The management had lost not more than fifteen hundred pounds on the entire production, which was just about the sum that Richard had taken away from it. It was then taken out on the road by Mr Grayson, who called it a Popular London Success, beseeched the north and south of England to Hear What the London Critics Said, swore (in a fanatical spirit) that it came Straight from the Coburg Theatre, London, and fell into the excessively severe financial quandaries besetting all reformers and enthusiasts.

Jackie was only a month out of work – her next engagement being with Mr Marsden at the 'Barnstormer' Theatre.

Jackie did not see so much of Mr Marsden now, but this was more her fault than his. They had not quarrelled, of course, over her alliance with Richard. They could not do so. An appeal, barely necessary, to the academy, would have at once established that Mr Marsden Happened to be one of those People who Greatly Believed in Minding their own Business and Not Poking their Noses into Other People's Concerns. This needed no reaffirming. Nevertheless, it was possible, Jackie found, to be virtuous in this respect to a fault. It was possible, indeed, so keenly Not to Poke your Nose into Other People's Concerns, as to ask People out to lunch three times a week purely in order Not to. Jackie often wished that Mr Marsden wouldn't not poke his nose into her concerns such a lot, for she really felt that it was not his business not to.

'There is a certain (what shall I call it?) reticence about you at times, Jacqueline,' said Mr Marsden.

The play which Mr Marsden was about to produce at the 'Barnstormer' Theatre was called 'The Woman of Temperament', and it had been translated from the French by Mr Marsden. This is neither a very clever nor very difficult thing to do, but in conjunction with his monocle, and double-wound bow-tie, accumulated for him a certain prestige. Which prestige was added to by the imprint (as it were) of the 'Barnstormer' Theatre. The 'Barnstormer' had been gaining prestige ever since its inauguration three years ago. This it had done principally by being a Mission Hall in the first place, and subsidiarily by a sharing system amongst the actors playing there, no orchestra, an air of a rather nice Maidenhead moving-picture place, and a far situation in Hampstead, only approachable by enthusiasts . . . From such causes it had become a prevalent rumour that the management was not working In the theatre so much as For the theatre. Jackie was coming across a lot of people who were working For the theatre, these days. The Rockingham Hard Court Tennis Club was all For the theatre, and so was Mr Marsden. (It will be remembered that it was his God.)

But Jackie, who knew her Tennis Club, and knew her Mr Marsden, and knew her 'The Woman of Temperament', and who had no very great taste or admiration for any of them, rather resented this altruism. *In* the theatre, if you like, thought Jackie, but not For the theatre, please.

Indeed, Jackie had lost some of her desire to get in touch with her profession, by now. Instead, she was beginning to be rather afraid that she had done so.

2

'The Woman of Temperament' was one of those weighted dramas in which a gentleman ends (after really hideous provocation; in calling a lady a Harlot. Which, causes her to stagger, as though she has been struck, and no wonder either. Or if he does not call her a Harlot, then he says that there is Only One Name for her, and any shrewd London audience knows what *that* means. It means that she is a Harlot, and she reels just the same. Her only retaliation is that all these years he has made her his Belonging, which is the sort of thing he should most decidedly *not* have made her.

And in the middle of this type of drama, which enacts itself in private rooms or public lounges of enormous hotels in Mentone (three years later), one young person tells another young person, very slowly, and looking most miserably at a non-existent wall, that it is because she loves him – because she *really* loves him – she is Sending him Away ... And he froths off in high dudgeon, and there is clearly not much left in life for the young person ...

This type of drama naturally gives ample scope for those in the theatre self-sacrificially For the theatre, and those associated with Mr Marsden in this venture were all on the side of the angels ...

His leading lady, in fact, was unexceptionable in this respect, being (it was rumoured) not only the divorced wife of a Russian Aristocrat (whatever that may have meant), but bearing the name of Jenya Poyoleff, and having the reputation of having acquired her reputation in Moscow and Berlin. Moscow and Berlin meant very little to Jackie, for she knew little of either place, but she was aware that these centres, so far as the theatre was concerned, presupposed altruism. Also Miss Jenya Poyoleff excelled in her Godfather, who had been King Leopold of Belgium. This caused a great stir. The rich shadow of the monarch overhung the entire production.

The rest of the cast, which was a small one, included Mr Percy Natton, Mr Robert Loade, Miss Janet Logan, and Mr Earle Scott, and a few others. Of these, Mr Natton resembled a clean-shaven butcher, and had indeed been one – Mr Loade was a self-effacing gentleman of enormous height and razor-like thinness who had been to America (but disapproved of it) – Miss Janet Logan was a rather pretty young girl who had never had a job before, and Mr Earle Scott was a wavy-haired, golden young juvenile, who spoke with a lisp and kept his head in one steady, fixed, embarrassed position, as though the beautiful thing might at any moment come off.

But from these and Jackie there was no danger of eclipse for Miss Poyoleff. There would have been no danger of eclipse for her anywhere. She spread her invincible personality about. The company watched her from sly corners, as she lolled about on the set during rehearsals. She filled the stage as she sat there. You were seeing something. There, in the flesh, was Jenya Poyoleff – her legs languidly crossed, her voice coming lethargically from her regal throat, the smoke from her cigarette going up into the air, and her Godfather – all the time, and even as you watched her – being King Leopold of Belgium.

3

It was a peaceful production, for the most part.

'But – but she is charming,' said Miss Poyoleff of Jackie.

Miss Poyoleff did not say this because some one had accused Jackie of not being charming, but merely because she belonged to the But school of conversationalists. 'But she is quite too fresh and pretty, is she not?' Miss Poyoleff would ask, when Jackie had excelled herself. Or, 'But the little English thing is shaping excellently – No?' (She was also a member of the No school of conversationalists.) She made laborious subterranean attempts to have Jackie removed from the cast, but failed.

It was not, of course, an entirely peaceful production. Mr Marsden, as producer, was the victim of two very distressing scenes. The first of these was caused by Miss Janet Logan, the young girl in her first part, who, on the fifth day of rehearsal, infuriated Mr Marsden by her obtuseness. Which obtuseness manifested itself in an inability to pronounce the line 'Really, this is impossible 'in the manner in which Mr Marsden desired it to be pronounced.

'Now let's have that again,' said Mr Marsden, looking a trifle severe. 'Really – this is impossible.'

'Really, this is impossible,' said Miss Logan.

'No,' said Mr Marsden, with patience. 'Not Really, this is impossible. *Really* – this is impossible.'

'Really,' said Miss Logan. 'This is impossible.'

'*Really,* this is impossible,' said Mr Marsden.

'Really, this is impossible,' said Miss Logan.

'*Really*,' said Mr Marsden, 'this is impossible.'

'*Really*,' said Miss Logan, 'this is *impossible*'

There was a pause.

Mr Marsden took a breath.

'*Really* – this is impossible,' said Mr Marsden.

'Really, this is impossible.'

'My God!' cried Mr Marsden. 'Now you're saying Really this is impossible!'

'Oh, I'm sorry,' said Miss Logan. 'I thought I was saying Really this is impossible.'

'May I ask,' cried Mr Marsden, 'whether you're trying to say Really this is impossible or Really this is impossible?'

'I'm trying to say Really this is impossible.'

'Oh,' said Mr Marsden. 'Then why don't you say it?'

'I am. I said Really this is impossible.'

There was a pause.

'Let's start again, shall we?' said Mr Marsden.

'Yes,' said Miss Logan.

Mr Marsden took another deep breath. 'Really—' began Mr Marsden.

'Sorry,' said Miss Logan, parenthetically.

'What?' asked Mr Marsden.

'I only said I was sorry.'

'Oh,' said Mr Marsden.

They looked at each other.

'*Really*,' said Mr Marsden, leaning forward. 'This is impossible.' Miss Logan leaned backwards.

'*Really*,' returned Miss Logan, leaning forward. 'This is *impossible*.'

'*Really* this is impossible,' said Mr Marsden.

'Really, this is impossible,' said Miss Logan.

'*Really*. This is impossible.'

'Really, this is impossible.'

The couple, now resembling two very energetic persons at a giant double saw, swaying forwards and backwards in unison, paused to rest.

'*Really*. This is impossible.'

'Really. This is impossible.'

'*Really*. This is impossible!'

'Really. This is impossible.'

The situation having now become, really, impossible Mr Marsden made an error. He forgot the play, and clenching both hands, and lifting his eyes to heaven, alluded to the situation.

'Really!' declared Mr Marsden, with conviction. 'This is impossible!' He turned away.

Miss Logan thought she could do this.

'Really,' said Miss Logan. 'This is impossible.'

They again looked at each other.

'Is that right?' asked Miss Logan.

'No. It is not. Let's start afresh.' Mr Marsden now changed his tactics, and tried to stress his 'impossible'.

'Really,' said Mr Marsden. 'This is *impossible*.'

'*Really*, this is impossible.'

There was a heavy silence.

Mr Marsden now placed himself in the wrong.

'REALLY!' bellowed Mr Marsden. 'THIS – IS – IM – POSSY – BULL!'

Miss Logan also had a temper.

'REALLY!' rejoined Miss Logan. 'THIS – IS – IM – POSSY – BULL!'

'Thank you,' said Mr Marsden, but he was speaking ironically.

The other occasion upon which Mr Marsden was led into an exhibition of spleen was on the ninth day of rehearsal, when Mr Marsden, taking it into his head to have an extra chair upon the stage, quietly bagged one that he had discovered in the prompt corner, and innocently continued the rehearsal.

In doing this he offended the susceptibilities of the theatre carpenter and general factotum, Mr Crabbe (a man of great distinction in this actual theatre), who had taken a furious dislike to Mr Marsden already, and who had had orders from his own immediate employer that this chair was not to be moved.

Mr Crabbe, therefore, at the earliest opportunity, and with a view to saving discussion, had quietly come forward and returned it to its place.

Which self-reliant action, taking place unobserved by Mr Marsden, caused some mystification in that producer five minutes afterwards. He had no difficulty in finding the chair again, however, and again placed it on the stage.

Which equally self-reliant action was not unobserved by Mr Crabbe, who, after the polite lapse of another five minutes, and taking advantage of a moment when he thought Mr Marsden was not looking, again walked away with it.

Which intensely impertinent action, being watched from the corner of Mr Marsden's eye, caused that gentleman to come forward, with some firmness, and to place it stoically upon the stage.

Mr Crabbe being downstairs at this moment, on other business, the rehearsal was allowed to continue for a full quarter of an hour, and Mr Marsden went and sat down in the stalls. At the end of which period, and during a most affecting moment in the drama, a figure emerged from the wings, and quietly removed a chair.

Whereat Mr Marsden, jumping up from the stalls, very violently replaced a chair, and jumped down again.

Whereat, after the lapse of two minutes, a figure emerged from the wings and removed a chair.

Whereat Mr Marsden jumped up and replaced a chair.

Whereat, barely a moment after Mr Marsden had reached the stalls again, a figure came forth and removed a chair.

At which it seemed that something of a deadlock had been reached.

There was, however, one expedient left to Mr Marsden. He could jump up and replace this chair. He availed himself of this. The company looked slightly baffled. '*Please* go on. Don't take any notice,' said Mr Marsden to the company.

But there was, unhappily, a similar expedient open to Mr Crabbe. He also made use of it.

At which Mr Marsden spoke.

'Will you kindly leave that chair alone?' asked Mr Marsden.

'You can't 'ave *this* chair, Mr Marsden,' said Mr Crabbe. 'Mr Bringham said it wasn't to be moved.'

'Will you kindly put that chair back?' asked Mr Marsden.

'No, Mr Marsden. Mr Bringham said it wasn't to be moved.'

'Will you kindly obey my orders and put that chair back?' said Mr Marsden.

'I take my orders from Mr Bringham, Mr Marsden.'

'See here, my man, put that chair back, or there'll be trouble for you!' said Mr Marsden.

'Oo you calling "my man"?' asked Mr Crabbe, offensively.

'*I'm* calling you my man!' cried Mr Marsden, arrogantly, and he jumped up upon the stage.

'Oo you bloody well calling "my man"?' asked Mr Crabbe.

The antagonists glared into each other's eyes, and there was a pause.

'There's no need to Get Sanguinary,' said Mr Marsden, measuredly, and holding his opponent's eye with a reproachful and deadly look.

'Oo you calling "my man"?' said Mr Crabbe, but his voice was drowned in that of Mr Marsden.

'There's no NEED to get SANGUINARY!' bellowed Mr Marsden.

There was a hideous silence.

'Oo you calling—'

'NO EARTHLY NEED TO GET SANGUINARY!' thundered Mr Marsden.

There was another hideous silence.

'You happen to be amongst gentlepeople,' muttered Mr Marsden.

'Oh, *do* I, indeed?'

'You HAPPEN,' repeated Mr Marsden, in measured tones, 'to be amongst GENTLEPEOPLE!'

Mr Crabbe did not reply to this, but glared a great deal.

'Not used to it, I fear,' said Mr Marsden, with a bitter sneer.

'Not used to gentlepeople?' asked Mr Crabbe, defiantly.

'Not USED to it, I FEAR!' thundered Mr Marsden.

Mr Crabbe succumbed. 'Well, you wait and 'ear what Mr Bringham says, that's all,' he said.

'Not used to it, I fear!' said Mr Marsden, with a derisive laugh, and he turned away.

'You just wait till Mr Bringham comes along, then,' said Mr Crabbe, and walked off the stage.

'Not used to it, I fear!' muttered Mr Marsden, pacing up and down, in a sinister manner.

The company stared submissively at Mr Marsden.

'Come. We've had enough of this,' he said. 'The rehearsal's finished. We'll start again this afternoon, at half-past two.'

The company dispersed.

Shortly afterwards Jackie encountered Mr Marsden in a passage.

'Well, thank God,' said Mr Marsden, smiling grimly, 'that whatever else, one can at least Preserve one's Sense of Humour.'

Chapter Eleven

TEMPERAMENT

1

'THE WOMAN OF TEMPERAMENT'S' first night obtained a mild reception, and the translator, having stood palely trembling for some time in the wings, felt justified in coming forward and making a speech. Mr Marsden said that he could Only say Thank you, but succeeded in only saying this for a period of five minutes without stoppage. The members of the audience were rather vague as to what he was thanking them about, but felt sure they had done something very pretty, and thanked him back with their hands.

The play was only booked to run a week at the 'Barnstormer' – it being hoped that it would soon afterwards find a home in Town. But it did not do this. It came off on Saturday and was never heard of again. The labour of the rehearsals took on an ineffectual aspect. Mr Marsden had lost his temper for nothing.

2

Jackie, however, was lucky enough to get another engagement almost immediately afterwards, and again at the 'Barnstormer' Theatre. This she did through the influence of Mr Bringham, who had taken a fancy to her performances.

The new show was entitled 'North', dealt with mounted policemen in another continent, and was produced by Mr John Grashion, a young American, who also took the leading part. This show also came off at the end of the week and was never heard of again.

Mr Grashion's producing technique was unlike any Jackie had encountered so far. His method was rapturous praise for all and everything, tempered by palpitating suggestions of his own. Only his suggestions were not corrections – merely blissful inspirations for improving the almost unimprovable. And the word 'Bully' was Mr Grashion's medium of joy.

'That's Bully!' Mr Grashion would cry. 'That's jes' Bully! ... Keep it like that, old boy – keep it like that! ... Don't budge an inch! ... That's jes' Bully! ... Of course, if you *cared* to take it a Bit quicker, old boy, it *might* improve it just a *weeny* bit ... But don't trouble, old boy; it's Bully.

Jes' Bully! ... And if you *could* face the audience a little more towards the end of that long speech, it might look better, just from the *front*, as it were, old boy. But I don't want to worry you. It's Bully ...'

'It's all right, then?' he would be asked.

'All right, old boy? All right! It's Bully. It's jes' Bully! Of course, we'll have to find some business for you while you're watching him speak. You're looking a bit lost just for a moment or two. But you can easily work something out, can't you? And otherwise it's fine – *fine*!'

There would be a pause.

'Now let's have *all* that again,' Mr Grashion would add, with a sweep of his hand. 'It's Bully. Jes' Bully.'

Jackie's performance was described as Bully.

3

It was in this show that Jackie made her first acquaintance with what she believed was called Temperament. This was provided by Mr Richard Leggitt, a very clever young actor of about thirty-five, who had lately risen to some fame and popularity within the circle of the play-going public.

Mr Leggitt, on the sixth day of rehearsal, and during a scene of grave moment and excitement, all at once threw up his hands, lifted his eyes to heaven, clasped his head, and paced over to the other side of the stage.

Here was an interested silence.

'What's the matter, old boy?' asked Mr Grashion, with humility.

'It's all right, old boy,' said Mr Leggitt. 'It's quite all right. I can't act, that's all. I can't act.'

'Why, old boy,' said Mr Grashion, 'I thought it was bully.'

Mr Leggitt did not reply to this, but paced up and down with his hands clasped behind his back, and his eyes cast upwards, as one who suffers in his stomach.

'Nothing to worry about in *that*, old boy,' said Mr Grashion.

'It's quite all right,' said Mr Leggitt, waving Mr Grashion's helpfulness aside with his hand. 'I've merely forgotten how to act. Just forgotten. That's all it is.'

The stage-manager said that he personally thought that Mr Leggitt had been acting better than ever, and the rest of the company diffidently grunted an endorsement.

There was a long pause.

'It's just Temperament, that's all,' said the stage-manager, reassuringly ...

'It's quite all right,' said Mr Leggitt, looking at the floor, and speaking to himself. 'I simply cannot *Act*. I simply *Can – Not – Act*. It's quite all right.'

They were clearly not to worry. It was, if anything, rather nicer not to be able to act, than to be able to. There was no cause for alarm on his behalf.

Time passed.

'What's that damn line?' asked Mr Leggitt.

The rehearsal proceeded.

This, however, was not the sole glimpse of Temperament afforded to Jackie during this show. Mr Grashion was also attacked. The company was not to worry about Mr Grashion, either. He Simply Could not Remember a line. That was all. It was quite all right.

He put his head in his hands, as he sat in the chair.

'Why not give it up, old boy?' asked Mr Leggitt.

For a long time Mr Grashion did not reply.

'Just want to cry,' murmured Mr Grashion at last, in a husky voice, from his hands ...

'Come along, old boy, give it up.'

'Jus' cry,' murmured Mr Grashion. 'Sit 'n weep ...'

'Now then, old boy.'

Mr Grashion rubbed his hands with his eyes, like a sleeper casting off a dream, looked around vaguely, murmured 'Forgive me all you people,' and plunged his head into his hands again. He emitted a sob.

A Breakdown, obviously. Mr Leggitt now spoke a trifle less kindly. This was not only because Mr Leggitt had half intended to have a Breakdown himself, a little later, and had now, through delay, let some one else get in first: it was also because he felt that in any case Mr Grashion was poaching upon his own temperamental preserves. He had, indeed, an annoyed feeling that Mr Grashion was cribbing.

'Well, old boy,' he said. 'If you won't come off ...'

Mr Grashion, detecting annoyance in his friend's voice, spitefully decided to go on with his Breakdown. He was aware, in his heart of hearts, that he was cribbing, but was sure he could do as well as Mr Leggitt when once he got started. He therefore sprang to his feet.

'Take it away!' he cried. 'For God's sake take it all away!'

He was alluding to the theatre in general. A truly awful moment. To such can hysteria reduce a man.

Breathing hard, he was led off by Mr Leggitt and the stage-manager. He put his wrists together as they urged him along, vaguely confusing himself with a condemned criminal, and feeling the lack of handcuffs.

Chapter Twelve

THE NIGHT

1

And then, with amazing suddenness, the whole of Jackie and Richard's routine was changed, and they were packing up to go on tour again. They were going out in a domestic drama called 'The Chatterers', which was being backed by its author, Mr H. L. Crawley, who wished Jackie and Richard to play the leading parts. Mr Crawley, a quiet little man with the knack of successful plays, had a great admiration for Jackie and Richard, whom (he declared) he hoped to see one day established as the English Guitrys. He himself, indeed, desired to aid them towards that achievement. Richard and Jackie thought it would be rather a good idea to be the English Guitrys – provided some one was going to pay for it – (and the cost, they believed, would be enormous) – and they accepted Mr Crawley's offer with some scepticism but little hesitation.

'The Chatterers' was first to visit Sheffield, and then Birmingham, and then Manchester, and then Edinburgh, and then Aberdeen – and then it was to come to Town.

But Jackie and Richard never got farther than Sheffield.

2

That last night, in their Kensington flat, was crowned with a sweet peace and nearness to each other such as Jackie, ever afterwards, did not dare recall. It was almost as if they knew. They sat over the fire, as on their first night together, and they did nothing but talk. She sat on the floor, and held his knees, and prodded the soft parts of the coal with the poker (a passion of hers), and watched the flames playing over his warm and contented face. And every now and again he would kiss her, and then she would go on prodding . . .

And at a quarter past eleven, just as they were going to bed, they had a great surprise. The little bell rang, scaring them out of their wits.

'Burglars!' whispered Jackie.

But it wasn't Burglars, as Jackie, if she had only thought for a moment, would have realized, and as a dressing-gowned Richard went downstairs to demonstrate. It was Charles.

He had only arrived in London that night, and was full of explanations for the late call (he was off to Brussels for a holiday to-morrow), and the fire was restarted, and the drinks were got out, and they all stayed up till half-past twelve.

A strange but cheerful trio, at the top of a Kensington flat at midnight. There was a kind of spell over that night, Jackie thought afterwards. And it seemed that Charles, too, in some magic way, was aware of its enchantment and curiousness, and was aware of what was to befall. She noticed how he kept on looking about him, at the furnishings, the pictures, at the whole flat, and most strangely, and in a rather too prolonged way, at herself and Richard. He knew, too, though it was quite impossible to know.

But she thought all this afterwards. She was very happy on this night. And when Charles went (he insisted on going), they went upstairs laughing and calling to each other, and having a great deal of fun.

3

But at half-past three that morning another curious thing happened.

Jackie awoke. She never awoke at this time. Half-past six was her time for waking.

Richard's bed was the other side of the room, by the window. In the blank darkness she listened for his breathing.

She was puzzled because she could not hear it. She looked over in his direction. He was not sleeping at all. There glowed through the darkness the fiery little point of his cigarette.

She was frozen with surprise – almost terror. She dared not speak or move ... How little she knew of him! Cigarettes in the small hours!

The silence was complete. He gave a little quiet cough, and all was black quiet again ... Strange, that he should never have told her that he did this sort of thing. She felt, for a moment, as though a kind of estrangement had come between them ...

What was he thinking about – at this moment? Abysses in his character opened up before her. She would ask him in the morning. It would be rather fun. She turned over and went to sleep.

Chapter Thirteen

RICHARD

1

The thing began, during the matinée on Wednesday afternoon at Sheffield, with flirtation.

'And how's my Richard?' asked Jackie. She had just come off (to an agreeable little round of applause) and had seen him standing, with his hands in his pockets, against a flat.

It was his point of honour to be fractious when he met her coming off.

'Extremely Ill,' he said.

'Ill?' said Jackie. 'I'm very sorry to hear that, Richard.'

'Extremely Ill,' he repeated. 'At Death's Door.'

'Very well, then, Richard. You must see a *doctor*.'

'I won't.'

'But you *must* see a doctor if you're at Death's Door, Richard.'

'I won't.'

'But, Richard, you *must*.' And then, in the old manner:

'But you're not *really* Extremely Ill, are you, Richard?'

It was here that it began.

'No, darling,' he said. 'I'm all right.'

She looked up in amazement. Who on earth had said that he wasn't all right? He was looking away.

She had to go on again, at this moment, and she forgot about it.

2

They came out of the stage door together at half-past five. He took her arm.

'Well, Richard darling, where are we going to have our tea?'

'Where does my darling want her tea?'

'Well, *she* wants to have it at a hotel.'

'Very well, then, she shall.'

They walked on.

'What about going home, though, Jackie? Don't you think it'd be better? . . . Sort of freshen up?'

'No,' said Jackie, firmly. 'I want it at a *hotel*.'

'Very well, then, dear, you shall *have* it at your old hotel.'

Your 'old' hotel? She immediately detected the flaw in

his good-humoured idiom, and looked up. She found him smiling awkwardly to himself. She had never known him smile to himself.

'Richard, dear? Do you *want* to go back?'

'No, darling. Let's go to the hotel.'

'No; but, Richard, I believe you really want to go back.'

'No, dear. I only thought we might sort of freshen up for the show this evening.'

'We'll go back, darling.'

'No, dear, let's go to the hotel. I'm all right, really.'

Who, in heaven's name, thought Jackie again, had said that he wasn't all right?

'Richard, dear? Aren't you feeling well?'

'Absolutely. Come on. We'll go to our hotel.'

'Darling, you're not feeling well. What's the matter? You look all right. What's the matter?'

'No, I'm all right, Jackie darling. Only a bit of a chill.'

'A bit of a chill?'

'Yes.'

'What does it feel like?'

'Sort of all cold. Come on, dear. It's nothing.'

'We're going back, Richard. Come on. We'll take a tram.'

She guided him in that direction, and he made no demur.

'I wish you hadn't got to go on to-night, Richard,' she said.

'Don't be mad, darling. I've got to go on.'

(Who, in heaven's name, thought Jackie, had said that he hadn't?)

3

They caught a tram, after some waiting about in the wind ('Go on, put your collar up, Richard,' said Jackie, and he did), and they went clanging up to the top of the town, where their rooms were situated.

These were expensive theatrical diggings, and, for Sheffield, of a high-class nature. They were placed in a rather respectable street adjoining a very foul slum, whence could be heard, all day, the cries of children. And there was a grocery, and a butcher's shop, and a sweet-shop in this slum, and at the sweet-shop the children could obtain toffee-apples and skipping-ropes – both of which were greatly in favour. The rooms themselves were clean, and the dining-room contained innumerable portraits of famous variety stars, affectionately dedicated to the landlady – who was a sinister, tall, thin, widowed character in black (undoubtedly a murderess), who spoke little, and with an air of extreme forbearance and rectitude when she did. Richard and Jackie had already had much fun at her expense.

It was dark by the time they got there, but they soon had their gas alight (a very asthmatic and bright green gas), and poked the fire – and then Jackie went to the top of the stairs to see the landlady about Tea. The landlady said that she had Understood they were not coming back. (She was a great Understander of things.) But she thought something could be Managed. (She was a great Manager, as well.)

When Jackie returned to Richard, she found him sitting back in an arm-chair by the fire.

'Feeling better, darling?' asked Jackie.

And he smiled up, rather wearily, without replying, and she went and sat on the arm of his chair, and stroked his hair.

When the tea came, she would not let him get up, but brought him over a cup by the fire. And then she herself came and sat down on the floor in front of him. And they looked into the flames and did not speak very much.

'I'll tell you what, Jackie,' he said, after a while. 'Suppose I go upstairs and have a little Lie Down?'

'A little Lie Down, Richard?'

'Yes. Sort of freshen me up for the evening. We've got an hour before we need start, haven't we?'

'That's right, Richard. Will you go now?'

'Yes,' he said. And he sprang up, very suddenly . . .

She took his arm as they went up the stairs, and led the way into the bedroom, where they lit a candle. It was very cold.

'You must wrap up,' said Jackie.

'Yes. I'll take off my coat, and get under the quilt thing.'

She took off his coat, and she arranged a pillow for him, and wrapped him round, and kissed him. Then, when the candle was out, she said through the cold darkness: 'Call you in an hour, darling.'

'Right you are, Jackie,' he said.

And she left the room, softly closing the door.

She stirred the fire again, when she got downstairs, and brought a book down to the arm-chair, and tried to read it.

But she did not find herself able to do this. Quite apart from this little accident, there was something troubled, hushed, uneasy over everything to-night. And she had never been left by Richard at this time of evening before. They generally had such fun, and were so noisy together, at this time. And it was quite horrid to think of him lying there, alone in the dark, upstairs.

And then she found herself listening, she did not know why, to the noises in the slum near by – to the cries of the children – to the incessant echoing cries – now loud, now soft – now single and whining, now in sudden chorus – on and on ... And brisk manly footsteps came hurrying past her window, and faded away in the distance ...

And how black and dark was the night outside! She could not see a light from here. Only the reflection of the room in which she was sitting, and the dirty tea-things ... She should pull down the blinds. She had not the energy to get up and pull down the blinds ...

So dark, and yet only six o'clock ... The top of Sheffield at six o'clock ... In her present state there was something frightening in the mere thought of it ... It seemed a wicked Universe which could have arrived at such a thing as the top of Sheffield at six o'clock ... Inexplicable event in time and eternity! A truly mysterious Universe ...

And she, alone in Sheffield – and the only human being

in Sheffield to feel the weight of these mysteries . . . Another pair of feet went hurrying past her window . . .

She was getting nervous. She wished that Richard would come down and say that he was better. When she was in Richard's arms the Universe could do what it liked.

4

She went up ten minutes before the time agreed.

She went over to the bed in the darkness, and said softly: 'Richard.'

There was no answer.

'Richard.'

And he did not reply to that.

'Richard,' she said, more loudly, and struck a match.

With the little tearing noise of the igniting phosphorus, he sat up suddenly, and looked into her eyes.

'Hullo, Jackie,' he said. He seemed dazed. She lit the candle.

'It's nearly time, Richard dear.'

'I've been right off.'

'How are you feeling?'

'Rather foul. I wish I had an understudy.'

She sat on the bed and took his hand. It was wet and clammy. And his face was flushed, now.

'Look here, Richard. You can't go on to-night.'

'Who's going on, then? The stage-manager?'

'Well. Couldn't he?'

He released his hand, and got off the bed.

'Come on, Jackie. It's no use.'

'But you mustn't, Richard, if you're ill. And you're *looking* ill.'

'No, I'm not. I'm better now.' He put on his coat, and kissed her, and led her downstairs.

'Well, we must have a taxi, there and back, that's all,' said Jackie.

'Shouldn't think we could get one.'

She asked the landlady. The landlady had no idea where one could get one.

'Come on, Jackie, we'll be late.'

He had his way.

On their way to the tram, and walking arm in arm (with their spirits slightly improved by the fresh air), he all at once made the most outrageous little sound in his throat. It was a kind of tremulous sob, a swift hiccoughing intaking of breath – as though in sudden horror of something, as though he had seen a spirit.

He smiled weakly at her, after it had happened. It could not pass unnoticed, and there was nothing else to do.

She did not say how horrified she was.

5

She almost forgot about him in the hurry of changing and making up, and the next she saw of him was from the o.p. corner as he acted. She could detect no difference in his performance (his laughs were coming as pat as ever) and the paint hid whatever there was of illness in his face. Only once, during a long speech from his fellow-actor, did his look become slightly strained as he covered his mouth to give a little harsh cough.

'*He's* all right,' thought Jackie.

But because the stage was freezingly cold, she went away to fetch her own cloak to put round him as he came off.

He was trembling a little (but then so was she) as he came off, and he let her put the woman's thing round him without demur. And they stood together, strangely silent, at the back of the set.

The stage-manager passed them as they stood thus. He was an agreeable, smiling, youngish man.

'Wrapping him Up?' asked the stage-manager.

'Yes,' said Jackie, smiling.

And they all three smiled, and were silent.

6

At half-past two next morning Jackie was standing, fully dressed, in the sea-green light cast by the gas of the sitting-room.

She had her back to the fireplace, and she was in the silent presence of a quaint, bowed, bald, common little man, with a white moustache and watery blue eyes. This was Mr Broggen, a permanent lodger in an attic of the house, who had just been out to knock up the doctor. That unknown, unseen, but existing and clearly conceived individual might be along any moment . . .

Downstairs in the kitchen the murderess, dressed in a nightgown and dressing-gown, was making Cocoa for them all.

Upstairs, in the bedroom, Richard was lying, propped up in candle-light (the gas had gone wrong and they could not adjust it), with flaming cheeks, and in the noise set up by the labour of accomplishing forty-five respirations a minute. He was, however, for all the ardour of this, surprisingly comatose.

Jackie could think of nothing to say to Mr Broggen, as they stood there. The little distressed man, hat in hand, gazed with a kind of weak commiseration at the tablecloth . . .

They waited.

7

Jackie told herself to pull herself together as she left the house next morning at half-past ten, on her way to the theatre.

Influenza ... There was nothing the matter with that. The only thing she had not liked had been the doctor's air. 'There's nothing at all *serious*, is there?' she had asked him. 'Oh, dear no, I don't think so,' he had replied, as though the idea had been almost fantastic. She did not like such an idea descending to the plane of the almost fantastic.

And he was, if anything, slightly better this morning. Besides ...

She had an awkward interview in front of her.

There was no one in the company down at the theatre when she arrived (except the carpenter), and she had an unpleasant quarter of an hour waiting about on the cold stage and in the colder passages. But at last there arrived the woman who played the housekeeper (with whom she had a small chat), and then the stage-manager, smiling as ever.

'Well, how are we this morning?' he asked.

'Well,' said Jackie. 'As a matter of fact, I'm afraid I've some rather bad news. My husband's rather ill.'

'Oh, dear. What's the matter?'

'It's a sudden attack of 'flu, I'm afraid. He's been awful last night. We've had the doctor.'

A very great silence fell. The stage-manager looked at the floor.

'Dear, dear, that's bad. Won't he be able to go on tonight, then?'

'No, I'm afraid he won't. He's really too bad. His temperature's something terrible. Is there anyone who can go on for him?'

The stage-manager pulled a wry smile.

'Well, some one'll have to go on, won't they?'

There was a silence.

'You're sure he can't get down?'

'No. I'm afraid he really can't. You see . . . '

There was another silence.

'I'm very sorry,' said Jackie . . .

'Well, it's not your fault, is it?' said the stage-manager. '*You'll* be able to come down all right, won't you?'

'Oh, yes.'

'Oh, well, we'll manage somehow, I expect. I'll have to go on myself.'

There was yet another silence.

'Well, I must be rushing back, I'm afraid,' said Jackie, smiling weakly and moving away. 'You'll tell everybody, won't you?'

'Yes. That's all right.'

'Hope he's better,' said the stage-manager, calling after her.

Jackie smiled again, and left.

Whatever else might be in store for her, there was no sympathy awaiting her in this crisis.

8

That night Jackie played.

The company were full of sympathy for her. 'Tell him he must buck up and get *well*,' said the woman who played the Colonel's wife, and, 'It's this cold stage,' said the woman who played the housekeeper. 'No wonder he caught a cold.'

'He shouldn't have come down last night,' said the rather queer man who played the butler. 'He ought to have stayed in bed.'

Nevertheless, it was all a bit of a lark for them all. It was great fun to see how the stage-manager was going to shape, and all agreed that he did remarkably well.

'You would have thought,' said the woman who played the housekeeper, 'that he'd been playing it ever since we opened.'

'Yes. Isn't he good?' said Jackie.

And, 'Well, I do hope he's better when you get back,' said the same lady, as she smiled Good-bye to Jackie, amid the grind and clatter of almost final trams, just outside the theatre, at half-past eleven.

'I expect he will be,' said Jackie.

9

She had quite believed that he was going to be better when she returned. He was to have smiled weakly at her as

she came in, and the nurse was to have been professionally cheerful.

But he was no better, and the nurse's face was the same.
Jackie might have been absent no more than two minutes,
instead of nearly four hours. There had been no upheaval,
no adventure, in the drama of his illness. It had proceeded
in her absence with all its grim, feebly-lit quiet. The nurse
did not so much as punctuate her duties with a smile, as
Jackie came in.

He was lying there, like a drunkard thrown down,
utterly unconscious, impotent and trusting in the fearful
battle which his heart had been called upon, and had gallantly undertaken, to fight for him.

He was in a state of perpetual climax. Each sharp breath
seemed to be the straining and decisive one, but the decision was never forthcoming . . .

She sat down by the bed and watched him . . . For one
passionate and angered moment she felt that she must
shake him, wake him up, reproach him, plead with him.
She must bring home to him the terrors he was bringing
upon herself and himself. She must tell him where he was,
what was happening, that this was Sheffield, that they were
in rooms on tour. She wanted to tell him, even, that he was
not married to her . . .

Then the night nurse came, whom Jackie did not like so
much as the other. She was an elderly woman, with a slight
cold, and she went about the place sniffing.

10

He was a little better in the morning (the doctor admitted as much), but by three o'clock she was in a panic, and had wired for Charles. She should have done this before. He was still in Brussels, and there was no chance of getting him for another day ...

Presumably she acted that night: but she was conscious of next to nothing of it. She was conscious of the faces of the actors and actresses, apprehensively sympathetic under their chromatic colouring – of the ebullient sea of the audience – and of the orchestra clashing in the intervals. The orchestra clashing, on Richard's last night on earth ... She knew everything now.

And at twenty-past one that night Richard's heart, competent and courageous in the emergency to the last practicable moment, abruptly accepted the fate of the organism for which it conspired, and was still.

Jackie was not in the room at the time, but downstairs in the dining-room, sipping and gulping at a cup of coffee. The nurse ran down the stairs and told her.

She arose, without speaking, and walked straight out of the room. It was not as though she had learnt that the man she loved was dead. It was as though she had been told of some domestic mishap, and was going to rectify it.

She ran firmly up the stairs, with her shoulders held back, and her slim body straight. The pall of her grief was too dense and black for tears or thought. She could see nothing beyond it, and did not try to do so.

She reached his bed, knelt down, covered her head with her arms, felt for his hand, and with the quietness of the dead man himself, was absolutely quiet.

Book Three

THE FAILURE

Chapter One

MOMENTS

1

Twenty to two in the morning, five months later. A train flying through Lancashire at fifty miles an hour, and Jackie huddled surlily in a corner with her eyes closed in disgust. A grey light from the terribly yellow little bulb above, and the roar of the rails, and three young men, in the same company as herself, talking to each other and drinking whisky out of the top of a thermos flask.

Three young men of about thirty – the stage-manager, the A.S.M. and the leading man – Mr Brands, Mr Crewe, and Mr North. The latter, to-morrow night, at half-past nine, will smother Jackie with an alcoholic and cosmetic embrace. They have offered her whisky, but she has smiled and said No.

This is her fourth week with Mr Edward Granger in 'The Reckoning'. Mr Edward Granger, the well-known London actor-manager, who has not been seen in London for over three years, but a great deal in Canada, and South Africa, and the provinces of England (where he is amassing a vast fortune), has heard of Jackie's plight (it is common talk), and employed her in his company, and treated her with very great kindness altogether. She is very grateful to Mr Granger, and Mr Granger is rather grateful to her, for she makes Mr Granger feel large.

But Jackie has no gratitude in her heart at the moment. The three young men are in jovial spirits, and chaffing one another.

'No, honestly, old boy, why don't you write a book?' Mr Brands is saying. Mr Brands is an embarrassed little man, not much good as a good fellow, and given to flattering the leading man. 'That was really jolly good – that bit in that letter there.'

'And come to you for the copy, eh, old man? Come on. Drink up. Drink up.'

'Oh, well, you might do worse, old man. (Thanks, old boy.) But honestly, old boy – why don't you? "The Diary of an Unsuccessful Actor". What about that?'

'The Diary of a *What*?' cry both the other young men, simultaneously, and Mr Brands looks a little sheepish.

There is a gust of laughter in the compartment, and then Mr Crewe comes down.

'My Dear Old Boy! My – Dear – Old – Boy! You have

Dropped it, old boy – this time all right. Poor old North! Poor old boy! Did he ever think he'd be called that!'

'No, old boy. Just a good title, that's all,' says Mr Brands, but Mr Crewe will have none of that.

'You – have – *Dropped*, old boy, *The* Brick! The Pro Verbial *Cube* – of Baked Clay, old chap! I mean I've never heard anything like that. *The* Pro Verbial Cube, old boy, I mean!'

'No, old boy, don't be an ass,' says Mr Brands, but Mr Crewe will have none of that, either.

'*The* Historic *Oblong*, old boy! *The* Identical and Actual *Oblong*! Well I *Never*!'

'No, old boy—'

'I mean Absolutely Ripped it up, old man. I mean you left nothing Undone, old chap. Ruthless, I mean. Poor old North. I don't think he'll ever get over that. Too bad. Cheer up, North, cheer up.'

'No – listen, old man—'

'As an Actor, old chap – doubtless very fine. But for Tact, old fellow … For pure Diplomacy, old man … I mean to say we won't mention Corns, old boy. Nor Sensitive Spots, old man. I mean we actors have our Susceptibilities, you know. I mean one Simply Doesn't, old fellow. Not straight to a fellow's face. Of course it's what we *all* think really, but there are certain Well-defined Limits, if you understand … Oh, that was too good … I say, we're getting up a pace.'

'Be in by two,' says Mr North.

And Jackie listens, and the train roars on, and the time is

ten to two. And she supposes the landlady has got her letter, and she trusts the landlady will be up, and her headache is fearful, and she thinks she has a cold coming on, and she'll take some Aspirin when she gets there, if she hasn't forgot to pack them (which she rather thinks she has) ...

And she is without love or protection in this world. She is utterly desolate, and ill, and alone. But she doesn't care two pins. She will never have another emotion.

She looks at a photographic advertisement of a watering-place in Wales.

2

It is half-past eleven in the morning. Jackie is in the front room of her Margate lodgings, and Little Minnie, her land-lady's daughter, is going to do the Charleston.

There has been a lot of talk about it, and Jackie's land-lady thinks that Jackie wouldn't be half amused, just to see it like.

But Little Minnie, standing there by the door, is Shy. Little Minnie is three feet high, and eats her thumb.

'Now then, dearie,' says Jackie's landlady. 'Show the pretty lady how you do the Charleston. Go along, dearie. Show her! Don't be Shy.'

But Little Minnie continues to eat her thumb.

'Go on, dearie. Do the Charleston. Do the Charleston, dearie.'

But Little Minnie continues to eat her thumb.

'She won't do it, will she?' says Jackie's landlady.

Jackie smiles.

'Go on – like you did it before, dearie ... Oh, you silly girl! Are you Shy of the Lady? She won't eat you. You're Shy of the Lady, aren't you?'

But Little Minnie, not committing herself on this point, continues to eat her thumb.

'Silly little girl,' says Jackie's landlady ...

And then, all at once, and before they are ready, the spirit moves Little Minnie. And Little Minnie's arms are suddenly lifted up, and a strange and awe-inspiring spasm shakes Little Minnie's body, and a hideous silence falls, and Little Minnie's face takes on a horrible smile ... And Little Minnie's legs begin to turn outwards and inwards.

Little Minnie is Doing the Charleston.

'Look! She's doing it! She's doing it!' cries Jackie's land-lady. 'She's doing the Charleston!'

'Oh, *isn't* that good?' says Jackie, with enormous glee. '*Isn't* that good?'

'Go on, dearie. Don't leave off! Go on, dear. Do the Charleston!'

But Little Minnie wouldn't stop the Charleston now, if you asked her.

'That *is* good, isn't it?' says Jackie. 'I'm sure I couldn't do the Charleston like that.'

'Look – she does it just like them, doesn't she?'

'Just,' says Jackie.

Little Minnie suddenly reverts to thumb.

'And *what* did you say the Lady was yesterday, dearie?'

Little Minnie looks flirtatiously at her mother, but does not reply.

'Go on', dear. What did you say?'

Little Minnie pauses. 'Pri,' says Little Minnie.

Pretty! The child has surpassed herself! There is an explosion of laughter and the little thing is bundled out. 'You must come and do the Charleston again before I go,' says Jackie. And then Jackie, by herself again, walks over to the window.

And she stays at the window for a long time, gazing out. And then she comes back to the sofa, and looks at the fire.

And then she puts her head into the cushion, and begins to cry, and tell the cushion things.

'Oh, *why* weren't you here, Richard?' she asks. 'To see Little Minnie do the Charleston? You shouldn't have left me to Little Minnie, Richard. I do hate her so . . .'

And, 'Richard dear, it's my birthday to-day . . . And I'm twenty-seven, Richard dear! I am . . . Oh, Richard, Richard, *Richard*! . . .

3

Sometimes Jackie would wake in the night and wish him back just to round it off. She wanted just one little word of exposition and farewell.

He would come in the dark and be close to her. And, 'That's all right, Richard,' she would say. 'There's nothing to fret about. It was quite wonderful while it lasted, wasn't it? And we got the best out of it. If we'd only known we had such a little time, we might have wasted it less, but it was perfect while it lasted . . . It was a perfect year. Do you realize it was just a year and five months? . . . And it's quite all right, isn't it, Richard?'

And he would say, 'Yes. That's right, Jackie. There's nothing really to regret. It's only over. Good-bye, darling.'

Then, she thought, he could go back, and she could go on. It would be a mere aching tragedy – no worse.

And if he could kiss her, in the dark, once, for the last time . . .

4

But then Jackie was always waking in the dark these days, and it was wearing away her spirit.

She had worries now – even earthly and monetary wor-ries – things which had not touched her before.

And nowadays Jackie's mind would continually revert to the days when she had first arrived in London – to the days when she had come up with all the dignity of her virginity and youth behind her – to the days when life had been too simple for her conquering. And nowadays she would examine that early attitude, and see it for what it was.

And she would see it as one enormous bluff, an astounding optimism which had so far borne her up – a colossal assumption that she was to take the prizes and rare things of life. And had she taken them? No. And was she going to take them? And was there any reason for supposing she was going to take them?

She wished she could recover that early dignity.

And in twelve years' time one would be forty. What did one do then? It was all getting too much for her.

5

It was in the o.p. corner of the stage of the Theatre Royal, Brighton, and at about 10.15 at night, and on the last night of the tour, that Jackie hit upon a temporary solution to life. She would succeed.

She would succeed in this business. She had always meant to do it. Her ambition had been temporarily diverted. Now she would return to it – with renewed vigour and wisdom.

The solution came quite suddenly. She was watching, with wide eyes and a dreamy air, Mr Robert Granger driving his wife round a very tropical-looking hut with a whip.

There was a great deal of cracking and screaming going on, and the audience were looking up with a strained, serious, pince-nez'd, and rather anxious expression, as much as to say Tut Tut, he shouldn't do that (though they knew to what drink led a man, in the tropics).

She would succeed. She would start right again from the beginning and succeed. She would be back at West Kensington to-morrow, and out of work. But she had her art. Yes, she had the right to say that now. She had her art, and could live for that alone.

She would write letters to every manager or producer she knew, and force herself upon London. And she would come to the top.

And when she had got there? . . . She could not answer that . . . But she now had something to work upon. She would use all her forces and die in the attempt.

By the time she had reached this conclusion, Mr Granger, having swallowed (on the mistaken impression that it was whisky) a large tumblerful of what was not, was rolling about, in a painful and arsenical manner, upon the floor. And at this point Jackie was joined by the company's carpenter.

'The Old Gent's Busted himself,' murmured this carpenter to Jackie.

That this carpenter, after having witnessed the Old Gent Bust (even if that was the right word to employ) himself in this way for over fifty nights at the least, should now have the naïveté, the effrontery, the spirit even, to announce, to the leading lady on the last night of the show, that his employer had done it again – was a surprising tiling to Jackie. Nevertheless, Jackie felt a peculiar sympathy arising towards this sardonic carpenter. He had an attitude towards the drama which appealed to her.

'I know,' said Jackie, and smiled at him. He smiled back. He was the most winning carpenter.

She was surprised by that smile. It brought her back to life again. She was one with human kind, after all.

When she had taken her call (and the Saturday applause was reassuringly violent) she ran up to her dressing-room with quite a light air – humming. She was going to succeed.

Chapter Two

THE ASPIRANT

1

Jackie kept her promise to herself when she got back to West Kensington, and in a week's time she had her card in the 'Telegraph' and over a dozen letters written to managers and producers of her acquaintance. Some of these received no reply whatever, others procured examples of the if-anything-comes-along-will-remember school of replies, and others obtained interviews for her.

These interviews were generally fixed for eleven o'clock in the front of a theatre, and they either took place at one o'clock or not at all. There was generally another young woman, rather like yourself, hanging about at these interviews – or else an Apollo-like young man (with a Plum) who at last got very testy and said

Well, *he* had been told he could see Mr So-and-so at eleven *thirty*, and strode away with a very slim waist but manifestations of spleen.

If, however, you succeeded in obtaining precedence over these lounging rivals, you at last found yourself in a small room, where your producer (or whatever he was) would by slow degrees familiarize himself with your hand, look into your eyes, and murmur, '*You* don't want a job. What do *you* want a job for?' Your producer did not say this because he really thought you *didn't* want a job (he knew you would give your soul for one) – but because he was not, at the moment, concentrating upon his profession, but dallying with matters nearer his heart.

Indeed, if he was greatly afflicted in this direction, he would forget himself so far as definitely to kiss you (in a prolonged manner), or, in very severe cases, to express his good-will by a curious tendency to Produce you on the spot – or at least artistically to mould, and make appreciative manual experiments upon, your figure – as though the first steps in production were purely personal, and he really had to see where he was . . .

It was all in the business, and if you were an actress of normal spirit, when you came out from such interviews you rushed pantingly to your nearest friend and exclaimed, 'Oh, my dear, the Embraces!' But if you were a Jackie of life you took a dreary train back home to lunch with a jaundiced outlook on life.

*

432

Not that all Jackie's experiences with producers were of this nature. There was also that type of producer which believed that the Theatrical Profession Happened to be a Business. And this type of producer didn't have Whole Mornings to Waste. And it Knew Actors and Actresses In and Out. And they Knew it Knew Actors and Actresses In and Out, and that was where the trouble lay (for the actors and actresses).

And this type of producer possessed a very telling nose, and much urbanity, but it did not leave off writing when you came into the room. On the contrary it said 'Do take a seat, please,' in a suave voice, as though it was keeping its temper very well this morning, and would continue to do so provided *you* didn't start any calumny. And it went on writing for about fifty seconds ... Then it clipped two bits of paper together ... Which was accompanied by a soft humming noise. Also by 'You're Miss Mortimer, aren't you' – as much as to say 'That's a pretty bad state to have got into – to be Miss *Mortimer*.' You admitted, not without a decent awareness of guilt, that you were. But it didn't follow up your affirmative, because it wasn't quite satisfied about those two bits of paper, which were by now in the little basket on the desk ... Either it thought that they weren't clipped together properly, or else that they weren't quite the right bits of paper to put in that basket – at any rate, it was sure something was wrong, and it picked them up and glanced over them suspendedly – lifting up the top bit, running its eyes down the bottom bit, and fiddling about until it was satisfied, when it tossed them back again. All this was keeping you waiting, of course; but being, by now, a confessed criminal, you obviously did not deserve much consideration. At last, however, in the same suave voice, and sharpening its pencil, 'Is there anything I can do for *you*?' it asked.

You only wanted to know, really, if it Had anything for you.

It rested its elbows on its chair, and joined its middle fingers. There was a silence.

It wanted to be let see – what had you been doing lately?

You stated your latter engagements.

Oh, you weren't HAZEL Mortimer, were you?

No. You didn't know anything about Hazel Mortimer ...

Oh. It thought perhaps you were Hazel Mortimer. It had been getting confused. Of course *she* was pure Legitimate, wasn't she?

So were you.

Oh, you WERE?

Yes. You were.

But by now it was getting rather dissatisfied about other bits of paper on its desk, and was picking them up and putting them down right and left, as though it had lost its paper-knife. It continued to talk, vaguely, while it did this, and then, suddenly alighting upon the most important piece of paper in the world, commenced to Stamp. This was done with a little rubber handle, which produced a very half-hearted mauve lettering, but which demonstrated, beyond the last growlings of Doubt, that the Theatrical Profession Happened to be a Business. There it was Happening to be it. It was a positive Post Office of a profession.

Well (stamp), it said, there certainly wasn't anything going around just now. It wanted to be let see – 'The Knocking at the Gate' you had said? (Stamp.)

You had.

Had you got (stamp) any programmes of that?

Felon that you were, you at last showed a little stiffness at this. No, you didn't think you had.

Your stiffness was not unobserved. (*This* was a curious bit of paper to find on one's desk! Stamp-stamp!)

Such a thing would be useful, it said.

You hadn't thought that such a thing would be necessary.

And some cuttings, too, would be useful, really . . .

You rose. Well, then, there wasn't anything doing just at present?

It had the grace to rise as well, and take your hand. No – but it would remember you if anything came along. Would you give your address in to the girl downstairs? You knew her room, didn't you? Good morning.

It was back at its desk before you had shut the door.

The whole result being that, by the time you had given in your address to the girl, who was prejudiced against taking down such a loathsome address from the beginning, but could not help herself – and by the time you were out in the street, you were alluding vulgarly to this type of producer's shows as Dirty shows, and asseverating (in the same low form of speech) that you would not enter them if you were given Two Hundred Pounds. But you knew, unhappily, that they were actually very desirable shows, and that even if so many as £195 were subtracted from your idiomatic amount, and you were given the chance, you would be in them like a shot.

2

After various experiences of this nature, and various other experiences wherein she found herself in stage-door passages with five or six young women of the same age and appearance, and the same manner of looking at their wrist-watches with serious doubt as to whether they could go on waiting about for the same interview for the same part as Jackie herself was seeking – and after various other experiences still, when, on being so lucky as to obtain intercourse with one of the dozen or so actor-managers of established repute in London, she was treated with the utmost deference, sweetness, and consideration, but a lack of optimism – Jackie found herself losing heart in her letter-writing, and made a concentrated attack upon the agents.

She did not, however, do any better with the agents than she had done with the producers. She tried them all. From the lowest kind of agent, at whose offices she would be kept waiting in a sparsely furnished outer room with a mumbling crowd of defeated professionals who said that it really wasn't worth their while, and of course they wouldn't dream of doing it under Fifteen, and it Knocked them Flat (old boy) and poor old Johnnie was trying to Touch them for five bob again (just as though they were defeated professionals in rather bad fiction) – up to the highest and newest kind of agent, who made appointments with you, but could afford not to keep them. Also she visited various female and peculiar agents, who dwelt in Gloucester Road, or thereabouts, and asked you if you had Done Anything of This Sort Before.

She kept her patience very well. Only once, in an interview with the Mulligan agency, did she nearly give way. She was seen, not by Mr Mulligan himself, but by an extremely pretty young chit of about seventeen years of age who dwelt in a middle room. This young chit was at the top of her profession, Mr Mulligan being the best-known (theatrically) and most influential of agents at this time, and it being the business of this young chit to keep people at a distance from Mr Mulligan.

She was discovered, by Jackie, seated at a desk, at the far end of the room. She did not get up when Jackie entered, but wheeled round, smiling majestically but forgivingly, and indicating a chair.

'And what can I do for you?' she asked, joining her middle fingers (like the rest of them), and looking with courteous interest at her visitor.

'Well, I'm just looking for work, really,' said Jackie.

'Oh, yes. Now, let me see. I'm sure I know your work . . .'

She screwed up her eyes and looked at the ceiling. 'What *were* you in last?'

'I've been with Robert Granger lately.'

'Oh, yes. But there was something before that … Weren't you in one of your husband's plays?'

'I was in "The Knocking at the Gate" – yes.'

'Oh, yes.' She glanced at Jackie, held the arms of her chair, and gazed at her desk. 'I thought so … Well … I don't know at all …'

There was a long silence as the child gazed at her desk, not knowing at all …

'Been up to the Greshams,' she suggested at last.

'No. I was told they were full up.'

'Yes – but you never know what they may be doing … Let me see, now … I – don't – know … You might try Strickland, of course, mightn't you? Have you tried him?'

'No. I haven't.'

'He might be worth trying.' She looked up, and her smile again forgave Jackie.

'I'll go up there, then,' said Jackie.

'Yes. You might do worse than that … Yes … Well … Well, that's all I can really think of for the moment. Of course, we'll put you down, and let you know if anything comes in.'

She switched a brief, more than usually tolerant, and utterly dismissing smile upon Jackie, and without another word, took up her pen, referred to a paper, and commenced to write. 'Thank you,' she murmured …

The interview was closed.

An incredulous Jackie was therefore left to get up by herself and walk to the door.

'Good morning,' said Jackie, at the door.

But the interview being already closed, this was rather pointless, and the rejoinder came tartly.

'Good morning,' she said, and naturally did not turn round, or leave off writing.

3

It was shortly after this episode, and in the twelfth month of her new attack upon London, and in the small hours of the morning (a very cold and dark one) – that Jackie decided to plunge her little legacy from Lady Perrin, which she had kept intact all these years, into theatrical speculation.

This she did partially because she thrilled (in those small hours) to the gamble of it, partially because she had become twenty-eight one day, partially because her spirit could not sustain unemployment and rebuff any longer, but mostly because she would be able, with money behind her, to walk straight through, at a given time, into Mr Mulligan's office, give a light nod to the chit on the way in, and another light nod on the way out, having spent the meanwhile discussing high finance behind a closed door.

A closed door and portentous financial mumblings for the chit, and just a light nod . . .

Chapter Three

LUNCHES

1

It was at this period that she had a rather strained little passage with Charles. It took place at lunch. He very often came up from Southshore and took her out to lunch nowadays, and they were very friendly indeed with each other.

This particular lunch, however, was the last one she was to have with him before he went to Australia. He was going there to play cricket for his country. It was a very great delight to be seen in public with the brown marvel. She was conscious of participating in history.

'Are they engaged, then?' said Jackie, speaking of a couple they knew.

'Yes. Rather,' said Charles, and after a silence, he added: 'And are *you* ever thinking of being engaged, Jackie?'

'Me?'

'Yes.'

'Oh, no,' said Jackie . . .

'I don't think so,' added Jackie, and looked at the table-cloth, as he looked at her – mentally worked out the entire faint pattern of the table-cloth, as he looked at her . . .

'And when are *you* going to be engaged, Charles?'

'Me?'

'Yes.'

'Oh, I'll never be engaged.'

'Why not?'

He lit a cigarette. 'Well, to tell you the truth, Jackie, I'm coming to the conclusion that nobody loves me.' He smiled.

Jackie smiled too, and looked a fool.

'Don't be a fool,' said Jackie . . .

2

Mr Marsden, also, was still taking Jackie out to lunch. But they were not so affable with each other as they used to be.

It had been Mr Marsden's habit, since the disaster of Richard's death, and when speaking on the subject to his friends, to state that he was Not the Sort of Person who Said he had Always Told you so. Which enabled Mr Marsden, in a very clever manner, to say, without shame or stint, that he had always told you so. He had not always told you that Richard was going to die, of course, but he had always told you that nothing but catastrophe could result from an alliance with Richard.

Jackie was not unaware of Mr Marsden's back-biting, and perhaps she showed her awareness in her slightly cooler behaviour to him. At any rate, she sensed a difference in their relationship, which she was unable to describe otherwise than as ⌐.

This curious symbol had been brought into being by Mr Marsden himself, who, taking advantage of an always extremely illegible handwriting, now concluded his letters to her no longer with

Yours ever

but with

Yours ⌐

which evasion, though it left Jackie in the dark as to the precise state of his emotions, she found quite extraordinarily expressive.

It was the most subtle thing. They looked at each other, during pauses, over the lunch-table, and perceived it. He was neither amicable nor hostile to her. Merely ⌐. Their relationship was ⌐. And would remain so.

Chapter Four

MANUSCRIPTS

1

The uncanny but immediate galvanization of the theatrical profession on Jackie's running up the little flag of her £700 legacy, had a slightly depressing effect upon her.

Indeed the comparison of herself to one who, in a beleaguered garrison several degrees beyond the boot stage, miraculously produces, and is observed to be blandly consuming, a handsome supply of roast beef and Christmas pudding (hot) – was the kind of comparison in which Jackie could have indulged more than once. Though it would have been, of course, an exaggerated kind of comparison. Actually, the eyes of the various gentlemen whom she visited with the news that she knew for certain Where (as it was put) she could Place her hands upon the Money, did not even light up. But the aforesaid gentlemen invariably said 'Oh—', and paused in a curious manner by the mantelpiece, and rubbed their left ears contemplatively with their right forefingers and thumbs ... Also there was an immediate decline in hand-holding (though not a complete deletion thereof), and premature production became a thing unknown. Also her daily post became much less type-written, but much more cordial and illegible, and she had to be very clever at pretending that the author's name on various manuscripts sent her, was *not* the pseudonym either of the gentleman who had sent it, or of the wife of that gentleman ... But it was, so often, that it became rather tedious to keep up the pretence ...

It was an engaging game, for the time – this game of manuscripts – and Jackie had never realized before how many there were playing it. Jackie, of course (quite uncorrectably perverse and obtuse creature that she was) did not play it according to the best traditions. If she had done that, she would have leant back in wicker chairs at the Rockingham Hard Court Tennis Club, said 'My dear, I've got *Three Plays* to read before to-morrow morning!' and lifted her eyes jadedly to the skies. And she would have pronounced 'Three Plays 'as a perfect spondee – (like 'God's Worst 'or 'Don't Ask!' or 'I Mean!' or other prevalent theatrical spondees – the profession, when emphatic, being very much addicted to this foot) – and she would have gone on to say that of course one |Can Not| Simply| Find a decent play these days, and that it was very dreadful altogether.

But Jackie was no use at this sort of thing, and few would have guessed how many manuscripts she got through, with her chin in her hands over her gas-fire at West Kensington of a night, in the month or so that followed her decision to speculate.

Nearly every day she received another. And they were all bound in red, or brown, or (in extreme cases) yellow: and they were most perfectly typed, with the name of a superior typist in an addressed circle on the title-page verso, and they were rather cleaner than new pins. And their titles were imposing though vague – 'Temptation' – 'Error' – 'Aggression' – 'Vindication' – 'Retribution' – 'Abdication.' Though sometimes you came across a very stern title, such as 'The Rupture'. Or even 'The Thrashing' – which was sterner still.

Of course, what Jackie was looking for, and what Jackie had stipulated upon when asking for these plays, was a Part for herself. She found quite enough parts, and as many thwarted and articulate heroines to interpret as she might wish. Unhappily, though, she also found that the greater part of these heroines, while possibly preserving a quite natural and sober demeanour during the drama as a whole, at moments of crisis were the type of persons who '*go off into a high hysterical laugh, lasting some moments, and then, suddenly reeling, fall upon the settee and commence a slow, regular sobbing, steadily increasing in power.*' Now from observations made, and information received, on the subject of life and manners, Jackie had little (or no) faith in the prevalence, or even existence, of this mode of self-expression. She had had some experience of affliction herself, yet she had difficulty in conceiving any set of circumstances which could compel her *either* to go off into a high hysterical laugh lasting some moments, *or* (suddenly reeling) to fall upon a settee and commence a slow, regular sobbing (steadily increasing in power). Or at least singly these two manifestations might have been credible, but both together they were inconceivable. She kept an open mind upon the matter: she knew it was only her point of view: but there it was.

And if this was her feeling, then if she undertook such parts, she would be giving an insincere, and therefore inartistic, performance. And Jackie did not want to give that ...

2

It was at the end of about her fourth month of flirtation with manuscripts that Jackie discovered an old play of Richard's (which he had never mentioned to her) entitled 'World's End'. This title, being comparatively flippant, immediately attracted her attention, and she sat down and read it all the morning. She arose with the intention to speculate upon 'World's End'.

This was an early play of Richard's, and the part for herself was not very good. But she felt she could touch the manuscript up, and the play on the whole was far ahead of anything else she had yet read. Also the idea of putting her heart and soul into anything that Richard had done, however long ago, was an attractive and healing idea.

She did not play the part, however, in the long run. Her fellow-backer, Mr Dyman Bryant (a gentleman of some wealth who spent the greater part of the year in a drunken state at Antibes, and who had been introduced to her by the Mulligan agency), was understood to be secretly demanding a Name in the part. A meeting was held (at Mr Mulligan's office) and Cards were lain upon the table. Jackie held out for a long while, and all at once gave in. There were two males against her, and there was no male to protect her.

And she was like that, these days. She had lost, for the most part, interest in life, and was continually being over-taken by a pernicious desire to slide ...

Besides, a few sleepless and agonized nights, shortly after her bluff had been called and she had blundered into active commitments with respect to the money, soon reduced her to a more or less contented frame of mind in which she realized she had lost her little legacy for ever and for no conceivable purpose. And she might as well lose it one way as another.

The play went into rehearsal in the Autumn, and was produced by Mr Gerald Gandon (a young man, who had lately produced a success) at the Empress Theatre, Charing Cross.

By the time the first night in London arrived, she had become quite excited again. At times she felt quite ill with excitement.

She was getting ill these days. Headaches, and giddiness, and a malaise after lunch. And one night the right side of her face was all swollen, and the right eye contracted. (It was better in the morning.)

Chapter Five

EAVESDROPPING

1

It is half-past five on a winter's afternoon. Jackie is standing in the stalls of the Empress Theatre, and looking at the stage. To-night will be the first night of 'World's End', and the four black hours have commenced.

The four black, uncanny hours, when the stage has been left for the last time, and the last actor has gone mumbling away from the last call . . .

A door upstairs in the gallery bangs in the draught . . . The whole auditorium is in glowing darkness, and the set itself, with the curtain up, stands alert, silent, uncritical, in the grey drear illumination of the one dazzling pilot above . . .

Half-past five. And outside, dimly, she can hear the

roar and explosion of London. London at tea. A brawling London at tea ...

An unearthly interim – and no one in the theatre but herself to witness it ... The actors and actresses ... They, too, are having tea, and keeping up their spirits. Here is their stage. What do actors and actresses know about their stage? ...

But she has an inkling now ... The door in the gallery bangs again: the flimsy flats give a sudden creak: she stands very still in the glowing darkness, and the Genius of the theatre creeps out, and whispers in her ear ...

Then she goes and has some tea herself.

2

When Jackie, stepping out of a taxi from West Kensington, arrived at the foyer of the Empress, ten minutes or so before the show commenced, she did not know whether to be gratified by the courtesy, or angered by the insolence of those who had come to witness the spectacle she had brought into being. In either case she wanted to enlighten them.

It was their assumption of reality that startled her. 'But really, you shouldn't have bothered to dress, you know,' Jackie wanted to say, on the one hand. 'Believe me, this is only one of Richard's old plays, and it's all my doing. This festive air, this smooth automobility, this shingled-ness, this dazzling green-cloakedness, this identifiable and traditional air of an occasion – I never dreamed you would take it as seriously as all that. You're assuming that this is a genuine production, aren't you? Well, it's very good of you, and I suppose it is, if you say so. But why have you come here? Surely you can't think you're going to enjoy yourselves. Surely you can't think that that senseless welter of repetitions and mechanicalities which we have been grinding out for the last three weeks – is a thing to afford you pleasure. I'm afraid you're being rather done.'

But there was the other feeling as well. She did not quite like the carriage of the heads, and the affronted shudder in the cloaks of the various ladies present. And there was a subtle air of tittering amusedness which she did not like. After all, thought Jackie, this was poor dead Richard's play, wasn't it?

And then, 'I *Beg* your pardon,' said one extremely frilled gentleman, as he nearly bumped into her, going down to the stalls. Jackie had not expended seven hundred pounds to be rather facetiously bumped into by an extremely frilled gentleman ...

It altered everything so much when you were responsible for the show yourself – when you were dependent upon the crowd. She experienced all the delights and fears, and inner thwarted ironies, of an unrecognized hostess ... Or an eavesdropper ...

It was not, however, until the first interval, when she came down from her box in the circle (which she was sharing with Mr Bryant and his wife and friends), that she reacted fully to these things. Then she went home.

3

She went home because she was unhappy and puzzled and chilled, and had remembered Richard at the wrong time.

She stood alone in the unrelenting electric glare of the foyer, underneath a large portrait of the leading lady, and amid the sheen and sparkle and chattering, gossipy air of release on the groups about her. And over the great general ripple of chatter, at once blurred and distinct, and as ebullient as that of a class deserted by its master, there was a pervasion of bars and refreshments, and cloak-room doors closing and opening. And the sound of the orchestra came through from the auditorium. And near her stood Mr Gerald Bassett (the famous author) in a thoughtful attitude against the wall, and nearer still stood a large blond American discoursing to his friends. (He had Jus set down An made up his mind (had this American) that he wasn't going back this time without having met John Gauls *Worthy*.) And a young woman, of undoubted means, but no talent for dressing herself, came rushing upstairs with another young woman, and brushed past Jackie with 'My Dear! I was *Hooting*!' This young woman meant that, at the time she was alluding to, she had been unable to contain herself with laughter. Jackie did not know whether this was at the play, and she did not really care. But she resented this young woman brushing away her legacy with a missish Hoot, and criticized her dress roughly in her mind. Then she began to listen to the various remarks around her . . .

'Oh, but, my dear, I *am* responsible. I *brought* you here . . .'

' . . . not wisely, I'm afraid, but too well . . .'

'I say, Ronald, old boy, is that man I just met a Famous Surgeon?' 'Famous *Surgeon*, old boy – what's the matter? . . .'

'No – but as a first act pure and simple, I mean . . .'

'Ah, but, my dear, I'm getting a violent Higher Thought complex myself these days!'

' . . . Famous Surgeons on the brain . . .'

'Oh, but you must be careful now we've got a novelist in the family! . . .'

'That's nothing, my dear. I go to *Palmists*!'

' . . . though only in strictly heavy parts.'

'My dear! CRYSTAL-gazers!'

' . . . and *when* sober, the most enchanting creature imaginable.'

And as Jackie stood there, in the crush, wondering what it was all about, and what Richard would have thought of it all, and whether they were liking this very second-rate play – a tune she was very fond of, all at once, came through from the auditorium . . .

And it caused her suddenly to recall, in a sad mist, the very great beauty of their little time together. And it struck her that her spirit had been alive and poignant then, and that it was dead and beautiless now, and that this ornate chattering and idle gossiping around her, this foolish orchestra and foolish play, this tawdry, stuffy, smoke-ridden foyer – were irrelevant and very paltry phenomena to one whose spirit had once been alive.

And then the young lady who had Hooted returned with her friend. 'A Succession of Violent Snorts, my dear!' said this young lady, as she passed.

Jackie went straight upstairs, made her apologies to her friends – who had not been Hunting Madly about the Place for her (as they said they had), but who were extremely concerned and puzzled by her decision to leave – and came down and left the theatre just as the first lines of the second act were reverberating hollowly upon a newly awed, breathless, shirt-creaking, slightly coughing, and romantically darkened house.

She refused a taxi, and walked in her evening cloak to Charing Cross. It was a curious thing to have done: but she was without feeling.

In fact, she had entirely lost interest in the matter by the time she had reached the station, and on seeing a newspaper placard:

'39 IN BURNING BUILDING'

she bought one to see whether they had got out. She looked at it in the train. They had.

Chapter Six

OBSERVATIONS

1

Jackie had many other opportunities for eavesdropping in the next few weeks' run of 'World's End', the publicity for which was being capably handled, and which, with a mixed Press, was doing fairly well.

It was the gallery crowd with which she at last became intrigued the most. She had never taken much interest in this part of the theatre before, having conceived of it as little else than a vaguely seething locality to which (as a slight concession and an evidence of your competence) you Spoke Up, so that every line could be heard at the back. But now she came into closer touch with her gallery.

It began with an enormous feeling of gratitude, on her part, towards those submissive little queue-lengths she would observe, as early as half-past six, forming and coagulating (like odd attracted atoms blown from the swirl of a home-going metropolis) outside the back doors of the Empress Theatre. She could never get over her sense of imposture and feeling of pity at this sight. She did not know what it was, but there was something so abject, so ingenuous, so altogether friendly and dependent in this spectacle, judged externally, that she quite experienced shame on their behalf. 'Really, you poor, dumb things,' she wanted to say. 'I need you indeed, if I'm ever to get my money back, but I would never have considered *you* like that. Why don't you go to a nice show (preferably a musical one) and enjoy yourselves? Who on earth told you you could get your money's worth here?' Such was Jackie's first attitude towards her galleries.

It was not until one Saturday afternoon, when, out of the spirit of curiosity and the desire to learn more of her profession, she herself queued up and planked down her hurried one-and-twopence for an Olympian view of 'World's End', that she changed her opinion. It was then borne in upon her that she was not amongst dumb cattle, but amongst Disinterested Theatre Lovers.

Jackie had heard a great deal about Disinterested Theatre Lovers, but now that she found herself face to face with the type she did not think that it was a very enjoyable thing to be. Nor yet a very valuable thing. Indeed, if the theatre (as an art) was to be judged by the standard of its most Disinterested patronage (and by what more valid criterion could it be judged?), she did not think the theatre would come out very well from the ordeal.

In fact, from the long queues of pasty-faced and over-worked typists, dowdy and genteel young women from obscure Universities, genteel and toothless ancients from Bayswater boarding-houses, suburban harridans with canvas stools, spotty-faced young men peering at bent-back books, out-of-work actors and medical students – all lined up stodgily between the wall and the gesticulatory histrionic parasitism of the down-at-heel but impudent queue-performer – Jackie derived the most depressing sensations. It was not that she reacted so much against the almost plodding beautilessness of these patrons themselves (though she did do this): it was that the whole scene was antipathetic to her own concept of art. For Jackie's concept of art was that of a thing bringing light-heartedness, and beauty, and joy into the hearts of its devotees, and there was very little evidence of that here. On the contrary, there was a certain grimness and aggressiveness here, which made itself felt from the moment the door clicked hysterically open, and that unpleasant, wolf-like rush up the hollow-clanging stairs (lit garishly by smudged, barred windows) commenced. If art was joy – a not very promising approach to the temple of joy!

And when upstairs, on a dizzy level with the ceiling, and in the wretched dimness cast by the blazing spanglements of the chandelier, and amid the brusquerie of medalled war-veterans, and the casual manners of unresponsive programme-girls – the atmosphere was even more chilling. Also an extraordinary touchiness developed in the crowd as the place filled up (which it did very rapidly).

There grew up, in fact, a constrained atmosphere of 'This is Engaged, I'm afraid' – or, 'Is this Engaged, please?' and, on a cool affirmative, an abrupt and rather unpleasant 'Oh' – or, 'If you'll move along a little to the right, we'll all be happier, won't we?' To say nothing of various muttered but indubitably testy 'Of course, Why People want to Wear Such Hats—' and occasional pure outbreaks of 'Other People, want to See as well as you, you know!' and appeals to the veterans.

Such was theatre love. And then, as the lights plunged down, and the curtain swished up, and a hush fell, and a late arrival went Stamp-Stamp (or even Plonk-Plank) on the wooden floor as he tried to blunder into a seat, Shshshshshsh ! hissed the gallery, and *Shshshshshsh!* (more angrily), and SHSHSHSHSHSH! And leant over, with glistening eyes, as the marvels of 'World's End' were unfolded beneath it.

Jackie developed an aloof and doubtful attitude towards theatre love.

2

But then matinées always had this kind of effect upon Jackie. That ineffectual assumption of darkness and

electric-lit revelry at three hours after noon in a theatre surrounded by a swirling, heavy-labouring and over-lunched
London, stole the last shreds of enchantment from her
calling. She could see the drama as a whole, and without
emotion, at such times, and she was slightly appalled.

3

Jackie, you see, was crying for faith ... She was for ever,
nowadays, examining and appraising the eminences to
which she still aspired.

If she was going to be a successful actress, if she was to
be given, that is, a medium of self-expression – she wanted
to know what awaited her.

Concerning that medium itself she had her doubts. Her
medium would be a slightly uncanny, elongated, three-
walled, glue-smelling, bright lemon-coloured interior world
(a form of symbolism, to begin with, from which the imaginative mind recoiled); and in this world she would walk
about with a feeling of peculiar mental undress, knowing
that every one of her movements and utterances was espied,
embarrassed, and generally eaten up by the spiritual mag-
netism of a fourth and non-existent wall – to which wall all
the settees were obviously sprawled (like sun-rays), all the
silent and dreadful speeches were made, and all existence
was subtly but inescapably referred. (Those sinister glassy
eyes of actors and actresses on a first night!)

But although this wall played so large a part, it did not really exist. You could not even look at a picture on this wall (and Jackie had tried this) without getting a laugh ...

And when there were a lot of people present at the same time in this world, the person speaking spoke three times louder than he would have ordinarily, and all the other people either remained queerly silent and attentive, or spoke amongst themselves three times more quietly than they would have spoken ordinarily, and stood extraordinarily close to each other, like conspirators ... With discrepancies and eccentricities of this nature this world was filled, and it was, on the whole, a grouped and arranged world as little resembling actual life as Frith's selected picture resembles Derby Day.

Such, normally, would be her vehicle, and she did not complain. It was undoubtedly the business of the actress to subdue these disadvantages to her own purpose. She now came to the use to which she was to put that vehicle.

Now Jackie was quite clear on this point – as far as she herself was concerned. She desired simply to convey to others as much as possible of her own personal observations and spiritual experiences in this world. Not only did she wish to indicate, in a lighter vein, some of the inconsistencies and piquancies and unadjustable ironies besetting herself and her fellow-creatures in their thwarted social endeavour; she also thought that she could, if given the opportunity, touch upon some of the higher and more mysterious and beautiful intimations she had had from time to time. She had had exalted moments, she knew – she had had her day in the rain on the Sussex downs, and she knew a great deal about many lovely things . . .

Moreover, she was convinced that these things had said something uniquely to herself, and that she very keenly desired to express that something to others, and that she would be able – she did not quite know how, but somehow or other with her gestures or her voice (which had great scope and flexibility at times) – to summon, and perhaps half mystically to suggest these appeals . . .

And that was all there was to it. She was (she now understood) neither a very clever nor exceptionally sensitive being: but she had the straightforward desire to express and unburden herself in these respects.

She found, however, that so far from being permitted to express her own self in this vehicle she had chosen, she was to be called upon to interpret the mostly obscure and always half-heartedly conveyed ideas of another. And more than that, these ideas, before coming under her control, had not only to pass filtrated through the whims and urgencies of the mime-master himself, but to be embarrassed and effected by the exigencies of her fellow-performers.

Actually she had heard in the theatre, abroad and unashamed, talk of gallantries and selfishnesses with Sympathy. If she was to be a true artist she knew that she could not possibly recognize such a word, and what freaks of characterization and falsities of sentiment, what ludicrous games of emotional Snap-dragon, were in progress around her, she did not dare contemplate.

And over and above this, there was the actual quality of the ideas which, after infinite waylayings, she would in general have the opportunity of interpreting. And taken all in all, from her present experience and general observations, she did not think that they were likely to prove either very noble, clear, or shrewd ideas. Indeed the world of the average play was a world she did not know. For although it was beyond measure preoccupied by the topic of love (and what more vital, imposing, and absorbing topic could there be?) – for one who had had her day on the Sussex downs in the rain, and observed what she had observed then, its treatment of this subject was too irrelevant and silly altogether.

But then it was an irrelevant world. It was a world in which purity consisted either of abstention from contacts which Jackie (and her actor and actress friends) believed to be perfectly decent and human contacts – or else of a sentimental idealization of a still rather reprobate escape from that abstention. It was a world in which Comedy was either the pat utterance of humorous quips, or a series of creaking Situations in which somebody discovered somebody else doing something he shouldn't, and watched him trying ineffectually to hide it up. And it was a world in which Tragedy was unalterably confused with self-sacrifice.

4

But even with all this she would be content. Again she told herself that a great actress (and though she had never yet observed one in action, she was convinced that there must be some such thing) could defeat and weld these conflicting factors to her own purpose.

And if there was also such a thing as a great drama, then the fault lay with herself and not with her profession.

But, taking into account these conflicting factors, she was overwhelmed by the enormous arduousness of the task facing her fellow-professionals ...

Whereat she was immediately appalled by the frivolousness with which these demands were habitually met.

Indeed actors and actresses (from what she knew of the greater part of them), so far from spending their entire undisturbed mornings closeted in rooms for the purpose of practising inflexion, tone, rhythm, modulation and gesture, till they were sick of their own voices and themselves – so far from observing, note-taking, and harassing their producer or author to the breaking-point – so far from debating every doubtful point amongst themselves until a working agreement was reached (and she had heard famous producers being derided for entering into the entire past history, place of birth and upbringing, illnesses and unique vices of the character to be portrayed) – so far from this, they were up to all sorts of daily occupations of which the

Rockingham Hard Court Tennis Club was but one shining example.

The obvious stumbling-blocks and difficulties of this art (if it was to be an art) being so much greater than those of any other, a supremer effort (she felt) was called for. She was therefore disturbed to observe that in this, of all arts, the least effort was being made.

She found, in fact, that those who had set out to hold the mirror to life and manners, were not merely as subjectively involved by that life, and those manners, as the rest of human kind, but, in a curious way, a great deal more so . . .

5

This was a distressing conclusion, which she took some time in reaching. She commenced to observe it shortly after her acquaintanceship with the Rockingham Hard Court Tennis Club, and her first inkling of it arose, possibly, through Crashes in the War . . .

Now in her social contacts, both apart from and in the theatre, Jackie had naturally encountered several individuals who had had Crashes in the War. They were quite easy things to have had. But, however accessible, they did, she found, confer a certain obvious distinction (even in her own mind) upon their victims – and particularly if they were Crashes . . . To have been severely wounded would not have been quite the same thing (though she personally would rather have put it like that) ... There was something expansive and livid about a Crash ...

Now it is strange that these accidents (and talk of these accidents) should have led Jackie to the unique conclusion she at last formed concerning the temperament of actors and actresses, but there it was. For she found that, however much the world in general might indulge in Crashes in the War, the theatrical world was indulging in them a little bit more, and a little more heavily ...

It was the most subtle thing on earth. It was not even as though these casualties were mentioned more often or more solemnly in theatrical circles than in others: it simply was that, in an ineffable way, they lay more heavily and more self-consciously upon those who had suffered from them ...

It was almost (almost – not quite) as though actors were endeavouring to imply that *they* could have Crashes in the War as well as anybody else ... It was almost as though you had made some accusation ...

Now when once Jackie had alighted upon this discovery with respect to Crashes, she commenced to apply the same line of thought to various other manifestations of the same kind of thing ... All this was far from being confined to Crashes. It was, rather, in the literary, lingual, scholastic, and most particularly social spheres that she identified the same atmosphere again. And in these other instances it was the perpetually recurring introduction of the two words 'Of Course' which principally attracted her attention.

Jackie could have multiplied the theatrical 'Of Courses' indefinitely. They were always applied to other people in the theatrical profession, for to have applied them to yourself would not have been quite modest – but they conferred distinction on the profession ... There was Of Course Getting his blue at Cambridge for Rugger: there was Of Course speaking German and Norwegian like a native: there was Of Course coming from really *the most* (old boy) English County Family: and there was Of Course being a Cousin or something of Lord Ladaming. There was Of Course Really Understanding all about Baroque, and all that: there was Of Course having a Really Quite Astonishing Army Record: there was Of Course not being able to get any Polo since he came back: there was Of Course having to trail off at an Unearthly Hour of the morning to look over a Horse he was purchasing (there were a lot of equine 'Of Courses'): and there was Of Course getting into Fearful State finishing this new book of his ...

But Jackie (assuming Socratic naïveté) could really not see *why* these things were taken as such a matter of course. A great deal of these activities, to her mind (which was that of a struggling young actress), appeared to involve the expenditure of time and money which she herself could certainly not afford – let alone take for granted. (She wished that *she* was the cousin – or even the something – of Lord Ladaming. Wouldn't she just make him back plays!) And though it was very nice to be able to speak so many languages, and buy so many horses, and know such a lot about

Baroque, and attend such exclusive functions – it was not so very difficult, really, if you had the time; and in view of her present concepts of the arduousness of the actor's task, she doubted if the time was there.

Or if the time was there – should not these things be relegated to a subsidiary or even recreationary functioning? But this was not the case. For just as War Crashes had attached to themselves that curious over-emphasis noted above, so did all these manifold interests and occupations undoubtedly make themselves felt in a more heavy and self-conscious manner than they did with those who could devote themselves to such things wholly.

Indeed at times she grew so weary of listening to this kind of talk, and observing this kind of talk being translated into everyday and week-end action, that she would often think that the philosopher who had suggested that actors and actresses were so busy being ladies and gentlemen that they had no time left in which to be actors and actresses – had not spoken quite accurately. She rather thought that it would have been more apt to say that these ladies and gentlemen were so busy being actors and actresses that they had no time left in which to be ladies and gentlemen – what with rehearsals, and playing at night, and looking for jobs, and visiting agents and one thing and another.

Chapter Seven

A PLEASANT SURPRISE

1

It was shortly after having arrived at (or dallied with) various conclusions of this nature, that Jackie came into the belated (but not displeasing) knowledge that she had Done Something. Her Work, in fact, in certain quarters, was Known.

Jackie had not previously been conscious of having Done anything — let alone work (indeed, looking back on the last ten years, she could not remember a stroke); but the tacit assurance that she had, gave her the same agreeable sensation one would experience on coming into a trifling but unexpected legacy.

Suffering from one of those periodic scares (to which human nature is subject) that she had no friends in this world, and must either come out and mix with her fellows or remain eccentrically recluse for ever, she began at this time to lay herself open to as many invitations as might come her way in the direction of social intercourse.

The aura of affluence and slight mystery which had surrounded Jackie since the production of 'World's End', stood by her well in this. She was asked a great deal to dinner, and here it was that she first became aware that she had Done Something and that her Work was Known.

There were quite a lot of other people, it seemed, who were similarly placed. In fact, several of these nightly concourses she attended were positive Dinners to People who had Done Something . . .

Dinners to People who had Done Something were rather damp affairs. Those who gave them were not persons of means, and they generally took place somewhere in St John's Wood, and they began with a rather insecure and electric-bell-ringing prelude during which the diffident exponents of achievement arrived and were made softly acquainted with each other. They then worked themselves up (with the aid of gin and Italian vermouth) into a slightly brighter and more loquacious plane, before an invasion was made into the dining-room, where seats were found and taken in a large but good-humoured silence.

Conversation at Dinners to People who had Done Something, when at last it got going, ranged from prolific mutual registration of places visited abroad, to light-hearted inquiry into the final values of civilization and evolution. And there was generally at least one gentleman present, probably of the theatrical but possibly of the journalistic persuasion, who would ask, 'But what *are* morals? Do tell me, please. I want to know. What *are* morals?'

Jackie herself had little faith in morals (as has been shown), but she rather thought she had got beyond the 'But-what-are-morals?' stage.

Humour at these dinners was mostly confined to Repeating Humour.

'My dear Johnnie,' a lady would say. 'I don't approve of your bowler hat.'

'You don't approve of my bowler hat?'

'No. I most decidedly do *not* approve of your bowler hat.'

The baffled owner would turn to Jackie.

'She doesn't approve of my bowler hat,' he would say.

'She doesn't approve of your bowler *hat*,' Jackie would reply.

'Poor old Johnnie,' a new-comer would say. 'They don't approve of his bowler hat.'

Mr Marsden attended as many Dinners to People who had Done Something as he was asked to.

2

'World's End' was withdrawn after a two months' run, and she saved about £300 from its debris. She considered herself lucky.

She wished, of course, that she had spent the other

£400 on herself instead of the public, but she considered herself lucky.

She wrote to Charles, who had adopted, in his letters, at first a discouraging, and then a very helpful and solicitous attitude towards her speculation, that she had 'just got out'.

3

One night Jackie (a little while after 'World's End' had come off, and she had been going round and round for jobs again) thought she had got influenza or something.

She went to bed, under the directions of Mrs Lover, who brought her hot brandy and aspirin, and she tried to get to sleep. But she was trembling so, and going first hot, and then cold, in such an unusual manner, that she could not do this, and lay tossing for hours.

Illness was a very dreadful thing, she thought. So far she had reckoned with many things, but she had not reckoned with illness.

She lay in the darkness and heard the trains thundering away to Baron's Court beneath her. She was alone in London, and without friends. Others might be ill, she thought, but she could really not afford it ...

West Kensington ... She had no background for an illness ...

Her teeth chattered and another train thundered by ...

Chapter Eight

THE CHANCE

1

And then, all at once, her skies cleared, and her chance came.

One morning she came down to breakfast and found two letters on her table. And one of these letters was from Mr Ronald Drew (the producer), who asked to see her at eleven o'clock that morning, and the other of these letters was from Mr Andrew Cannon (the producer), who asked to see her at eleven o'clock that morning.

At eleven o'clock that morning she was (it need hardly be said) at the offices of Mr Andrew Cannon. On reading his letter she had lost colour. Actresses of greater repute than Jackie have lost colour on receiving a summons from Mr Cannon, and personal friends of such actresses have been known to assume very sickly congratulatory smiles on hearing of such actresses having brought it off with Mr Cannon (for there is envy in the theatrical profession). And the even doubtful rumour of Mr Cannon being in Front, circulating round stage passages at about 9.30 of a night, has had a bracing effect upon more dramas than could be counted. For this producer, by means of various talents (mainly, perhaps, a lack of highmindedness and a distaste for golf) had forged for himself an eminence in the theatrical profession such as it will be difficult to excel in the future.

How Mr Cannon had now come to send for Jackie was a thing beyond her understanding. But the ways of this terrifying man were notoriously dark, and he had pounced upon many a nonentity, to elevate them, with a contract, to fame, before now. Not that Jackie had never met Mr Cannon. He had been at school with Richard, and after her performance in 'The Knocking at the Gate' she had had the fortune to have been personally congratulated by him.

She entered Mr Cannon's offices at eleven o'clock, and she came out at twenty to one (after half an hour's interview with Mr Cannon) with the prospect, nay promise, of a year's contract, commencing at £5 a week in January. It was now November.

Jackie had quite forgotten what it was to be drunk with bliss, and she now found it as agreeable a sensation as you could have.

She walked down Villiers Street, and when she reached

Charing Cross District Station she went straight into a telephone box.

She did this in order to try and get a friend to come to lunch with her. She would have entertained every one of her friends, at the same time, if she could have done so, and dropped the news, with extravagant casualness, over the cocktail ...

It is a pity that Jackie should have been as spiteful as all this – but she had suffered a good deal of late.

2

And now commences the queerest part of Jackie's story, for it was on the afternoon of this day that Jackie, all unknowingly, sealed her own fate. For on this afternoon, after a lunch which included a cocktail but was taken alone (for none of her friends were obtainable), Jackie, feeling in a still joyful, and also slightly aggressive mood, decided to follow up the other letter she had received that morning. She had completely ignored this in the flutter caused by Mr Cannon's communication, but now, by use of the telephone (and the employment of chicanery), she succeeded, without loss of honour, in obtaining an appointment for half-past four.

From this appointment she emerged with a script under her arm and a definite engagement to play what was described as a Sort of Lead in a play entitled 'The

Underdog', to be produced at the Cumberland Theatre, St Martin's Lane, in three and a half weeks' time. On reaching home that night she read the part and the play.

It was a very fair play, she thought, and the part itself was interesting. As she re-read some of the lines she paced about the room, trying them softly out ...

She was to be produced, she understood, by Mr Lionel Claye. She knew Mr Claye, having acted with him in 'North' – a long while ago. But she had barely spoken to him at that time, and she had not been aware that he was a producer. She wondered how she would get on with him.

She was another creature as she got into bed that night.

Chapter Nine

CORRESPONDENCE

1

And then, on top of all this, and the very next day, a letter from Charles. Charles had, of course, been back from Australia a long while now (he had hurt his foot and it had been a slightly disastrous trip for him), and he had been up to see her several times. She had spent the day with him, in fact, the day before her interview with Cannon.

DEAR JACKIE,—

I got back all right last night, and hope you did. You'll be surprised to hear that the old gentleman we collided with was in the same compartment as mine going down, and on hearing who I was (i.e. Cricket), thrust out his hand and said 'Let me shake

hands with you, sir! My boys adore you!' So you
see we made a hit with him after all. Or at any rate
with his boys.

But this is not what I'm writing to you about. I've
got something much more grave to say. And as I'd only
write thousands of letters if I didn't come straight to
the point, I'm going to say it straight out. I want to
know if you'll marry me, Jackie. Don't be shocked
when you read this. I'll try and explain.

I don't know that there's anything to explain really.
It's all so simple. I just love you, and that's all I can
say. I know it sounds sudden, and all that – but I know
it now, and I've always known it. Yes – even while
Richard was alive. I couldn't have done anything else.
I don't really see how anybody could.

I know it must sound ever so strange to you, but
there you are. I can never tell you how sincere I am, or
what a lot it means to me. I love you truly, Jackie.

You may think it strange that I've never hinted
much of this before. But I didn't know how you were
feeling about everything, and perhaps it's taken all this
time, and that long absence, to realize how completely
I adore you.

Will you marry me, Jackie dear? I can't say
anything else – except how badly I want you to think
it over. Of course I know you can't answer all at once,
but will you think it over, for as long as you like, and
then let me know? Unless of course the answer is *too*

obviously on the wrong side, and then you must put me out of my pain as soon as possible.

If you could only love me a bit we could really have such fun. Of course it would be rather difficult if you wanted to go on acting, but you could if you liked. And we'd have quite enough money. They're making a golf-course on the estate now, and everything's moving in the right direction. And I'm sure you'd be happy here. The gardener's simply infatuated with you (by the way I never knew you'd met him), and they're all in love with you, from Mrs B. downwards. And one can live really well down here, if one knows how to.

Stating his qualifications now! I don't think I can say any more. Don't hurry your reply, and when thinking it out just remember how terribly I want you.

Yours ever, CHARLES.

To which Jackie, after a day's labour and contemplation, sent the following reply:

DEAREST CHARLES,—

Thank you most terribly for your letter. I think it's wonderful of you to have written like that, and I don't know how to reply or thank you.

I wish I could just say Yes. But I just can't do this, there are too many reasons. First of all I don't think I love you properly in that way, and thousands of other reasons.

I would have to give up the stage if I married you
(I'd certainly insist on doing so in any case), and I
just can't do this. You can never know what it means
to me. I've banked such a lot on it so far – giving up
everything – and I simply dare not fail. It would be
running away. If I don't succeed, after all I've done
and risked, I might as well throw myself in the river.
I've got an absolute spite on about it. I want to make
good just to spite them. Really. And I'm going to.

And anyway, I know that you're only asking me just
because you're wonderful about things, and want to
make me happy. But really I'm quite happy – getting
along wonderfully really.

But I can never thank you enough for your
ripping kindness and thoughtfulness. That sounds
nothing – but *really*, Charles, I mean it. I think you're
marvellous and always will

Yours ever, JACKIE.

This document, which was as sincere a one as Jackie
had ever composed in her life, received no reply. She was
vaguely and unreasonably disappointed . . .

Chapter Ten

A DAY IN THE THEATRE

1

And now it would be wise to advance, without further delay, to the day which, with the exception of a day spent upon the Sussex downs, was of the gravest moment in the life of that-lonely, striving, optimistic, egoistic but harmless organism that was Jackie.

This day occurred late in November, and was the fifth day of rehearsal of 'The Underdog' – and must be described in detail.

It began with her leaving Talgarth Road at ten o'clock, and taking a short walk in the vicinity of St Paul's School with the object of going over her words to herself.

She was well wrapped up, for it was the coldest day of the year as yet, and a great wind was blowing the clouds over a scudding and vaguely sunlit sky. It was, indeed, as though the first big guns of the coming winter were pounding out, and she felt strangely invigorated in that bombardment.

The trees lining St Paul's playground, with their battalions on battalions of leaves, whirling with lyrical and ascending buoyancy from their seething branches, as though they had waited all the long, drooping summer for this one bounding moment, and were now going to make the best of it, touched her heart altogether, and made her feel like a happy leaf herself.

And by the time she had walked round and reached West Kensington Station again, with a flushed face (and a rather pink nose), she had forgotten all about her words. She had forgotten about her whole profession, indeed, and was merely conscious of the privilege of being alive.

On reaching Earl's Court Station, where she changed, she was accosted by a young, nervous, and very pretty girl (nine years her junior at least), who asked her if she was on the right platform for Wimbledon.

'No,' said Jackie. 'You must go up these stairs, and right along to the right, and then down the stairs again, and it comes in on the farthest line.'

'Oh, thank you so much,' said the very pretty young girl, as she moved away.

'Only,' said Jackie, 'you must see that it has Wimbledon written on the front, because they sometimes run trains to Ealing on that line now.'

She then smiled, and went bustlingly downstairs to her own train. She was surprised (and not a little proud) at the almost maternal fluency and calm with which she had carried off this little episode. And she remembered how, on her own first day in London, she had tremblingly sought direction on precisely the same spot.

And she felt maternal. She thought of a few of the things that had happened to her since then.

2

It was the fifth day of rehearsal. The actors and actresses had reached that phase wherein they made pleasant jokes at each other's expense, and were very friendly in public, but very malicious in the innumerable private lunch and tea combinations which had already formed.

Jackie herself, lonely as she was, was not unpopular – the anger which had arisen in the breasts of her fellows on slowly comprehending that such a pretty and insignificant figure had an important part, having been partially alleviated by her treatment at the hands of Mr Claye.

Of the first four days of rehearsal nothing need be said. Jackie was too hardened now to feel the blows in running the emotional gauntlet of production. At least she told herself she was too hardened. She had been telling herself this, with great conscientiousness and keenness, for the last four days.

Mr Lionel Claye had certainly been unusually difficult. Mr Claye would have been a great deal nicer, Jackie
thought, if he had not been so Infinitely Patient. Endless-
Painstaking-with-Actresses was also a thing which she put
as a black mark against his character. They were doubtless
very valuable things in their way (thought Jackie), but the
betrayal of the fact that they were, at the expenditure of
enormous self-control, being exercised at all times upon
herself, revived in her an old frame of mind, which she was
loath to revive, but in which the broken edges of bottles figured largely. Also the combination of Infinite Patience with
white flowing hair (brushed back), pince-nez, a thin, emaciated face, a soft collar one inch larger than its neck, an
old blue suit, a thick voice, and a reproachful (but infinitely
patient) smile – was not a pleasing combination to Jackie.

She left the sunny London day outside, and entered
the dark, board-banging mumble of the theatre at eleven
o'clock precisely. The curtain was up, the stage was half
lit, and the various actors and actresses were standing in
groups about the stage. She was only just in time.

The stage-manager was seated at a table, and Mr Claye
was in deep converse with Mr John Sheridan (the heavy
man) who was seeking instruction on some subtlety in his
part. For the purpose of attending to this gentleman's que-
ries, Mr Claye's arm was placed affectionately around his
interlocutor's shoulder, and he was looking thoughtfully
at the floor. And as Mr Sheridan spoke, Mr Claye accompanied his speech, as though beating the time, with a slow

(and infinitely patient) nodding process, and the enuncia-
tion of 'Ye-e-es ... Ye-e-es ... Ye-e-es ...' in a manner that
implied that so far from being about to punish this actor
for upping and speaking his mind, he quite encouraged this
sort of thing.

Then, 'Well, you play it just how you feel it, will you,
Sheridan, old man?' said Mr Claye, in his slow voice. 'And
then we'll see how it comes out, shall we?'

And it was the smile, conciliatory and all-embracing,
which Mr Claye at this moment switched upon Mr
Sheridan, that subtly warned Jackie to prepare herself for
an even larger dose of infinite patience than she had yet
had to swallow.

'Miss Mortimer here?' asked Mr Claye, looking around.
'Ah! ...' he said.

And he smiled at her too ... She smiled back, and set
her teeth.

3

Her scene began in half an hour's time. This opened with
her entrance, and was played alone with Mr Maddox.
Mr Maddox was an altogether brilliant and also very
courteous little actor, with a reputation worth having but
the habit of spending many months (about nine in every
year, for instance) Out. During which periods his appearance, which was that of a hungry but very well-dressed

wolf – underwent emphasis. His natural skill, however, made it a joy to play with him, and Jackie thought she could be very happy in this scene.

It began three minutes after her entrance.

'Now, shall we have that again, Miss Mortimer?' asked Mr Claye.

An impression was given, from the complacent manner in which Mr Claye asked this, that it was merely a casual suggestion which she might veto at will.

'Where from?' asked Jackie. 'The entrance?'

'The Entrance,' affirmed Mr Claye, nodding. The first impression was subtly nullified.

Mr Maddox changed his position. Jackie returned to the doorway.

'Hullo, Ronald,' said Jackie. 'Where have you been?'

'Been?' said Mr Maddox. 'Only just round to Sector's – why ? You're not—'

'Yes, Miss Mortimer,' said Mr Claye. 'But we're not just dropping in to tea, are we?'

There was a silence.

'I thought,' added Mr Claye, 'that we were just getting our first suspicion of our husband's misconduct.'

There was another silence in which Mr Claye and Jackie looked at each other.

'Eh?' said Mr Claye, and he now, with some conscientiousness, looked into the script to verify what he had said. There was obviously a sturdy argument for those of the conviction that at this moment of the drama we *were* just dropping in to tea, but he personally, when *he* had read the play, had had an intimation to the contrary. 'You mean you want it more tense?' asked Jackie. 'Oh, yes. A great deal more tense, Miss Mortimer.' Jackie returned to the doorway.

'We want to let ourselves right out in this, don't we?' said Mr Claye. 'Oh,' said Jackie.

Being of the strong personal belief (after a close study of her part) that this was the exact moment at which she held herself In, so as to give whatever value there was to her later stormings, Jackie was thrown back forcibly upon 'Oh.' This is a nasty monosyllable to employ during production – and one which creates bad feeling – but she had no alternative.

'Eh?' said Mr Claye, in an off-hand and agreeable way, and looking up at the proscenium arch. Mr Claye knew how to quell his 'Oh' insurrections at once and without mercy.

'Yes. Perhaps so,' said Jackie, coming to heel, and the production was allowed to proceed.

She now played with Mr Maddox for seven minutes without interruption. This concluded with a two minutes' speech on her part, into which she put every ounce of knowledge, skill, and energy that she had at her command. She then looked, with some optimism, at Mr Claye.

This producer, however, appeared to have become suddenly rather blasé about his production, and was merely gazing upwards, in a spirit of friendly contemplation, at the second border. There was a long pause.

'Ye-e-es,' said Mr Claye, at last – and there was another long pause . . .

'Well,' said Mr Claye. 'You'll have to come farther down for that, Maddox. And we'll have to find some business for you while all this is going on.' (This was a reference to Jackie's speech.) 'We'll have some drinks there, of course, when the time comes. Otherwise that's very good, old man.' Mr Claye made pencil marks in his script. 'Now you, Miss Mortimer . . .'

Mr Claye came forward to Jackie, and she came forward to him. They faced each other.

'Now,' said Mr Claye. 'We've got two hands, haven't we?'

'Yes,' said Jackie.

'Well, then,' said Mr Claye, looking into her face. 'Shall we try to make use of them?'

'How do you mean, exactly, Mr Claye?'

Mr Claye now adopted a slightly sterner tone.

'Well, they're simply expressing nothing at the moment, are they?'

Jackie blushed. 'What should I do?' asked Jackie.

'Well, to begin with – as you're supposed to be in a very nervous state all through this scene, don't you think you might try to express that a little? You're just wriggling them about in the air at the moment.'

'Oh,' said Jackie.

'What about a little Clenching?' suggested Mr Claye. 'And standing up a little stiller – so.'

Mr Claye stood at attention, and Jackie followed his example. They looked into each other's eyes.

'Eh?' said Mr Claye, expansively, as much as to say that *that* was better.

Jackie found it quite easy, while facing Mr Claye, to stand up stiffly and clench her hands. She was also clenching her teeth and her toes. But Mr Claye did not know that. Mr Claye was more hazardously situated than he guessed.

4

These little passages in Jackie's day are being related without extraneous comment. Each of them was to have some bearing on the general result of her day, but she had no idea of this at the time.

She had lunch in a slightly foetid atmosphere at the 'Jerry' Lunch and Tea Rooms in Rupert Street. These rooms were owned and run by Miss Stella Gladdon, the sister of the well-known Miss Billie Gladdon, and existed almost exclusively for the profession. But Jackie would have known she was surrounded by professionals without knowledge of this fact. About the women she could sometimes remain in doubt, but the men she could now detect at sight. That infinitely minute tendency to Waist, that slightly shabby swagger, that distant air of dissipation and emaciation, that too perfect simulation of gentlemen who

were anything in the world but actors, that elusive effeminacy – could never, nowadays, escape her.

In the noise and knife-clatter of the ill-ventilated place,
and the roar of London around her, she sat over her
coffee – nonchalantly reading her paper, and having imaginary conversations with Mr Drew (Mr Claye's partner
in this venture, who had actually given her the part), to
whom she intended to appeal concerning her treatment at
the hands of Mr Claye. If he did not look in at the theatre
this afternoon, she would go to the 'Barnstormer' Theatre
at Hampstead, where she knew she could find him, in
the evening.

'You see, I know how terribly good he is,' she would say.
'But he's started so early he's getting me all worried ...'

Mr Drew, of course, was Hand-holding, wasn't he ? ...

'No – honestly, Mr Drew. *Honestly* ...' She would meet
his eyes ...

It was a day like any other day to Jackie.

5

Only Mr Claye, Mr Maddox, the stage-manager, and
Jackie were present at rehearsal that afternoon. It was a
rehearsal exclusively for Jackie. The others had been sent
away on the explicit, widely credited, but entirely false
assumption that they were going to attack their words.

Mr Claye was in the best of tempers on arrival, and all

went fairly well until about 4.30. At this period his patience assumed the infinite proportions to which Jackie took such exception.

'Now, *once* again, *once* again,' said Mr Claye, in a singsong voice. 'We'll go ver-ry slowly, shall we, till we get it right? Now, watch me closely.' Mr Claye came forward to demonstrate.

Mr Claye faced Mr Maddox, at the distance of three paces, and lifted his hand as though he were going to paint a picture of him.

('What's the line?' asked Mr Claye.

'*Ronald-I'm-tired-of-all-this-acting*,' muttered the stage-manager.)

There was a pause.

'Ronald!' said Mr Claye, in a stern voice, and stiffened his body. There was another pause.

Mr Claye took three serious-minded paces over to Mr Maddox.

'I'm tired of all this——' said Mr Claye, and paused again.

'*Acting*,' said Mr Claye, bitterly, and having looked deeply into Mr Maddox's eyes with what he had a little while before described as a Frank, Challenging look, turned with a modest flourish to Jackie. 'There.'

Jackie faced Mr Maddox at a distance of three paces.

'Ronald,' said Jackie.

'*Ronald*,' said Mr Claye.

'*Ronald*,' said Jackie.

'*Ronald*,' said Mr Claye.

'*Ronald*,' said Jackie.

'Better, better,' whispered Mr Claye.

'*Ronald*,' said Jackie. Mr Claye made no comment. She started again.

'Ronald,' said Jackie. 'I'm tired of all this acting.' And she tried to walk on the line, in a weak endeavour to circumvent her instructor, whose style of acting was neither her style at all, nor (she believed) the style of any intelligent human being.

'NOnonononononoNO!' cried Mr Claye. 'Wait till you get there before you start "I'm tired"!'

'Ronald,' said Jackie, and took three paces over to Mr Maddox. 'I'm tired of all this acting.'

'But *pause* before "acting"! *Pause* before "acting"!' cried Mr Claye.

'I'm tired of all this acting,' said Jackie.

There was a heavy silence. Mr Claye came over, and looked at her as though he would at last have to punish her.

'Miss Mortimer,' said Mr Claye. 'Is it that you can't do this, or that you have some objection to it?'

'Well, to tell you the truth,' said Jackie, who was nearly in tears, 'I *don't* really feel it. I don't think it's quite natural, somehow.'

'You don't think it's quite natural?'

'No,' said Jackie, who had detected her own tears, and wanted to cry at the thought that she might cry in a moment. 'I think it's rather mechanical.'

'You think it's rather mechanical?'

'Yes,' said Jackie.

'Yes, Miss Mortimer, but *I'm* looking at this show from the front, aren't I? . . . Now, let's try that again, shall we? We'll get this if we go on long enough . . . *Ronald!*'

'*Ronald,*' said Jackie.

At 5.30 the rehearsal concluded. By this time the blandness of temperament habitual to Mr Claye had returned to him. He assumed a suave and sing-song voice for his summing-up.

'Yes, that's very, very much better, Miss Mortimer. We've still got a long way to go, but I can see you're trying your best, and if we work together we'll manage to hammer something out. So will you go home and think over all those things I've been telling you?'

'Yes,' said Jackie. 'I will.'

'You see, all these things are a question of technique, Miss Mortimer, aren't they? We can all take ourselves as seriously as we like, but it's a slightly different thing when we're faced by the problem of putting it across. I have no doubt that you've got the Music in your head, but now it's a question – well—' Mr Claye here switched on his most winning smile, '—of learning to Play the Piano. Do you follow?'

'Yes,' said Jackie. 'I see.'

'So you go home and Slog like anything at that to-night, and when you come again in the morning we'll start afresh, shall we?'

'Yes,' said Jackie. 'I will.'

'Good.' Mr Claye smiled again, and turned away. 'You coming my way, Lockyer?'

The stage-manager and Mr Claye commenced to pack their attaché-cases.

'Well, I'm off,' said Mr Maddox. 'Good-bye all.'

'Good-bye.'

'Good-bye.'

The pass-door slammed behind Mr Maddox as he left. The time was twenty to six. Rehearsal was done. A great silence and awe seemed to creep up from the untenanted but still vigilant stalls. Something prompted Jackie to come forward to the floats, and look out and around in the darkness of the auditorium ... Mysterious hour, she thought ... Mysterious way of spending your afternoon ...

'Well – ten-thirty to-morrow, then,' said Jackie.

'Ten-thirty to-morrow,' repeated the stage-manager.

'Sharp,' added Mr Claye, agreeably, and sharply snapping his attaché-case.

She left.

She wished he had not said 'Sharp' like that. It had leapt so neatly from his suavity, and yet was like the crack of the whip of his ascendancy over her. And what an inexplicable ascendancy it was! Truly, human nature would submit to all things, to achieve its own purposes.

When she reached the stage-door, she found that she

had lost a glove. She turned back to seek it on the stage. Approaching this, by a dark passage, she heard Mr Claye's upraised voice.

'*Will Not Learn!*' Mr Claye was saying. 'Will Not *Learn*. A lot of infantile notions of their own, and Will not take the Trouble to do *Conscientious Work*.'

She could not hear what the stage-manager replied.

'Well, if she doesn't do what I tell her to-morrow, I shall have to get rid of her, that's all. That's all there is to it . . .'

It seemed as though Jackie's whole theatrical career collapsed about her, as she heard these words. She had laboured for ten years, and she had reached this.

She went back without her glove.

6

'"Will Not Learn" . . .' reflected Jackie, as she had tea. She was having this at a little table by a little window overlooking the Haymarket in the Thistle Tea Rooms. And on one side of her, down below, was the swirl and grind of the spacious one-way street, and on the other was the china clatter and eager feminine loquaciousness of an inflowing matinée crowd, full of the sights it had seen and the sounds it had heard. She observed the latter with a certain mimical and professional interest. In a vain and struggling endeavour to be one of those who catered for such, she had given ten years of her life. They were all too unaware of the sacrifice.

'Will not learn,' reflected Jackie. 'Ronald' – pause – three paces – 'I'm tired of all this' – pause – 'Acting! ...' And then she was to meet his eyes with a Frank, Challenging Look ...

Mr Claye was right. She was not good at this at present. Perhaps, in another ten years, she would have become so.

7

Seven forty-five that evening saw Jackie, standing up in a tube which was flying through Belsize Park, on her way to Hampstead. She wore a coat and skirt, and excited little attention amongst those (many in evening dress) who were bound for the same destination. Her expression in the splitting, infernal din to which all were airily and uncomplainingly submitting, was that of thoughtfulness, and she looked upwards as her body swayed slightly with the motion of the strap ...

Going up in the lift she heard a conversation between two old ladies, whose bared heads were dressed for the theatre.

'Of course, you know that Eileen's on the stage now?' said one of them. 'She's got a job with a Shakespearian Company.'

'Oh – really?' said the other. 'Well – I'm not sorry to hear it ...

'I mean,' she added, 'with talent like that it really would be a pity to *Waste* ...' They agreed with each other.

Jackie wondered how Eileen would fare.

Probably much better with Mr Claye than herself, she thought. Another rival. She wished *she* had all that talent.

8

Arrived at the theatre, where business was very quiet, she obtained a complimentary seat for herself, and looked about for Mr Drew. She was unable to spot him before the curtain rose, and decided to go behind after the first act. She had some interest in the play on account of Miss Edna Radley, who was playing the juvenile, and who had been a friend of hers for some time.

Miss Radley's performance was, she thought, lamentable. The play also was very bad, she thought – but being a war play of an emotional nature it caused her to shed many tears.

Miss Radley was very pleased to see her. 'My DEAR!' she said ...

And, 'Well, my dear, what am I like?'

'My dear,' said Jackie. 'Mar-ar-ar-arvellous. I've been absolutely howling! '

'No, Jackie. Honestly.'

'No, *honestly*, dear. You were wonderful. You were really.'

'Well, how are you getting on with Claye?'

'Oh, ghastly. That's what I've come up to see Drew about.'

'I *know,* my dear, isn't *he foul?* So SWAIVE and SLIMY . . . You feel you can knife him!'

'Oh, have you had any, then?'

'Oh, rather. But it's no use appealing to Drew. He believes in him *implicitly,* my dear. He thinks he's God's Own.'

'Oh, no – he *doesn't?*' said Jackie, appealingly, but, 'He DOES, my dear, he DOES!' affirmed Miss Radley.

She met Mr Drew in the foyer after the second act. He was in a hurry. 'Ah-ha, Miss Mortimer,' he said. 'Getting on all right with the part?' And he held her hand.

'Well, I'm getting on all right,' said Jackie. 'I don't know what Mr Claye thinks about it.'

'Good. I must fly, I'm afraid,' said Mr Drew. 'I'll be down there to-morrow. Good-bye.'

'Good-bye.'

And that was that.

After the show she stayed some time with Miss Radley, who was with an admirer.

This young gentleman, who was in the chartered accountant business, behaved coyly in the presence of Art, but offered to give Jackie a lift in his car as far as Piccadilly. But Jackie refused, and seeing them off, and waving her hand to them, walked over the deserted street to the deserted station.

As she got into the train, and as the train moved out of the station, she observed that she was sitting opposite Mr Reginald Byndon. She knew Mr Byndon slightly, and he had been acting in the play she had just seen. But he did not recognize her. He was about sixty years of age and extremely (indeed professionally) stout: he wore his glasses, on his round red face, in a diagonal fashion which gave his eyes a bleared, profoundly muddled, and blundering expression: and he was smoking a pipe. He was very well-known amongst actors and playgoers, for he had been for forty years in this business. He was looking far from triumphant at the achievement, and he was now, doubtless, going home. Jackie was glad that he had not recognized her, as it was interesting to sit in a corner and observe Reginald Byndon going home.

Reginald Byndon going home ... In the roar of the tube it was impossible to read his thoughts. His pipe was out, though still held weakly in his mouth, and he was obviously very weary. Sometimes his eyes would close, and you might think that he slept; but then, all at once, they would be open again, gazing limply down at a point somewhere near Jackie's ankles ... Reginald Byndon was deep in contemplation of some nature.

Were there not echoes and memories of all those forty years? wondered Jackie. Could he not hear now, in the clash and roar of the train, the clash of all the rehearsals, and the roar of all the applauses, and see again all the fluster and seekings and victories and thwartings that had filled his career? ... And now it had come to this. A confused old man (who should have been in bed a long while ago) sitting alone and unrecognized in a late deserted train from Hampstead.

You would call Reginald Byndon a failure, she supposed. His successes, of course, were innumerable. His crowning achievement, seven years ago, in 'Bobby', had coloured and given substance to his whole career. And since then and before then he had never failed of recognition and particular notice ...

And the sum of all these successes equalled, in the end, participation in a second-rate production at Hampstead, and a late train home at night ...

She endeavoured to conceive him as a young man again, in the flush of his first progresses. His chubbiness and cheerfulness and redness and roundness must have carried all before them at the time. What wisdom he must have acquired since then! – in forty years. He could, indeed, well afford to take pride in his wisdom, but she could detect no pride. His attitude, as he sprawled out in the jolting vehicle, was very patient and even a little suppliant. 'You young people,' he had once said to Jackie ... His wisdom flew over to her, unashamed, as she sat there, and dropped at her feet ...

And the train roared on, and his eyes opened again, and his eyes shut, and he held the same position. And to-morrow morning, by eleven o'clock, he would be up and about. And it would be Reggie this, and Reggie that, and 'What sort of business are you doing up there, Reggie?' and 'Pretty fair, old boy, pretty fair.' But to-night it was Reginald Byndon – a lonely, sleepy old gentleman with forty dazing years of the theatre behind him, and about three years of life ahead (and his pipe out), going home . . .

9

And she also had to be up in the morning, to face the same tasks that Reggie had had to face in all those years. Even Reggie, for all his age and acquired prestige, was not immune . . . 'And just a spot quicker, Reggie, old boy – we're playing too long already. You won't forget that, will you? 'No, no. I won't.' 'I mean one can't *stop* to make points just here, old boy. Don't you agree?' 'Yes, yes. I see.'

What was this coercion to which she and Mr Byndon were so inextricably and submissively committed? What preliminary urge was it, that had led Mr Byndon and herself into this hazardous mode of life? And what good had it done either of them? Mr Byndon's eyes closed again at this, as though there were no reply.

And what part did he and she fulfil in this world? At best, she supposed, they were a couple who, in the indescribable complexity of modern civilization, spent their evenings in a very harassed and obstructed endeavour to mirror or portray some remoter emotional or intellectual complex of that civilization. She was careful to say at best, for so far she had done nothing of the kind. High Hysterical Laughs and Ronald – pause – three paces – I'm tired of all this – pause – Acting had been the level of her art to date ...

She must think about all this some time. At present she had to succeed. She would work at her part to-night, and surrender, hands down, pauses and all, to Mr Claye in the morning.

And there was her contract with Cannon, wasn't there?

It was past eleven when her train came in at Charing Cross. She went on the escalator, and up on to the platform of the District Railway. She ran into the returning theatre crowd.

10

There was nothing but them. They filled the whole platform with the murmur of their talk, and the shuffle of their glittering feet, in the green depressed light of the station. They were at once blasé and yet bedecked for an occasion – a curious contradiction. And they were returning to Sloane Square, or Turnham Green, or Ealing; she knew which was doing which. The elder lot were for Sloane Square, and the ladylike young things, with red cloaks, escorted by gentlemanly young things, with mufflers, were bound for Turnham Green or Ealing. She passed unnoticed amongst them.

And these, she reflected, were her masters. To such as these she had devoted, was now devoting, her life, and ambition and energy. Mr Byndon had done the same. Such was their choice in life.

She was unlucky in her choice of a compartment, in the Ealing train. This was a small one, adjoining a first-class one, and was filled almost exclusively by the escorted young. There was a party of four which had just been (Jackie observed from the programme) to 'The Last Thing' – a drama in which she herself, in an extremely damp interview five weeks ago, had sought to play.

And the names of the members of this party were, she discovered, Gladys, George, Diana, and Bobby.

The atmosphere was sprightly. George was the principal sinner. His wit and innuendo were irrepressible. 'Oh, shut TUP, George!' cried Gladys. 'Will you Shut TUP!'

'Oh, George, *will* you remember wheah you AH!' . . .

'My dear George, I shall give you a seveah smacking in a moment.'

An attempt to give George a severe smacking was made, and there was laughter.

'Here, give me that programme,' said George, and he snatched at it.

They then discussed 'The Last Thing'.

'I know,' said Gladys. 'Wasn't she a shriek!'

This, Jackie gathered, was an allusion to the young actress who had played the part she herself had sought.

*

And now Jackie, though she could not quite analyse the feeling, began to feel a kind of cold anger arising at this spectacle – an anger which increased as it developed before her eyes. It was not that she resented their light-heartedness and disinterest towards the things which had meant so much to her (though that distressed her somewhat): it was that she suddenly seemed to see life as a whole, and herself in relation to it. And she saw herself as a human being committed to an occupation which, in one of its manifestations at least, led up to, laboured for the benefit of, and finally resulted in, this suburban quartet.

And at the same time, in a sudden access of vision, the infinite disadvantages, humiliations, follies, idlenesses, lyings, self-seekings and base submissions of that occupation itself, flooded in upon her, with ten years made a moment, and set her thinking as she had not thought before.

Ten years of it . . .

And then she thought of Mr Claye, and of to-morrow morning. Mr Claye, who would never guess, could never conceive, her thoughts to-night. Mr Claye, with his infinite patience, who so far from imagining that she was using him for her own ends, considered himself an end in himself, and a highly excellent one at that . . . How very much she desired to enlighten Mr Claye . . .

And all that suave and untroubled portentousness for which he stood . . . All the Mr Clayes of life . . .

Mr Claye's 'technique' . . . Mr Claye's belief in himself as an artist . . .

Why was it that she, an independent human being, should be expending the prime of her life in playing tear-stricken pupil to Mr Claye's expansive schoolmaster? An independent human being . . .

'What fun it would be,' thought Jackie, as the train swept in at West Kensington Station, 'if I gave it up altogether.'

As she walked down Talgarth Road she played with the idea as with a fascinating toy.

No more rehearsals, she thought, no more agents, no more hand-holding, no more submissions, no interviews, no maulings, no highmindedness, no first nights. She could elaborate the idea indefinitely.

If it had not been an idle thing to do.

11

She had to wash a lot of stockings that night, and by the time she had had her bath, and got into bed, it was well past midnight.

It began, as she lay on her back, and just before she was going to turn over to go to sleep.

Now if she were placed differently, she thought, she might have had a pleasant flirtation with that idea . . .

If she had been a success, for example – if she had justified herself, if she had demonstrated that she at least could mount to the eminences which she now secretly disparaged – then she might turn from them with immunity from the accusations of failure.

But until then – until then ... 'Oh, yes, she was on the stage for a long while, but never did any good at it ...'

Iris Langham ...

Did human beings, at a certain age, and after a certain amount of affliction, find themselves losing their early pride? She hoped this was not happening to her. She turned over to go to sleep.

Of course – if she did particularly well in her contract with Cannon ...

A contract with Cannon would be enough – a stamp of success in itself ...

Of course, thought Jackie, there were two ways of never returning to the stage, weren't there? One would be to make known your intention, with some solemnity, never to return to the stage. And the other would be never, from this very instant, to return to the stage ...

In that case you would not have to face Mr Claye in the morning ... Surely no one had ever left the stage like that ... Surely no living creature, overnight, and in a sudden access of enlightenment, had ever decided to leave the stage, and done so at once ... Decided it in the dark at night ...

Wouldn't it be fun, though, to lie here, sleeping on in the morning, while at ten-thirty (Sharp) that rehearsal was commencing ... commencing up there ... lying here sleeping on ... commencing up there ... Mr Claye walking about ... Mr Claye growing suaver and suaver ... sleeping on ... Mr Claye mutely deciding to dismiss her ... sleeping on ... Mr Claye himself dismissed ...

Mr Claye had said 'Sharp'. Suppose she, with one magic gesture, relieved herself, slipped out from the chains of that bland ascendancy. Suppose Mr Claye had made miscalculations as to the persons he could say 'Sharp' to ...

This was unprofitable. She must sleep now, or it would be all the worse for her in the morning. She turned over.

But Mr Claye's Face ... when he learnt that the bird had flown ... learnt that he was not indispensable to life ... learnt that he was on the same footing as his pupil ...

This was pure naughtiness. She must go to sleep.

And then, all at once, in the darkness of the second hour of the morning, Jackie stiffened herself in her bed, and listened to a voice from within her. And this voice urged her to be just as naughty as she liked ...

12

And five minutes after that Jackie sat straight up in bed, and stared, with glowing eyes, into the darkness.

'I'm *not* going back!' she said. 'I'm *never* going back!'

She threw back the bed-clothes, and fumbled weakly and tremblingly into her slippers.

'Oh, God!' she said. 'I'm never going back!'

She ran over to the window, not knowing what to do

with herself, and drew back the curtains, and looked down at the quiet street. She was a convert. She was free. She understood what it was to be a convert.

13

Free! She turned from the window, she clasped her hands, and the word surged through her like a rejoicing melody. Free! Not so much from all she had suffered as from her own aspiration! She surrendered and she was free. But from all she had suffered, as well. It seemed as though the weight of ten years had been lifted in a moment. It was too simple. Why had she not thought of it before?

To-morrow morning – *now* – she was a free woman! She could pass a stage-door, she could meet an actor, she could hear of a likely new show, and it would mean nothing to her! She could look the whole world in the face! She could take a walk to-morrow morning, and read a book in Kensington Gardens! She *would* take a walk to-morrow morning and read a book in Kensington Gardens! She was childish, she was impish, she was disembodied with joy. She was without care. She had lost desire. She had all her desire. She was a failure. She had the courage to be a failure – the originality to be a failure.

She walked up and down the room, she returned to the window, she swung round and clasped her hands.

14

A complete failure, thought Jackie (as she lay snuggled up again), and now she could hug the thought to her bosom like a child. There were no half measures about it – her humiliation was perfect, and she gloried in her humilia-tion. A stage-struck little fool who never, at one point, had brought it off. She could go back with nothing to her credit. She had no theatrical technique, no theatrical gossip, no ideas (save a few very decided ones) on the theatre, and no earthly interest in the theatre. She knew no one of repute intimately, she had no Christian names at her disposal, she had never had a job worth calling a job, and the whole West End acting world, with its social intrigue and garrulity, remained a closed door to her – a thing beyond her. They had defeated her. A silly little stage-struck idiot who had made an attack upon London and failed on every side. And now (final and most delicious disgrace!) she was going to try and settle down! ...

There were one or two things to be done, of course. There would have to be a wire to Mr Claye in the morning, and a letter to Mr Drew ... How very sweet it was to be letting some one down for a change! She had wanted all her life to let some one down.

And to-morrow afternoon she was seeing Charles ... It was very lucky that Charles should have chosen to-morrow to come up ... And Charles would hear all about it ... Charles ...

It was all rather dreadful about Charles ...

She thought for a long while about him, and then she decided it would be better not to think about him any more ...

And then, before she knew she was doing any such thing, this slightly unscrupulous (but still very harmless) girl, went to sleep.

Chapter Eleven

DOUBTLESS BUYING A NEW HAT

1

The time was twenty to eleven and the full company of 'The Underdog' was on the stage of the Cumberland Theatre. Faint traces of a slightly unnatural elevation were discernible in the general countenance of the company (as it stood, conferring softly, in groups), and a casual observer might have had difficulty in detecting the cause of this elevation. One in possession of the facts, however, would have put it down to the undoubtedly bracing influences of Trouble Ahead.

The rehearsal should have commenced ten minutes ago.

Mr Claye, in the infinitude of his patience, stood apart with his stage-manager. His hands were in his pockets, and he was gazing, very benignly, at the floor! The stage-manager murmured something to Mr Claye.

'Oh,' said Mr Claye, so that all the company could, and did, hear what Mr Claye was saying. 'Doubtless buying a new hat.'

It must be understood that Mr Claye said this with the utmost detachment, affability, and tolerance. Anything more natural or proper than his leading juvenile (during these rather curious moments) buying a new hat, could not be conceived. Mr Claye had probably observed, only yesterday, that she wanted one ... Very good. Let her get on with it. *He* could wait.

The minutes passed.

A vague vision of hat after hat, fastidiously rejected and strewing the drawers, floor, and shelves of a neighbouring milliner's, filled the mind of the company present ...

The stage-manager again murmured something to Mr Claye.

'Oh, no,' said Mr Claye. 'Patience does it. Patience does it.'

Mr Claye then made an indistinct speech to his stage-manager, preluded by the words 'Of Course', and including the words 'last straw' and 'finished'. But Mr Claye's patience did not desert him. Mr Claye had perfect mastery of the situation. He was (to be quite truthful) enjoying himself immensely.

At this moment the stage-door keeper appeared and handed a telegram to Mr Claye.

Mr Claye, humming lightly, opened this telegram.

'*I am tired of all this acting,*' read this telegram, '*so will not come up to-day.*' It was from Jackie.

*

Mr Claye gazed at this telegram for some time. His hand trembled slightly. 'Ah,' said Mr Claye. He was fighting for time ...

'Er – here – *you*,' said Mr Claye, recalling the vanishing stage-doorkeeper. 'Has this – er – Come – er—?' He got no further.

Now although Mr Claye deserves commiseration in his fight for time at this crisis, the silly man should have kept silent, and not asked whether this telegram had Come. For anybody could see that the thing had Come (how could it have been given him otherwise?) and the rather baffled doorkeeper told him as much.

'Yessir,' said the door-keeper, gazing at him queerly. 'Juscumsir.'

'Oh,' returned Mr Claye, heavily, and as though worlds of things had hung upon the man's reply. 'Oh.'

He folded it up. 'Well, we'd better commence upon the second act,' he said.

The stage-manager bustled about, and the actors and actresses got themselves ready.

'This chair's still to be right down-stage, then, Mr Claye?' asked the stage-manager.

Mr Claye leapt from dreams.

'What? Oh. Ye-e-e-es,' drawled Mr Claye. 'Ye-e-e-es. Right down-stage. That's right.'

The rehearsal commenced.

Chapter Twelve

THE TAXI

That afternoon Jackie met Charles, at the Waldorf Hotel, for tea.

There was an elusive humour and alteration in their relationship even before she had told him. 'Anything the matter?' asked Charles. 'No – nothing the matter,' said Jackie ...

She had more difficulty in telling him than she would have believed possible. 'Of course, you'll think me *quite* mad,' she said ... But as soon as it was out, and as soon as he had gazed at her in a baffled way, and as soon as he had told her how very wise indeed he thought she was, and as soon as she had observed how truly happy it seemed to have made him – an indescribable elation began to steal, like a film, over Jackie's soul – a happiness which could not but expand as the time wore on and they spoke ever more intimately to each other.

And they did truly awake to a new intimacy. They did not speak of her future, for 'That can wait — for the present, anyway,' said Charles. Instead they discussed a thousand little things in the past, as though it had all been a rather dreadful ordeal from which they had both just emerged . . .

And they paused to smile at each other, over the table, in the wide, hushed, spoon-clinking place, and were glowingly delighted with each other.

Until at last, just as they were getting up from tea, and the music in the restaurant behind had just begun its appealing strains, a height of calm happiness was reached by Jackie, such as she had seldom experienced before.

'I say, Jackie,' he said. 'Let's go somewhere for dinner to-night.'

'But, Charles dear,' said Jackie, and it was at this moment that that calm triumphant height was reached, 'you've got to go back to Brighton'.

'No, I haven't. I can 'phone up, and I'll sleep at the club. There's no difficulty.'

'And I'd have to go back to change, wouldn't I?'

'Well, that's all right. I'll see you off now. You see, I feel we really must do something about it to-night. Everything's so different now — isn't it, Jackie?'

'Yes — I suppose it is, Charles,' she said, smiling; and she was on a height at that moment, too.

He led the way out, and when they had reached the street he said that she must have a taxi all the way back to West Kensington. She cried out upon this, but he called one before she was ready, and she got into it, and sat alone.

Then Charles had a small conference with the driver, inaudible amid the noise around, and coming back, to see that the door was fixed, said, 'This *is* paid for, Jackie. See you at seven,' and smiled. And as she was swept away, they smiled and lifted their hands ...

It comforted her extraordinarily to know that this taxi was paid for, though she could not quite analyse the feeling ... She felt a great pride in taking this from Charles – and yet she felt that she had a right to do so ...

The taxi sped at a great pace through London, and it was one of those chill November twilights (with a little red still in the sky, but the lights already twinkling emerald, all the way along, in a mist) which she knew so well ... Rather like those red, cool skies to which she used to return, after those days in the country, with Richard ...

Jackie did not lie back in her taxi to-night. She sat up, and observed her London. She really felt that she could afford to do so. Her prolonged and ancient grudge against this city that had so stolidly, insidiously, and inactively defeated her, was miraculously lifted to-night. Indeed, whizzing through the grave (though sparkling and busy) streets, she had an enormous sensation of forgiveness and friendliness – a friendliness which was, she fancied, in some blind way, returned. And there might have been several ways of accounting for this new amity, but principally, she thought, it was because this was, after all, a farewell.

For she knew now, with a calm and sweet assurance that replaced and was more glad than reason, that the end had come to her sojourn here, and that very soon she would be taken away.

Taken away, thought Jackie, taken away. And she lay back.

And then she began to think of Charles . . .

And the night fell, and the taxi jolted on, and she observed the driver's jerking and unknowing black shoulder as he worked the machine. How many of those shoulders had she seen, at work for her, and what a furious and foolish round of locomotion it had all been!

She liked watching that shoulder. Its surly owner had so little interest in her, and yet he called to mind so much. London . . . In her great new gladness she felt a great pity arising for the poor Cockney in front of her.

To buy any of our books and to find out
more about Abacus and Little, Brown, our authors
and titles, as well as events and book clubs,
visit our website

www.littlebrown.co.uk

and follow us on Twitter

@AbacusBooks
@LittleBrownUK